When I was a kid, my parents took me to all sorts of specialists to find out what was wrong with me. I wasn't afraid of anything, not spiders, snakes, heights, wild animals—nothing. That's when they figured out that if there was a fear gene, I was missing it. So I guess you could say I'm fearless. Like if I see some big guy beating up a little guy I just dive in and finish off the big one—and I can, because my dad trained me to. He figured if I was going to keep getting myself into trouble I might as well have the skills to protect myself. And my dad knows trouble—he's in the CIA. At least I think he is. I haven't seen or heard from him since, well, since something happened that changed our lives forever.

Anyway, you'd think that because I'm fearless my life would be pretty great, right? Wrong. In fact, if I had three wishes, one of them would be to know fear. Because without fear, I'll never know if I'm truly brave. That wouldn't be my first wish, though—my first wish would be to have my dad back. For obvious reasons. My last wish . . . well that's kind of embarrassing. I'd like to end my unlucky seventeen-year stint as Gaia-the-Unkissed. Do I have anyone in mind? Yeah. But I'm beginning to think it'll never happen. . . .

Don't miss any books in this thrilling series:

FEARLESS™

Available from SIMON PULSE

FEARLESS™

Double Edition #2
Sam (#2) & Escape (#26)

FRANCINE PASCAL

SIMON PULSE
New York   London   Toronto   Sydney   Singapore

First Simon Pulse edition March 2003
Sam text copyright © 1999 by Francine Pascal
Escape text copyright © 2003 by Francine Pascal

Cover copyright © 2003 by 17th Street Productions, an Alloy, Inc. company.

SIMON PULSE
An imprint of Simon & Schuster
Children's Publishing Division
1230 Avenue of the Americas
New York, NY 10020

Printed in the United States of America
10 9 8 7 6 5 4 3 2 1

ISBN 0-689-85812-4

Sam and *Escape* are also published individually.

Double Edition #2
Sam (#2) & Escape (#26)

SAM

To Molly Jessica W. Wenk

. . . with
her back to
him and his
gun dug
into her
head,
she was
almost
defenseless.

two

things

IT REALLY WASN'T *THAT* FAR.

Gaia Moore studied the small garden four stories below her window. Well, it wasn't *her* window, exactly. It was one of

Jones

three back windows that belonged to the top floor of the New York City brownstone of George and Ella Niven, her so-called guardians. George was a CIA friend of her dad's from way back when. "Way back when" was typical of the vagueness you got when living with spies and antiterrorist types. They didn't say, "You know, George, the underground assassin I met in Damascus?"

"Gaia?"

Gaia flinched at the voice materializing in her ear. Ella Niven's voice didn't seem to react to air molecules in the normal way. It was breathy and fake intimate, yet carried to the far reaches of the house without losing any of its volume.

"Guy-uhhhhhhh!" Ella bleated impatiently from her dressing room one floor below.

Gaia inched open the window. The window frame was oak, old and creaky with its lead chain and counterweight.

"Gaia? The Beckwiths will be here any minute! Come down now! George asked you to set the table twenty minutes ago!" Now Ella sounded downright whiny.

Gaia could smell bland, watery casserolelike odors

climbing up the stairs and mixing with Ella's strong, spicy perfume. George was a sweetheart and a terrible cook but probably a better cook than `potato-brained Ella`, who wasn't a sweetheart and never set foot in the kitchen except to whir up a fad-diet shake. The unspoken rule when they had company was that George prepared the food and Ella prepared herself.

Gaia grabbed a five-dollar bill from the top of the bureau and stuffed it in the pocket of her pants. Keys or no keys? That was the question. Mmmm. No keys, Gaia decided.

When the window was open just enough, she climbed out.

Although Ella might think otherwise, Gaia wasn't having dinner with the Beckwiths. They were old State Department people, certain to ask questions about her parents, her past, and her future, her parents, her parents. Gaia could `not deal`. Why was it that people over the age of thirty felt the need, when confronted with a "young person," to ask so freaking many questions?

Gaia had never agreed to make an appearance tonight. In fact, when Ella had demanded her presence a few hours earlier, Gaia had told Ella she would jump out the window before she'd have dinner with the Beckwiths, and she wasn't kidding.

The autumn air was scented with dry leaves and

frying garlic from the Italian restaurant on West Fourth Street. Distantly Gaia smelled chimney smoke and felt a moment's longing for a different life, when she'd had parents and a pretty house in the Berkshires with a fire in the fireplace every autumn and winter night. That life felt like it belonged to a different person.

She knelt on the narrow windowsill and gripped it with both hands before she lowered herself down. Errg. Her feet tapped blindly for her next toehold while her fingers began to tremble with the exertion of holding up the full weight of her body. Wasn't there a window top or trellis around here somewhere?

At last the toe of her sneaker found purchase in a deeply pitted slab of brownstone. She sank her weight into it, releasing her cramping fingers. And just then, the brownstone cracked under the weight and she fell.

She winced in surprise and annoyance, but she didn't scream. Her mind didn't abandon its rational sequence.

She fell several feet before her hands jammed against the windowsill of a third-floor window, and she miraculously arrested her fall, saving her skull from the slate patio below.

God, that hurt. Angry nerve endings throbbed in her palms, but her heart beat out its same steady rhythm. Air entered her lungs in the same measured breaths as always.

That's why Gaia Moore was different. A freak of nature. Gaia knew that any normal person would have been afraid just then. But she wasn't. She wasn't afraid now, and she wouldn't be ever. She wasn't born with whatever gene it was that made ordinary people feel fear.

It was like something was missing from her genetic tool kit. But doctors weren't sure exactly what it was. They only knew it seemed to affect her reaction to fear. Scientists know the basic setup—there's a master gene that triggers a series of minor genes that in turn control fear reactions. After extensive testing they came up with the theory that one or more of Gaia's genes in that cascade might be inactive or just plain missing.

Something moved on the other side of the window and Gaia squinted to get a better look.

Oh, crap. It was Ella.

Obviously hearing a noise, Ella swiveled her head from the mirror where she was gunking up her eyelashes with mascara and stared into the darkness outside. Ella was both dumb and otherworldly alert. She was self-obsessed but controlling at the same time. Gaia felt her blood start to boil at the mere sight of George's young, plastic wife. Whenever Ella was around, Gaia began to wonder if Mother Nature had given her extra capacity for anger and frustration when she'd left out the capacity for fear.

Gaia's fingers were straining so hard on the windowsill, she felt her muscles seizing up. *Go away, Ella. Go away now!*

A less annoying version of Ella would have figured the noise was just a pigeon or something and gotten on with her elaborate primping ritual. But this being the `actual Ella`, she came right over to the window and started to open it. Gaia glanced back over her shoulder, eyeballing the distance between her dangling feet and the patio. It had been reduced to twelve or fifteen feet.

Ella succeeded in throwing open the sash, narrowing her suspicious eyes. "What in the . . . ? Oh, Christ. Is that Gaia? Gaia!"

Gaia raised her head from her painful perch, and their eyes met for a fraction of a second.

It was weird. Ella was vapid and worthless at least nine-tenths of the time, but when she got really mad, her face became sharp and purposeful. Almost vicious. Like if `Barbie` were suddenly possessed by `Atilla the Hun`.

Ella's fingers were only inches from Gaia's. "Oh, hell," Gaia murmured, and let go.

Wump. Her feet took the brunt of the impact, then her knees, then her hands slapped down to steady her. Her knees stung, and she rubbed her hands together, doubting whether she'd ever have feeling in her palms again.

"Gaia! Get back here now!" Ella shrieked.

Gaia peered up momentarily at Ella's white face leaning out of the window. Gaia really hadn't wanted to make a scene. Poor George was never going to hear the end of it.

"Guy-uhhhhhhhhhhhhhhhh!"

Without another look behind her, Gaia ran for the back of the garden. Briefly she paused to glance at the seven fat goldfish swimming in the tiny pond before she leaped over it. She scaled the five-foot garden fence with exceptional grace.

Ella's supersonic voice followed her all the way to Bleecker Street and then dissolved amid the noisy profusion of shops, cafes, and restaurants and the crush of people that made the West Village of Manhattan unique in the world. In a single block you could buy fertility statues from Tanzania, rare Amazonian orchids, a pawned brass tuba, Krispy Kreme doughnuts, or the best, most expensive cup of coffee you ever tasted. It was the doughnuts, incidentally, that attracted Gaia.

She walked past the plastic-wrapped fruit laid out on beds of melting ice and into the deli, where the extravagant salad bar at its center emitted a strong, oily aroma. It was called a salad bar, but it was filled with the least healthful stuff Gaia could imagine (apart from doughnuts, anyway). A trough of deep-fried egg rolls, chicken blobs floating in a sea of pink grease,

7

and some slop vaguely resembling potato salad if you quintupled the mayonnaise. Who ever ate that stuff? Gaia didn't know for sure, but she would have bet her favorite Saucony sneakers that the smelly egg rolls she saw now were exactly the same smelly egg rolls she'd been seeing for the last month.

She made a beeline for the doughnut shelf. Crullers? Cinnamon cakey ones? Powdered sugar? Glazed? Chocolate?

Oh, who was she kidding? She'd been jonesing for a sticky chocolate doughnut all evening. Why pretend any other kind came close? Her mouth was watering as she laid the crumpled five on the counter. The pretty young Korean woman took the bill and gave Gaia her change without really looking up. Somehow, in spite of the fact that they saw each other nearly every day, Gaia and this woman never made any sign of recognition. That was a New York thing— pretend anonymity—and frankly, Gaia liked it. It was perfect, what with Gaia being a not-very-friendly person with a lot of secrets and an embarrassingly large appetite for doughnuts.

Gaia said no thank you to the plastic bag and carried her box of doughnuts in her still-numb hands out of the store, along Bleecker Street toward Seventh Avenue. She figured if you weren't woman enough to carry your doughnuts with pride, you shouldn't be eating them.

Her feet went into auto-walk. They knew their way to Washington Square Park by now. That was her favorite place to eat doughnuts or do just about anything. She chose the perfect park bench, clean and quiet, and sat under a canopy of red-turning leaves that carved the glowing night sky into lace. Hungrily she tore open the box.

Yum.

This moment suddenly contained the entire universe. Hell was eating George's food, watching Ella flirt shamelessly with Mr. Beckwith, and fielding questions about her parents she couldn't imagine answering. This doughnut, this bench, and this sky, on the other hand, were heaven.

"DON'T MOVE."

No Bullet

Okay. Gaia's pupils sped to the corners of her eyes, but she didn't turn her head. Okay, it felt very much like the cold barrel of a gun pressed against her neck. Okay, if Gaia were to feel fear, now would be an obvious time.

The drying leaves were rustling sweetly overhead, the picturesque little puddles cast the glow of the streetlamps back up into the sky, but there wasn't a soul in sight besides the heavy-breathing, perspiring young man crushing the gun into her trapezius muscle.

He was standing behind the bench, but she could make out enough of him through her straining peripheral vision to recognize the nasty little hoodlum she'd seen in the park many times. His name was CJ Somethingorother. She'd not only beaten up his friends but identified him in a police lineup two weeks before as the gang member who'd stabbed Heather Gannis in the park. It didn't tax her imagination to think of why he wanted to scare her. Even hurt her. But kill her?

"Don't freakin' move an inch, bitch."

She sighed. She glanced longingly at her box of doughnuts.

"I *mean* it!"

Ouch. Jesus, he was going to puncture her flesh with the goddamned thing.

He was breathing heavily. He smelled like he'd been drinking. "I know you killed Marco, you sick bitch. And you're gonna pay."

Gaia swallowed hard. Suddenly the doughnut was a bitter clump in her mouth that she couldn't choke down. This guy's voice didn't carry the usual stupid bravado. He wasn't just trying to feel like a man.

Sweat trickled from his hand down the barrel of the gun.

He was dead serious, partly scared, maybe crazy.

Gaia had wondered what had become of Marco. He was a vain, annoying loudmouth, the most conspicuous of the thuggy neo-Nazi guys who contaminated the park. She could tell from the new graffiti she'd seen around the fountain that one of their number was dead.

Now it made sense. Marco was gone, and his boys believed Gaia killed him. That wasn't good news for her. Gaia felt sure there was any number of people who would have wanted to kill Marco.

"I didn't kill Marco," she said in a low, steady voice.

"Bullshit." CJ dragged the gun roughly from her neck to her temple. "Don't mess with me. I know what you did. That's how come you're gonna die."

She could feel her pulse beating against the dead, blunt metal.

CJ steadied the gun with both hands, breathing in deeply.

Oh, God. This was bad. Gaia eased her left hand along the thickly painted wooden slats of the bench.

"Don't move!" he bellowed.

Gaia froze, cringing with pain at the pressure of the gun against her head. A surge of anger ripped through her veins, but as badly as she wanted to break his neck, she recognized that in this position, with her back to him and his gun dug into her head, she was almost defenseless.

She tried to subdue her anger before she opened her mouth.

"CJ, don't do it," she said tightly. "It's a mistake. You're wasting your time here—"

"Shut *up!*" he screamed. "Don't say *any*thing!"

His hand was poised on the trigger. He was going to do it. He was going to kill her right here, right now. If she moved, he would just kill her sooner.

She prayed for an intervention of some kind. A noise, a voice, even a car horn. She could turn the tiniest distraction into an opportunity. If he even flinched, she could wrench away the gun and demolish CJ with a couple of quick jabs. But the park and its surrounding streets were eerily calm.

Her mind entered into that dream state, in which you process things without quite believing them. This was it? This was the end? This was what it felt like to die?

The barrel shook as he tightened his grip on the trigger. She could see the taut, quivering muscles in his forearm.

The wind had ceased. It seemed there was no one alive on the planet. The night was so silent, she could hear the grinding of his teeth. Or was it her teeth?

His muscles strained, her heart stopped, her eyes squeezed shut. He pulled the trigger.

Her mind was in free fall. Perfectly blank. Then, like the burst of a firecracker, came a searing moment of understanding and regret, so complete and profound it shouldn't have been able to fit into a small fraction of a second—

Click.

What was that?

She turned her head. She realized her whole body was shaking. CJ looked just as shocked as he stared at the gun.

It hadn't fired. There was no bullet lodged in her head.

Not yet, anyway. Thank God CJ was an incompetent cave boy. Now, if she didn't get off her butt quick, she'd lose the only chance she had to save it. She shot up to her feet, grabbed CJ by the arm that held the gun, and used it to flip the bastard right over her shoulder. His body smacked hard against the pavement. The gun skidded off the path and into the brush.

She stared at his seizing body for a second. Under normal circumstances she would have stayed to pummel him like he deserved, but tonight she was too genuinely freaked out. She needed to get out of there. Her brains, thankfully, were still safely in her skull, but her emotions were splattered on the pavement.

Gaia ran. She ran as fast and gracefully as a doe. But not so fast that she didn't hear the tortured voice screaming behind her.

"I will kill you! I swear to *God* I will kill you!"

Tonight, as I sat on the
park bench waiting for my head to
explode, I had one moment of clarity in which I learned two things.

1) I have to find my dad.

I just have to. As angry as I am, as much as I hate him for abandoning me on the most awful, vulnerable day of my life, I don't want to die without seeing him one more time. I don't know what I'll say to him. But there's something I want to know, and I feel like if I can look in his eyes—just for a moment—I'll know what his betrayal meant and whether there's any love or trust, even the possibility of it, between us.

2) I have to have sex.

Oh, come on. Don't act so shocked. I'm seventeen years old. I know the rules about being safe. If my life weren't in very immediate jeopardy, maybe I would let it wait for the exact right time. But let's face it—I may not be around next week, forget about

happily ever after. Besides, I've
been through a lot of truly awful
things in my life, so why should
I die without getting to experience one of the few great ones?

Who am I going to have sex with?

Do you have to ask?

All right, I have an answer. In
that moment, when my fragile mind-
set was shattered, the face I saw
belonged to Sam Moon. Granted, he
hates me. Granted, he has a girlfriend. Granted, his girlfriend
hates me even more. But I'll find
a way. 'Cause he's the one. I
can't say why; he just is.

I wish I could convince myself
that CJ wouldn't make good on his
threat. But I heard his voice. I
saw his face. I know he'll do any
crazy thing it takes.

I won't go down easy. But I'd be
stupid not to prepare for the worst.

Am I afraid? No. I'm never
afraid. But the way I see it,
dying without knowing love would
be a tragedy.

She hated
that pale
blond hair,
a color
you **desperate**
rarely saw
on a person
over the age
of three.

"YOU SOUND WEIRD."

"How do you mean?" Gaia asked.

"I don't know. You just do. You're talking fast or something," Ed said as he clenched the portable  phone between his shoulder and his ear and eased himself from his desk chair to his wheelchair.

Ed Fargo was honest with Gaia, and Gaia was honest with Ed. He appreciated that about their relationship. With most girls he knew, girls like Heather, there were many mystifying levels of bullshit. With Gaia he could just tell her exactly what he was thinking.

Ed's mind briefly flashed on the hip-hugging green corduroys Gaia was wearing in Mr. McAuliff's class today.

Well, actually, not *everything* he was thinking. There was a certain category of thing he couldn't tell her about. That's why it was often easier talking with her on the phone, because then he couldn't see her, which meant he had fewer of those thoughts he couldn't tell her about.

"I had a bad night. That's probably why," Gaia said.

Ed wheeled himself down the shabbily carpeted hallway of his family's small apartment. Family photographs lined the walls on both sides, but Ed didn't seem to see them anymore. "A bad night how?" he asked.

18

"I almost got shot in the head."

Ed made a sound somewhere between laughter and choking on a chicken bone. "You w-what?"

That was another thing about Gaia. She was always surprising. Though too often in an upsetting way.

Gaia let out her breath. "Oh, God. Where to start. You know that guy CJ?"

Ed slowed his chair to a stop and clenched the armrests with his hands. "The one who slashed Heather? Isn't he in jail?" he asked with a sick feeling in his stomach.

"I guess he got out on bail or something," Gaia said matter-of-factly. "Anyway, CJ's friend Marco is dead, and he thinks I killed him."

Ed groaned out loud. How had his life taken such a turn? Before he'd first laid love-struck eyes on Gaia in the hallway outside physics class, he wouldn't have believed he would ever have a conversation like this.

"Marco is dead? Are you sure?"

"Only from what CJ told me."

Ed sighed. The really crazy thing was, in the brief time he'd known Gaia, so many violent and alarming things had happened, this wasn't so staggeringly out of the ordinary.

"Hey, Gaia? If trouble is a hungry great white shark, then you're a liquid cloud of chum."

Gaia's laugh was easy and comforting. "That's a beautiful image. I love it when you get poetic."

Ed resumed his roll down the hallway and into the galley kitchen. His late evening phone reports from Gaia, distressing as they sometimes were, had become as precious a ritual as his eleven o'clock milk shake.

"So tell me," Ed prodded, hoisting himself up a few inches with one arm to reach the ice cream in the freezer. "Tell me how it happened."

"Okay. I was sitting in the park, minding my own business—"

"Eating doughnuts," Ed supplied.

"Yes, Ed, eating doughnuts, when that loser came up from behind and shoved a gun into my neck."

"Jesus."

"I didn't take it seriously at first. But it turns out this guy is half crazed and deadly serious."

"So what happened?" Ed asked, milk shake momentarily forgotten.

Gaia sighed. "He actually pulled the trigger. I thought I was dead—a wild experience, by the way. It turned out he must have loaded the gun in a hurry because there was no bullet in at least one of the chambers. I took that opportunity to throw him."

Ed's mind was spinning. "Throw him?"

"You know, like flip him."

"Oh, right," he said.

"You're making fun of me again," Gaia said patiently.

20

Ed shook his head in disbelief. "I'm not, Gaia. It's just . . . you blow my mind."

"Well, speaking of, I think this guy CJ is dead set on killing me. I'm scared he's really going to do it," Gaia said.

"You're scared?" Ed asked a little nervously. Having seen Gaia in action, he would have imagined it would take more than a pimply white supremacist with a borrowed gun to hurt Gaia. It would take something more on the order of a hydrogen bomb. But if Gaia was scared, well, he had to take that seriously.

"Figure of speech. I'm scared *abstractly*," Gaia explained.

Ed rocked a tall glass on the counter. "Gaia, you worry me here."

"Don't worry," Gaia reassured him. "I mean, think about it. CJ is kind of a moron, and I happen to be okay at self-defense."

Ed felt reassured. That last part was an understatement to rival "Marilyn Manson is an unusual guy." He could hear Gaia thumping her heel against her metal desk. He realized the ice cream was melting and spreading along the countertop. He absently scooped some of it into the blender.

Prrrrrrrrrrrrr.

"Ed! I hate when you run the blender when we're talking," Gaia complained loudly.

"Sorry," he said. By the time she finished

complaining, the milk shake was frothy and smooth. That was part of the ritual.

"I don't want to die," she said resolutely. "You know why?"

"Why?" he asked absently, sucking down a huge mouthful of vanilla shake.

"I haven't had sex yet."

Ed spluttered the mouthful all over his dark blue T-shirt. Cough, cough, cough. "What?"

"I don't want to die before I've had sex."

Cough, cough.

"Right," he said.

"So I need to have sex in the next couple of days, just in case," Gaia added.

Cough, cough, cough, cough, cough, cough, cough, cough, cough, cough—

"Ed? Are you okay? Ed? Is somebody around to give you the Heimlich?"

"N-No," Ed choked out. "I'm (cough, cough) fine."

In fact, he had about four ounces of milk shake puddled in his lung. Could you die of that? Could you drown by breathing in a milk shake? And shit, he'd like to have sex in the next couple of days, too. (Cough, cough, cough.)

"Ed, are you sure you're okay?"

"Yesss," he answered in a weak and gravelly voice.

"So anyway, I was thinking I better do it soon."

"It?"

"Yeah, it. You know, *it*."

"Right. It." Ed felt faint. Milk shake, as it turned out, was much less handy in your veins than, say, oxygen. "So, who . . . uh . . . are you going to do *it* with? Or are you just going to walk the streets, soliciting people randomly?"

"Ed!" Gaia sounded genuinely insulted.

"Kidding," he said feebly, wishing his palms weren't suddenly sweating.

"You don't think anybody's going to want to have sex with me, do you?" Gaia sounded hurt and petulant at the same time.

"Mmrnpha." The noise Ed made didn't resemble an English word. It sounded like it had come from the mouth of a nine-month-old baby.

"Huh?"

"I . . . um . . ." Ed couldn't answer. The truth was, although she made every effort to hide it, Gaia was possibly the most beautiful girl he had ever seen in his life—and that was including the women in the Victoria's Secret catalog, the *SI* swimsuit issue, and that show about witches on the WB. Any straight guy with a live pulse and a thimble full of testosterone would want to have sex with Gaia. But what was Ed going to say? This was *exactly* the category of conversation he couldn't have honestly with her.

"Anyway, I do know who I'm going to do it with," Gaia said confidently.

"Who?" Ed felt his vision blurring.

"I can't say."

Ed definitely wasn't taking in enough oxygen. Good thing he was in a chair because otherwise he'd be lying on the linoleum.

"Why can't you say?" he asked, trying to sound calm.

"Because it's way too awkward," Gaia said.

Awkward? Awkward. What did that imply? Could it mean . . . ? Ed's thoughts were racing. Would it be too crude to point out at this juncture that although his legs were paralyzed, his nether regions were in excellent working condition?

He felt a tiny tendril of hope winding its way into his heart. He beat it back. "Gaia, don't you think you'll need to get past *awkwardness* if you really plan to be doing *it* with this person in the next forty-eight hours?"

"Yeah, I guess." He heard her slam her heel against the desk. "But I still can't tell you."

"Oh, come on, Gaia. You have to."

"I gotta go."

"Gaia!"

"I really do. Cru-Ella needs to use the phone."

"Gaia! Please? Come on! Tell."

"See ya tomorrow."

"Gaia, who? Who, who, who?" Ed demanded.

"You," he heard her say in a soft voice before she hung up the phone.

But as he laid the phone on the counter he knew who'd said the word, and it wasn't Gaia. It was that misguiding, leechlike parasite called hope.

One Small Comment

THE TIME HAD COME. HEATHER Gannis felt certain of that as she slammed her locker door shut and tucked the red envelope into her book bag. She waited for the deafening late afternoon crowd to clear before striking out toward the bathroom. She didn't feel like picking up the usual half-dozen hangers-on, desperate to know what she was doing after soccer practice.

Okay, time to make her move. She caught sight of Melanie Young in her peripheral vision but pretended she hadn't. She acted like she didn't hear Tannie Deegan calling after her. Once in the bathroom she hid in the stall for a couple of minutes to be sure she wasn't being followed.

Heather usually liked her high visibility and enormous number of friends, but some of those girls were so freakishly *needy* some of the time. It was like if they missed one group trip to the Antique

Boutique, they would never recover. Their clinginess made it almost impossible for Heather to spend one private afternoon with her boyfriend.

Heather dumped her bag in the mostly dry sink and stared at her reflection. She wanted to look her best when she saw Sam. She bent her head so close to the mirror that her nose left a tiny grease mark on the glass. This close, she could see the light freckles splattered across the bridge of her nose and the amber streaks in her light eyes that kept them from being the bona fide true blue of her mother and sisters.

Her pores looked big and ugly from this vantage point. Did Sam see them this way when he kissed her? She pulled away. She got busy rooting through her bag for powder to tame the oil on her forehead and nose and hopefully cover those gaping, yawning pores. She applied another coat of clear lip gloss. For somebody who was supposed to be so beautiful, she sure felt pretty plain sometimes.

She wished she hadn't eaten those potato chips at lunch. She couldn't help worrying that the difference between beauty and hideousness would come down to one bag of salt-and-vinegar chips.

As she swung her bag over her shoulder and smacked open the swinging door, she caught sight of the dingy olive-colored pants and faded black hooded sweatshirt of Gaia Moore. Heather's heart picked up pace, and she felt blood pulsing in her temples.

God, she hated that girl. She hated the way she walked, the way she dressed, the way she talked. She hated that pale blond hair, a color you rarely saw on a person over the age of three. Heather wished the color was fake, but she knew it wasn't.

Heather hated Gaia for dumping scorching-hot coffee all over her shirt a couple of weeks ago and not bothering to apologize. Heather hated Gaia for being friends with Ed Fargo, her ex-boyfriend, and turning him against Heather at that awful party. Heather *really* hated Gaia for failing to warn Heather that there was a guy with a knife in the park, when Heather was obviously headed there.

All of those things were unforgivable. But none of them kept Heather up at night. The thing that kept her up at night was one small, nothing comment made by her boyfriend, Sam Moon.

It happened the day Heather got out of the hospital. Sam was there visiting, as he was throughout those five days. He had disappeared for a few minutes, and when he got back to her room, Heather asked him where he'd been. He said, "I ran into Gaia in the hallway." That was all. Afterward, when Heather quizzed him, Sam instantly claimed to dislike Gaia. Like everybody else, he said it was partly Gaia's fault that Heather got slashed in the first place.

But there was something about Sam's face when he said Gaia's name that stuck in Heather's mind and wouldn't go away.

Heather's mind returned again to the card floating in her bag. She sorted through the bag and pulled it out. She needed to check again that the words seemed right. That the handwriting didn't look too girly and stupid. That the phrasing didn't seem too . . . desperate.

She'd find Sam in the park playing chess with that crazy old man, as he often did on Wednesday afternoons. And if not, she'd go on to his dorm and wait for him there. She'd hand him the card, watch his face while he read it, and kiss him so he'd know she meant it.

She was in love with Sam. This Saturday marked their six-month anniversary. He was the best-looking, most intelligent guy she knew. She loved the fact that he was in college.

She had made this decision with her heart. Sam was sexy. Sam was even romantic sometimes. He wasn't a guy you let get away.

So why, then, as she wrote the card, was she thinking not of Sam, but of Gaia?

> *Dear Sam,*
>
> *These last six months have been the best of my life. Sorry to be corny, but it's true. So I wanted to celebrate the occasion with a very*

special night. I'll meet you at your room at eight on Saturday night and we'll finally do something we've been talking about doing for a long time. I know I said I wanted to wait, but I changed my mind.

You are the one, and now is the time.

Love and kisses (all over),

Heather

He smiled at
her. This **lonely**
time it
was sweet, **hearts**
open, real.

"THAT STUPID PUNK WILL NOT KILL Gaia!" he thundered. "Do you understand?"

He strode to the far end of the loft apartment and kicked over a side table laden with coffee mugs. Most rolled; one shattered. One of the two bodyguards who hovered in the background came forward to clean them up.

Remarkable Girl

He spun on Ella. He hated her face at moments like this. *"Do you understand?"*

"Of course I understand," she said sullenly. "I wasn't expecting her to climb out the window," she added in a scornful mumble.

"Learn to *expect* it!" he bellowed. "Gaia is *not* an ordinary girl! Haven't you figured that *out?*"

Ella's eyes darted with reptilian alertness, but she wisely kept her mouth shut.

"Gaia is no use to me dead. I will not let it happen. I don't care how crazy the girl is. I don't care if she throws herself in the path of a bus. I will *not* let it happen!" He was ranting now. He couldn't stop now if he wanted to. He'd always had a bad temper.

"Show me the pictures," he demanded of Ella.

Reluctantly Ella came near and put the pile in his hands.

32

He studied the first one for a long time. It was Gaia sitting alone on a park bench. Her face was tipped down, partly obscured by long, pale hair. Her gray sweatshirt was sagging off one shoulder. Her long legs were crossed, and a little burst of light erupted from the reflective patch on her running shoe. A box of doughnuts sat open on the bench next to her.

Her gesture and manner were so familiar to him, he felt an odd stirring in his chest. Though Gaia was undeniably beautiful with her graceful, angular face, she didn't resemble Katia. Katia had dark glossy hair, brown eyes flecked with orange, and a smaller, more voluptuous build.

In the next picture Gaia's head was raised, and in the shadow behind her was the boy pointing the gun at her head. The boy looked agitated, his eyes wild. Yet Gaia's face was impossibly calm. He brought the picture close. Remarkable. Utterly fascinating. There was no fear in those wide-set blue eyes. He would know. He had a great gift for detecting fear.

Gaia was indeed everything he had heard about her. All the more reason why he could not accept another ridiculous close call like this one.

He glanced at the next picture. The boy was leaning in closer, his face clenched as he prepared to pull the trigger.

"Keep that boy and his stupid friends away from her," he barked at Ella.

"Yes," she mumbled.

"He will not get that gun anywhere near Gaia!"

"Yes, sir."

He glared at Ella with withering eyes. "Hear me now, Ella. If *anyone* kills Gaia Moore, it will be me."

Ella's gaze was cast to the ground.

He studied the next picture in the pile. This one showed Gaia standing in all her ferocious glory, flipping that pitiful boy over her shoulder. Her face was wonderfully alert, intense. She was magnificent. More than he could have hoped for.

No, Gaia didn't resemble Katia, he decided as he studied the lovely face in the picture. Gaia resembled him.

SHE PROBABLY WOULDN'T EVEN BE there. Why would she? She'd be avoiding him if she had any sense.

Sam Moon hurried into Washington Square Park with his physics textbook tucked under his arm. Then again, if *he* had any sense, he'd be avoiding *her*. Instead he was darting around the park at all hours like some kind of timid stalker, hoping to catch a glimpse of her.

Like a Drug

He approached the shaded area where the chess tables sat, surveying them almost hungrily. No. She wasn't there. It verged on ridiculous, the physical feeling of disappointment that radiated through his abdomen.

He kept his distance, reviewing his options. He didn't want to plunge right into chess world because then all his cohorts would see him and he'd be stuck for at least a game or two. And he'd found out the hard way that when Gaia was on his mind (and when wasn't she?), he was a lot worse at chess.

Maybe she had come and gone already. Maybe she'd caught sight of him from a distance and taken off. Maybe she really did hate him—

"Moon?"

Sam practically leaped right out of his clothes. He spun around. "Jesus, Renny, you scared the crap out of me."

Renny smiled in his open, friendly way. He was a wiry-looking, barely adolescent Puerto Rican kid who was quickly becoming a lethal chess player. "You looking for Gaia?"

Sam's face fell. Was his head made of glass? Was his romantic torment, which he believed to be totally private and unique, available for public display? Was everybody who knew him talking and snickering about it? Even the chess nerds, who wouldn't ordinarily notice if you'd had one of your legs amputated?

"No," Sam lied defensively. "Why?"

"I figure you're getting tired of whipping the rest of us. Gaia could probably get a game off you, huh?"

Sam studied Renny's face for signs of cleverness or mockery. No. Renny wasn't being a wise guy. He wasn't suddenly Miss Lonely Hearts. Renny was thinking the same way he always thought, like a chess player.

Sam let out a breath. He tried to relax the crackling nerve synapses in his neck and shoulders. There was a word for this: *paranoia*.

"Yeah," Sam said in a way he hoped was nonchalant. "Maybe one or two. If she was on her game."

"Yeah," Renny said, "she's unbelievable." Renny's eyes got a little glassy, but Sam could tell he was fantasizing about Gaia's stunning end play, not about her lips or her eyes.

Unlike Sam.

"Yeah," Sam repeated awkwardly.

"See you." Renny clapped him on the back agreeably and waded into chess world. Sam watched Renny take the first open seat across from Mr. Haq, whose taxicab was predictably parked (illegally) at the nearest curb. That was the downside of playing Mr. Haq. If the cops came, he abandoned the game and put his cab back into action. And no matter how badly you were creaming him, Mr. Haq would always refer to it afterward as "an undecided match."

Sam found his way to a nearby bench with a good

view of the chess area. He opened his physics book, lame prop that it was.

What had happened to his resolution to forget about Gaia? He'd decided to put her out of his mind for good and focus all of his romantic energy on Heather, but Gaia was like a drug. She was in his blood, and he couldn't get her out. He was a junkie, an addict. He knew Gaia was bad for him. He knew she'd undermine his commitments and basically ruin his life. But he obsessed about her, anyway. Was there a twelve-step program for an addiction like this? Gaia Worshipers Anonymous?

He remembered that antidrug slogan that had scared him as a kid. *This is your brain.* He pictured the sizzling egg. *This is your brain thinking of Gaia.*

Clearly his decisions, vows, determinations, and oaths to forget Gaia weren't enough. Maybe it was time to try a different tack.

What if he attempted to relate to her as a normal person? Just talk to her about everyday things like school and extracurricular activities and stuff like that? Maybe he could demystify the whole relationship.

Maybe he and Gaia could even have a meal together. You couldn't easily idolize a girl while she was stuffing her face. She would probably order something he hated like lox or coleslaw. She would chew too loudly or maybe wear a bit of red cabbage on her front tooth for a while. Maybe she would spit a little when she talked. Afterward she would have bad breath or maybe a grease spot on her pants, and voilà. Obsession over.

Yes. This was a practical idea. Demystification.

Because after all, although Gaia came off as a pretty extraordinary person on the outside, on the inside she was just the same as anybody else.

. . . right?

SHE WAS A MESS.

She was a nightmare.

She should have her license to be female revoked.

Gaia turned around to look at her backside in the slightly warped mirror that hung on the back of the door to her room.

A Lame Come-on

Earlier that day she'd picked up a pair of capri pants off the sale rack at the Gap in an effort to look cute and feminine. Instead she looked like the Incredible Hulk right after he turns green and bursts out of his clothing.

What kind of shoes were you supposed to wear with these things? Definitely not boots, as she could plainly see in the mirror. Was it too late in the year to wear flip-flops?

Sam was not going to fall in love with her. He was going to take one look and run screaming in the opposite direction. Either that or laugh uncontrollably.

Why was she torturing herself this way? In her ordinary life she managed to pull off the functional style of a person who didn't care. She had no money, which occasionally resulted in the coincidental coolness of thrift shop dressing.

But now that Gaia actually cared, she had turned herself into a neurotic, insecure freak show.

Caring was to be deplored and avoided. Hadn't she learned that by now?

She stripped off the pants and pulled on her least-descript pair of jeans. She pulled a nubbly sweater the color of oatmeal over her head.

Better ugly than a laughingstock. That was Gaia's new fashion motto.

She had to get out of the house before Ella sauntered in and recognized the beaded necklace Gaia had "borrowed." Ella was a whiny, dumb bimbo, but she had a nose for fashion trends. Gaia had every intention of returning the necklace before it was missed, so why cause a big fuss by asking?

Gaia thundered down the three flights of stairs, slammed the painted oak-and-glass door behind her, turned her key in the lock, and struck out for the park.

And to think she'd come home after school to work on her appearance.

She hurried past the picture-perfect row houses. Lurid red geraniums still exploded in the window boxes. Decorative little front fences cast long shadows in the late day sun, putting Gaia's shadow in an attenuated, demented-looking prison.

After a few blocks, Gaia suddenly paused as the sound of heavy guitar music blared through an open basement window, followed by a raspy tenor voice. "framed/you set me up, set me out and/blamed/you tore me up, tore me down and/chained/you tied me up, tied me down and . . . " It was that band again—Fearless. For a fleeting moment Gaia wanted to shout through the window and ask them where they got their bizarrely Gaia-centric name, but she had to keep moving.

She didn't have much time. CJ probably wasn't crazy enough to open fire on her in daylight, but once the sun got really low, she had to be ready for it, especially hanging around the park. How typical of her new life in the biggest city in the United States that the guy she wanted to seduce and the guy who wanted to shoot her hung out in exactly the same space.

Her stomach started to churn as she got close. What was she going to say to Sam?

"Hi, I know you have a girlfriend and don't like me at all, but do you want to have sex?"

On the one-in-ten-billion chance that he agreed to

her insane scheme, what then? They couldn't just do it on a park bench.

Suddenly the actual, three-dimensional Sam, sitting on a bench with a clunky-looking textbook open on his lap, replaced the Sam in her mind.

Oh, crap. Was it too late? Had he seen her?

"Gaia?"

That would mean yes.

`Swallow`. "Hi." She tried out a friendly smile that came off more like the expression a person might make when burning a finger on the top of the toaster.

He stood up, his smile looking equally pained. "How's it going?"

She hooked her thumbs in the front pockets of her pants. "Oh, fine. Fine." What was she? A farmer?

"Yeah?"

"Yeah."

"Great."

Oh, this was awful. This `come-hither Gaia` was a complete disaster. Why couldn't she be cute and flirty *and* have a personality?

He was clearly at a loss. "Do you, uh . . . want to play a game of chess?"

She would have agreed to `pull out her toe-nails` to escape this awkward situation.

"Yeah, sure, whatever," she said lightly. God, what a wordsmith she was.

"Or we could just, like, take a walk. Or something."

"Great. Sure," she said. Had her vocabulary shrunk to four words?

"Or we could even sit here for a couple of minutes."

"Yeah," she proclaimed.

"Fine," he countered.

"Great," she said.

They both stayed standing.

This was pathetic. How was she possibly going to have sex with him when simply sitting on the same bench involved a whole choreography of commitment?

She sat. There.

He sat, too.

Well, this was progress.

She crossed her legs and inadvertently brushed the heel of his shoe. With lightning-fast-reflex speed they both swung their respective feet to opposite sides of the bench.

Or not.

Gaia studied Sam's face in profile. It made her a little giddy to realize what a hunk he was. A classic knee weakener. He belonged on television or in a magazine ad for cologne. What was he doing sitting near *her?*

He looked up and caught her staring (slack jawed) at him. She quickly looked away. She pressed her hand, palm down, on the bench and realized her pinky was touching the outer edge of his thigh. *Uh-oh.*

Should she move it? Had he noticed? Did he think she had done it on purpose? Suddenly she had more feeling, more nerve endings (billions and billions at least) in her pinky than she ever thought possible. All of the awareness in her body was crammed into that pinky.

Now it felt clammy and weirdly twitchy. A pinky wasn't accustomed to all this attention. Did Sam feel it twitching? That would be awful. He'd think it was some kind of lame come-on. Either that or she'd lost muscle control.

Well, actually, this *was* some kind of lame come-on and she *had* lost control.

The problem was, if she took away her pinky, he would know she noticed that she was touching him, and that would be embarrassing, too.

He moved his leg. Suddenly Gaia's pinky was touching cold, lonely, uncharged air. She felt the piercing sting of rejection. Jerk. Loser. She was ready to give up on the whole project.

Then he moved it back and practically covered her entire pinky. Oh, faith! Love! Destiny! Could she propose to him right there?

He smiled at her. This time it was sweet, open, real.

Her stomach rolled. She smiled back, fervently

hoping it didn't look like a grimace and that her teeth didn't look yellow.

She heard a noise behind her. She jerked up her head.

She realized that the sun had dipped below the Hudson River and the streetlamps were illuminated. Oh, no. Could it be? Already?

She had to go. Fast. She wasn't going to turn into a pumpkin, but she was very likely going to get shot in the head. That could easily put a damper on this fragile, blossoming moment.

The sound resolved itself into a footstep, and a person appeared. It wasn't CJ, but just the same, it put an end to the encounter as powerfully as a bullet.

It was Heather. The girlfriend.

Her adrenaline was pumping now. Her muscles were **cold** buzzing with intensity. **blood** She was an easy target this close.

THERE WERE MOMENTS IN LIFE WHEN

words failed to convey
your thoughts. There
were moments when
your thoughts failed to
convey your feelings.
Then there were mo-
ments when even your
feelings failed to convey your feelings.

Cunning Intelligence

This was one of those, Heather realized as she
gaped at Sam and Gaia Moore sitting on the park
bench together.

They weren't kissing. They weren't touching. They
weren't even talking. But Sam and Gaia could have
been doing the nasty right there on the
spot, and it wouldn't have carried the intimacy of
this tentative, nervous, neurotic union she now wit-
nessed between them.

Maybe she was imagining it, Heather considered.
Maybe it was a figment of her own obsessive, jealous
mind.

She'd almost rather believe she was crazy than that
Sam, *her Sam*, was falling in love with Gaia. It was too
coincidental, just too cruel to be real. Like one of those
Greek tragedies she read for Mr. Hirschberg's class.
Gaia was the person she most despised. Sam was the
person she loved.

Had she done something to bring this on herself?

What was it the Greek guys always got smacked for? *Hubris,* that was the word—believing you were too good, too strong, invulnerable. The world had a way of teaching you that you weren't invulnerable.

Heather was paralyzed. Anger told her to get between them and make trouble, Pride told her to run away. Hurt told her to cry. Cunning told her to make Sam feel as guilty and small as possible. She waited to hear what Intelligence had to say. It never spoke first, but its advice was usually worth waiting for.

Her mind raced and sorted. Considered and rejected. Then finally, Intelligence piped up with a strategy.

"Sam," Heather stated. Good, firm, steady voice. She stepped around to the front of the bench and faced them straight on.

Sam looked up. Shock, fear, guilt, uncertainty, and regret waged war over his features.

Staring at them, Heather made no secret of her surprise and distress, but she overlaid a brave, tentative, give-them-the-benefit-of-the-doubt smile.

The effect was just as she'd intended. Sam looked like he wished to pluck out both of his eyeballs on the spot.

"Hey, Gaia," Heather said. Her expression remained one of naive, martyrlike confusion.

Gaia looked less sure of herself than Heather had ever seen her before. Gaia cleared her throat, uncrossed her legs, straightened her posture, said nothing. Heather detected a faint blush on her cheeks.

Now Heather looked back at Sam. She applied no obvious pressure, just silence, which always proved the fiercest pressure of all.

"Heather, I—we—you—" Sam looked around, desperate for her to interrupt.

She didn't.

"I was just . . . and Gaia, here . . ."

Heather wasn't going to help him out of this. Let him suffer.

"We were just . . . talking about chess." With that word, Sam regained his footing. He took a big breath. "Gaia is a big chess player, too."

Heather nodded trustingly. "Oh."

Sam looked at his watch. There wasn't a watch. A moment's discomfort. He regrouped again. "I gotta go, though." He stood up. "Physics study group." He offered his textbook as evidence.

"Right," Heather said. "Wait, I have something for you." She fished around in her bag and brought out the red sealed envelope. "Here. I was looking for you because I wanted to give you this." She smiled shyly. She shrugged. "It's kind of stupid, but . . . whatever." Her voice was soft enough to be intimate and directed solely at him.

He had to come two steps closer to take the card

from her hand. This required him to turn his back on Gaia.

Sam glanced at his name, written in flowery cursive, and the heart she'd drawn next to it. When he looked at Heather again, his eyes were pained, uncertain.

He cleared his throat. "Why don't you walk with me, and I'll open it when I get to my dorm?"

Heather nodded brightly. "Okay."

He pressed the card carefully between the pages of his physics book and anchored the book under his arm. Heather took his free hand and laced her fingers through his as she often did, and they started across the park.

Sam said nothing to Gaia. He didn't even cast a backward glance.

But Heather couldn't help herself. She threw a tiny look over her shoulder. Then, without breaking her stride, she planted one fleeting kiss on Sam's upper arm, just the place where her mouth naturally landed on his tall frame. It was a casual kiss, light, one of millions, but undoubtedly a kiss of ownership.

"See ya," Heather said to Gaia, silently thanking Intelligence for dealing her yet another effective strategy.

It was funny, thought Heather. Intelligence and Cunning so often ended up in the same place.

WHAT GOOD WAS IT BEING A TRAINED fighting machine when you couldn't beat the hell out of a loathsome creature like **Not Yet** Heather Gannis? Gaia wondered bitterly as she stomped along the overcrowded sidewalks of SoHo.

What a catty piece of crap Heather was. No, that was too kind. Cats were fuzzy, warm-blooded, and somewhat loyal. Heather was more reptile than mammal—cold-blooded and remote with dead, hooded eyes.

Gaia was supposed to be smart. When she was six years old, her IQ tested so high, she'd been sent to the National Institutes of Health to spend a week with electrodes stuck to her forehead. And yet in Heather's presence Gaia felt like a slobbering idiot. She'd probably misspell her name if put on the spot.

"Oops. Sorry," Gaia mumbled to a man in a beige suit whose shoulder she caught as she crossed Spring Street.

Trendy stores were ablaze along the narrow cobble-stoned streets. Well-dressed crowds flowed into the buzzing, overpriced restaurants that Ella always wanted to go to. Gaia strode past a cluster of depressingly hip girls who probably never considered wearing boots with capri pants.

Gaia caught her reflection in the darkened window

of a florist shop. Ick. Blah. Blech. Who let her out on the streets of New York in that sweater? Exactly how fat could her legs look? High time to get rid of the—

Suddenly she caught sight of another familiar reflection. He was behind her, weaving and dodging through the throng, staying close but trying to avoid her notice. His face was beaded with sweat. One of his hands was tucked in his jacket.

Oh, shit. Well, at least you couldn't commit fashion blunders from the grave, could you?

She walked faster. She jaywalked across the street and ducked into a boutique. She wanted to see whether CJ was just keeping tabs on her or whether he intended to kill her immediately.

Gaia blinked in the laboratory-bright shop. The decor was spare, and the clothing was inscrutable. In the midst of all the chrome shelving and halogen lighting there seemed to be about three items for sale, all of them black. It made for poor browsing.

CJ stopped outside. He knew she knew he was there.

"Excuse me, miss." An impatient voice echoed through the stark, high-ceilinged room.

Gaia spun around to see a severe-looking saleslady pinning her to the floor with a suspicious look. Salesladies in SoHo had a sixth sense for whether you could afford anything in their store. It was a superhuman power. It deserved to be investigated on *The X-Files*. This particular woman obviously knew that Gaia couldn't afford even a zipper or sleeve from the place.

"We're closed," the saleslady snapped. Her outfit was constructed of incredibly stiff-looking black material that covered her from her pointy chin to the very pointy tips of her shoes. Gaia couldn't help wondering if she ate breakfast or watched TV in that getup.

"The door was open," Gaia pointed out.

The woman cocked her head and made a sour face. "Apparently so. But we're closed."

"Fine." Gaia glanced through the glass door. CJ was pacing in an area of about two square feet. He was ready to pounce. She was pretty sure that the hand concealed in his roomy jacket held a gun.

"In the future, when you're closed," Gaia offered, trying to bide a little time, "you should consider *locking* your door. It's a common business practice. It not only alerts your customers to the fact that your store is closed but can help reduce crime as well."

"Are you done?" the woman asked, rolling her eyeballs skyward.

"Um, yeah." Gaia glanced out the door reluctantly. It opened outward. The glass was thick and well reinforced.

"Please leave."

Gaia backed up a few feet. "Okay," she said.

One . . . two . . . three . . .

Gaia slammed into the door at full strength.

Just as she'd hoped, the door flew open and caught CJ hard in the face, knocking him backward. She heard his groan of surprise and pain. It gave her the moment she needed to run.

SoHo, with its single-file sidewalks and indignant pedestrians, was not a good place for sprinting.

"Ex*cuse* me!"

"Yo, watch it!"

"What's your problem?"

Gaia left a stream of angry New Yorkers in her wake. "Sorry!" she called out in a blanket apology. It was the best she could do at the moment.

She heard CJ shouting behind her. Then pounding footsteps and the protests of more unhappy pedestrians.

Gaia hung a quick left on Greene Street. She navigated the sidewalk with the deftness of a running back.

She heard screams as CJ (presumably) crashed into a woman with a screechy voice. He was gaining on Gaia. He cared less than she did about thrashing innocent bystanders.

Gaia hooked onto Broome Street and ran west. CJ was just a few yards behind. The street was clotted with traffic, and she needed to cross to the south side,

53

where the sidewalk was clear. The crosswalk was too far. She heard more screams and then a man's voice.

"That kid's got a gun! A *gun!* Everybody down!"

"Damn it!" Gaia muttered. Her adrenaline was pumping now. Her muscles were buzzing with intensity. She was an easy target this close. Now what?

Parked cars were nose to tail at the curb without a break. Gaia pounced on the first parked car she came upon, putting both hands above the driver's side window and vaulting herself onto the roof. She was in full flee mode now, and she didn't have the luxury to care about making a spectacle. Thin metal thundered and buckled under her feet. She surveyed the traffic piled up behind the light. She jumped to the roof of the next-nearest car and picked her way across the street from car to car the way she'd use stones to traverse a river. Cars honked. Cabbies shouted. A shot rang out to her left. Oh, man.

CJ had beaten her to the other side of Broome Street. The idiot was shooting at her in front of hundreds of witnesses. God, she wanted to wring his crazy neck! It was no fair going up against someone with a gun and no sense.

The traffic light was about to change. Any second, the stones under her feet were going to start moving downstream. She hopped her way back to the north side of the street in half the time and sprinted along Broome Street to the east now. A fast left took her zigging up

Mercer. Her breath was coming fast now. The muscles in her legs were starting to ache.

This lower stretch of Mercer was nearly deserted. If she just ran north, she could cut over a couple of blocks and get to the park. She could run her way out of this. She had her Saucony sneakers on her feet. Footsteps sounded behind her, and she accelerated her pace. She knew that if CJ paused to take aim, he'd lose her. *Faster, faster,* she urged her protesting leg muscles.

"You're dead!" he shouted after her.

Not yet, she promised herself. She could see the lights of Houston Street. She was getting close.

Suddenly her escape route was obscured by a large, silhouetted figure. As she got closer she realized his presence wasn't coincidental. In the side wash of a streetlight she recognized the face. She didn't know his name, but she'd often seen him with CJ and Marco and the other thugs in the park. A blade winked in his hand.

Ka-ping! CJ fired a shot, which bounced off the cobblestones several feet away.

Oh, this sucked. This really sucked. Another wave of adrenaline flowed through her limbs and sizzled in her chest. She dragged in as much air as her lungs could take.

She juked, but he wouldn't let her pass. CJ was hard on her heels, so she couldn't think of stopping. CJ would succeed in shooting her in the back if she gave him any time at all. The space between CJ and his accomplice was closing fast.

Come on. Come on. Come on.

The guy in front of her raised the blade. Gaia didn't stop running. She lifted her arm, drew it back, and without losing a step punched him as hard as she could in the middle of his face. "Sorry," she murmured to him. Judging from the sting in her fist, she'd broken a tooth or two.

A bullet seared past her right shoulder. Another past her knee. The toe of her trusty sneaker caught in a deep groove between the cobblestones and she went down hard, scraping the skin of her forearms and shins.

Shit. Oh, shit.

Her mind was dreamlike again. She didn't feel any pain from her ragged, bleeding skin or from the impact to her wrist and knees. There wasn't anything wrong with her nervous system. It was that every cell of her body was fiercely anticipating the dreaded shot. Some atavistic impulse caused her to bring her hands over her head and curl her knees up in the fetal position.

Time slowed to an eerie, inexplicable stop. Although CJ had been within a few yards of her, the shot didn't come. She took big gulps of air. There were no footsteps. No bullets. She heard nothing.

Slowly, slowly, in disbelief she lifted her head from the street. She turned around cautiously. Her legs shook as she straightened them under the weight of her body.

She peered into the dark, desolate street.

He wasn't there. He really wasn't. CJ had disappeared, just when his duck had finally sat.

It was impossible. It made no sense to Gaia. Something told her there was no reasonable explanation for this. But she also knew it would be a mistake to hang around and try to figure out why.

Sometimes I worry
there's something wrong with me.
Sometimes I worry I don't actually feel things like regular
people do. Often I'm watching the
world rather than actually living
in it. It's not just that I feel
distant from the world. The thing
that worries me is that a lot of
times, I feel distant from myself. I watch myself like I'd
watch an actor in a movie. I
think, I observe, I process, but
I don't *feel* anything.

Have you ever felt that way?
Have you ever sat at the funeral
of your great-aunt, for example,
and worn a solemn expression on
your face and tried to tell yourself all the ways in which it was
sad, without actually feeling sad
at all?

Have you ever met somebody who
said, "Oh my God, that's so
funny!" all the time, but never
actually laughed? I'm worried
that's me.

When my parents split up when

I was in fifth grade, I said all of the things a sad kid says in that circumstance. I even wrung out a few tears. When they got back together ten months later, I shared in the happiness. But for me it was abstract. I could sort of talk myself into feeling something—or at least into believing I felt something—but it didn't come naturally. The emotions certainly didn't rush over me like a wave. I was their eager host, never their victim.

Maybe that's really lucky; I don't know.

But the flip side of experiencing pain abstractly is that you experience pleasure that way, too. Sometimes Heather and I will be eating a romantic dinner together or making out in the park, and it feels really good and everything, but I find myself wondering if I'm missing out on something.

I think this is the reason I can't get over Gaia Moore. I

think it's the reason why I'm intensely attracted to her and re-
pelled by her at the same time.
When I'm with her—when I even
think of her—I feel things. I
feel a wave brewing just out of
reach, building and swelling into
a breaker of dangerous proportions.

So maybe you can see why I
have mixed feelings about getting
close to Gaia. I'm not sure I
want to lose control. I mean, who
would willingly turn himself into
a victim?

Maybe that's what love is—I
don't know.

Sam couldn't
help smiling.
"Yeah, I'm
getting **hazards**
lucky.
Very lucky."

GAIA IS IN DANGER.

Tom Moore looked up from his laptop computer. He'd been thinking vaguely of Gaia all evening—there was nothing unusual in that—but this was the first time a specific thought coalesced in his mind.

An Ocean Away

For most of his life he'd discounted notions of telepathy with a certain scorn, but his last five years in the CIA had opened him up to almost any possibility. Was Gaia truly in danger? He felt the familiar worry roiling his stomach.

He looked out the window of the airplane. The plane was either crossing desert or ocean because the sky was almost clear of cloud cover and beneath him was blackness. There wasn't a single light or other sign of human life. He felt terribly lonely.

He wasn't worried about danger in any ordinary sense. Gaia could get herself out of most situations. Tom, of all people, would know. He was the one who'd taught her. In the case of a mugger or purse snatcher going up against Gaia, Tom would frankly fear more for the criminal than her. Gaia was intensely strong, a master of martial arts and most commonly used weapons, and moreover she was free of the fear that compromised ordinary people. Or at least she *was*—

Was.

What did he know of her now?

He knew where she lived and where she went to school. Twice a year he received a heavily encrypted notice of her safety and general progress from the agency. He looked forward to those updates with the fervor of a man grasping for a lifeline, even though they were absurdly short, stiff, and uninformative.

That was it. He knew nothing of her friends, her habits, her pleasures, her emotional state. He had no idea how she was coping with her losses or how close the danger was.

"Sir?" An attendant offered him dinner on a tray. The smell further distressed his stomach. The food on U.S. military planes was even worse than on commercial flights.

"No. Thanks. Maybe later."

"We should be landing in Tel Aviv in approximately seventeen minutes, sir."

"Very well."

Tom looked back at his computer screen. His current briefing involved hundreds and hundreds of pages that had been downloaded via satellite during the course of the flight. One couldn't escape even for a matter of minutes anymore.

He couldn't give his mind to the intricacies of desert diplomacy right now.

There were other dangers to Gaia. More insidious ones that struck close to home. And how could he possibly protect her? Apart from his memories, that was the worst pain he faced.

In the old days, when Gaia was still a child, he'd been purely blown away by her abilities. She was a miracle. His greatest gift. Her brilliance, her beauty, her athleticism, and most of all her God-given sense of honor astonished him every single hour he spent with her. He couldn't imagine what he had done in this life to deserve such a child.

But in these strange days he found himself wishing and praying that his darling, magnificent Gaia were a meek, ordinary creature, likely to catch the attention of no one. A daughter he could trust, above all, to stay out of trouble.

"MAN, WHAT HAPPENED TO YOUR teeth?" Tarick asked. His eyes were bugged out the way they got when he was excited about something.

A Threat

Marty put his hand over his mouth. He was embarrassed. One front tooth was gone, and the smaller one to the side of it was cracked down the middle. "The girl got in a lucky punch."

CJ snorted and leaned back against the fountain in Washington Square. "The girl laid him out for like five minutes," he explained. "The girl kicked his ass." He was relieved that Gaia had busted somebody else for once.

Tarick turned cold eyes on him. He got up off the fountain wall and paced. "And you, my man. Not having a lot of luck, either?"

CJ could feel his face fall. He'd been dreading this little talk with Tarick for a good reason. "She's tough, man. She's, like, supernatural. And now she's got somebody watching her back. I had a bead on her down on Mercer Street. I had her, I'm telling you, and somebody wearing a parka and a ski mask bagged me from behind and ran off."

"Who was it?" Tarick asked. He looked doubtful.

"Somebody. I don't know. I told you—I couldn't see a face," CJ said.

"You're getting real creative about coming up with excuses," Tarick said.

CJ glared at him. It was unfair. "I am totally serious, man. Marty woulda seen 'em, too, but he was out cold."

Marty looked hurt, but he didn't say anything.

Tarick shook his head. He looked at his watch. He sighed, like he was holding back his temper.

CJ was starting to feel really uneasy. The midday sun had disappeared, and clouds were rolling in from the west. The October air was suddenly cold against CJ's bare head. He felt goose bumps rising all along his back, coursing up his neck and scalp.

"CJ, my man," Tarick started slowly. "This is not hard. You got a powerful weapon. You know where this girl lives. You gotta do what you said you were gonna do."

CJ nodded.

"And you gotta do it, like I said, by midnight Saturday. We're not fooling around here, are we?"

CJ shook his head.

Tarick sat back on the fountain wall just inches away. He put a hand on CJ's bald scalp. "I need to be able to tell the boys we avenged Marco, you know what I mean?"

CJ wished Tarick would remove his hand. It wasn't supposed to be comforting. It was a threat.

"Yeah," CJ mumbled.

"So let's make it crystal clear here, okay?" Tarick increased the pressure of his palm against CJ's shrinking scalp. "Saturday at midnight. If Gaia's not dead . . ."

Tarick paused, and CJ stared at him expectantly.

"Then you are."

SEARCH: THOMAS MOORE
```
No Match Found
```

Search: Special Agent
Moore

```
Arlington, Virginia
No Match Found

Search: Federal Agent #4466
No Match Found

Search: Michael Sage
No Match Found

Search: Robert W. Connelly
No Match Found

Search: Enigma
No Match Found

Search: My goddamned father, you
stupid morons.
No Match Found

Search:
```

Gaia threw the mouse at the monitor. She was getting frustrated. She'd hacked her way into the files of the appropriate federal agency, but the search engine refused to recognize her father's name, his old badge number, or any of his old aliases.

Was he with the agency anymore? Was he even still alive?

She'd always told herself the government would notify her if he were dead. The agency was the only place that knew her whereabouts. She'd also told herself that her dad had to have been up to some pretty covert and important stuff—like single-handedly saving the planet, for instance—to have abandoned her this way.

She told herself these things, but that didn't make them true.

Gaia heard a noise. Oh, no. If Ella was home, she'd have to jump out the window again. A moment spent with that woman was like `chewing tinfoil`. And this was not Gaia's computer to be performing illegal operations—or actually any operations—on.

She crept to the door of George's office on silent feet. The house was still. She crept back to the computer. According to the time in the right corner of the screen, she had seven minutes before Ella was due home. George wouldn't be home till after seven.

Okay. Now what? She drummed her fingers on the mouse pad. She didn't know the name her father used. She didn't know where he lived. She didn't know where he was working. He'd never, in almost five years, made any attempt to contact her. Not quite your doting father.

She felt the old anger building. Time for a little distraction. As far as Gaia was concerned, a little distraction was worth a lot of solution.

Okay. Plan 2. Sam. She had been less successful with plan 2 than plan 1, if that was possible. Could you get lower than zero? Was it appropriate to bring in negative numbers for the sake of comparison?

She aimed her fingers back at the keyboard. She called up an address-locator web site and typed in Sam's basic information.

Aha! All was not lost! Within seconds she had a definitive answer:

SamMoon3@culdesac.com

She was just one (borrowed) computer away from direct and private conversation with Sam.

Ha!

And she'd done it while leaving one full minute to hide before Ella got home.

Getting Lucky

SAM LAY IN HIS LUMPY, STEEL-frame twin bed, considering Heather's note. He didn't need to look at the note to consider it because he had stared at it so long, he'd committed it to memory.

Heather was ready. How long had he wanted to hear those

words? How long had he fantasized about this very thing?

God, and after seeing him with Gaia, he'd expected her to be pissed or at least suspicious. But she wasn't. She was angelic and totally trusting. And he was an undeserving bastard who was about to get unbelievably lucky. Almost too lucky to be true.

So what was the problem?

Forget it. There wasn't a problem. He wasn't going to get derailed by thinking about the problem.

If there was a problem, that is. Which there wasn't.

He was really, really happy as hell, even if he didn't realize it one hundred percent yet.

Time to think about Saturday night. That was only two days away. Heather was coming here, to his dorm room, and they were going to . . .

Oh, man. He was starting to feel tingly. He stared up at the stained acoustical tile on the ceiling. It wasn't the most romantic sight. He glanced at the piles of clothes around his room. He looked at the mound of chess books, magazines, and clippings blanketing his desk. He eyed the new box of syringes he'd just bought for his diabetes treatments. He propped himself up on his elbow and studied the grayish sheet covering his mattress. Exactly when was the last time he'd washed that sheet? Had it been gray to start out with, or was it born white? The fact that he couldn't remember the answer to either question wasn't a good sign.

Wait a minute. Heather. Gorgeous, perfectly dressed, sweet-smelling Heather was going to come into this room? This pigpen? This landfill? Was he seriously thinking of lying her down on this filthy bed? It wasn't only unromantic; it was probably a health hazard.

He sat up with a jolt and swung his legs off the bed. He swept up a pile of clothes and threw them on the bed beside him. Lurking under the pile were dust creatures that belonged in a horror movie. Thank God his mother couldn't see this.

In his freshman year he'd kept up some semblance of hygiene (if you defined the term very loosely) because he had a roommate. But this year he had his own minuscule room, attached to a common room shared by three other guys. He pretended to get indignant when the other guys left spilled beer on the vomit-colored carpet in the common room or ground Cheetos into microscopic orange dust underfoot. But that didn't mean he'd spent even one second looking after his own room. Usually if Heather came around, they hung out in the common room and watched TV or raided the minifridge. She hadn't inspected the frightening cave where he slept.

It was high time to reacquaint himself with the laundry room in the basement. He'd sweep out whatever flora and fauna were growing under his bed. He'd get rid of the altar to Gary Kasparov—no need to subject Heather to a full-on dork fest. Besides, the knitted brow of Kasparov didn't exactly put you in the mood.

He was just consolidating his massive clothes pile when the door swung open.

"Hey, Moon."

It was Mike Suarez, one of his suite mates.

"Does the word *knock* mean anything to you, Suarez?" Sam asked.

"Does the phrase 'lock your friggin' door if you don't want company' mean anything to you?"

Sam laughed. "The lock is busted. Half the time you turn the knob, it falls off into your hand." He made a mental note to get that fixed before Saturday.

Suarez watched him clean for a minute.

"You planning on getting lucky?"

Sam paused and rubbed his nose. Dust bits were flying in his nostrils, making them itch. "What do you mean?"

"I can think of only one reason why a guy cleans his room," Suarez said suggestively.

Sam's energy sagged at the thought of being such a cliché. He tossed the ball of laundry on the ground.

"So?"

Sam couldn't help smiling. "Yeah, I'm getting lucky. Very lucky."

"SHE FOUND NOTHING, OF COURSE,"

Can He Resist?

Ella stated, her voice ringing shrilly through the wide-open loft space, bouncing around its few polished surfaces.

"I see. And you were there watching her for the duration of her search?"

Ella's face showed impatience. "Certainly."

He pressed his lips together to signal his own waning patience. Ella, with her sleek body, her colorfully revealing clothing, and her poorly concealed moodiness acted as much the angry teenager as his bewitching Gaia. But as potently as Ella annoyed him, she had a value far beyond the `dog-loyal bodyguards` who remained within fifteen feet of him at all times. "Did she display any knowledge of her father's whereabouts?"

"No. Nothing current."

He flicked a tiny piece of lint from his dark blue slacks. "I see." He sipped coffee. "And he has made no attempt to contact her?" The question was rhetorical. He didn't even know why he'd asked it.

"No," Ella confirmed.

"How can he resist?" he mused in a quiet voice, mostly to himself.

"Sir?"

"How can he resist making contact with Gaia?

73

She's all he has in the world after what happened to Katia. He adores her. He needs her. He knows she's bound to get into trouble." He was really talking only to himself.

"Yes, sir. Would you like me to continue to keep a record of her computer activity in case she makes any strides toward finding him?" Ella asked. Even when her words were perfectly dutiful, her tone was `petulant`.

He made a sharp exhale through his nose, which was the closest he came to amusement. "She won't find him. Although I despise Tom, I can't pretend he's an idiot, can I? She'll never find him, although you're welcome to leave a few red herrings that will keep her busy trying. I'm banking on the belief—no, the knowledge—that Tom will find *her*."

He picked up the impossibly slender computer from the table beside him. He'd just had a very simple and appealing idea. He sat back and crossed his legs, the computer perched on his knee. "Tom will come for her, and when he does, he's mine."

There's one thing I want more than anything else, and I know I can never have it. I don't mean Sam or finding my dad. I'm talking about something inside myself.

I want to be brave.

And I'm not brave, in case you're wondering. Maybe I could have been brave, but I guess I'll never know.

The reason is that you can't separate bravery from fear. This is something I've thought about a lot. The people with the most fear have the greatest opportunity to be brave. A woman who is terrified of the water would be braver sticking her big toe in the swimming pool than I would be surfing a thirty-foot breaker in the Pacific Ocean. She would be overcoming something. She would be challenging herself. She would experience the pleasure of expanding her world, the freedom of exercising her will. I would be surfing a wave.

My mom used to say that a poor person who gave a dime to charity was more generous than a rich one who gave hundreds of dollars. In this example, I would be Bill Gates. Only richer.

I know for a fact that my mother was claustrophobic. And most especially, she was afraid of tunnels. Deeply, seriously afraid. I think it had something to do with her childhood in Russia, which was pretty tough. Anyway, the reason I know is because when I was seven, all my friends were taking gymnastics class a few miles away and I was desperate to go. My mom didn't want to take me at first, but I begged and pleaded. I wouldn't shut up about it. Finally my mom agreed. It turned out you had to go through a tunnel to get there. So even though I wasn't a very sensitive or nice kid, I realized my mom was basically flipping out in that tunnel. Her hands were dripping wet on the steering wheel, and her skin was whitish gray. She made these weird little moaning sounds. When we finally got out of the tunnel, she pulled over on the shoulder, rested her head on the steering wheel, and just stayed like that. I was upset, but she held me and promised me everything was fine.

Every Saturday for almost two years after that, my mother drove me to gymnastics and picked me up.

When I think of that, I'm filled with horrible, wrenching, miserable guilt. I wish so much I would have dropped that stupid gymnastics class and never gone back. But I didn't. And I can't change the past.

So instead of that, I wish that for one single moment in my life, I could be brave like my mom.

Sam's long, **fragile**
beautiful **under-**
body
claimed **standing**
all of
her senses.

DEAR SAM,

I have a very strange favor to ask you. I know you don't know me that well, and what you know of me you probably don't like. I am really, truly, sincerely sorry for what happened to Heather in the park and for the part I played in it. I know she's your girlfriend, so what I'm about to ask will sound particularly insane, but

Dear Sam,

There's this guy named CJ, a friend and fellow neo-Nazi of Marco's, the guy who tried to kill us after slashing Zolov in the park. Well, would you believe Marco is dead and CJ thinks I did it? CJ has completely lost his mind and is now hell-bent on killing me. And I came to this realization that before I die, I really want to

Dear Sam,

I know I must seem like trouble to you. I know it must seem like bad luck follows me around. I know you probably wish you'd never seen my face, which I

can totally understand. And lucky for
you, after this coming weekend you'll
most likely never have to see me again.
But before then, I was wondering if you
wouldn't mind

Dear Sam,
    I am confessing to you in total con-
fidence that in my seventeen years,
I've had very little romantic experience. Okay, none. Well, actually there
was this kid in seventh grade who kind
of liked me but—
    Anyway, I've been thinking about you
a lot recently, and I was wondering
whether—

Dear Sam,
    Will you have sex with me? Saturday
night, no questions, no commitment.

    Oh, shit. Ella was home. Gaia had to get out of
George's office right away. Ella would lose it if she
found Gaia in here and there was no way Gaia wanted
to deal with the witch in her present state of mind.
    Oh. Oh. Gaia's eyes flew over the computer monitor.
What should she do? Should she save one of these horrible letters to finish later? She had so many windows

open on the screen, she couldn't keep track of them. She heard Ella's heels clicking down the hallway. Oh, no. Um. Um.

In desperation she clicked on the Send Later icon. She clicked the X in the top-right corner to exit the on-line service. Ella was slowing down. She was right outside!

Gaia threw herself under George's desk and held her breath.

Ella paused in the open office doorway.

Don't come in here! Gaia commanded silently. *Go away* now!

Ella paid no heed to the telepathic messages. She walked right up to the computer and stared, squinting, at the screen.

Gaia knew for a fact that Ella was seriously near-sighted. But the woman was too vain to wear glasses and too stupid to put in contacts.

Ella placed her hand on the mouse.

What could she possibly want with the computer? Gaia wondered. No interface was user-friendly enough for Ella. Gaia had often snickered at the full library of "Such and Such for Dummies" titles on Ella's bookshelf.

Ella continued to stare dumbly at the screen. Her feet were a matter of inches from Gaia's shins. *Don't look down,* Gaia ordered in her head. *Do* not! Gaia tried to make her body as absolutely small as possible.

Ella clicked the mouse. Gaia heard the modem dialing up the on-line service and, within a few seconds, connecting. "Hello," the synthesized computer voice chirped.

What was going on? Gaia had never seen Ella in the same room with a computer before. Had she suddenly discovered the joy of on-line sex? Had somebody told her about the Victoria's Secret web site?

Ella squinted at the screen for another moment and clicked the mouse again.

Please don't be long, Gaia begged silently. Her knees hurt, and her back was cramping. It was so dusty under George's desk, she felt a sneeze threatening. If Ella was going shopping, it could take hours.

Then, as though obeying silent orders, Ella stood up, turned around and walked away. She walked right back down the hallway and up the creaky stairs.

Gaia's heart soared with relief. She uncrumpled her limbs and climbed out from under the desk. She was so busy congratulating herself, she didn't bother to look at the screen at first. Then the blinking box caught the corner of her eye. She came closer to read it.

"Your mail was sent."

A shiver crept down Gaia's spine. What? What mail had been sent? Probably just something of Ella's, Gaia tried to comfort herself.

She clicked on the file icon to investigate. Then she

clicked the Mail Sent icon. She was starting to get a very bad feeling in her stomach.

It was one of Gaia's files. Somehow, by going online, Ella had sent a Send Later file. But which one? Gaia clicked twice on the file.

It came up instantly, the letters twice as big and black as any others on the screen. She felt like someone had kicked her brutally hard in the middle of her chest.

Dear Sam,
    Will you have sex with me? Saturday
night, no questions, no commitment.

TOM MOORE WAS CROSSING ANOTHER endless desert. For a man who traveled tens of thousands of miles every week of his life, he certainly spent a great deal of time in the same chair, studying the same screen. For a man who hadn't seen his daughter in five years, he certainly spent a great deal of time thinking about her.

Gaia Sighting

Hundreds, thousands of pages of briefings swam

before his eyes. He closed the document and looked around him. He was so accustomed to the hum of jet engines, he could hardly sleep without it. The only other passenger, his personal assistant, was asleep.

The ever present satellite connection allowed him to get on-line. He'd promised himself he wouldn't do this, but tonight, well, tonight his mind was once again burning with worry for Gaia, and he couldn't ignore it any longer.

His first search for her name called up nothing. That was as it should be if the U.S. government was doing what they'd promised. Then he reduced the search to just her first name and conducted it globally, typing in a series of passwords that allowed him a degree of access allowed to only a handful of people— access to virtually all e-mail posted on the web, for example. This turned up an enormous list. He allowed himself a look into one file. Just one. He'd pick it wisely, then he'd stop this nonsense and get back to his work.

He scrolled through the upper part of the list. He stopped on a note tagged by the re: field. It read:

re: supergaia

He opened the file:

To: jackboot
From: stika

Gaia sighting at WSW. Call set for
2100 Sat. 2 guys and metal.

It was an unfortunately good guess. Tom's worry in-
tensified as he read easily between the lines. He felt dis-
tressingly sure this Gaia was his Gaia. He could see that
the posting had come from the New York City area and
could easily assume that WSW meant Washington
Square West, a very short distance from George's home
and the school Gaia attended.

Now that he'd opened Pandora's box, the ghosts
were all around him. He'd known this could happen. Now it didn't matter how critically his presence was
needed in Beirut. He pressed the button for the inter-
com that connected his voice to the cockpit.

"Gentlemen," he said calmly, "I'm afraid I need to
order a change in destination. Let's touch down for re-
fueling. We'll be crossing the Atlantic tonight."

GAIA PADDED QUIETLY DOWN THE
darkened hallway. She'd never been
in a college dormitory before.
When she reached the room number she'd gotten from the student
directory, she paused. She combed

Urgent
Longing

her fingers through her hair, pushing long strands back from her face. She pulled self-consciously at the hem of her exquisitely soft red velvet tank dress. Taking a breath, she turned the heavy brass knob and swung open the door.

Her breath caught. He was there. He lay on his bed, his strong arms folded behind his head, propping his upper body against the bed frame. The rest of the room was oddly indistinct, shadowy and blurred. Sam's long, beautiful body claimed all of her senses.

He looked at her. He wasn't surprised. He wasn't upset. He wasn't happy, exactly, either. He looked . . . serious. Had he known she would come now? Had he wanted it?

His feet were bare and crossed at the ankles. His loose gray sweatpants were turned up a few times at the bottom. Keeping his eyes on her face, he swung his knees over the side of the small bed and stood. He started toward her, then stopped, leaving two feet between them. Slowly he reached his arm, making a bridge across the air, and placed two fingers on the inside of her elbow, that vulnerable place where oxygen-thirsty blood coursed closest to her surface. A chill stole up her neck and dispersed over her scalp.

She'd come prepared with a storm of explanations in her head: (1)Why. (2)Why now. (3) Why him. But in this moment, stating them felt like it would break the tentative, fragile understanding, nurtured and protected by silence.

She took a step closer. This was hard for her. She bent her elbow and wrapped her fingers around his wrist. Was he pulling her, or was she pulling him? She wasn't sure. All she knew was that she was now close enough to feel the warmth radiating from his skin. He put his arms around her. She felt his fingers on the nape of her neck. Suddenly her arms were circling his taut waist, pressing him against her, crushing her breasts against his broad chest.

God, she was dizzy. She was light-headed, giddy, tingling with excitement and disbelief. Her heart was too full to stay in her rib cage. Tears gathered under her lashes.

He bent his head down so close to hers, she could feel his soft breath on her cheek. Oh God, how she wanted this kiss. She'd waited a lifetime for it. She breathed in his subtle, masculine smell and faint mixture of clean sweat and eucalyptus-scented shaving cream. She lifted her mouth to his.

Her mind was a tumultuous sea, with thoughts listing and bobbing there. And all at once an image arrived. It was an image of her body, scarred and wounded, becoming whole and perfect under his healing lips. The picture was beautiful, and she wished she could keep it, but a wave crashed through, sending thoughts spinning and surfing in the chop.

Please, kiss me, she found herself wishing. *Please. I need you.*

And then, in a cruel trick played by fate, Sam not only failed to kiss her; he dissolved completely. He vanished into air. He was replaced by dim, grayish sunlight, a tangle of mismatched covers. The magical night in his bed was replaced by a harsh, wrenching morning in hers. No, not even in hers. In one that belonged to George and Ella. Her velvet dress was replaced by a worn-out T-shirt from Jerry's Crab House.

She turned over and buried her head in her pillow. Tears stung in her eyes. The loneliness was almost unbearable. As reality spread out before her, its stark contrast to the dream made it that much harder to take.

She wanted so much to retrieve the feelings . . . and that image.

What was that image again?

In that first moment of waking, it teased her with its closeness. It danced and sparkled on a wavelet at her feet. But then the vast ocean pulled back the tide into its dark, infinite belly, and now Gaia was faced with the terror of never finding it again. If she could only find it, she felt sure it would give her strength and maybe hope.

But she was left with nothing but the taste of Sam—her fantasy of Sam—on her lips and an urgent, painful longing in her heart.

You may have noticed my name sounds familiar. I share it with a number of people, but most importantly the great scholar, statesman, and saint Sir Thomas More, born in England in 1478.

My mother was a devout Roman Catholic, and I assumed she picked the name to remind me of piety above all else. To remind me to choose God-given principles over king or scholarship or art . . . or even family.

Since I was a child, I felt the pressure of this name. I took it seriously. That's the kind of person I am, I suppose. I wanted to serve my country. I wanted to serve God. And if sacrifices were called for, I wanted to possess the courage to make them with honor.

My namesake set forth an almost impossible record of bravery. He watched his father imprisoned by King Henry VII because of his own deeds. He wrote a brilliant critique of English

(SIR) THOMAS MOORE

society in his work <u>Utopia.</u>
Ultimately he was canonized for
putting his head on the chopping
block rather than compromising
his basic beliefs for the benefit
of King Henry VIII.

I never questioned the right-
ness of More's example until
after I lost Katia and then Gaia.
Now the question haunts me every
day of my life.

In an ironic and unfortunate
twist of fate, not long after my
mother's death, I read a letter
she'd written to her father
around the time I was born. In it
I discovered she didn't name me
after Thomas More, honored saint
and statesman. She named me after
Thomas Moore, the Irish romantic
poet.

But maybe
he would be
curious. **about**
And maybe a
tiny bit **sex**
interested?
Was it
possible?

"GAIA MOORE? ARE YOU WITH US?"

Gaia snapped her head up. She glanced around at the un- **A Creepy** sympathetic faces of her class-mates. Which class was this? What were they talking about? **Pervert** She gave her head a shake to dislodge her heavy, demanding preoccupations.

Let's see. Ummmm. Ms. Rupert. That would be history. European history. Which century were they in now? Which country? She hadn't looked at her textbook in a while.

"No, ma'am, I'm not," Gaia replied truthfully.

Ms. Rupert's eyes bulged with annoyance. "You're not, are you? Then would you be so kind as to share with me and the rest of the class what you find so much more captivating than the court of King Henry VIII?"

Gaia drummed her fingers on her desk. Did Ms. Rupert *really* want to know the answer to that question?

"Yes, Gaia? I'm waiting." Her hands were on her hips in a caricature of impatience.

Apparently she did. "I was thinking about sex, ma'am. I was thinking about having sex," Gaia stated.

The class disintegrated into laughter and whispering.

Everybody was staring at Gaia. It wasn't nice laughter. Since the incident with Heather getting slashed in the park, Gaia wasn't exactly Miss Popularity. She shrugged.

Ms. Rupert looked like she'd swallowed her tongue. She spluttered and turned deep crimson before she could get a word out. "G-Gaia Moore, get out of my class! Go to the principal's office *now!*"

"Yes, ma'am," Gaia said agreeably, striding to the door.

This was a lucky break, she thought, walking down the deserted hall with lightness in her step. The vice principal would keep her waiting outside his office for ages as a phony display of his importance and full-to-bursting schedule, and it was much easier to obsess about Sam without Ms. Rupert droning on about Henry VIII and all the various people's heads he'd chopped off.

What was Sam thinking? That was the central question nagging her. Assuming he'd received her psychotic e-mail and could tell it was from her, what must he be thinking?

That she was a nympho, for one thing. That she gave new meaning to the word *desperate*, for another. That she was an opportunistic couple wrecker, for a third.

But maybe he would be curious. And maybe a tiny bit interested? Was it possible?

95

She hardly dared hope.

In some ways she was happy she'd gotten the ball rolling, even if the note did make her seem like someone who deserved to be arrested and put under a restraining order. At least she'd opened up the conversation. At least it would give her the opportunity to say, Hey, Sam, I know this is weird, I know I seem like a complete sex-starved lunatic, but can I just explain?

She ascended a flight of stairs and was just passing the computer lab when she stopped. Hmmm. The room was dark, empty, and filled, not surprisingly, with computers. She needed only one, and she needed it only for a minute or two. Ms. Rupert would eat her own arm if she knew Gaia was making a detour, but so what?

Gaia crept to the back corner of the room and revived the sleeping monitor. Quickly she located the Internet server and signed on. She went to the site where she kept a mailbox and typed in her password.

Oh, God. There was mail! She held her breath and clicked on the envelope symbol. Her heart leaped. It was from Sam Moon! He had replied!

Was this good? Was this bad? At least it was something.

Now, calm down, she commanded herself. Okay. She clicked on the letter to open it.

```
Dear Gaia13,
   Your letter was an unbelievable turn-
on. I've been hard since I read it. You
name the time and place and I am there,
honey. I am all over you. I will make
you scream, baby. I will make you beg
for more. Once you feel my—
```

Gaia swallowed. She couldn't read any more. Her stomach felt queasy. This wasn't what she . . . she couldn't quite believe he...

Her eye caught on something in the routing information at the bottom of the letter. A phrase of coded gobbledygook in which she picked out the word *Canada*. She clicked on another series of boxes to get Sam Moon's personal profile.

```
Name: Sam Moon
Home: Victoria, BC
Age: 62
```

Gaia's body was flooded with relief. She almost had to laugh. She had blatantly propositioned a sixty-two-year-old Canadian man. She exited the program and turned off the computer.

On the bright side, her beloved Sam Moon wasn't a creepy pervert, although he shared his name with one. On the less bright side, she was back to square one.

"SO *WHAT* IS THE PROBLEM?" DANNY

Bell wanted to know. He said it so loudly, Sam had to hold the phone a few inches from his ear.

How He Feels

"Well, I guess . . . I don't know." Sam scratched the back of his scalp absently. "I'm not really sure how I feel about her."

Sam watched colorful pipes weaving three-dimensionally through the computer screen that sat on his crowded dorm-room desk. He'd set the screen saver to come on after ten minutes of idleness, but when he was talking on the phone or procrastinating, the damn pipes seemed to take over his screen every thirty seconds.

"You're not sure how you *feel* about her?" Danny didn't go far out of his way to hide the incredulity in his voice. "Let me get this straight. You have a stupendously gorgeous girlfriend who you've been with for six months. She wants to have sex, and you're suddenly not sure how you *feel*?"

Sam could picture exactly the look on Danny's face, even though he was three thousand miles away. Danny was his oldest and closest friend from the neighborhood in Maryland where he grew up. In fact, Danny was the only friend he had from the old days, before Sam had remade himself from a stammering, buck-toothed chess nerd into a decently dressed, mainstream guy who went out with beautiful girls and cared what other people thought.

It was funny. Sam had changed, but Danny hadn't. Danny was still an unapologetic lover of chess and Myst and Star Wars. He was an engineering student at Stanford University, which was probably what Sam would have been had he stayed the course.

"Okay, there's a little more to it than that," Sam confessed. "See, I met this other girl."

"Aha," Danny said in a know-it-all way. "I had a feeling there was something more here. So what happened? Did you go out with her behind Heather's back?"

The pipes were hypnotic. "No, not exactly."

"But you're attracted to her."

Sam let out a groan. "Yeah, you could say that."

"What's she like?"

"Well . . . she's different from any girl I've ever met," Sam began slowly. "She's an uncanny chess player, for one thing. She's probably at my level or close to it."

Danny was silent for at least thirty seconds. "No way," he said at last.

"I'm serious."

"Jesus. What's her name? Have I heard of her or read about her?"

"No. She's mysterious like that," Sam explained. "She hasn't come up through the normal chess ranks.

I don't know anybody who's played her in competition. I don't know how she learned. She's just . . . brilliant."

"Are you sure you're not just stupid when you're around her?" Danny asked.

Sam laughed. "I *am* stupid when I'm around her. But she really is good. The other guys who play chess in the park worship her—and not for her body, either. I wouldn't even play her again 'cause she'd probably beat me in a matter of seconds."

Danny was struck to the point of speechlessness. "So, what else do you know about her?" he asked finally.

"Well, I guess her parents aren't around anymore, and from what I can tell, she has very few if any friends. She just moved to New York, but I don't know from where."

"That's awful. Did you ask her where she came from?" Danny asked.

"No." The pipes were now making Sam nauseous. He moved from his desk chair and paced the three available feet of space in the room. One of the few benefits of a minuscule room was that the ancient phone cord reached every corner of it. "I can't explain why, exactly. It's like . . . I don't know. She doesn't give you the feeling that she really welcomes questions. She seems kind of . . . haunted in a way. I guess she's been through a lot in her life. I had this weird reaction to her the first time I saw her, like I knew everything about her even though I didn't know anything. I was intensely attracted to her and sort of scared off at the same time."

Sam heard Mike Suarez and one of his other suite mates, Brendon Moss, firing up the TV for a baseball game. He moved to close the door to his room.

One of the great things about Danny was that he wasn't cool. He wasn't jaded or sarcastic. He wasn't embarrassed about having a real conversation. Sam could tell Danny things he wouldn't consider telling his other friends.

"Does that make any sense?" Sam finished.

"Um. Not really," Danny answered.

Sam sat down on his bed. (Now covered with a clean, nearly white sheet.) "Yeah, I know," he said. "I guess I'm hesitant to ask her anything because I'm not all that sure I want to hear the answers."

"Huh," Danny said. "Maybe she's a spy. Or an alien. Did you ever see that movie *Species*?"

Sam laughed again.

"So what does this girl look like?" Danny asked. "She can't be as pretty as Heather."

Sam thought that one over for a minute. "In a way she's not, and in a way she's much, much more beautiful. She doesn't dress like Heather, or wear jewelry, or keep her hair nice. You don't get the feeling she's trying to be pretty. And she's got this kind of hard, angry expression on her face a lot of the time. But if you can get past that and really see her face and her eyes . . . she's by far the most amazing-looking girl I've ever met. I can't explain it."

"Wow," Danny said. "So why don't you try it out with this girl?" he suggested after considering it for a few moments. "It sounds like she's gotten under your skin."

"She has. That's exactly what it is," Sam said, rearranging his long legs as the weary dorm-room bed groaned under his weight. "But first of all, there's Heather to think of. And also, this girl is all about trouble. I can't even begin to explain to you the kind of trouble she causes. Heather is safe, and she's great. And she's . . . ready."

Danny laughed. "Yeah. God, I wish I had your problems."

Sam walked over to the window and looked out at the courtyard. In New York City they called it a courtyard even if it was ten square feet of poured concrete, overfilled with plastic garbage cans and piles of recycling. "It's not as fun as it sounds," Sam said.

"Well, there's one obvious thing to do," Danny pointed out.

"Yeah, what's that?"

"Take out a piece of paper. At the top put Heather's name on one side and the other girl's name on the other, and make a list."

Heather	_Gaia_
My girlfriend	_Not my girlfriend_
My parents love her	_Would frighten my parents_
Not good at chess	_Great at chess_
Belongs in a magazine	_Doesn't_
Safe	_Trouble_
Loves me	_Probably doesn't give a shit_
Ready	_?_

Sam studied his list for a moment, crumpled it in a tight ball, and tossed it in the garbage. What was he, some kind of idiot?

His heart,
his life,
his sense
of life's **ghosts**
possibilities
was shaken.

TOM MOORE KNEW HE WAS CRAZY TO BE

Remembering Katia

doing this. He walked down Waverly Place in the West Village with his head throbbing and his heart full. Just two blocks from here, in a tiny bookshop, he'd first laid eyes on Katia. It was probably the most important moment of his entire life, and yet he hadn't been back here in twenty years.

It was, without question, love at first sight. It was a freezing cold day in February, and the city was bleak and dismal. The previous night's snow was no more than a brown, muddy obstacle between sidewalk and street. He'd been looking for a rare translation of Thucydides for his graduate thesis. He was stewing about something—that his adviser hadn't credited him in a recent publication. He'd seen her as soon as he'd opened the door. The shop was a tiny square, for one thing. But Katia seemed to draw every atom in the place to her. In that moment Tom's entire life evaporated and a new one started.

She was sitting cross-legged in the corner, bent forward with a book on her lap. He remembered she wore gray woolen tights, under battered rubber boots and a red knit dress. Her hair was long, dark, and straight, falling in a shiny column on either side of her face. She was devouring a stack of books the way a starving person would devour a plate of food. He would never forget that image of her.

Up until that point, he'd had many relationships with women. Fellow college and grad students, pretty ones he'd met through friends. He'd traveled with girlfriends, even lived with one for a few months. And yet his heart had never been stirred until the time he saw Katia, a naive nineteen-year-old with cheap, old-fashioned Eastern Bloc clothing and a thick Russian accent. And then it was shaken.

His heart, his life, his sense of life's possibilities was shaken. In her eyes he became somebody he could believe in.

He paused after crossing Seventh Avenue. He shouldn't be here at all. He'd learned in the hardest possible way that a man who'd made enemies like his could not afford to have a family. His disguise was minimal. His presence was needed in Beirut. He could walk straight into Gaia if he wasn't careful. He was drowning his usually sane mind in a riptide of memories.

Still he continued on. And then stopped dead in his tracks. Of course. Of course. Virtually every single thing in New York City had changed in the last twenty years, and that bookstore remained. Katia was gone. The person he'd been with Katia was gone.

Their beautiful daughter, the greatest pleasure in their lives, was alone. And the damn bookstore winked at him smugly. The riptide threatened. It dragged on his feet. Tom walked faster.

If he had any sense, he'd get back on that plane, his home away from work, and resume his mission. It was all he could show for the terrible sacrifices he'd made.

But he couldn't. He needed to see Gaia just once. From afar, of course. He'd drink her in with his thirsty eyes, make sure she was safe, and get back to his work.

Although Thomas, sainted statesman, had boarded the plane back in Tel Aviv, it appeared that the romantic poet had disembarked here in New York.

Darts

"WAIT, SO YOU'RE NOT GOING TO Robbie's tomorrow night?" Melanie asked Heather, scrambling to keep up with her friend's long, efficient strides. "According to Shauna, it's a two kegger with zero parents."

Heather shook her head. "Nope. Other plans." She smiled in a way that was mysterious and maybe a tiny bit smug. She glanced up the crowded block of Eighth Street. There were two good shoe stores before they even got to Patricia Field, and Melanie and Cory Parkes were already loaded down with shopping bags and struggling to keep up. Heather was famous among her friends for being a very fast walker and an intensely picky shopper, but the truth was, she no longer had a duplicate of her parents' credit card, the way many of her friends did.

"Other plans?" Cory demanded, gulping up the bait as always.

"Sam and I are . . . getting together," Heather offered.

"So bring him to the party," Melanie said, falling back for a moment as she rearranged her bags between her tired hands.

"I promised him we'd be alone for once," Heather explained.

"Oooh. Does this mean you're taking things to the next level?" Cory asked.

Heather smiled ambiguously. "It's a thought."

Melanie was getting that look. Her face crumpled a little when conversation turned to Sam, partly because she was envious that Heather had a mythically desirable boyfriend but also because it got in the way of Melanie's supercontrolling go-girl solidarity. Heather had a pessimistic feeling that Melanie's allegiances would change once she found a guy she thought was worthy.

"Besides," Heather said. "You know I can't drag

him to high school parties anymore." She pulled up short at Broadway Shoes, one of their regular destinations. "Do you want to go here?" she asked.

"Let's go straight to Patricia Field," Melanie said. "They have these really cute mod dresses."

Cory strode alongside Heather eagerly. "Are you going to get the orange skirt with the thingies along the bottom you tried on last time? It looked so, so cool on you."

Heather shrugged. "Maybe. The lining was kind of itchy." The lining was only mildly itchy; the skirt cost ninety-five dollars.

They were a few yards down the block from Ozzie's Cafe when Heather's stomach dropped. It was funny. She saw Ed Fargo most days of her life. It had been over two years since they'd broken up. Yet still her physical reaction on seeing him was always the same—sometimes stronger, sometimes weaker, but always present.

He was sitting in his wheelchair at a front table by the window, seeming to scan every person who passed. His dark hair was crying out to be combed, and his awful midnineties cargo pants belonged in a Dumpster. But Ed managed to be powerfully attractive nonetheless. His jaw was a little sharp and his straight nose was a little long, but he had possibly the most beautiful mouth that had ever graced the face of a man. The parts of his face, though not flawless the way Sam's were, came together in a striking and disarming way.

As often happened, Heather had that strange, sad feeling of disconnect, knowing the ghost of the person she'd loved desperately, the one with legs that worked, was lurking within the person in the ghastly wheelchair, who needed special ramp entrances and kneeling buses.

She was shallow. She knew that. Ed was still the same person inside. He was still the same person inside. No matter how many times she said it and thought it, she couldn't make herself believe it.

She stopped abruptly and rapped on the glass. Ed looked up and smiled. It was a guarded smile. She was in a position to know the difference.

Her friends were already several steps ahead, but they had stopped now and were waiting for her. "Go ahead," she called, waving them on. "I'll meet you there in, like, five minutes." When they paused, she gestured again, less patiently. "Go. I swear I'll be there in a couple of minutes."

Once her friends started walking again, Heather stepped into Ozzie's and was embraced by the thick smell of coffee. "Hey, Ed," she said, sitting down in the empty chair across from him.

"Hey," he said back. "What's going on?"

"Nothing. Just, you know, shopping with the girlfriends."

Ed nodded.

"You're waiting for someone?" Heather asked. Before he had a chance to answer, she said, "Let me guess. Gaia Moore, right?"

He looked uncomfortable. "No, not really."

"Oh, come on."

"What?" Ed said defensively. "Sometimes she comes by here after school and we have coffee. Sometimes I have coffee by myself."

Heather put her index finger on a drop of coffee that had spilled on the table. She spread the liquid in a widening circle. "You guys have gotten to be good friends, it seems like."

"Yeah."

Heather laughed at a memory, pretending it was impulsive. "Did you hear about her classic line in Rupert's class today?"

Though still guarded, Ed now looked interested in spite of himself. "No. What?"

"Rupert asked her why she wasn't paying attention, and Gaia said, and this is an exact quote, 'I was thinking about sex. I was thinking about having sex.'" Heather laughed again. "What a freak. People were mimicking her all afternoon. I'm surprised you missed it."

Ed waited for her to finish without even a smile. What had happened to the guy's sense of humor?

Heather needed a way in. She needed to make Ed

talk to her. She sat back in her chair and rolled a piece of her hair between her finger and thumb.

"I've heard Gaia's stoking a major crush," she said, tossing a dart into the winds.

Ed remained wary. "Oh, yeah?"

"So says the rumor mill," Heather said provocatively. She took a calculated risk with a second dart. "Word is, the crush is on you. Tannie got a look at her notebook in precal...."

Bull's-eye. Ed's cheeks flushed. He met her eyes with poorly masked excitement and curiosity.

On the one hand, Heather was pleased that her instincts served her so well. On the other hand, it pissed her off that Ed was obviously falling victim to Gaia, too. Had Gaia Moore been put on earth to punish her?

Ed crumpled an empty sugar packet tightly between his fingers. "I don't know about that," he mumbled. Guarded as he was, he did want to talk. "I think it's more about sex."

Heather yawned. Once she got started, it was genuine. "What do you mean?"

"Oh, I don't know." Ed seemed to wave a thought away. "She wants to lose her virginity. I guess if she's telling Ms. Rupert's class about it, it's not a big secret."

Heather looked in her purse, ostensibly for lip balm. "And who's the lucky guy?" she said suggestively.

"She hasn't said. It's a mystery."

113

"Aha." In near perfect detail, Heather's mind called up the image of Gaia and Sam sitting together on that bench in the park. Heather was starting to get an unpleasant feeling about this.

Heather located the tube of Chap Stick and ran it over her lips. "It's not a mystery to me," she said confidently.

"What do you mean?" Ed asked tentatively, crushing the bit of paper in his palm.

"It's obvious," Heather said, getting up from the table, "that the lucky guy is you."

It was a mean thing to say since Heather didn't believe it, but when she saw the naked hope and pleasure in Ed's eyes, her anger took over and she told herself he deserved it.

Stupid,
moron,
shit-head
CJ **impossible**
was
sticking
his stupid
gun in her
face again.

EVER SINCE SHE'D WOKEN FROM THAT

dream, Gaia was so distracted, she could hardly remember to breathe regularly or feed herself or put one foot in front of the other when walking.

The Vigilante

Ow. She kicked her big toe hard against a ledge in the cracked cement sidewalk and stumbled forward.

She certainly couldn't be bothered to come up with appropriate kiss-ass behavior for the vice principal, which was why she'd sat through detention, which was why she was walking home late.

She arrived at the corner of the park. Cut through or take the long way?

In her state, the right thing to do was go around. How was she going to make the dream happen if she got shot today?

She cut through, anyway. To do anything else was purely against her nature.

Would Sam be at the chess tables today, and if so, what should she say? It was time to get serious about her plan. No more being shy. No more being awkward. Her dream emboldened her.

Oh God, and there he was. She spotted him from the back, playing chess with Zolov. His elbow rested on the edge of the table, and he cradled his head in his hand. The last of the day's sun turned his tousled hair

116

into gold. She could see a bit of his profile, the sensual curve of his mouth.

It was the perfect opportunity to proposition him, but she couldn't seem to make her feet go forward. She called up the dream again, but far from emboldening her, it turned her cheeks red and made her feel very shy. Those were the lips that had made her feel ...

She heard scrambling behind her and spun around. *Oh, shit.* She took off at a run. CJ was lying in wait, of course, as she certainly knew he would be. Why was she so stupid? Couldn't she give up the death wish for even a day or two? At this rate she *deserved* to die a lonely, bitter, parentless virgin.

She cursed herself as she sprinted through the park and westward toward Sixth Avenue. It would be busy there this hour, hopefully busy enough to lose him.

Gaia raced onto the avenue. *Beeeep! Beeeeeeeeeeeeep!*

"Get the *hell* out of the *street!*" somebody screeched.

A maroon commercial van swerved to avoid her and plowed into the back of a taxicab. Gaia heard the crumpling of metal. The taxi rear-ended a black Mercedes-Benz convertible. The Mercedes drove up onto the sidewalk and crushed its headlight against a parking meter.

Oh, Jesus. Gaia ducked behind a stopped garbage truck as the air filled with shouting drivers slamming doors and the excited buzz of pedestrians crowding to watch the show. No one was hurt, Gaia was pretty sure of that, and the chaos gave her a second to collect herself. She spotted CJ on the curb, his eyes wildly scanning the street for her.

Don't move, she told him silently. *I'll be right there.*

This was all she needed—a chance to see him without being seen. She noticed with huge relief that he'd stuffed the gun back in his jacket. The sidewalk where he stood had largely emptied of people, who were drawn to the activity a little ways down the street.

Ducking as she crept along, she used the line of stopped cars to conceal herself. She had him directly in her sights, not ten feet away. *Now go!*

She pounced. In a single graceful move she captured both of his arms and wrenched them behind his back. She dragged him several yards off the busy avenue to the relative backwater of Minetta Lane. CJ growled and twisted his body to free his arms. He succeeded, or at least he thought so. The truth was, she was happy to let him come at her as long as the gun stayed out of his hands.

"Bitch," he hissed at her with a snarl. He took a step back to get some leverage, drew back his right arm, and launched his fist at her face. She dodged it easily. She felt relaxed, even—shamefully—a little excited. For Gaia a fistfight against one other person hardly drew a sweat. And CJ was just the kind of asshole she most enjoyed putting in his place.

He hauled off again, this time aiming the punch at her stomach. She caught it long before it landed. His exertion threw him so far off balance, she used the offending arm to lay him out on the pavement with the smallest effort.

He quickly found his feet and stood up, bellowing a long string of obscenities. He was squaring off, spitting mad, trying to find some way at her.

All right. It was tempting to linger but not a good idea. Time to close this thing out. He leaped at her sloppily, swinging both arms. She ducked and landed a swift, hard jab in his stomach. He doubled over, unable to breathe. She kicked him on the shoulder and sent him sprawling to the pavement. Now she knelt by his head, wrapped her forearm around his neck, and pulled him up onto her lap. She plunged her other hand roughly into his jacket, feeling around for the gun.

CJ gaped at her with surprise and fear, still unable to catch a breath. He probably thought she was going to kill him. And he did deserve it. What a joy it was to reverse their roles, to have him right where she wanted him. He should have known he didn't have a prayer against her one-on-one. Few people did. That wasn't bragging; it was just a fact. The gun was what threw everything.

"Don't you know better than to open fire in a crowded street, you stupid bastard?" she barked at him. Where was the damn gun? She tightened her grasp on his neck and made her way through his pockets. CJ's dark red wool cap got pushed to the side, revealing his stubbly bald head.

Unpleasant as it was, Gaia jammed her hand down his shirt. She saw the ugly black hieroglyphs carved into the skin of his chest and made a mental note to never, ever consider getting a tattoo.

Okay. Now she was getting somewhere. She felt the cold butt of the gun with her fingertips. What a huge relief. In a rush of hopefulness she felt the possibility of this whole insane episode coming to an end and the world stretching out with her alive in it.

Maybe she could calm down about this sex thing and go about a relationship like a normal human being. Maybe she could take on the search for her dad in a thoughtful and intelligent way.

She gripped the gun, which CJ had secured in the tightly belted waistband of his pants.

Maybe she could—

Gaia shouted in surprise as an arm closed around her own neck. Her thoughts scattered, and she lost her hold on the gun as she was wrenched backward.

"Leave the kid alone!" a voice thundered much too close to her ear. She snapped her head around to look over her shoulder. Less than a foot away was the red face of a very large man in a disheveled suit jacket and tie.

What—?

The large man dragged her back another few feet. By now CJ had sprung to his feet and lightly patted the gun still tucked in his pants.

"Did she get your wallet off you?" the man asked CJ, concern clear in his voice. "You go tell the police all about it, son. There's a squad car around the corner."

Unbelievable. Gaia was speechless.

This guy wasn't a friend of CJ's, a fellow thug from the park, as she'd briefly imagined. This was a suit-wearing, forty-something-year-old, white-collar stranger on his way home from work. This was an angry citizen taking justice into his own hands. A vigilante. He believed she was mugging CJ. He was *protecting* CJ!

What an awful joke. CJ, out on bail, concealing an illegal weapon, had every reason not to seek the help of New York's finest. He only stayed long enough to sneer at Gaia, pull his hat back down over his ears, and smile.

"You're dead!" CJ shouted over his shoulder at Gaia as he took off at a run into the bedlam of the Village on a Friday night.

The big guy was practically strangling Gaia, but she was too miserable at the moment to do anything about it.

"I've heard about girl gangs," the man was saying, not to Gaia, but not to anyone else, exactly. "That kid may not want to turn her in, but you can be sure I'm not letting her go."

Obviously the man meant it because he started

yanking Gaia toward Sixth Avenue. Was there any point in telling him the magnitude of his mistake?

"Um, sir?" She loosened his grip around her neck so she could breathe and speak. "You have to let me go now." She locked her feet on the pavement and stood firm.

He stood up tall and puffed out his chest in indignation, even as he attempted to crush her trachea. He was at least six feet four and very powerfully built. His hair was dark and thinning on top. He looked like an ex–offensive lineman. Unless he was some kind of wretched, hypocritical wife beater, he probably wasn't used to fighting girls.

"Kids like you gotta be kept off the street," the man told her. "I don't want to hear any sob stories. You can save it for the cops."

Gaia sighed. Things were not going her way. "Look, sir," Gaia said reasonably. "I don't want any more violence tonight, but if you won't let me go, I'm going to have to force you, and it could hurt."

The man looked at her in disbelief. Then he laughed dryly. "You're going to hurt *me?*"

"I don't want to. I realize you're just trying to help out. I appreciate that."

He laughed again.

"I'm serious," Gaia said. "Let me go now."

He stared at her with undisguised amusement. "You're scaring me."

"Sorry, then," Gaia said flatly.

She gave him about ten more seconds to withdraw. She actually did feel bad, but what was she supposed to do? She wasn't getting booked and spending several more hours of her life in a police station. It brought back memories of the worst hours of her life. There was just no way.

She placed both of her hands on the man's arm that circled her neck. Without any more force than necessary, she took a deep breath and flipped him over her shoulder onto the ground.

He landed hard, what with being so huge and old. He let out a terrible squawk. As he lay there writhing in discomfort, staring at her as if she'd grown second and third heads, all traces of amusement disappeared from his face. She hoped very genuinely that he would feel better tomorrow.

"Sorry," she said again before she ran off.

"THAT'S HER! THAT BLOND GIRL!"

No More Thinking

Gaia was rounding the corner of Bleecker Street less than sixty seconds later when she heard another commotion behind her. Gaia turned her head partway, and out of the corner of her eye she saw two police-men pointing after her. The big man in the suit had managed to sic the cops on her in record time.

She didn't turn her head any farther or slow her steps. The cops hadn't really seen her face yet, and she meant to keep it that way.

It was wrong and bad to run away from cops, but Gaia was really tired now, and she hadn't done any-thing illegal, except maybe flip the balding guy, but he was strangling her, and he deserved it. Furthermore, she had given him ample warning.

She would just run away from them this one time, she promised herself. In the future she would be extra friendly and helpful to the police.

She was coming up on her favorite deli when she had a brainstorm. The hatch to the basement, a sprawling black hole in the sidewalk in front of the store, was open. She could disappear without having been seen, and the cops would probably be happy to forget about the whole thing. Were they really going to blame a high school kid for roughing up a guy three times her size? She practically dove into its darkness. She pulled the heavy metal doors shut be-hind her and clung to the top of the rickety conveyor belt used to stock the supply rooms. She heard foot-steps banging along overhead. Hopefully they be-longed to the cops.

Ugh. The place was pitch black and smelled awful.

It was unfortunate to be winded and gasping for breath in a place where the air was thick with dust and rotting food. There were certainly rats down below, but she didn't want to think about that too much.

Gaia glanced at the glowing hands of her watch. Five minutes took several hours to pass. At last she opened one of the doors a crack and peered out. Never had New York City air smelled so fresh. No sign of any police.

She opened it another few inches. She was either home free or a very easy target. Still no sign. Time to make her move. She threw open the hatch door and climbed out. Once on the sidewalk, she spun around.

What she saw made her freeze. Her blood seemed to stop in her veins. Black blotches clouded her vision. She put her head down to prevent herself from fainting, and when she looked up again, he was gone.

It wasn't a cop. It wasn't CJ. Who knew where he'd gone? The man she'd thought she'd seen in that split second looked uncannily familiar. He looked, although she was sure she'd imagined it, like her father. It couldn't have been. She was low on oxygen, overtired, overwrought. It couldn't have actually been him. But it shocked her to her core just the same.

On trembling legs she found her way home. She stopped at the bottom of the stoop, trying to regain her breath and her sense of balance. She prayed Ella wouldn't be home yet.

Deep, cleansing breaths. In, one, two, three. Out, one, two, three. She put her hands on her hips and bent her head low to keep the blood flowing into it. She wasn't going crazy. There could be people in the world who looked a little like her dad. Was that so impossible?

It was a crazy night. With all she'd been through, who could blame her for a minor hallucination?

"Say good-bye, bitch."

Gaia choked on her cleansing breath. Stupid, moron, shit head CJ was sticking his stupid gun in her face again. How much more could she take in one night? She was completely beyond reason. She was exhausted and mad and frustrated and totally freaked by the sight of that familiar man.

Without thinking, she shocked both herself and CJ by wrenching the gun right out of his hand and throwing it as hard as she could down Perry Street. She wanted him away from her. Now. That was it.

CJ ran after it.

"Can't you leave me *alone* for a couple of *hours*, you little *shit*?" she screamed after him.

Then she lumbered up the stairs to the front door, carrying with her the discomforting knowledge that in addition to losing her heart and her pride, she had also lost her mind.

The only thing she'd managed to keep was her virginity.

Wearing Patience

"THAT STUPID, STUPID GIRL!" HE paced the floor of the loft, pausing briefly to kick an ottoman out of his way. "Ella, did I not order you to kill that lowlife the same way you killed his friend? What is the problem here?"

Ella glared at the parquet floor. "I said I'm trying, sir."

"Clearly not very hard. You are a trained assassin, need I remind you, and he is a pathetic, imbecilic teenager. Do you honestly need backup?" He beckoned to his two omnipresent bodyguards, who stood at attention several yards away.

"No," Ella said firmly.

He glared irritably at Ella. Was she not adequately frightened of him anymore?

He methodically took a gun out of his drawer, walked over to her, and pressed the barrel to her forehead. "Ella, you know I would as easily kill you as ask you this a third time?"

She didn't meet his gaze. "Yes, sir."

"I've taken some pains placing you with that doormat George Niven, so I'm forced to be patient with you. But know this, Ella. My patience is wearing."

No, she wasn't frightened enough. He fired the gun so that the bullet nearly grazed her nose and ruptured

127

a windowpane with a blast of noise. Ella jumped back in shock. Her eyes were momentarily filled with fear.

There. That was better.

"Trust me, Ella, if something happens to that girl, I will kill you and everyone you have ever cared about. I need Gaia, and I need her alive."

He walked to the wall of windows, watching the dying sun set flame to New Jersey's sky in a lurid show of color.

Perhaps it was time to move forward. Perhaps it was time to bring Gaia in.

HOW LONG HAD HE BEEN SITTING

here? Tom wondered, looking up at the ceiling of the diner absently. Cracks riddled the surface of the plaster, buried under multiple coats of high-gloss light orange paint. The color was the same as the bun sandwiching the burger that sat on his plate, which he hadn't found the appetite to eat.

Clinging

He truly hadn't expected to see Gaia. He hadn't prepared himself for it. Now his fragile hold on life's priorities were shattered once more.

His baby. His child. His and Katia's. His throat ached at the memory of her face. He'd known she'd be grown-up now, much like a woman, but he didn't *know*. He hadn't been ready for it.

He'd always imagined she would grow up to be a beautiful woman, being Katia's daughter, but he was surprised by precisely how. She wasn't petite like her mother. She was tall and lanky, like him. Her hair had stayed that glorious pale yellow. He would have guessed it would fade and darken, as most child hair did, but hers hadn't. It had remained straight and soft looking. Her eyes were still `deep, challenging blue`. Some blue eyes looked pale and watery—more an absence of color than a color itself. But Gaia's were rich with pigment, a dense, tumultuous, changeable blue.

He'd desperately wanted to go to her. To hold her for just a few minutes. To tell her he loved her and thought of her every hour of every day. He needed her to know that she would never be alone; she would never be unloved as long as he was alive.

And if he had, what would she have said to him? Would she have glared at him in anger? In hurt? `Could she ever forgive him for abandoning her?`

Tom pulled his eyes back down from the ceiling, pinning them to the chipped Formica table on which his hands rested. What was the use of imagining it? He couldn't hold Gaia. He couldn't talk to her. To contact her would be selfish and put her in greater danger than she could ever know. His presence here at all was a terrible, senseless risk.

Five years ago he'd clung to Katia, and in doing so he'd as sure as killed her himself. He couldn't do that to Gaia. He'd already hurt her enough.

His desire
rose to an
unquenchable **from**
thirst as he **the**
burrowed his
lips **waist**
in her soft, **down**
buttery
hair—

"GAIA, IS THAT YOU?" ED FARGO stared at the pretty brunette in the wide-brimmed straw hat, sunglasses, and flowery dress standing in the doorway of his family's apartment.

Condom Shopping

"Yes. Duh," she replied somewhat impatiently.

Ed studied her for another moment in confusion. "Why are you wearing a wig?"

"What wig?" Gaia asked.

"Have you been a brunette all this time and I just didn't notice?" Ed asked, feigning innocent surprise.

Gaia rolled her eyes. "I'm not wearing a wig, smarty-pants. I colored my hair with washable dye," she explained reasonably.

"Oh. Aha. Okay, then."

Ed shut the door behind him and locked it, and he wheeled along next to her down the hallway to the elevator. Gaia, typically, didn't offer any more information.

"Would you mind if I asked why?" Ed asked as the elevator arrived and Gaia pushed him in.

Gaia tapped her foot on the linoleum floor. "What happened to your promise not to ask questions?"

"I meant I wouldn't ask questions about big stuff," Ed said defensively. "Parents, past, unusual abilities. Not hair color. But fine. Don't tell me if you don't want."

Gaia sighed huffily. "Fine, I will tell you. But don't chicken out on me, okay?"

Ed put his head in his hand. "I have a feeling I'm not going to like the explanation very much."

"Okay?" Gaia pressed.

"Okay," Ed replied weakly.

The elevator arrived at the lobby, and the doors opened.

"Remember I told you CJ was out to get me?" Gaia asked, following him out of the elevator. "Well, he's still out to get me, and I'm sick of hiding out in my room. I wanted to go on this errand with you, but I don't want him to open fire again, particularly not at you. So that's why I look like this."

Ed swallowed. He let his wheelchair roll to a stop. "CJ is likely to open fire in the middle of the day?"

"Not if he doesn't recognize me," Gaia said breezily.

"But if he does?" Ed demanded.

"Yeah. Probably." Gaia took hold of the back of his chair and rolled him to the entrance of the building.

"Gaia! What do you think you're doing?"

"You said you wouldn't chicken out," Gaia reminded him, rolling contentedly along.

"I didn't realize my *life* would be in danger," Ed complained.

"It won't be," Gaia assured him without sounding at all convincing.

"Gaia! Stop pushing me! I'm being hijacked here!"

133

Gaia stopped. She took a breath. "Sorry," she said, like she meant it. She turned him around. "You're right. I'll take you back."

"No. I'm not saying . . . I'm just—" Ed sputtered. Why was Gaia so frustrating all the time? How did she always manage to stay in control of every situation? "Gaia, stop! Just stop."

Gaia stopped. She let go of the chair.

"Thank you," Ed said. He looked around the dull gray lobby with its drab fifties decor and hoped that no one he or his parents knew was within hearing distance of this conversation. "Now, don't roll me anymore."

"I'm sorry," Gaia said. "I really am. I won't do it again."

He glared at her in silence.

"Do you want to come or not come? It's totally up to you," Gaia said solicitously. "I promise I won't *touch* your chair."

She actually looked sweet as she waited for his response. Man, she made a fine brunette. Errrg. He knocked his knuckles against the armrest. Of course he would go with her, even if he *was* going to get shot at. That was the really pitiful thing.

"All right, Gaia," he said after he'd made her wait long enough. He wheeled into the bright sunshine of First Avenue, and she followed. "But slow down, okay? You're making me nervous."

"I'll try. It's just that I've had a rough couple of days, what with not getting killed and all."

"Right," Ed said, wondering how he'd ended up with such a friend.

They walked across the avenue and took East Sixth Street past all the Indian restaurants toward Second Avenue. Ed could smell the curry.

"So where are we going?" Ed asked.

"To buy condoms," Gaia replied.

(Cough.) "To buy"—Ed paused to clear his throat so his voice wouldn't come out squeaky—"condoms?"

"You gotta be safe," Gaia pointed out.

Ed scratched his head behind his ear. "Yes. Yes, you do," he said slowly. "Can I ask who they're for?"

"Me," Gaia said.

"Um . . . Gaia?"

"Yeah?"

"I don't know if you ever got to the unit in health class where they covered this stuff, but . . . uh, condoms are usually intended to be worn by the—"

Gaia punched him on the shoulder playfully but still too hard. "I don't mean I'm going to *wear* one, dummy."

He waited for her to offer some corrected version of her plan, but of course she didn't.

"So you're buying them for a guy?" he tried out.

"Yes," she said.

"And that guy would be . . . ?"

Gaia looked at him over her dark glasses. "Remember how I told you I wanted to have sex?"

"Yeah?" That was a hard conversation to forget.

"Well, obviously I'm going to need some condoms," Gaia explained as if she were speaking to a person with a very low IQ.

"Obviously," Ed said. His heart was racing, and he was feeling a bit queasy. He was miserably uncomfortable both with the remote hope that Gaia intended to have sex with him and the idea that she was planning to have sex with somebody else.

"Can you tell me who the lucky guy is?" His choice of words made him think of the conversation he'd had with Heather the day before. Had Gaia really written something about him in her notebook? As hard as Ed was trying to sound light and carefree, he felt his life's happiness was hanging on her answer.

"Nope," Gaia said.

Ed felt oddly relieved. "Okay. Let me ask you this. Have you told this person you're planning to have sex with him?" He hated himself for fishing, but he couldn't help it.

Gaia suddenly looked ill at ease. "No, not exactly."

"So you're just going to pounce on him in the dead of night?"

Gaia looked offended. "No. I'm not," she replied stiffly.

"Then what?"

"When I'm ready, I'm going to just go to where he

lives and . . . ask him," Gaia explained a little defensively.

"Just ask him."

"Right."

"I see."

"Does that sound so bad?" she asked. Were her eyes searching, or was he imagining it?

She stopped in front of a discount pharmacy on Third Avenue and gallantly held open the door while he passed.

"Kind of unorthodox, I guess, but not . . . *bad*, exactly."

Gaia was already studying the selection hanging on the wall behind the counter. "So what do you think, Ed?" she asked him, squinting at the labels. "Lubricated? Ribbed? Ultrasensitive?"

Ed tried to breathe evenly. For a girl who'd been concerned about awkwardness a couple of days ago, she was really `taking this in the teeth`. "Jeez, I don't know," he said feebly. He scanned the back wall, which was jam packed with every brand of embarrassing merchandise—birth control, tampons, pregnancy tests, laxatives, hemorrhoid medicine. What sick mind decided that all that stuff went behind the counter where you had to ask for it by name? "You pick."

She pointed out the package she wanted to the cashier man, who wore a sweater vest and a name tag that said, "Hi, my name is Omar." Omar, looking curious and somewhat amused, spent an extra-long time locating Gaia's choice. At last he slapped the bright red box on the counter, and Gaia paid up. Ed realized Omar was giving him approving, go-get-'em looks.

"Have fun," Omar said as they left the store.

Ed was certain his face was probably the shade of a ripe strawberry. He suddenly wished he weren't wearing a bright orange tie-dyed T-shirt.

"Do you think the guy is going to say no?" Gaia asked as they started back in the direction of his building.

"I'm not saying that."

"But you're thinking that," Gaia accused.

"No, it's just . . . I mean, look, Gaia, it's not your everyday thing to do to a guy."

Gaia nodded thoughtfully. "I realize that. I do. But I'm a little desperate here. I figure I can stay alive till tomorrow, but maybe not after that. If there's any chance of losing my virginity before then, I've just got to do it. Tonight."

"Tonight?" Ed couldn't hide his shock.

"Yeah."

"Tonight," Ed repeated numbly.

"Yes, Ed. Tonight. Saturday night."

Ed's brain felt like it was shutting down.

"So I'm just going to go right to his room and ask. Nicely, of course. I won't insist or anything. And if he seems really reluctant or . . ."

"Freaked out," Ed supplied.

"Or freaked out," Gaia allowed, "I'll just tell him the truth."

Gaia paused to let him say something, but when he didn't, she surged ahead. When she was with Ed and her mouth got going, there was no stopping her.

"The truth is good. The truth is your friend. Seriously. I'll just say to him, Look, I'm probably going to get shot in the head tomorrow, and I really want to have sex before I go, so would you mind?"

Gaia looked at Ed again for some response. He couldn't even work his mouth anymore.

"And even if he thinks I'm completely repulsive and would rather have sex with his aunt, well, he probably still won't want to refuse a girl's dying request, will he? What do you say?" She turned to Ed with a genuinely hopeful look on her face.

Ed struggled for words. "I—I say. I say . . . have fun."

The Wrong Girl

"PLEASE TABULATE YOUR RESULTS according to the format Dr. Witchell presented in the lecture on Thursday."

The very droopy-looking kiss-ass teaching assistant droned on as Sam pictured the way Heather would look when she appeared in his room that night.

It was unfortunate that his lab section of biochemistry had to meet on Saturday. It was especially unfortunate on *this* Saturday, when his mind was impossible to contain.

Would she wear that short black skirt that made him drool? Maybe one of those miniature T-shirts she had that showed off her belly button? And what about under it? It probably wasn't a good idea for him to go there right now, but he couldn't help it. He pulled his chair up so his waist pressed against the table and further obscured his lap with his notebook. It was highly embarrassing to get excited in class—something he hadn't done since seventh grade.

He'd made his way into Heather's sexy satin bras before. That was a pleasure he was looking forward to. But it was the new frontier that piqued his interest. Would she wear satin panties to match, like the women in those lingerie ads?

Suddenly he wasn't picturing her clothes anymore; he was picturing himself taking off her clothes. He couldn't help that, either. And as the fantasy evolved he wasn't under the harsh fluorescent lights of a science lab anymore but in his (now almost clean) dorm room in low romantic light (he made a mental note to buy a candle). His body pressed against her soft skin, his hands exploring her luxurious curves. Her soft, dark hair tickled his chest. His lips trailed up her neck and under her chin.

He sighed (almost inaudibly) and kissed the lids of those mysterious eyes, the bridge of her thin, straight nose, the plains of her bewitching face. His desire rose to an unquenchable thirst as he burrowed his lips in her soft, buttery hair—

Sam looked up in alarm. The blissful fantasy screeched to a stop with jarring suddenness. It felt like somebody had ripped the needle off an old vinyl record spinning a Mozart symphony.

He wasn't kissing Heather. Where had this fantasy gone so far awry? Heather didn't have hair or eyes or legs like those. Somehow Gaia had arrived in his reverie uninvited. He should have been jolted, surprised, even repulsed by her sudden presence in his bed, but was he? No. The look and feel of her had sent his desire into some completely new stratosphere.

This was not good. This was very bad. What was he going to do?

"Sam . . . ? Sam, uh . . . Moon, is it?"

Sam blinked several times. It took him a moment to bring the TA's face into focus. When he looked around the lab, he realized that except for the TA, he was all by himself. The class was gone, over. The TA was gazing at him as if he were a particularly puzzling specimen in a petri dish.

"I've kind of got to close up here, if you . . . uh . . . don't mind," the TA pointed out.

"Sure. Sorry," Sam said feebly, trying to coordinate his limbs to lift him out of his chair and walk him out of the classroom. "See you," he said over his shoulder.

Still in a fog, he walked down the corridor of the science building and out into the windy courtyard, where the bright, hopeful afternoon sun was threatened by blotchy gray clouds gathering on the horizon.

Little-Known Facts about me:

The summer before my sophomore year, I fell in love. It was the most idyllic summer you could possibly imagine. My family had rented a house in East Hampton that year. My mom and sisters and I stayed for the whole season, and my dad came out on weekends. Those were the days when my dad's business was doing really well.

Ed Fargo was spending the summer at his aunt and uncle's place just a few blocks away. Ed's folks are teachers, but his aunt is this big-time lawyer with a beautiful house right on the beach.

I was working at the farmers' market in Amagansett, and Ed was working at a surf shop on the Montauk Highway. Ed is a year older. You've met Ed, so you know he's seriously good-looking, funny, charming, self-deprecating, super-sharp, and generally a great guy. He was also an amazing surfer. This all took place before his accident, as I'm sure you've already guessed.

Anyway, our love story would take too long to describe here, but it was the most magical time of my life. Someday I'll turn that story into a romance novel, maybe somebody will even make a movie of it, and I'll earn millions of dollars.

The climax of that summer, so to speak, was a night in August, when Ed and I made love on the beach. The moon was full, and the surf was so gentle, we lay together in it. It was the first time for both of us. It was too perfect ever to be described in words, so I won't try.

One month later Ed was paralyzed from the waist down. He spent the next several months in the hospital and in physical therapy. He lost a year of school. Now he's sentenced to a wheelchair for the rest of his life.

Technically, I didn't break up with him. But I would have. Ed let me off the hook by doing it for me—that's the kind of guy he is. I was under a lot of pressure from my parents and everything. They didn't want me spending my youth taking care of a guy in a wheelchair—a guy they felt no longer had "possibilities."

Ed never acted like he hated me after that. In fact, we're still sort of friends. But in his eyes, when I have the courage to look, I see profound disappointment that can never be repaired or forgotten.

I don't need to tell you my parents love Sam. Gorgeous, brilliant, world-class-chess-playing, premed Sam. I'm only eighteen, but they'd be overjoyed if I married him tomorrow. It would relieve some of their financial pressure, I suppose.

You're probably wondering why I told Sam I'm a virgin. The reason is because Gaia is a virgin. I know it for a fact. I don't want Gaia to be able to give Sam something I can't.

Here's a little-known fact

about Ed Fargo: He has a personal fortune of twenty-six million dollars. Probably more now because the settlement came over a year and a half ago, and money like that earns a lot of interest. His parents, acting on the advice (and guilt, I guess) of his aunt, sued over the accident, even though Ed begged them not to and he refused to testify.

Ed won't let anybody touch the money. He will never tell anyone he has it. I only know because I read about the windfall in the newspaper—no names, of course, but I'm one of the few people who know the strange circumstances of the accident. In fact, I first heard about the case because Ed's parents contacted me about testifying.

Here's another fact about Ed. His reproductive organs, to put it clinically, still work perfectly well. Not that it matters to me anymore.

Heather
paused at
the door,
hesitant **ready.**
for some
or
reason to
not.
commit
herself to
this strange
night.

GAIA WAS AS CLOSE TO NERVOUS AS

a girl who lacked the physical ability to feel nervous could be. She had taken a long bath and spent hours picking out a bra and underpants that wouldn't be completely embarrassing if revealed. She'd brushed her teeth twice.

She spent several minutes naked in front of the mirror, worrying that she was too fat. After she talked herself out of that, she worried she was too skinny—bony limbed, underdeveloped, and flat chested.

She couldn't stop herself from making comparisons to Heather. Her body wasn't as feminine as Heather's. Her breasts weren't as big as Heather's. Her feet were definitely much bigger. Her hair wasn't as thick as Heather's.

Gaia had even reverted to the tactics of a seventh grader by calling Sam to make sure he was in his room, then hanging up as soon as he'd answered.

Now, standing in the middle of the floor, wearing the slinky pink dress she'd "borrowed" from Ella and a pair of heels, she felt like a big, oafish fraud. Why was she even putting herself through this? Sam would take one look at her and tell her to get lost. Why did she think he would be attracted to her? Why in the world would he consider going behind Heather's back for *her*? Even if Gaia *was* going to be out of the picture by tomorrow.

She glanced at her watch. Arg. Urmph. It was

almost eight o'clock. If she didn't leave now, Sam would probably head out for the evening, and she'd go to her grave a virgin.

She took one last look at herself. No, this wasn't going to work. She was no seductress. She wasn't going to fool anybody. She pulled the dress over her head and kicked off the heeled sandals. If she was going to go, she'd go as herself. She'd be honest. She pulled on jeans and a T-shirt and dug her bare feet into her running shoes. She thrust the package of condoms into her bag.

As a safety measure she tucked her hair into a wool cap, which she pulled low over her eyes, wrapped a scarf over most of the bottom of her face, and slipped on a pair of glasses with heavy black frames. Not exactly sexy, but neither was a severe head wound.

Thankfully Ella was out, so Gaia could walk down the stairs like a sane human being. She locked the door behind her and struck out into the cool October night, knowing that this was going to be the greatest single night of her life or a complete and total nightmare.

"THE GREEN OR THE BLACK?" HEATHER
asked her sister Phoebe.

Hesitant

Phoebe leaned back on her elbows on Heather's unmade

bed and sized her up. "The green is prettier; the black is sexier."

"Black it is," Heather said, pulling the close-fitting sweater over her head. "Can I borrow that gauzy dark red skirt?" she asked, scanning the many piles of clothing that covered her floor.

"Big night tonight?" Phoebe asked suggestively.

"I hope so," Heather answered in a way that was mysterious but didn't openly invite further questioning.

On the one hand, it was annoying that Phoebe came home from college almost every weekend. She was a sophomore at SUNY Binghamton and hated it there. She referred to it as Boonie U. and was constantly composing the personal essay for her transfer application. Heather reasoned that if Phoebe spent even half that time on her courses, she could actually make the grades to transfer. Heather didn't mention this to Phoebe, of course. Phoebe's old room had been partitioned off and rented out, so Phoebe stayed in Heather's room, and she was quite the slob. On the other hand, Phoebe had managed to accumulate lots of nice clothes—who even knew how—and usually let Heather borrow them.

"Sure," Phoebe said. She got up from the bed and planted herself in a chair at Heather's vanity table. Phoebe leaned close to the mirror and pursed her lips. "Only it's dry-clean only, so don't mess it up."

"Yes, ma'am," Heather said, locating the skirt and pulling it over her hips. Phoebe was taller, but Heather was a little slimmer. "How does it look?"

"Fine," Phoebe said without even giving her a glance. She was rooting through her capacious makeup bag. "Have you seen my brandy wine lip liner? It's Lancôme, and it cost like twenty bucks. I'm sure I had it when I came last weekend."

Heather ignored her. Phoebe was always losing things and subtly blaming other people.

Heather slipped on her black nubuck loafers and checked her hair and makeup one last time. She felt keyed up and a little shaky. She wasn't sure where excitement ended and nervousness began. She checked her purse again to make sure she had the condoms.

"Okay, Phoebe, I'm taking off. See you later."

"See ya," Phoebe said absently, without taking her eyes from her reflection in the mirror.

Heather paused at the door, hesitant for some reason to commit herself to this strange night.

"Wish me luck," she added in a quiet voice, wishing in a way that this were a night from their innocent past in which the two sisters would practice gymnastics in the living room for hours and try to stay up late enough to watch *Saturday Night Live.*

But Phoebe was already too deeply involved in her cosmetics to respond.

"OUCH. SHIT," SAM MUTTERED, putting his index finger in his mouth. He'd tried lighting the candle, but the wick was buried in the wax, and when he'd dug for it in the hot wax, he'd burned himself.

Sincere

He lit the wick again. It took this time, but the flame was sputtering and underconfident.

He sniffed at the air. Crap. The candle was advertised to smell like vanilla, which he'd hoped would cover any residue of dirty-room odor, but instead it smelled like floor cleaner.

He was nervous. He couldn't help himself. He glanced again in the mirror. It seemed stupid to take pains with his clothing when the whole point of this evening was to be taking them off as quickly as possible. He'd actually brought his khakis with him into the bathroom and taken an extra-steamy shower in the hope of getting out some of the wrinkles. He'd put on his softest oxford shirt and carefully rolled up the cuffs. It reminded him of Christmas Eve. All those hours he spent wrapping and tying up presents, when it was all torn up and discarded in a matter of moments.

It was already after eight. His suite mates had gone out. The place was eerily quiet.

He was ready for this. He wanted it. He wanted Heather. As he repeated those words in his head, he felt like a quarterback in the locker room, revving himself up for a big game.

He conjured up an image of Heather's lush body and felt his hormones starting to flow. And it wasn't just sex that he wanted, although face it, what guy could turn that down? He cared about Heather. He really did.

Sam found himself pacing the small (clean) room, reassuring himself. He wanted to do right by Heather. Her honesty and openness were genuinely touching to him. He wouldn't betray that or ever make light of it. Sure, he'd wrapped himself up nicely tonight, but she was the one giving the gift.

When the knock on the door came, the sound seemed to reverberate in his bones. He went to the door slowly, knowing who it was, of course, telling himself he wanted her fervently and yet wishing in a way it were somebody else.

A Failed Experiment

AGAINST HIS BETTER JUDGMENT, TOM Moore saw Gaia rounding the corner of West Fourth Street and followed at a safe distance. As a father he needed to see her safely to her destination, wherever that was. Then he would get on a plane back to Lebanon and resume his mission, leaving romantic notions and painful memories behind.

Based on her strange outfit, Tom guessed Gaia knew she was in danger. With her remarkable hair stashed away under her hat and a scarf and glasses obscuring her face, she was almost unrecognizable. Gaia was well adapted to taking care of herself, he told himself as he followed her east toward Fifth Avenue. He'd taught her the skills she'd need, and her miraculous gifts more than outstripped his teaching and his own abilities, in truth.

Tom, too, had been a prodigy. He had an extraordinary IQ, almost perfect powers of reasoning, and an intuitive genius for understanding the motivations of the human mind—particularly the criminal mind. He had been virtually fearless until he lost Katia. After that he wore fear like a coat of chain mail every day of his life. Tom sometimes imagined that he represented nature's first—though failed—experiment at an invincible creature. Gaia represented its subsequent and much more perfect attempt.

Gaia paused for a traffic light, and Tom took the opportunity to pull out his cell phone. He pushed two buttons, connecting instantly with his assistant. "We'll fly from the base at nine-thirty," he told him.

It was with some sense of relief that he watched

Gaia approach the door of a large building flanked by stone benches on either side. He could see from the awning that it was an NYU building, a dorm. It seemed a safe and relatively ordinary place for a girl to begin her Saturday night. He chuckled to himself at the pleasure it gave him to think that Gaia had friends and an active social life.

Maybe she would be okay. Maybe she could actually be . . . happy. The thought suffused him with unexpected joy.

Suddenly he was glad he had come. He was reassured. He could imagine his Gaia thriving here in New York. That knowledge would strengthen him for almost any trial.

He was just backing off when a glint of metal caught his eye from across the street. His thoughts and perceptions went into warp speed. It was a young man standing in the shadow of a tree, holding a .44-caliber pistol. The young man brought it up to eye level and trained it directly on Gaia.

Tom was across the street in a fraction of a second, never diverting his gaze from the gun. He was nearing his target, ready to throw his weight into the man, when suddenly the young man withdrew the gun. The young man's gaze was still trained on Gaia, but the hand with the gun hung at his side. Tom pulled up short, backing up against the side of a building to escape the young man's notice. When Tom looked back across the street, he realized that Gaia had already disappeared into the building.

Tom closed his eyes for a moment and caught his breath. Had that gun actually been trained on Gaia? Could he have been imagining the danger to her? With a sense of foreboding, Tom watched the young man conceal the gun under his shirt and stroll across the street, stopping under the well-lit awning. The young man glanced into the building and then took a seat on one of the stone benches. Tom knew he was settling in to wait.

Distress mixed with frustration as Tom took out his phone once again and pushed the same two buttons.

"Make it eleven," he told his assistant in an unhappy voice.

My views on Luck:

Before my accident, I used to think I was the luckiest guy in the world. Then I had my accident, and I sort of believed I deserved it because nobody stays that lucky. I used to think that luck got around to each of us equally. When things went badly, you were sort of saving up for a stretch of good luck. When things went too well . . . You get the idea.

According to this theory, I would be in for some good luck, right? I mean, a guy who's in a wheelchair shouldn't have parents who bicker constantly, for example, or an older sister who's ashamed of him. He shouldn't be abandoned by the girl he believed to be his one true love.

But the theory is wrong. Luck doesn't shine her light on each of us equally. She is arbitrary, irrational, unfair, and sometimes downright cruel. There are people who spend their entire lives basking in her glow, and others never seem to get one goddamned break.

Luck is powerful. Don't mess with her. Accept her for what she is and make the best of it. I can't stand that people are constantly blaming other people when bad stuff happens to them. Somebody trips on a sidewalk, and they sue some innocent bastard for millions of dollars. It's *not* always somebody else's fault. Sometimes it's just luck. Bad luck.

Luck is unpredictable. She's not your friend. She won't stand by you.

Maybe in heaven it's different. I do hope so.

But here on earth, my friend, those are the breaks.

He couldn't
hold back
much longer
without a
really good
reason.

SAM HAD A NEW RESPECT FOR
biology. Although his mind
floated somewhere near the
acoustical tiles on the ceiling, his
body did all the things a body
needs to do in order to successfully propagate the species.

The Big Moment

He gently, efficiently removed
Heather's sweater and expertly navigated her tricky
front-fastening bra. He gazed at her lovely breasts
hungrily, feeling the blood flow to his
nether regions quadruple in under two
seconds. He pulled her skirt over her perfectly
shaped hips, revealed dark purple satin panties equal
to his daydreams, and forced himself not to go further yet.

Biology was exerting so much force, Sam had to
battle himself not to remove that last bit of Heather's
clothing or to pick her right up off the floor, put her
on his bed, and hurtle forward into the main event.
But he was a gentleman. He'd toughed it out before,
and he could do it again. His older brother once told
him that if you found you were undressing the girl
and yourself, take a break and ask yourself whether
you're pushing too hard.

Sam stuck to the advice, although it seemed
like hours before Heather got around to removing
his shirt. She seemed a bit tentative to

him. Not scared, but not entirely sure of herself, either.

"We can stop anytime," he murmured against her ear, although biology was begging her not to take him up on the offer.

"No, I'm good," she whispered back.

She punctuated her point by sliding her hands under the waistband of his khakis. From his perch on the ceiling he heard a moan come from deep in his chest.

Now he saw his pants on the floor and only his blue-and-green-plaid boxers standing in the way of nudity. Soft, delicate lips poured kisses over his chest and stomach.

It was weird. His body was fully aroused and responsive, and his mind was remote. Was there a psychological term for this? Was there a treatment for it? Was this at all what death felt like?

He bitterly wished he could get his mind into the action. He'd picked a fine day for a complete out-of-body experience, he mused ironically.

"Ready?" he whispered, taking her hand and leading her to the bed.

Before taking a step, he studied her expression, waiting for her cue. Her face was flushed and intense, but not exactly the picture of lustful ecstasy. Was she holding back? Was she regretting this?

Or was he projecting *his* feelings onto her?

He took his eyes from her body so that biology would ease its choke hold for a moment. "Are you sure, Heather? We don't have to do anything you don't want. We've got plenty of time."

In response she sat down on the bed, placed a hand on either side of his waist, and pulled him down on top of her. She commandeered his mouth with kisses so he couldn't ask any more questions.

"I'm sure. I'm sure I want to do it now," she said against his ear. Why did her tone suggest more grim determination than arousal? Suddenly he felt her hands on the elastic waist of his boxer shorts, pulling them down. Another moan escaped him. He couldn't hold back much longer without a really good reason.

"I love you," she whispered to his chest. He couldn't see her eyes to gauge the depth of her words.

"Mmmm," he said, knowing that wasn't the right answer.

Apparently she didn't need to hear more. She wriggled out of her own panties and pressed the full length of her naked body against his. His body was pounding with pleasure and anticipation. His mind was surprised by her assertiveness and her . . . hurry. It almost seemed like she was in a hurry.

162

The big moment was upon them, and biology was demanding they surge ahead. Sam felt for the condom on the table by his bed. With her help he put it on. With her guiding, demanding arms he entered her. Again he heard the deep groan thundering from his chest. He heard her breathy sigh. At last his mind was pulled down into the whirlpool. At last the sensations became so fierce and so pervasive, his body and mind joined together. At last he was consumed.

So much so that he didn't notice that a slight breeze from a crack in the door had snuffed the fragile flame of the floor-wax-scented candle.

THE HALLWAY OF SAM'S DORM

Cruel Luck: 1

looked surprisingly like the one in her dream, but Gaia's feelings were different. She didn't feel sexy and bold. She felt insecure and deeply self-conscious.

First she knocked on the outer door that read B4–7. Sam's room was B5, so it had to be through there. While she waited for an answer, she pulled off her wool cap and shook out her hair. She unwound the scarf and stowed the ugly glasses in her bag. Her eyes caught the package of condoms floating at the surface of her bag, and the eager box threw her confidence even more.

Gaia knocked again. She waited for what felt like two weeks, but nobody came. Had Sam managed to slip out between the time she'd called and now? She thought she heard a noise inside. Was it okay to go in? Was it kind of a public room?

The thought of trudging back home to Ella and George's house in defeat, potentially only to be hunted down by CJ, was so unappealing, she turned the doorknob and walked inside.

It was a good-sized room, housing four desks, a minifridge, a hot plate, bookshelves, piles of sports equipment, notebooks, jackets, a couch that looked like it had been retrieved from a dump, and a very large television set. Gaia took a deep breath. No people, though.

Could Sam possibly be in his room? Maybe he was sleeping and he hadn't heard her knock. What if she were to creep in and climb into bed with him? Would he start screaming and call the police? Or would they have a beautiful, semiconscious, dreamlike sexual encounter? Gaia's head began to pound at the thought.

She walked very quietly toward room B5. Her spirits lifted. It was just her luck. The door was open a crack, and she heard a sound from inside. It sounded almost like a sleep sound.

Gaia took another deep, steadying breath. *Do it,* she commanded herself. *You have to try.* She put out her hand and placed it lightly on the knob. The brass sphere was a little wobbly in her palm. She gave it the lightest push and let it swing open.

Physicists were always crowing about the speed of light, but in this case the light from the common room seemed to filter into the small chamber slowly, as though well aware it was not a welcome guest. In this case, light traveled at the speed of dawning horror, of rude awakening, of hopes being dashed—but no faster. Before Gaia's round, naked eyes, the form on the bed was illuminated.

Two forms.

SAM HAD BELIEVED HIS BODY

and mind joined together as he made love to Heather. But in truth, they weren't actually joined until several seconds later, when his senses alerted him, in fast succession, to the subtle creaking of the door, the surprising influx of light, and most importantly, the stunned face of Gaia Moore. That was *actually* the moment when his body and mind snapped back into one piece.

GAIA HAD NEVER SEEN ANYBODY
having sex before, so the image was raw, crude, strange, terrible, and electrifying at the same time.

21/

She should have dashed out of there instantly, but her astonishment seemed to lock her muscles, giving her eyes ample time to torture her with the sight of Sam's naked body, poetic even under these circumstances. His long, lean form was cupped against Heather's, their hips joined, dewy sweat shared between chests and arms, their legs a mutual tangle.

But by far the worst moment came when Sam turned and saw her. Her pain was too big to hide, she knew, and scrawled flagrantly on her face. Sam was baring his body, but she was caught exposing her soul. Her secret pain, her crushed hope, her sickly envy, and her queasy fascination were there for all to see. Worst of all, Sam saw her see him seeing all of this.

At last her muscles freed her, and she ran.

It wasn't until afterward that she realized she hadn't bothered to look at Heather. Heather didn't really matter much.

3

WHEN SAM LOOKED AT GAIA'S face, he thought his heart broke for her, but he realized later that it broke for himself.

Just Cruel

HEATHER WATCHED GAIA'S FACE with a disturbing sense of excitement. As full and complex as Gaia's expression was in that surreal moment, Heather knew she wouldn't forget it.

Heather realized later that she hadn't even looked at Sam's face. Somehow she knew his response without needing to look. At the time, it didn't really seem to matter much.

Just when
she'd settled
herself on
that bench
and he'd

the

gotten her
temple

chase

between the
crosshairs,
she'd taken
off again.

GAIA STRODE DOWN THE SIDEWALK, tears dribbling over her cheeks, past her jawbone, and down her neck, hair streaming in the breeze. Her hat and scarf and whatever were someplace. What did it matter? If CJ wanted to shoot her right now, he could be her guest. In fact, she might ask him if she could borrow his gun.

The Park . .

At that moment she would have burned her eyes out rather than have to see that picture of Sam and bitch-girl ever again. But now the image was stored in her brain for good. Or at least until one of CJ's bullets came to her rescue. "CJ!" she called out semideliriously.

She walked blindly under the miniature Arc de Triomphe that marked the entrance to the park. She staggered to a bench and collapsed on it. She hid her face in her hands and cried. Her shoulders heaved and shook, but the sobs were noiseless. Why did her life always go this way? Why did it always seem to take the worst-possible turn?

Whenever she made the mistake of caring, of wanting something badly, life seemed to take that desire and smack her in the face with it.

What had she done to deserve this? Was it because she was strange? A scientific anomaly? Just plain made wrong? If she had fear, like a normal girl, would she also have been allowed to have a mother and a father and a

170

boyfriend? And if so, was there any way she could go back and renegotiate the deal? Give me fear! she would say. Give me tons of it. Give me extra; I don't care.

No more caring, that was the golden rule. Forget about "do unto others" and all of that crap. Life's one great lesson was: Do not care. Not caring was a person's only real protection.

In the midst of sobs and tears and internal ranting, something made Gaia look up. Afterward, when she thought back, she couldn't say precisely what it was. But for whatever reason, she turned her tear-stained face up at that moment, and a terrible night became a perfectly mind-shattering one.

There, not fifteen feet away, standing against the trunk of a compact sycamore tree, was her father. In that split second she saw that he was thinner than he was five years before, that his face was more lined and angular, that his reddish blond hair was cut very short now, but he was unmistakably her father.

Gaia didn't jump to her feet as the result of any specific thoughts or decisions. One minute she was collapsed on the bench, and the next minute she was running toward him. He didn't run to her with open arms in slow motion the way long-lost relatives do in old movies. He gave her a look that was both surprised and pained, then he took off in the other direction.

Gaia followed him without thinking. She had to. She couldn't have stopped herself if she'd tried.

EXACTLY ON SCHEDULE, GAIA HAD seen him standing under the tree. They had locked eyes, and she had recognized him. As if on cue, she ran toward him, and he ran away from her. It's what her father would have done.

10th St. & 5th Ave.

Now he would lead her to his loft on the Hudson River, just as he had planned. He was about to meet Gaia face-to-face. Excitement, true excitement, bred in his heart for the first time in many years.

For this great meeting the playing field wouldn't be even, of course. But when was it? He would go into it knowing everything about Gaia Moore, knowing her present, her past, her mother . . . intimately. She would go into it believing he was her father.

CJ CURSED IN FRUSTRATION. HE was so completely consumed by anger, he couldn't think straight anymore. Just when she'd settled herself on that bench and he'd gotten her temple between the crosshairs, she'd taken off again. He

17th St. & 6th Ave.

stowed his gun before anybody saw him and followed her.

Now he was badly winded, running, walking, dodging throngs of pedestrians, weaving through wide avenues clotted with traffic, staying with her each and every step. Not for a second would he lose sight of her blond hair, which luckily for him practically glowed in the dark.

Tonight was his night. He'd make sure of it. This couldn't go on another day. Tarick and his boys had made it clear. If he didn't kill Gaia tonight, he'd be dead by morning.

TOM KEPT THE YOUNG MAN WITH

17th St. & 7th Ave.

the gun clearly in his sights as he ran. Here was an example of why agents were never allowed near the business of protecting their families. Tom had seen Gaia's face when she'd emerged from the dorm building, tear soaked and racked with misery, and he'd stopped thinking like an agent and started thinking like a father. He'd lost a step, screwed up.

Gaia had narrowly avoided a bullet, and now they were on the run.

SAM HAD NEVER PUT ON CLOTHES

faster. He felt disgusting about leaving Heather at such a moment, but his more urgent feeling was the need to catch up to Gaia and . . . what? He had no idea. Make her feel better? Make himself feel better? Tell her he wanted

Back Up a Minute

her desperately, body and soul, and the fact that he'd just been making love to Heather was an odd, irrelevant coincidence? That would be a complete lie, yet also true at the same time.

"Heather, I'm really, really sorry," he said to her numb-looking face as he raced for the door. He wasn't so sorry, however, that he waited for a response or even looked back at her once. He felt disgusting.

The elevator was many floors away. He ran for the stairs instead. He took them two and three at a time, stumbling at the bottom and practically crashing into the serene lobby like Frankenstein's monster. Gaia was gone, of course.

Sam ran to the door and scanned the sidewalk in either direction. No sign of her. Now what? If Sam hadn't felt the frantic pangs of a drowning man, he would never have involved the security guard in his predicament.

"Uh, Kevin, hey. Did you see a girl, a blond girl around eighteen, rush out of here?" Sam asked.

174

Kevin paused for an infuriating two and a half seconds to consider. "Tall, pretty, crying?" he asked.

Oh God, she was crying. "Y-Yeah, that's probably her," Sam snapped, feeling an irrational desire to cram his hand down Kevin's throat and pull whatever informative words he had right out of there. And Sam *liked* Kevin. He and Kevin talked about the Knicks five out of seven nights a week.

Kevin paused again, savoring his important role in Sam's drama.

"Did you see which way she went?" Sam prodded, wild-eyed.

Kevin sighed thoughtfully. "Coulda been downtown," he said at last. "I'm pretty sure she walked downtown."

Sam was already at the door and out of it. "Thanks, Kevin. I really appreciate it." Most of his thanks were wasted on passersby on Fifth Avenue.

He ran toward the park. Of course she'd gone to the park. Every major event in his brief life with Gaia (with the notable exception of this evening) had taken place in the park.

Suddenly Sam had it in his mind that this was a good sign. If Gaia had gone to the park—their place, really—she would want him to find her there. If she was in the park, that would mean Sam could somehow repair this disaster.

When he caught a glimpse of yellow hair, sagging shoulders, and a face buried in familiar hands on a bench near the entrance, his heart soared irrationally. He would take her in his arms; he didn't care. He would tell her he loved her. How weird was that? But it was what his heart was telling him to do. He did love her. He loved her in a way he'd never come close to loving anything before. He'd known it for a while, even if he was too cowardly to say it or act on it. Now he would cut through all the chaos and defensiveness and confusion. He would take a risk for once in his life.

I love you. I love you, Gaia. The words were on his tongue, he could practically feel her in his arms, and suddenly, without warning, without even appearing to see him, Gaia leaped off the bench and started running.

Sam was destroyed. But he did find a reserve of insanity that pushed him to follow her.

HEATHER SAT VERY STILL ON SAM'S

A Brief Visit with Heather

bed, half dressed, with her chin resting in her hands. The room was dark; the suite was perfectly quiet.

In her mind she knew she felt horribly wronged and betrayed and mistreated by Sam, but her insides felt strangely dry. She felt too dry for tears or any of the really muddy emotions. Why was that, exactly? Why did she feel so oddly calm and lucid?

When she thought of Gaia's ravaged face, she felt a burst of gratification and maybe even joy. They had a word for this in German, her mother's first language. *Schadenfreude.* It meant shameful joy—taking pleasure in somebody else's pain.

Heather knew she should have felt shamed by this, but she didn't. She should have felt shocked and furious at Sam, but she didn't quite. Maybe later.

Maybe she was just numb.

Or maybe in her heart she already knew that Sam had fallen in love with Gaia and that he had never truly been in love with her.

Or maybe it was really all because of Ed. Because of the awful things that happened with Ed, Heather's heart wasn't the soft, supple muscle it had once been.

And Another with Ed

ED FLICKED OFF THE LIGHT IN THE hallway. He wheeled back into his room and unbuttoned his shirt—his best, softest shirt. On the collar lingered a tiny whiff of the cologne he'd put on after his shower. It brought on a pang of wobbly self-pity, and the self-pity brought on anger and discontent. Self-pity was the single worst feeling there was, particularly if you happened to be in a wheelchair.

He hoisted himself into his bed and struggled to take his pants off his immobile legs. A close second, in the race of worst feelings, was helplessness.

Ed didn't need to brush his teeth. He'd brushed them twice two hours ago.

Why was he so sad? He didn't really think Gaia was going to come, did he? No, not really. Not rationally. But he'd made the mistake of listening, just a little, to the seductive whispers of that rotten, misleading bastard called Hope.

If there was some way Ed could have strangled Hope and put the world out of much of its misery, he would have.

Instead he laid his head down on his pillow and cast a glance at the glowing blue numbers of his clock radio. It was 10:02. Only 10:02. Not so late.

What if Gaia . . . it was still possible. . . . And maybe she . . .

Ed groaned out loud and put the pillow over his head. It did nothing to drown out the whispers.

If her own
father was
leading
her into **hell's**
an ambush,
what **kitchen**
was there
to live
for, anyway?

GAIA'S MIND WAS BLANK. HER existence was all and only about keeping the tall man in the gray sweatshirt—her father, she reminded herself—in her vision. At this point Sam, Heather, and CJ were strangers to her, inhabitants of a different planet.

39th St. & 11th Ave.

The fact that her father was running away from her was immaterial. The reasons for his presence here didn't cross her mind. She made no consideration of what she'd do or say when she caught him. Past and future no longer shaded her thoughts.

She wouldn't let him get away. She *would not* let him get away. Her consciousness was only as big as that thought.

Pedestrians, cyclists, cars, trucks, pets passed in an unobserved blur. She didn't pay attention to which streets she took and where they'd lead. Chasing was so much easier than being chased because it required no strategy.

The man—her father—was fast. He was clever. He almost lost her when she collided with the Chinese-food deliveryman someplace on the West Side. Her dad was still pretty nimble for an old guy. But Gaia was unstoppable. She was too focused to feel loss of breath or any ache in her muscles. Her father had trained her too well for him to have any hope of losing her.

Now they were in the West Forties, Hell's Kitchen, she believed it was called, and her father was showing signs of exhaustion. From Eleventh Avenue he peeled off sharply to the left onto a dark side street. Gaia pulled up short and turned to follow. In this creepy neighborhood the streets and sidewalks were virtually deserted. Streetlights were few and far between. She saw that the side street dead-ended into the West Side Highway. Her father had disappeared into a building. Which one, though? A second passed before her fine hearing picked up a thud. The inimitable sound of a closing door. Gaia traced the sound to the door belonging to the last building on the street, one overlooking the Hudson River. Quickly she raced around the corner to determine if the building had a second entrance on the river side. It didn't. She had him.

JESUS, WAS SHE EVER GOING TO

44ᵗʰ St. stop? CJ felt like his lungs were on the verge of collapse. He was in no shape to scramble thirty-some blocks uptown and all the way west to the river, much of it at a dead run.

Gaia was running away from him, but she never

once looked over her shoulder to see him coming. Not even when he'd nearly picked her off on Hudson Street, after she'd collided with the Chinese guy on the bike. He'd locked on her head at point-blank range, and she'd stopped to help the Chinese guy up! The girl had ice in her veins. She wasn't a regular person.

When she turned off on the side street, CJ skidded to a hard stop, almost losing his balance. Gaia slowed down, then walked to the entrance to the building at the very end of the street and stopped. CJ didn't move from the corner. He felt his heart pounding like a jackhammer. But now it wasn't just exhaustion. It was excitement, too.

He secured the gun in both hands. He brought it up almost to eye level. Why wasn't Gaia moving—getting her ass out of there? Didn't she know he was there? She was crazy! She was a dead woman.

He tensed his right index finger on the trigger. "This is for Marco," he whispered. And with a huge, heady surge of accomplishment, he pulled the trigger and blew her away.

TOM MOORE WATCHED THE YOUNG gunman from a distance. With deep concentration he observed the young man aim the pistol, aiming his own weapon almost **Bang** simultaneously. He pulled the trigger and heard two explosions, a fraction of a second apart. With fear spreading through his heart he watched the young man go down. It was a good wound. Enough to scare a guy like that off. For now, he was out of the equation, and all that mattered was Gaia. Tom bolted around the corner in flat-out panic.

Gaia was alive. She was standing at the entrance to a building, looking around to see whence the shots had come. She was unharmed. She didn't even appear particularly concerned. Had she any idea how close that bullet had come to ending her life?

Tom ducked out of sight again. With relief flooding his body, he slid to the pavement and allowed himself a moment of rest to slow his speeding heart. Then he took out his phone and connected with his assistant. "There's a man down. I need you to report it to 911. Make the call untraceable."

Gaia's Back

SAM WAS WEARY AND CONFUSED and fast losing his grip on reality. He'd chased Gaia for at least two miles of congested city streets up to this godforsaken neighborhood and onto a side street as dark and empty of people as a New York City street could be. What was she thinking? Did she have some plan in mind? And was he crazy, or was there more than one other guy following her?

What was Gaia into now? What had she really come to tell him when she'd barged into his room tonight? Nothing was clear to him anymore—except that Gaia was a source of astonishing complexity and trouble, and of course he knew that already.

Sam staggered along the street, catching a flitting glance of Gaia's back disappearing into an old loft building that faced the river. Now what the hell was he supposed to do?

He didn't pause to answer his own question. He just followed her, of course. He hoped she wasn't leading them both to their deaths. And at least if she was, he hoped he would get a chance to tell her that he loved her (in addition to finding her stupendously annoying) before he went.

GAIA FOLLOWED HIM UP THE STAIRS
on silent feet. Did he know she was still behind him? Did he know she could hear his footsteps perfectly well in the darkness? She was certain her father could have evaded

Her Father

her more skillfully than this. Was it possible he wanted her to find him after all? What could it mean?

Complicated questions were filling up the purposeful blank that had been her mind. Eleven floors up, he exited the staircase. The heavy cast-iron door banged to a close behind him. She waited a second before following.

This had the feeling of an ambush. Gaia knew she should be cautious and prudent, but on the other hand, if her own father was leading her into an ambush, what was there to live for, anyway?

She walked through the door and found herself suddenly in a vast, well-lit loft. The ceiling soared twenty feet above her, and the floor under her feet was highly polished parquet. Enormous floor-to-ceiling windows spanned the entire wall facing the river. She could see the lights of New Jersey across the way and a garishly lit cruise boat churning up the Hudson.

She blinked in the light, regained her bearings, and turned around. There, standing before her, not ten feet away, was her father. He wasn't running from her any longer. He stood still, gazing into her face.

"Gaia," he said.

The raw pain
that lived
hidden **not**
inside her
every **nothing**
day of her
life had
broken free.

GAIA'S HEART WAS VOLCANIC.

Tears threatened to spill from her eyes.

A Soulless Viper

It was really him. He was here with her. For the first time in almost five years she had before her the thing she'd yearned for most.

In those long, empty years she'd hardened her heart against him with anger and distrust, commanding herself not to care, not allowing herself the hope that he would ever come for her.

But now, in his presence, her heart's protective shell was cracking and threatening to fall away. She'd been so strong, so capable for all that time, and now she felt that the pressure of the misery and frailty and helplessness built up over those lonely years could flatten her in a torrent of sorrow and self-pity.

She was like the toddler who'd lost her mother in the grocery store, facing miles of grim, dizzying aisles and shelves with numb courage, not allowing herself the luxury of tears until she was back in her mother's arms.

Now Gaia's tears distorted her father's familiar features, the blue eyes so much like her own. It brought upon her wave after wave of memories that she hadn't allowed herself since he'd disappeared.

Her father scrupulously drawing castles when she loved castles, horses when she loved horses, boats when she loved boats. Making her waffles every Saturday morning through her entire childhood as she sat on the counter and told him stories. Teaching her algebra, basic chemistry, martial arts, gardening, marksmanship.

He was teaching, always teaching her, but he made it fun. On Mondays he would speak to her only in Russian, and she and her mother would make blintzes and potato latkes for dinner. On Tuesdays they'd speak only in Arabic, and she and her mother would make kibbe and hummus and stuffed grape leaves. He and her mother took her on hikes in famously beautiful places all over the country to teach her about the natural world.

Most other fathers Gaia knew were good for one game of catch on Sunday after the NFL games had ended. Gaia's was different.

Now Gaia's father took a step closer. She didn't move.

That blissful childhood was what made it almost impossible to survive the night her mother was murdered and her father disappeared. She needed him and missed him so desperately, crying for him every single night, not understanding at first that he was really gone. And it wasn't beyond his control, the way it was for her mother. He was still alive. He chose something else in his life over her, and even when she became so severely depressed that she could barely eat or sleep or talk for weeks and then months at a time, still he stayed away. He never once called her or wrote. She wanted to die then just so her father would know that he had broken her heart.

Could she ever forgive him for that?

He took another step closer. And another.

His face was close and vivid now. A question hovered in his eyes.

Gaia's heart was a war zone. On the one side was the happiness and devotion her father gave her for her first twelve years. On the other was the brutal neglect for the past five. Which side was more powerful? Would Gaia's love or the anger win out?

She was watching his face very closely.

"Gaia," he said again, tentatively. He reached out to her.

Suddenly the battle shifted. Gaia wasn't sure exactly why. It was something in the way his mouth moved, something indescribably subtle, that made her know that this man was different than the one she'd adored above everything else for twelve years. Something fundamental had changed between the way he was then and now. She couldn't put her finger on it.

The anger surged forward in a fierce offensive, beating back the love with ruthless energy. The victory in battle was so quick and so decisive that when her father came another step closer and reached out his arms to embrace her, Gaia recoiled. Feeling the brief touch of his hands on her shoulders, she experienced no warmth, no affection. Nothing.

Well, not nothing. Anger.

She experienced such powerful anger that she shoved him away from her. "I don't want to see you," she told him.

The anger was building. It was terrifying. The raw pain that lived hidden inside her every day of her life had broken free, and she couldn't control it. She shoved him again, harder this time.

There was sadness and confusion in his face as he stumbled backward, or some semblance of it. She couldn't tell. She didn't know this man. His expressions weren't familiar to her.

She drew back her arm and connected her fist with his jaw. It made a satisfying crack. It was horrible, unspeakable of her to do this, to treat her own father this way.

And yet his expression conveyed no pain. He never took his eyes from her.

She was hauling off for another blow when her arm caught behind her. She spun around and realized for the first time that there was another person in the room. Over her shoulder she saw a tall, very broad man with dark clothing, short dark hair, and a completely blank expression.

Who was this? she wondered distantly, from beyond her rage.

The man held Gaia's arm tightly and twisted it behind her back.

What could her father have meant by this? Gaia wondered, staring at him in indignant disbelief. Was this some kind of ambush after all?

It didn't matter. The oversized man provided an opportune release for Gaia's exploding rage. With some zeal she broke his grasp. Instantly she grabbed a fistful of his hair in one hand and shoved her other hand under his armpit. She positioned her legs for the greatest leverage and swung the son of a bitch over her shoulder, laying him flat out on the wood floor.

She waited for him to scramble back up to his feet before she buried another jab in his stomach and kicked him brutally in the chest.

She was dangerous now. She wasn't in control. She had to put him away before she really did harm. She calculated the exact spot on his neck and struck fiercely with the heel of her hand. The man crumpled to the floor without a glimmer of consciousness, just as she'd expected. He'd wake up in a while. He'd be fine. It was her own wildfire temper that caused her concern.

Her father watched her intently. Beseeching her. She couldn't look at him anymore. If she didn't get out of there, she would do something she would truly regret.

192

"It's too late. You stayed away too long," she muttered to him as she turned and walked away. He was no longer her handsome, magical father; now only a pale reminder of sickening betrayal and loss, she needed him out of her sight.

She wished he were dead. That way she could treasure the time she had with him. She could carry on in life with the belief that love was real and happiness could be trusted. Now that cherished time, the foundation of her existence, was fatally poisoned by the knowledge that her beloved father had been a soulless viper all along.

TOM MOORE STOOD SWEATING IN

The Dark Half

the dark stairwell on the eleventh floor of the largely abandoned loft building. He had a terrible feeling about this. Why had Gaia come to this place? He felt certain there was grave danger here. He sensed it so strongly, his brain clouded with dark, impenetrable fear. He hadn't had this feeling in a long time.

He was preparing to follow her when he heard the

metal door creaking open just a few feet away. He hurled himself backward, concealing at least most of his body behind dusty boxes in the corner of the landing. He crouched there silently.

Gaia staggered through the door and into the stairwell. Her face displayed `pure psychic pain.` He stopped breathing as she walked within inches of him. Clearly she didn't see him because she continued down the stairs.

Tom felt as if his heart were being ripped from his chest. This was too hard, being near Gaia, seeing her pain, and not being able to help. But he was involved now, and how was he ever going to pull away again?

He knew he would follow her, but before he did, he needed to see what was beyond that stairwell door. Gaia had emerged physically unharmed, but nonetheless something had `destroyed her` in there.

He had a bad feeling about it. A black curiosity. Even as he crept to the door, he advised himself against it.

He opened the door with ultimate gentleness, wincing in anticipation of the slightest creak. He pulled it open about a foot and took a deep breath. Slowly, silently he peered into the giant loft, his hand poised on the trigger of his gun.

Tom's glance lighted ever so briefly on a man of his own age and build sitting in the middle of the floor, elbows resting on knees, chin resting in hands, silently contemplating.

That man sitting on the floor was exactly Tom's build and exactly his age—to the hour. His face was more familiar to Tom's than any other, and yet Tom flew from the scene with the singular horror of a man who has seen the dead rise and walk.

Tom knew it was the man referred to, in his short, explosive life among the terrorist underground, as Loki, after the Norse god of the netherworld. But he also knew that the man's given name was Oliver Moore and that he was supposed to have died five years ago.

It was Tom's alter ego, his dark half, his brother.

If You Love Something . . .

"YOU LET HER GO?" ELLA ASKED IN disbelief, returning to the loft from the floor below.

Loki said nothing. He sat there, meditative.

"After all that, you let her go?"

It was a great failing of Ella's that she couldn't keep her temper under control. She was self-destructively trying to get a rise out of him, and he wasn't in the

195

mood to play. Ella made a grave error in allowing her dislike of Gaia to get the best of her.

For a man who had risen above (or perhaps fallen below?) his emotional impulses long ago, it was rather confounding to feel the sting of Gaia's rejection. He should have been delighted to see the rage and hatred she held for her father—or a man she believed to be her father, at any rate. Instead, in some primal way, he longed to see love in her eyes, no matter who she believed him to be. She was his daughter after all, genetically if not actually. She was the child of the woman he'd loved. In all of the sordid, black history between him and Katia and his brother, Gaia was the prize, and he meant to win her.

"You've lost her now," Ella prodded sullenly.

Loki stood and stretched. He walked toward the windows, admiring the sparkling panorama with fresh eyes. Suddenly he felt enormously hungry, like he'd woken from a very long sleep.

"Until Monday, perhaps," Loki informed her with a careless yawn.

"And why will she be back then?" Ella demanded snappishly.

Loki stood inches from the window, staring out, his hands pressed against the cold glass. He was in no particular hurry to answer Ella. He studied the dark precarious cliffs of New Jersey's Palisades for a long time.

"Because I've detained a certain friend of hers. We'll keep him. Weaken him for a day or so. On Monday morning Gaia will learn that if she doesn't come for him when I wish, I will murder him."

SAM LAY ON THE CONCRETE FLOOR,

Bad Choice

feeling the thumping ache in his shoulder and ribs, dully considering the pale shaft of light that crept into the far side of an otherwise black space. Where was he? Where was the light coming from? Why had he come here, and who wanted to imprison him?

He hadn't caught up to Gaia. He had no idea where she'd gone. But the insidious suspicion had taken root in his mind that she had led him here just to be beaten up and held captive by two large men in ski masks. Blind, lovesick moron that he was, he'd chased her right into a trap.

Why, though? What had he done? Who were these people, and what could they possibly want from him?

He heard the wail of sirens coming close and wished without much real hope that maybe they were coming for him.

This was a truly depressing twist. It was so awful that a part of Sam—not a part relating to his shoulder or ribs—almost wanted to laugh.

He'd had a choice between a safe, loving girlfriend and a seamy, mysterious troublemaker, and whom had he chosen? He had abandoned the culmination of a long-desired sexual encounter for a mad dash through city streets and the privilege of getting beaten up and locked up in a deserted building on the far West Side.

He had a choice, and he'd chosen wrong.

GAIA'S LIFE FELT BLEAKER AND more desolate than the trash-strewn street where she walked. In one night the few joys she'd had or hoped for were obliterated. Her father—the idea of her father—was irretrievable. She had no choice but to accept now that Sam would never be hers. In her misery she allowed herself to imagine the scene between him and Heather after she'd run off. Sure, they were embarrassed, but once they got over it, they probably had a good laugh at her expense and got back to business—Sam more passionately than before in his joy

Being Brave

and relief to have Heather in his bed and not a psychotic miscreant like Gaia.

She walked slowly down the forsaken street, wondering in the back of her mind where CJ was with his gun. She was ready for him now. Plans 1 and 2 had crashed and burned with equal horror. Not a single hope had survived the collisions. She officially had nothing to live for.

Chill winds blew off the Hudson. She was probably cold, she realized, but she was too numb to register it.

She looked around. Wasn't it just her luck that even CJ disappointed her when she wanted him?

Well, she reasoned, she could always load up her pockets with rocks and wade into the Hudson. She could always walk into the screaming traffic of the West Side Highway. She could find her way to the roof of any one of these buildings and leap off. It's not like her demise was dependent on CJ. *Suicide is the most cowardly act,* a voice inside Gaia's head reminded her. Where had she heard that?

For some reason, the smell in the air reminded her of the smell off the lake at her parents' old cabin in the Berkshires. Who knew why. This was gritty urban water, and that was pure mountain runoff.

For some reason, the smell reminded her of her mom, and the memory of her mom magically brought an image into her mind. It was her mom's face, clear and sharp—shaded by Gaia's raw feelings, maybe, but otherwise accurate. It was the way her mom looked dangling her bare feet off the dock, watching Gaia's attempts to fish for dinner, although she knew perfectly well that Gaia would end up throwing every single fish back into the lake.

It made Gaia's heart come back to life a little because this was something approaching a miracle. Gaia could never remember her mother's face clearly. It drove her crazy that she couldn't. And yet here, in the midst of Hell's Kitchen, was Katia's beautiful and beloved face.

And for some reason, seeing her mother clearly right now reminded Gaia of something else.

Although she had lost the two things she longed for, it somehow opened up the opportunity for something she wanted even more. She had the chance to keep on living, even though she didn't think she could.

At the moment it felt to Gaia like a chance to be brave.

ESCAPE

To Jon Marans

a most
explosive
attack
of
misperception

juicy

gossip

FAKE MOTHERS ARE THE ENEMY.

This had been Gaia Moore's credo for the better part of the last year. It was like a physical law of sorts. A mantra that had been engraved in her brain ever since she'd suffered through her prison sentence in that brownstone on Perry Street with the fakest of all fake mothers, Ella Niven.

Basket Case

Ella had been as fake as they come. Fake nails, fake red hair, fake eyelashes, and an inflatable chest faker than Britney's and Mariah's combined. But the fakest thing about Ella Niven had actually been hidden under that fake chest. Her fake heart. Make that her murderous heart. Yes, in Gaia's limited experience, fake mothers, for the most part, tried to kill you.

All right, maybe that wasn't fair. Ella, as it turned out, hadn't been *all* bad. In fact, she hadn't really been anything other than a victim. Just another one of Loki's helpless victims. But still, take away those last forty-eight hours of redemption in Ella's life, and all you had left was a jealous, vindictive, all too fake mom who had spent her last days on this earth trying to order a hit on her own adopted daughter.

Obviously the odds of Gaia ever trusting another fake mother after that were pretty goddamn slim. But nonetheless, here she was, stomping her way down the hall of her apartment, headed for Natasha's bedroom, with one very simple goal in mind: She had to forget absolutely everything she believed about fake moms.

Natasha Petrova was fake mom number two, and now, more than ever, Gaia needed to trust her. Not only did she need to trust Natasha, but she actually needed her help. And Tatiana's help, too. Because Gaia's father was obviously in serious danger, more serious than any of them had even imagined. And Gaia had learned an essential lesson in the last few weeks—perhaps the most essential lesson of all. She had learned that she wasn't alone.

She did not have to face all this impending doom in a vacuum. Now there was this *thing* in this apartment on East Seventy-second Street that was starting to look and feel more and more like a family. And not even a fake family. Gaia had to admit that each day, the nagging sensation that Natasha and Tatiana were nothing more than cheap and nefarious imitations of a mother and sister had receded a little farther into the distance. And now, after everything they had been through together, Gaia was beginning to remember one of the best things about a family—something she hadn't even thought about since her mother had died.

If Gaia's father really was in serious trouble, now at least *one* other person would care as much as Gaia did. That person always used to be her mother. Her *real* mother. But now that person was undoubtedly

Natasha. And whatever doubts Gaia might have had about Natasha in the past, one thing was for damn sure: Natasha loved Gaia's father. She truly loved him. And they were probably headed for marriage. She was the closest thing Gaia had to a real mother. Closer than Gaia was even willing to admit. And when Natasha heard about Gaia's encounter with the *real* Dr. Sullivan at the hospital, she was going to be just as shocked and infuriated as Gaia was. And just as ready to kick someone's head in.

Gaia knocked loudly on Natasha's bedroom door, barely waiting for her faint and groggy invitation. She slipped through the doorway and crouched down next to Natasha's bed, glimpsing the flashing clock on the bedside table: 7:03 A.M. Natasha had somehow managed to fall back asleep since Gaia had rushed off to the hospital, though Gaia couldn't imagine how. But Gaia's news would surely send her flying up from the bed and straight to the phone to check in with all her Agency contacts.

That was what they needed now. They needed the kinds of answers Gaia couldn't possibly obtain alone.

"What. . . what's going on?" Natasha croaked sleepily. Her eyes slammed shut when Gaia flipped on the bedside lamp.

"Something's wrong," Gaia said sharply. "With Dad. Something is really wrong."

Natasha squinted her eyes open and tried to get a better look at Gaia. "What are you talking about?

What time is it?" Natasha leaned toward the clock and then fell back to her pillow. "Did something happen at the hospital? Did you talk to Dr. Sullivan?"

"I did," Gaia said. "You need to be awake for this. Are you awake?"

Natasha jimmied herself up against the headboard and brushed her hair clumsily from her face. She pulled the covers up over her silk nightgown and tried to focus her eyes on Gaia's. "I am sorry," she uttered, clearing her throat before speaking again. "It has been such a horrible morning, I think I was just trying to recover. To. . . recharge for when you got—"

"Well, the morning just got worse," Gaia interrupted, sitting firmly down on the bed. "That call we got this morning, from Dr. Sullivan—that wasn't Dr. Sullivan."

"What?" Natasha tilted her head quizzically. "What do you mean?"

Gaia looked deeper into Natasha's eyes. "He was a fake. He was a goddamn *fake*. Dad is gone."

A long silence took over the room. Sounds of morning traffic and the muted chatter of New Yorkers snuck in through the barely open window. Gaia couldn't tell if Natasha was just dumbfounded or if she had already begun to think countermeasures. She prayed it was the latter. Wherever her father was, there was no time to spare on drawn-out explanations. Not that Gaia really had any explanations.

"What do you mean. . . a 'fake'?" Natasha asked.

Gaia's hand clenched with frustration, bunching up the covers, but she quickly relaxed it. She was being ludicrously unfair. Obviously Natasha was going to need a little more than that to go on. Even a clairvoyant genius would have needed a little more information.

"I'm sorry," Gaia said, dropping her head momentarily. "I'm sorry, I'm moving too fast. Listen. The phone call—the call we *thought* was from Dr. Sullivan—it was a complete fake. All that stuff he was spewing about some *clinic* and sending him off to *Switzerland?* I thought it all sounded so ridiculous, so *stupid,* but. . . but *he's* the doctor, right? He knows *everything.* But he *wasn't* the doctor. That's why we need to put out an APB. That's why we need to call in the Bureau or, you know, Interpol, or—"

"Gaia, Gaia, shhh. . . ." Natasha placed her hand gently on Gaia's shoulder. Gaia suddenly realized that she was talking a mile a minute, like some hyperactive five-year-old who'd neglected to take her Ritalin.

"I'm not making any sense," Gaia muttered, driving the palms of her hands deep into her eye sockets. She hadn't even realized how wound up she was until she'd started to speak. "I'm sorry, but we've got to do something. We've got to do something *now.*"

"Gaia, I am not understanding you," Natasha said calmly. "Did you speak to the real Dr. Sullivan or not?"

"*Yes.* At the hospital. I *saw* the real Dr. Sullivan. I *talked* to him. He told me that all of Dad's tests had come back negative. There was no hormonal. . . *whatever,* and he didn't know a damn thing about Switzerland or anywhere else. He didn't even know Dad was gone from the hospital. Dad is *not* in the hospital, Natasha, he's *gone.* Now I don't know if *anything* is true. I don't know if they took him to Switzerland or if he's still in New York somewhere or *what.* I don't even know who 'they' are. Who was I talking to on the phone? 'They' could be a million different people. I'd say it was Loki for sure, but he's practically dead—"

"*Gaia.*" Natasha clamped both her hands around Gaia's shoulders and pressed down firmly. "You have *got* to *calm down.*"

Gaia locked her eyes with Natasha's and tried to collect herself. She was a little out of control, she knew that. But what exactly did Natasha expect? After everything they'd gone through just to have a few calm and happy minutes as a family, how could Gaia be anything other than a basket case? How could Natasha stay so calm after hearing all of it?

"How can I calm down?" Gaia complained. "How the hell can I calm down right now? How can *you* be so calm? Why are we even still sitting here?"

"Gaia." Natasha's tone was soothing but patronizing. She loosened her grip on Gaia's shoulders, but she didn't let go. "Listen to me now. If all this information were true. . . then, of course, I would be out of my mind, like you. But Gaia. . . we don't know *anything* for sure. All you have right now is a prank phone call from a man you cannot even identify. Perhaps Dr. Sullivan is misinformed, uh? Or perhaps he is not aware of a decision to send Tom to this clinic in Switzerland? Believe me, Gaia, I have been doing this for a very long time. If I went running around with my head spinning every time I got a false lead or prank phone call, they would have locked me away long, long ago, you see?"

Gaia stared defiantly into Natasha's oddly vacant eyes. "No, I don't see," she said. "I don't see why we're not—"

"A few calls, of course, I will make a few calls, Gaia. But what we need to do now is stay calm. What we need to do now is *wait*. Wait for more information. Do you understand?"

Gaia turned her head toward the window with increasing frustration, watching as a tiny beam of light cut through the room like a laser beam—like the sun was trying to break in and light the carpet on fire.

She turned back to Natasha and examined her face, trying desperately to sift through the condescending kindness, and the sage wisdom of an experienced agent, and the generic innocence of her big brown eyes. Gaia wanted to see some of the desperation that she was feeling. The desperation that came with loving someone so much that the thought of losing him actually damaged your sanity. That was half of what she'd come into this room for. Not just the help, but the empathy. The empathy that only a family member could feel . . .

But she couldn't find it. These simply were not a mother's eyes. And they weren't a wife's eyes, either. Gaia didn't even know what these eyes were.

Maybe Natasha was just an incredibly disciplined agent. Or maybe she was just nothing like Gaia. Maybe she handled the traumas of her life with total passivity. Gaia tended to handle her traumas with a well-placed kick to the groin area. They were just . . . different. That was all. That was what was going on here. Two different people coping in two very different ways. This "new family" thing was going to be a long road.

"No," Gaia said finally. "No, I don't understand. If you need to wait it out, then you wait it out. But I'm not waiting for anything. I want to know what's going on. And I want to know it now."

"We need patience now, Gaia. Patience is the best way to—"

"Where's Tatiana?" Gaia interrupted. "I didn't see her in our room."

Tatiana wouldn't be talking any of this "patience" crap. The more Gaia thought about it, the more she realized how much better she knew Tatiana than Natasha, anyway. She'd hardly spent any real time with Natasha, at least not without being in a completely

9

delirious fever state. But Tatiana. . . Gaia and Tatiana had been through hell and back together. Tatiana didn't waste time. She didn't tiptoe around a problem waiting for "more information." When Tatiana heard about Gaia's trip to the hospital, she'd sprout claws and fangs and go to work with Gaia on finding her father. Tatiana had guts. She must have gotten them from her father.

"She left early," Natasha explained. "She said something about having coffee downtown before school. Gaia, please, don't worry, okay? I will make a few calls, all right? I will try to find out what we really know. We have to believe that Tom is okay. We have to—"

"I have to go." Gaia shot up from the bed and headed for the door.

"Gaia, come on, now, don't do that."

"Let me know how the waiting goes for you."

Gaia was out the bedroom door before she could even hear a response. *Two different kinds of people, that's all. Just two different kinds of people.*

She shot over to her room, shoved a few random books into her bag out of habit, and slipped right back out and down the hall toward the front door. She needed to get downtown and find Tatiana.

But first, there was one more door she needed to open in the house. One more emotionally baffling, still barely believable, highly complicated door.

THIS HAD ALREADY BECOME SAM'S

Sickly
Newborn

favorite part of the morning. The part when he heard her footsteps coming toward the door at that brisk, almost military pace. It was like being a child on a Saturday morning and waking to that first whiff of his dad's French toast. He remembered the smell of butter and cinnamon frying in a huge tarnished copper pan, along with the promise of Japanimation cartoons to follow and then a game of chess in the park. Very few things were as thrilling to Sam as a childhood Saturday morning. But the sound of Gaia's footsteps came awfully close. And right now, lying in his lumpy twin bed, staring up at the dusty ceiling, Sam felt just about as much like a child as he had back then.

He had to admit, this bizarre circumstance did have an unfortunate air of infantilization—just waiting there like a child for Gaia to open the door. In fact, ever since he'd woken up that first morning—the morning after he was sure he had died—he'd felt like some kind of sickly newborn. That was what it had felt like. Like he was some premature newborn trapped inside an incubator and denied just about all human contact—certainly the kind of contact he'd needed. He'd needed a gentle hand to wake him and tell him he was alive instead of the cold, gruff voices

11

and sharp needles of his prison guards. He'd needed someone to talk to, maybe even cry to, instead of four white walls and a mattress that seemed to be made out of bricks and mortar. Sam had had no idea that resurrection could be so lonely.

But of course, he wasn't being altogether honest with himself. It wasn't really a mother's touch he'd yearned for in that cell. It wasn't just any gentle touch he'd imagined a thousand times over. It was Gaia's touch. Only Gaia's.

Her knuckles rapped against the door, tapping out the secret signal. Sam leapt from his bed, knocking over three books and four magazines that were only a fraction of the mess that had surrounded him like a dusty fortress in the bed. He turned the knob, releasing the flimsy lock on the door, and stepped back to let Gaia in.

God, she was a vision. It was the exact same sensation every time he saw her—ever since he'd seen her face lying next to his, half passed out by the West Side Highway. The truth was, lying all those weeks in Loki's cold, ascetic compound, half conscious from morphine and whatever else they were giving him, Sam had honestly wondered from time to time whether it was all just some kind of dream. He'd considered it a very real possibility that he *was* in fact dead and that the compound was nothing other than a purgatory of sorts—some halfway nightmare place he'd been consigned to until they'd made up his room for him in heaven. But when he'd opened his eyes and seen Gaia's face just inches from his own, sprawled out in the dirt by that highway. . . that was the first time he'd truly believed that he wasn't dead. That was when he knew she was no longer the imagined Gaia of his dreams or his memories. She was the *real* Gaia, with that lightly freckled, delicately chiseled face that no memory could possibly do justice to. Every time he saw her again, it was like waking up from a dream.

"Are you okay?" Gaia whispered, closing the door behind her and locking it.

"I'm fine," Sam replied. "Why?"

"You just looked weird. I thought it was your back again."

"No, my back is fine," Sam assured her. "No pain today. No pain at all." Sam had paused for a moment to breathe her in completely, when he suddenly realized that Gaia was the one who looked strange. Every muscle in her face had tensed up, not to mention her fidgeting fingers and her tapping right heel. "Are *you* okay?"

"No," she said absentmindedly, looking back toward the door. "No, I'm not."

Sam was struck by a powerful impulse to wrap his arms around her. So he slid a pair of his wrinkled khaki pants on over his boxers and sat down in the chair next to the bed.

This was basically the system he'd been using since being hidden away in her apartment. It was an incredibly

13

simple system, really. Every time his body ached to get closer to her, he stepped farther away. Because he didn't know what else to do. Because there was no book called *How to Come Back from the Dead and Rekindle a Romance*. Hell, Sam wasn't even sure there *was* a romance to rekindle. Things had been such a disastrous mess between them before he had. . . "died." They'd had nothing but miscommunication and arguments for weeks, all thanks to the torture Josh Kendall had put him through. Gaia and Sam had broken up with almost nothing left to salvage of their relationship. But now . . .

Now Josh was dead. Now Loki was a vegetable in some hospital bed somewhere—talk about poetic justice. Yes, *they* were both basically dead, and *Sam* was alive. Now had almost nothing to do with then. It was as if the earth's clock had been set back to before Sam's "death." And as far as Sam was concerned, if they could set the clock back to before his death, well, then why not set the clock back just a little further? Set it back to before Sam had ever met Josh Kendall. To before Gaia's uncle had begun to sink his claws into Sam. Set it back to when he and Gaia were just in love. When there was nothing dangerous about being in love.

The only question was, did Gaia want to set the clock back that far? Even if she did want to, was she ready to? Sam couldn't tell. He could certainly tell that she was maintaining a certain degree of distance from him, but she could have been doing it for so many different reasons. After all, if you'd already seen someone disappear, it must be awfully hard to believe they might not disappear again. You couldn't have love without trust. And how could you trust a man who'd already up and died on you once?

All Sam knew was that he wasn't going to rush anything. He was prepared to carry on in this isolated, untouched, infantilized, incubator-prison world of awkwardness. Just as long as he saw her every single day.

"Well, what's wrong?" Sam asked. "What's going on?"

"It's my father. . . ," Gaia began, and then she trailed off. From out of absolute nowhere a tear had appeared on her cheek. She dumped her bag on the floor and crouched down against the wall, burying her head in her hands for a half second before visibly forcing herself to regain her composure.

Sam had no choice but to glue his fingers to the arms of his chair. The desire to crouch down next to her and hold her was like some kind of preprogrammed hypnotic command. His fingernails were turning white from clenching the cushy arms of the chair, but he knew a physical gesture would only turn into an awkward disaster.

"I'm sorry," she uttered.

"No," Sam said gently, feeling like he was calling to her from a hundred miles away, even though the room

15

was the size of the average rich man's closet. "Just tell me what it is. Tell me what I can do."

"I don't *know*," she replied. Her frustration was clearly near the boiling point. "I don't know exactly what's going on, but I know Dad is in trouble. They *took* him, Sam. They took him from the hospital. And I have no idea where. I don't know where he is and I have no idea who 'they' are."

Sam felt a flash of pure empathy for Gaia's father. He pictured her father being carried away with nothing to think about but how far he was being taken from his family—how far he was being taken from Gaia. Sam knew every one of those sensations far too well.

"Well. . . we have to find him," Sam declared. "That's all. We need to start looking for him right now. We don't want to waste any time."

Gaia froze for a moment and looked up at Sam. This rather obvious reply seemed to strike her in some surprisingly deep way, as if Sam had somehow said the thing she'd been longing to hear, even though he couldn't really imagine what else there could possibly be to say. If someone was missing, what else did you do but start looking immediately? Didn't they always say that the first forty-eight hours were some kind of critical period for finding missing persons? But still, Gaia's face had seemed to light up when he said it. Like he'd just solved some riddle she'd been mulling over all morning.

"Yes," she said, showing the first faint signs of a smile since she'd walked through the door. "Yes, that's right. *Right now.* I need to start looking right—"

"*We,*" Sam corrected her. "*We* need to start looking."

Gaia's smile faded from her face. "Sam. . . you don't need to be involved in any more of—"

"Gaia." Sam searched her eyes for some common sense, trying to ignore their mesmerizing shade of ocean blue so as to complete his sentences. "Whoever the hell I'm hiding from right now is out there somewhere. And I'd be willing to bet my second life on the fact that those same people have something to do with whatever is going on with your dad. So *we* need to start looking for him, Gaia. *We.*"

Gaia stared into Sam's eyes. And she kept staring. She stared long enough to confuse him terribly and make his heart beat twice as fast. The longer she looked, the quicker his heart beat.

"What?" he asked finally, praying for her to blurt out a `ten-minute monologue` about how much she loved him—how much she'd *always* loved him and had dreamed about him every night he was gone the exact same way he had dreamed about her. . . .

"I don't know," she said, lifting her bag off the floor. That wasn't what he'd had in mind. "I'm just. . . I need to talk to Tatiana. I need to—"

"Look, Gaia . . ." Sam stood up from his chair and took a step closer to her, trying not to make her feel

17

cornered. "I want to help you. And I need you to help me. If this is still your uncle doing this, then we both need to know that. If he's just a vegetable in a coma, then we need to figure out who *is* doing it. Either way. . . we . . ." Sam felt his throat beginning to close. "We *need* each other," he stated finally. He suddenly felt like he was wobbling wildly on a tightrope, waiting for her response.

Gaia dropped her head down toward her scuffed-up sneakers. The silence was unbearable. "I know, Sam," she uttered at last. "I know we do."

Sam felt his entire spine light up. Taking risks was beginning to grow on him.

"Why don't we meet up?" he went on, a bit too excitedly. "After you've talked to Tatiana or after you're done with whatever you need to do. Tonight. In my palatial headquarters here. And we can go over it all. We can go over what we know and what we don't know. We can try to plot out a strategy to find your dad."

Gaia took another moment and then looked up at Sam with a simple half smile that made him nearly lose his balance again. "Okay," she said. "Okay, you're right. We need a strategy."

Sam breathed out comfortably. "Seven-thirty?" he asked.

"Seven-thirty," she agreed. There was a brief, indefinable pause before she spoke again. "I have to go, okay?"

"Okay." Sam smiled slightly and then backed away

toward his chair. He felt like grinning from ear to ear, which made him a little sick. They weren't going to the movies, for God's sake, they were meeting to discuss a litany of horrible tragedies. He was just ecstatic that he had managed to earn a little bit of her trust back.

GAIA COULDN'T IMAGINE WHY TATIANA

An Army of Thirsty Penguins

would be so utterly stupid as to hang out at the Astor Place Starbucks before school. She'd told Tatiana at least ten times that the Village School's "master clique," aka the Friends of Heather, aka the "FOHs," gathered there in hordes at seven forty-five. They piled into Starbucks like an army of thirsty penguins—swaddled in black and white from head to toe, waddling around with their ice-cold attitudes, preening themselves endlessly, chirping frantically at ear-shattering frequencies, and guzzling down grande lattes like they were about to become extinct.

Gaia would have to try and dart in unnoticed, fish

Tatiana out of the nightmarish squall, and get her safely over to Taylor's Bakery, where they could have coffee priced within their economic bracket and actually hear each other talk.

As she approached the corner of Astor and Lafayette, she could already see through the floor-to-ceiling windows that the penguin show had begun. Starbucks was packed. She took a deep breath, ducked her head, swung open the door, and entered the storm.

The chirping stung her ears as she slid past the painful snippets of profoundly idiotic conversation.

"Does my nose look fat today. . . ?"

"Well, you really have to go to the Isle of Capri to get the best capri pants. . . ."

Hang on, Tatiana, Gaia thought as she tuned out the tragic sounds of elitist teen culture, scanning every cushy chair and wooden table for a sign of her quasi sister. She pictured Tatiana huddling somewhere on the outskirts of the room, cursing Starbucks and the state of American youth as the icy winds of popularity beat her fragile frame deep into the frozen tundra. *Just hang on. I'll save you. . . .*

But when Gaia finally did find Tatiana. . . she wasn't huddling in the least. And she certainly wasn't on the outskirts of the room, shivering in the winds of idiocy. No. When Gaia found Tatiana, she was, in fact, seated comfortably in the warm and sunny *center* of a ring of queen idiots. . . .

Gaia froze in her tracks and blinked twice, hoping her vision would clear. But the disturbing image remained the same.

Tatiana was dressed with her usual display of annoyingly perfect casual elegance. A formfitting black knit shirt and a lavender print skirt. Her hair was in its usual perfectly coiffed dancer's bun. But there was simply nothing usual about the seating. What was she doing on "the Platform"? The platform that was practically reserved for the FOHs? She wasn't grimacing with fear and loathing. . . she was *smiling* politely. She wasn't buried in the hard frozen tundra; she was sitting in one of the biggest cushy chairs, right next to Ed, *surrounded* by a giant circle of attentive rich girls from hell. Okay, Tatiana and Ed was a normal sight. Ed and the FOHs was not an entirely abnormal sight. He had, after all, gone out with Heather for quite some time back in another life. But *Tatiana and the FOHs?*

Shake it off, Gaia. You're seeing things. Either she was hallucinating, or else she was just experiencing an explosive attack of misperception. She stepped closer to try and correct her skewed vision. But stepping closer only made it worse. Seeing this bizarre congregation of individuals was one thing. But actually hearing what they were all discussing was a whole other level of disturbing.

"So, like. . . how blind is she?" Megan Stein asked, scrunching her face into her best approximation of seriousness. She had probably learned the expression by studying her favorite model-turned-news reporters on TV. "I mean, is she, like, *sort* of blind, or is she, like, *totally* blind?"

Heather. They were quizzing Ed and Tatiana about Heather. No, not just quizzing. *Grilling.*

"She's completely blind," Ed explained patiently.

"But I mean, what did it to her?" Tammie Deegan followed up, keeping her head tilted to the left to accentuate the swoop in her hair. "Was she taking drugs?"

"No," Ed replied.

"Was it some kind of symptom of bulimia or something?"

"*No,*" Ed puffed with frustration.

"Well, can she put on her own clothes and makeup?" Tammie's brown eyes filled with concern. "I mean, how does she pick her *clothes* now?"

"I, uh . . ." Ed shrugged slightly and shook his head, most likely as awed as Gaia by the inane and hopeless priorities of the Friends of Heather. The question was not how Heather was coping. The question was what Heather was wearing.

On one hand, Gaia supposed it made sense for them to be asking all these rapid-fire questions. After all, they really hadn't gotten any real time with Heather before she'd headed off for her semester of training at a school for the blind. But the truth was, Heather hadn't really wanted to make that time for her "friends." She'd known that all her loyal subjects would react to her blindness the exact way they were right now. Like it was another sensational piece of juicy gossip to sink their teeth into and devour.

Watching it all go down was making Gaia queasy. She could tell that Ed was just trying to be kind and informative, but what the hell was Tatiana doing there? Gaia had told Tatiana a fair amount about what had happened with Heather, but did she have to share it so shamelessly with the gossip-hungry hordes? Had she ever even *spoken* to these people before?

"I really don't think you need to worry about her," Tatiana assured them.

How did *she* know whether or not they needed to worry?

"Yeah," Ed agreed. "In fact, Heather has been so strong through this whole thing, I wouldn't be surprised if she bounced right back from—"

"*Oh my God!*" Megan suddenly leapt out of her chair like she'd just discovered the cure for cancer. "I just had the *best* idea."

"What?" the FOHs sang, seemingly in unison.

"I totally know how we can help Heather," Megan announced, nearly falling forward with enthusiasm. She scanned the faces of the entire group, peering at them like she was about to impart the secrets of life. Her entire posse froze with anticipation.

Megan slid the professionally shaggy strands of her

23

three-hundred-dollar blond hair behind her ears and brought her voice down to a near whisper as a smile spread across her proud face. "A *benefit*," she whispered loudly.

Gaia watched as a reverent hush fell over all their Stila-glossed lips.

Carrie Longman was the first to finally speak, though she could only muster one word: "*Totally,*" she agreed, nodding in slow motion.

"*Yes,*" Megan squeaked, basking in the glow of self-congratulation. "A *benefit*. Whenever people are suffering, my mom *always* throws a benefit. We should throw a *huge* party at some totally swank establishment. We charge at the door, and we donate all the proceeds to finding a cure for Heather's *blindness.*"

Gaia could no longer watch this madness from afar. Her mouth could not possibly stay shut at this point. She plowed through the two kids in front of her and stepped up onto the platform, searching Megan's sparkling eyes for the remotest indication of intelligence. "Heather is not a Cambodian refugee," Gaia announced flatly. "She doesn't need a *benefit*. She just can't *see*. And that's probably only temporary—"

"*Excuse* me, Gaia," Melanie Young interrupted. "But *one*, who asked you? and *two*, there's no need for you to worry: You're not invited."

"I think it's a brilliant idea," Laura Stafford announced, standing up from her chair.

"Genius, Meegs," Tammie agreed. "You are a *genius*."

Gaia dropped her head into her hands. A *benefit* for Heather? Could they possibly have come up with a more offensive excuse to throw themselves a big party? Just the thought of it was enough to snap Gaia's priorities back in order. She had not come to Starbucks to eavesdrop on this confederacy of dunces. She had come here to find Tatiana and tell her about her father's situation. And that was what she was going to do.

She turned to Tatiana to pull her off the platform and deliver her from this nightmare, but before she'd even reached for her arm, Tatiana's words froze Gaia's entire body in place.

"I think this is an *excellent* idea," Tatiana stated with a smile. "A benefit for Heather? I'd love to help plan it."

Gaia couldn't even be sure if her jaw had dropped open or not. She was too stunned to check.

like some

biker trying

to start a

fight **goddamn**

over **tornados**

who

had the

biggest

Harley

"ARE YOU KIDDING?" GAIA COUGHED

Starbucks Nightmare

out, staring dumbfounded at Tatiana. "You're kidding, right?"

Tatiana shrugged mildly at Gaia. "What? It's a *gesture.*" She turned to Megan. "This is a very nice gesture for Heather."

"Well, *thank you.*" Megan smiled, turning to Gaia and firing a ballistic missile of sarcasm at her face. "*I* thought so, *too.* . . ."

"A *gesture*?" Gaia scoffed. "Heather's blind, so let's have a swanky party? *That's* your gesture?"

"Gaia, come on." Ed smiled, too. "It's not that big a deal—"

Gaia cut Ed off with a harsh glance. If he thought being her boyfriend meant undermining her in public, then they would have to have a long discussion about the terms of this relationship.

"I think I know where we could do it," Tatiana announced. "Have you heard of this club Pravda? It has sort of a Russian flavor. Many different vodkas, Russian food—"

"No, it's totally impossible to book Pravda," Melanie explained. "We'll have to find—"

"Wait," Tatiana interrupted. "It is not *totally* impossible. I have a friend from Russia. She is friends with the owner. I think I could get us the place for sure. If I call her now, maybe even for tomorrow night."

Us? What the hell did Tatiana mean, she could book *us* the place? Were she and the FOHs an "*us*" now? Was this absurd dream ever going to end?

"Tatiana," Gaia grunted, stepping closer to her. "I need to *talk* to you—"

"*No way!*" Tammie squeaked, staring admiringly at Tatiana. Suddenly they all seemed to be staring at Tatiana with the same reverent bug eyes. "Wait. . . you could seriously get them to close down Pravda for our party? Tomorrow night?"

"I think so, yes." Tatiana smiled.

"Oh my God, *yes!*" Tammie howled at a ridiculously unnecessary volume. "This party is going to be *awesome*. Tatiana, this is so cool. This will be the kind of party Heather would have totally loved. I'm going to start inviting the right people ASAP! No, even better, I'm going to *make* invitations."

"I'll start thinking about decorations," Tatiana offered.

"Perfect!"

Gaia was beginning to feel faint. The entire scene was so sickening, she was actually feeling woozy. There was apparently very little oxygen on the Platform. The girls began to converge on Tatiana, quizzing her on her Pravda connection and her entire Russian history. Gaia quickly realized that her words would no longer suffice to maintain Tatiana's attention. She clamped her hand around Tatiana's wrist and simply dragged her off the Platform before she could offer the ladies yet another smile.

"What is wrong with you?" Tatiana complained, ripping her arm from Gaia's grip once they'd stepped down. "Why are you being so totally bitchy today?"

"*Bitchy?*"

"Yes, *bitchy.* What is your problem today?"

"What's my problem?" Gaia suddenly became very aware of being watched by the FOHs. Not to mention a rather disgruntled-looking boyfriend. She tugged Tatiana farther into the swarm of coffee-swilling penguins and lowered her voice, looking Tatiana deep in the eyes and trying to get down to business.

"What's my problem?" she whispered intensely. "My problem is that Dad is *missing. That's* my problem."

"What do you mean, missing?"

Gaia gave Tatiana a quick rundown of her visit to the hospital, informing her of Natasha's unfortunately lackluster reaction. Once she'd managed to maintain Tatiana's attention long enough to give her all the information, she let out a long, cathartic breath.

"*That's* what I've been trying to tell you since I walked into this godforsaken place." Gaia moaned. "So what are we going to do? How do you want to deal with this? Should we split up and research, or do you want to stick together? I don't want to waste any more time. I *can't* waste any more time."

29

Tatiana seemed to mull it all over for a moment, rolling her eyes up to the ceiling as she thought.

"I don't know," she said finally. "I don't really know what we *can* do, Gaia. If my mother thinks we should wait, then I think we just have to wait, don't you?"

Gaia felt her heart sink down to her toes. *This* was the best she could get from Tatiana? *Waiting?* She sounded just like her goddamn mother! Gaia had seen Tatiana fight her way out of almost every crisis they'd been through. How could she choose *now* to wimp out completely? Gaia stared deeper into Tatiana's eyes, wondering how she could possibly stay so calm and composed. But the answer was rather obvious, wasn't it? Of course she could stay calm. After all, it wasn't *Tatiana's* father who was quite possibly lying dead on some stretcher in God knew where. No, he wasn't really anything *close* to her father, was he?

"Why are you looking at me like that?" Tatiana asked. Her face began to fill up with regret. "I'm sorry, Gaia, I don't know what else to say. I don't know what we could do for him. . . ."

Gaia tried to force a false expression of acceptance on her face, just to let Tatiana off the hook, but she couldn't. She knew why she was looking at Tatiana "like that"; she just didn't feel the need to put it into words. She was looking at her "like that" because she had already realized, in only the last hour, that this "new family" of hers left a whole lot to be desired. Tatiana would probably come around in a few hours, maybe even a few minutes, but right now she felt about as much like a sister as all those rich bitches up on the Platform.

"Gaia?" Tatiana urged. "Can you talk to me, please? I'm not trying to be insensitive, you know? I just don't know how we—"

"No, it's fine," Gaia stated numbly. "It's fine. You're right. We should just wait and see what happens."

"Wait. Now you're not being honest with me," Tatiana complained.

"No, I am." Gaia's feet had already begun moving backward. "Let's just talk about it later, okay?"

"Gaia... Gaia, wait...."

"Yeah, *later*," Gaia muttered, swinging away from Tatiana to head for the door.

But the Starbucks nightmare *still* wasn't over.

The moment Gaia turned around, she bumped straight into a wall. A wall named Jake Montone.

"*Oompf*," Jake huffed, gripping Gaia's shoulders tightly to slow her down. "Jesus, Gaia. You're awfully clumsy for an all-powerful karate master."

Gaia shook free of Jake's grip. Her tolerance for his obnoxious martial arts-jock grin was at absolute zero. Jake could not have picked a worse time to mess with her. And his check-me-out gym-toned biceps and perfectly floofed hair only made her hungrier to drop him on his ass right here and now. "Can you move, please?"

31

Jake crossed his thick arms over his chest and stood his ground. "You know, Gaia, I've only been in this school for a couple of days, but I still feel qualified to speak for the entire senior class when I say... what the hell is your *problem*?"

Gaia's blood had been boiling so long it was beginning to froth. Her violent tendencies had been building slowly ever since she'd entered penguin hell, and if Jake didn't make way, she might just have to take it all out on him. And why the hell not? She'd already given him the judo pounding of his life once. Mr. Handsome New Guy or not, he was probably the only one in the entire school who could take it.

"I try not to speak in clichés, Jake," she uttered through clenched teeth. "But right now... my problem is *you. Move.*" She stepped to the left to pass him, but he countered with an ultra-annoying step to his right to block her again.

"Are you sure *I'm* the problem, Gaia?" He leaned a little closer. "Because I could swear you've had that same *screw-you-all* grimace on your face for the past... oh, say eight or nine *years.* Does that sound accurate to you?"

Just smack him, Gaia. Pummeling him with words takes too much time. When dealing with a primitive, there is no other choice but to use primitive tactics. "Jake, you've got three freaking seconds to get out of my way. Three... two..."

"No, no, *five* seconds." Jake laughed, waving his

hands wildly in fake desperation. "No, wait, *six*. Give me *six* seconds. . . ."

That was it. Gaia felt her restraint snap. Before she knew it, she had grabbed the front of Jake's tight T-shirt in her hand and yanked him violently forward so that they were face-to-face.

"*Listen* to me, Jake," she menaced, nearly ripping a hole in the center of his shirt. "There is an entire level that you are *not* getting here. The level on which my life, which you know *absolutely nothing* about, exists. The level on which I will *snap* your goddamn neck if you do not cut the seventh-grade-style antagonism and get the hell out of my way. *Do you understand?* Have I answered your questions to your satisfaction?"

Jake stared at her without budging an inch. He widened his excessively green eyes with a bizarre kind of confrontational glee and leaned in closer, nearly head-butting Gaia from above. If he was going to try the head butt, she was oh so ready to flip him straight onto his ass. Hopefully she could take a few penguins with her.

But he didn't go for the head butt. He surprised her and went verbal.

"Gaia," he said, only inches from her face, "I fear that this is the only way you can get close to people. Just remember. . . violence is never the answer. If you want to get closer to me, then you should really call my father and invite me out on a proper date." He smiled.

33

Gaia felt her free hand clenching up into a fist. He deserved it now. There was no question in her mind. He had earned it. She pulled back her fist and tried not to think about the lawsuit that would follow. . . .

"*Whoa*, there." Ed laughed, grabbing Gaia's arm from behind and gently guiding her away from Jake and his obnoxious grin. "Let's just *chill* for a moment, shall we?"

Ed pulled Gaia across the room as she watched Jake slowly disappear into the crowd. A moment more and Gaia realized how completely ridiculous she was being. She felt like some biker trying to start a fight over who had the biggest Harley. She felt like an idiot. And she had much bigger problems to deal with than the newest FOH jock and his tight T-shirt.

Ed pulled her to the farthest corner from the FOHs and settled back with her against a relatively private wall.

They sat for a moment in silence.

And then, out of nowhere, Ed smoothed her tangled hair behind her shoulder, leaned in, kissed her neck, and then released her hair, sitting back comfortably against the wall.

Ed truly knew her. He knew that his strange little kiss on the neck would basically be the equivalent of flipping her "human" switch back to the on position. She instantly felt her lungs expand and she began to breathe again. It was as if she hadn't been breathing for hours. Maybe she hadn't. She turned to Ed, and each of her senses began to return. As usual, his clear eyes showed no hidden agenda whatsoever, no ulterior motives. There was nothing behind his eyes that she couldn't trust. Just Ed. Ed, who was, as far as she could tell, perfect. Ed, who had sat her down here just to be next to her. And that was when she realized . . .

She had barely spoken to her boyfriend since she'd entered the room.

Why do I always feel like I'm losing her? Always. No matter how many times we seem to reach some kind of finish line, I always feel like the next day is an entirely new race.

I've proved everything I can prove to Gaia. I've proved my love and my friendship and my devotion. For Christ's sake, I've laid my life on the line for her more than once. So exactly what else can I do? What can I do to stop her from hovering?

That's Gaia. This beautiful girl hovering over her own life. Spinning like a top over school, over her apartment on East Seventy-second Street. Over the entire city. But I don't care about the geography. The problem is, she's hovering over *me.* Totally obsessed with doom and destruction and depression when I'm *right here.* It's all right here for her. Ed and Gaia—the antidote to her madness. The anti-Gaia. Hasn't she figured that out yet? Is it egotistical of me to think that? Is it totally self-aggrandizing and presumptuous of me to call our relationship an antidote?

Hell, no. Because it's not about ego. It's not that I'm the solution to Gaia's problems. If one thing has been made abundantly clear, it's that there *is no* solution to Gaia's problems. But "Ed and Gaia." That's a solution to something. I know that much. I can feel it every time we're together. I feel it in her. I feel her breathing more easily, and I see her smile, and I hear her laugh. Every time we're together, it's like she comes back to earth. She lands. So why the hell won't she turn off the engines and dodge all of her goddamn tornados and *stay awhile?* Why do I always need to follow her flying shadow around like some kind of emotional cowboy, swinging my lasso up in the sky and roping her back down to the ground?

It's so exhausting. Such an endless challenge to my perfectly
healthy ego. Truth be told, I'm not
even sure it's worth it. There's a
world of nondepressive, nonhover-
ing, non-tragedy-magnet women out
there for me to choose from. People
who could love me back on a regular
basis. People who could love me
back without. . .

Oh, who am I kidding? I'll
never be in love with anyone else
for the rest of my life. Even if
someday I was, I'd really just be
pretending. Loving anyone other
than Gaia would always be pretending. That is to say. . . I'm
screwed.

He could
practically
feel his tail
wagging with **twist**
anticipation
as he waited in **and**
his little
spasm
doghouse
for Gaia to
walk through
the door.

GAIA TILTED HER HEAD BACK AGAINST
the Starbucks wall. The
place was so crowded, the
management couldn't even
see them huddled in their little camp-out spot. She turned
to Ed, keeping the back of her
head glued to the wall.

Thousands of Thoughts

"Thank you *so much*," she sighed bitterly. "Thank
you for getting me away from that monster. I swear I
was going to—"

"Gaia, listen," Ed interrupted, swiveling his head
against the wall to face her. "Listen to me, okay?"

Her face turned a bit pale. It seemed the added
gravity in his voice had come through. She now
seemed to be dreading whatever it was Ed was going
to say. That certainly was not his intention. Or, then
again, maybe it was? Well, in any event, the goal was to
get her attention, and he had certainly done that.

"I'm listening," she assured him, locking her eyes
on his.

"Okay. The thing is—"

"Ed, I must have seemed like a total freak when I
came into Starbucks," she announced. She banged her
head twice against the wall. "And I didn't even say
hello to you when I walked in. I'm crazy, Ed. I'm total
Bellevue material, and I swear to God someone out
there is trying to finish me off. They're trying to take

down my entire family, and they're trying to drive the last freaking nail into my sanity. And all I have is *you,* and I didn't even say hello to you when I walked in. Okay, sorry, I'm listening. . . ."

"No, no, go *on,*" Ed insisted.

But Gaia turned her head away. He could practically see the thousands of thoughts and anxieties coursing through the veins of her forehead. "Ed, there's so much going on. . . ." She trailed off as she shook her head. "I don't even know where to—"

"Go on," Ed prompted her. "You don't know where to what?"

But he'd lost her again. He could tell. He'd lost her attention to that far-off star in outer space that was obviously far more compelling than her own supposed boyfriend.

"Gaia. . . ?" Ed sighed. "Gaia, where are you?"

Crawling with Lepers

THAT FACE. STANDING AT THE CASH register. Gaia had seen that face before. The pockmarked skin and the chubby cheeks of an ugly manchild. She never forgot a face. He might

41

not have been wearing his shiny blue jacket with the silver stripes across the back, but it was unquestionably his bloated nose and his pudgy fingers.

It was one of the obnoxious dirtbags who had come for her father that night. The EMT worker who had shown up with the ambulance, strapped her dad into a gurney, and then refused to let Gaia ride along with her own father.

It seemed like such a cruel coincidence, but there he was, standing there in his rumpled, off-duty attire: filthy beige corduroys, a stained white oxford shirt, and a tattered black messenger bag over his shoulder. There he was, ordering some beverage with a ten-word description and a Rice Krispie Treat. At 8:00 in the morning. Disgusting.

Ed suddenly faded off into the periphery of outer space as Gaia followed the man with narrowed eyes. Her blood began to boil as images of her father's limp frame being strapped to that gurney began to invade her mind. She could still feel this bastard's pudgy hands holding her back from the ambulance, denying her the most basic right to stay as close to her father as possible, to hold his hand as this whole pathetic course of events began.

What the hell was he doing at Starbucks? At this Starbucks? Right now? Could it be a simple coincidence? She supposed St. Vincent's hospital wasn't that far from here, only seven or eight blocks away. He could just be getting his morning latte before starting his shift—before starting another day of being egregiously insensitive to other victims and their freaked-out relatives. Maybe he lived around here?

But how often did the coincidences in Gaia's life turn out to be coincidences?

She could think of two other possibilities, as she watched him lumber over to the milk-and-sugar counter:

Though she was not particularly religious, this could be a sign from God. A sign that, like most signs from God, was meant to induce guilt. In this case, to slap a lazy-minded daughter in the face and remind her that while she was sitting here making goo-goo eyes at her boyfriend and bitching and moaning about Jake the Jock, her father was still out there somewhere, waiting for her to find him.

It was no coincidence. He was there for a reason—to check up on Gaia. Somehow, some way, due to a series of circumstances that made absolutely no sense. . . he was one of *them*.

But that theory seemed just about as far-fetched as they came. How could St. Vincent's hospital be involved in her father's disappearance? Unless the ambulance *hadn't* come from St. Vincent's? But that made no sense either because the ambulance had *taken* him to St. Vincent's. So what could it be? How could this disgusting, obnoxious, poorly trained ambulance schlub be part of some massive conspiracy to kidnap Gaia's father and put him out of commission? How could he be a part-time ambulance driver/part-time spy?

You're going crazy, that's how. Why don't you just head off to Texas and figure out who killed J.F.K. while you're at it. He's an EMT guy getting coffee before work, and he's the last person you wanted to see today. That's it. He can't do a damn thing for you.

He probably came here every morning for coffee. Gaia, of course, would never know, as she avoided the Astor Place Starbucks morning rush like the place was crawling with lepers.

Just take it as a sign, Gaia. That's all it is. Just a sign for you to get moving and find your father.

"Gaia?" Ed barked, waving his hand in Gaia's face. "Don't make me say your name again. And don't make me say 'Earth to Gaia.' You have no idea how tired I am of saying 'Earth to Gaia.'"

She glanced back at Ed and caught the surprising amount of sadness and defeat in his eyes. And for a moment, it hit her. Hadn't she just been in the middle of apologizing for ignoring him? Wasn't that the little bit of real life that had been happening here before Pock-mark had walked in? What a brilliant way to follow up an apology for ignoring Ed: Ignore him again.

"I'm sorry, Ed. I'm really sorry."

Ed shook his head hopelessly. "Gaia, we really need to talk. Big time."

"I know, I—"

44

Wait, did he just glance over here? Did I just imagine it?

Her eyes shot back to Pock-mark as he bit into his Rice Krispie Treat and dropped it back into the bag. She honestly wasn't sure. She could have sworn that, out of the corner of her eye, she'd just seen him glance over at her and Ed in their little private corner by the wall. But maybe she was making it up? She tried to make eye contact, but at that very moment, he rolled up his brown paper bag and shoved open the door, disappearing around the corner. Gaia felt an impulse to jump up off the floor and follow him, but Ed's hand grabbed onto her arm and pressed down firmly.

"Gaia, what the hell are you looking at? Are you even listening to me?"

She seemed to literally feel her brain rattling inside her skull. She was so mixed up at this point. What did she want to follow him for? Just to ream him out for his lousy bedside manner? Insult his choice of breakfast treats? Give him more evidence that she was completely deranged by asking him if he was one of *them*? No way. He was a cue, that's all. A cue to give up on this worthless Starbucks visit and get back to her search.

But you can't leave yet. For God's sake, look at Ed's eyes.

There was no other way to describe Ed's eyes but desperate. He was the least desperate person she knew, but she, and she alone, had managed to reduce him to a state of desperation. Why did he even bother trying to put up

45

with her? Why would anyone in his right mind actually continue to love her? The look in Ed's eyes was dead serious, and somehow Gaia knew that if she did not hold still and give him her full attention at this moment, she would be introduced to a whole new level of regret.

Five minutes. She had to give him at least five minutes of her full attention, and then it was back to search mode.

"I'M SORRY, ED." GAIA'S VOICE WAS tinged with that same old ugly futility, and Ed was getting so tired of it. He took her by the shoulders and tried to wake her out of her stupor with his eyes.

External Crap

"Gaia. . . ," he began, staring deep into her eyes. "We live in a very strange world. . . ."
Jesus, Fargo, get to the point.

"Yeah. . . ?" Gaia raised her eyebrow with confusion.

"Sorry, scratch that," Ed said, letting go of her shoulders. He gave the wall one good head-bang of his own and slid closer to her. "Okay, look, what I'm about to say will not make any sense to you, but you have to understand. You have to believe what I'm telling you even if you can't see it for the undeniable truth that it is right now. And you'll think it's pretty presumptuous, and you'll think that I'm way out of line, but—"

"*Ed*. You're babbling."

Ed cleared his throat. "Okay, here's the deal. I know that your life is in a total state of crisis basically twenty-four hours a day. I know that literally right this second, there is probably some incredibly urgent life-threatening thing you need to be doing. And I want you to deal with whatever that might be. And I want to *help* you deal with it. But the thing is this. . . Somehow, in the middle of all these crises, there is something that you *must* do tonight. Something just as essential to your survival as overcoming *all* those crises. Gaia. . . somehow. . . tonight. . . you and I must go out on a date."

Gaia's face was blank with confusion. "What?" she uttered.

"A date," he replied. "A *date* date. Like you see on TV. We pick a time, we put on unnecessarily nice clothes, I pay for numerous overpriced things, we make the occasional googly eyes, we discuss our dreams and life philosophies, we retire to one of our respective homes, and depending on how things go, we both get lucky."

"Ed," she began, with that same horrid futility in her voice. "Ed, I can't possibly take the time to—"

"*No*, Gaia, I *told* you. I *told* you that you wouldn't see

47

it at first. The importance of this date. The absolutely essential urgency of this date. So *listen* to me." He dug himself deep into her ocean-blue eyes and glued himself there, unmoving and unblinking. He did not even want to say the words out loud, but he had to now.

"We are drifting apart," he said, feeling a totally unexpected hitch in his throat as he said it. "We're drifting apart right now, Gaia, and to be honest with you, I don't even know *why*. But I know this: You do not want us to drift apart. You do not want that, Gaia. Do you not remember what it felt like for us to be apart? Like I said, I have no idea what's been going on the past couple of days, but you're dragging us *back*, Gaia. You're dragging us back into that torture chamber, and we *don't* want go there. Because the thing is. . . my life without you. . . absolutely, unequivocally *sucks*. And, Gaia. . . so does your life without *me*. Do you agree?" Ed was still finding wells of confidence he didn't even know he had. But these days, everything seemed to require the big guns. So he had no choice but to puke his entire heart out on the table.

Finally, Ed saw a touch of surrender in her eyes. "Yes," she said quietly. "I agree."

Hearing this was such a relief that Ed finally surrendered a bit himself, relaxing his posture and lowering his voice to a more intimate volume. With that one simple response, Starbucks had finally faded away. It was just the two of them again. At least for this moment. The way they were supposed to be. With none of that external crap clogging things up.

"It's a simple equation," he said. "My life sucks without you, and your life sucks without me. We *need* each other, Gaia. That's it. That's the whole thing."

"I know," she said, practically croaking out her words at this point. "I know we do."

"Then tonight? A date. An absolutely essential date. I pick you up at eight o'clock?"

"Ed. . ." Gaia began to look positively ill as she spoke. "I want to go on the date. But does it have to be tonight?"

Ed threw up his hands and laughed bitterly. "*Yes*, Gaia. Jesus, that's my entire point. Yes, it has to be tonight. Unless you're going out with your *other boyfriend*," he chuckled. Gaia looked white as a sheet. "Sorry. I'm being a jerk. Yes," he said sweetly. "Tonight, Gaia. Please."

He searched her eyes for the right answer. . . .

"Okay," she said, locking her eyes with his. "Tonight."

Ed let out a long and happy breath and he smiled. "Eight o'clock."

"Eight," she agreed.

"Wear a dress."

"Oh, God, don't do this to me, Ed."

He grinned mischievously and gave her a quick kiss on the lips. "Wear a dress."

"Ed. . . if you're trying to scare me. . . it's working."

School was obviously a non-option for the day. Especially after the whole Starbucks debacle. Once I realized how totally useless Natasha and Tatiana were going to be, I knew that the burden of finding my father was now entirely on me, and I sure as hell wasn't going to find him at school. So I split Starbucks and went straight to the New York Science and Medical Library to do some research—see if I could possibly drum up any leads.

"Research." "Leads." What a freaking joke.

I spent hours at the library trying to dig up anything I could possibly find. I tried absolutely everything I could think of. I cross-referenced his name and his symptoms with every single research lab and hospital database I could log into. I pulled any article I could find on Swiss institutes specializing in everything from poisonous substances to acute neurological trauma. I swear to God, I must have called almost half of them, trying to pull impossible information out of lowly paper-pushers about patients who'd been admitted in the last twenty-four hours.

Useless. All of it so utterly useless.

I even tried calling hospitals and *pretending* to be a nurse calling for Dr. Sullivan, just so I could get some more specific information on all their recently admitted patients. But that just turned into a long, fruitless acting exercise that left me with yet another big fat zero in the information department. I don't know why I kept kidding myself for the entire day. I was just spinning my wheels. I had nothing to go on. *Nothing.*

I got so desperate, I even called to check in with Natasha again, just to see if she'd made any of the "few calls" she'd promised me she would make. But

I couldn't even reach her. If she was looking into it at all, she wasn't letting me know a damn thing about it.

In fact, I was so focused on my useless research, I didn't even notice the day draining away. I didn't even notice when the sun had set. It was like I had looked up at the library windows once and seen a sunny and depressing New York morning and then looked up again and seen a black and depressing New York night.

And just like that, I had run out of research time. Thanks to my insane agreement to go out on that date with Ed.

But I have to go. No matter how much I might want to stick with this useless research, I have to go. Because Ed's right. Piece by little piece, and day by day, I've been doing it again. Thanks to my very own specific brand of misguided idiocy, I've been starting to push him away again, and I'm not going to let that happen this time. I'm not going to back away from him for his own "protection" again (a plan that has never done anything but backfire on us both completely). And I'm not going to take him for granted just because my life is in its usual state of pre-apocalyptic chaos. There has to be a way to keep him *in* the loop and *out* of danger at the same time, and I'll be damned if I can't figure out what that way is. I know that step one is to go on that date.

Which also means that the time has come. The time has come to face that inevitable drama queen's disaster I've created. The time has come to tell Sam about Ed. He's obviously going to want to know why I can't meet with him as planned. And I'm going to tell him. I have to tell him sooner or later. I have to. I'll just have to walk right into his room and detonate my own stupid land mine.

I'm just praying that the injuries in that tiny room won't be too severe.

But who am I kidding? The injuries are going to be disastrous.

Visual Jackpot

IT HAD CUT THROUGH HER LINE OF sight so quickly, she'd almost missed it. Like an irritating mosquito or a black mouse scurrying into a dark corner. Only it was so much bigger. It meant so much more. A black bag. Gaia knew it instantly. She was sure of it. All thoughts of broken hearts and obligatory dates had disappeared. Suddenly Gaia's attention had zeroed in on that bag like a high-powered telephoto lens. A few seconds later she had crouched stealthily behind a bookcase, peering through the available space between two huge red encyclopedic volumes. It was only a few moments more before she hit the `visual jackpot.`

There he was. The pock-marked EMT slob. In his white shirt and his grimy corduroys. The coincidence that never was.

Gaia's eyes narrowed as she watched him step over to his wooden table and glance furtively back toward the spot she had just been sitting in for hours. The spot that was now empty.

He'd stepped away. The idiot had stepped away from what was now quite obviously his little surveillance post, perhaps to stuff his face with more Rice Krispie Treats. Whatever the reason, the moment he had stepped away just happened to have been the moment that Gaia had shot up from her seat and

55

walked out. And now, it seemed, the poor bastard had lost his mark.

Gaia watched him scan the entire floor of the hushed library from left to right, searching for her. She watched him take a few steps out into the main aisle of the room, scanning a little more obviously now—a little more anxiously.

I'm over here, you idiot. Behind the bookcase.

But Gaia's pleasure in his utter ineptitude at surveillance quickly fell away. Because her mind had just come around to the full implications of this vision.

The worst-case scenario had quite suddenly revealed itself. All her most far-fetched thoughts while sitting in the corner of Starbucks had suddenly turned from ludicrous paranoid speculation to probable fact. He hadn't been just a random sighting. He wasn't just an off-duty EMT worker getting his morning coffee. A sighting at a downtown coffeehouse, she could chalk up to coincidence. But a second sighting, on the same day, at the library on East Fortieth Street? With him surveying the entire floor like the world's worst spy? It changed everything. It proved everything. Yet it explained absolutely nothing.

The longer Gaia spied on her appointed spy, the more chilling all the realizations became. If the ambulance driver who'd brought her father to the hospital was actually some kind of operative working for "them"—the Mystery Assholes, Loki's people or whoever—then that meant that there had never really *been* a hospital angle here. They'd had her father from the moment he was picked up. They were just using the hospital. Using it as some kind of holding station to shake off cover and leave Gaia completely in the dark.

They'd had him all along. The whole freaking time. They'd had her father from day one. And that meant that they definitely had him now. And they were watching her.

Gaia's teeth clenched tightly together. She'd had so many chances—so many opportunities to get her dad out of that ambulance or out of that hospital, away from these people. And she'd missed every one of them. She could feel her face heating up with the desire to pound her own face in for being so goddamn blind.

Pockmark did one last sweep of the room. For one millisecond Gaia thought he might have spotted her through the books, but his face proceeded to glide right by her. He looked flustered, to say the least. He tugged his bag over his head and bolted for the exit. She could see his frustration increasing with every step. But he really didn't need to worry. Yes, he had lost her for a moment, but in just a few minutes he was most definitely going to find her. Or rather, she was going to find him.

She waited the appropriate ten count before following him in full surveillance mode. Eyes wide open, feet barely touching the ground, appearing completely nonchalant while inching closer and closer.

Out the library doors and then out onto the brightly lit night on Fortieth and Fifth. The sidewalk was swarming with people, mostly men in suits headed home after putting in their extra `this-is-how-I-got-rich two hours`. The street had been transformed into a sea of metallic yellow, thanks to the bumper-to-bumper taxicabs and the amber streetlights. But Gaia's eyes were like two fast-motion cameras, shooting frame after frame of every one of Pockmark's lumbering moves. He slid between the taxis' bumpers as he crossed the street. Then he walked up the wide expanse of stone stairs to the palatial main branch of the Public Library, guarded on either side by two stone lions lying proudly on their stone pedestals.

The entrance concourse was reasonably empty at this point, what with the entire city headed home for dinner, and it was dark enough in certain corners for a little privacy. Gaia was in no mood to waste time. She decided that the moment had come for her and Pockmark to be reintroduced.

"Looking for me?" she barked, being sure to cut right through the street noise with a sharp tone.

She saw him stop in his tracks. But he didn't turn his head. He knew that his cover had been blown and that any contact with his mark would have his people pounding on tables in a rage and most likely pounding on him, too. And most of all, he hadn't turned around because he obviously knew all about Gaia. He knew what she was capable of doing to him, and he knew why she would do it. He was, after all, the man who had taken her father from her. Literally.

And so, rather than turn around, this pathetic, cowardly slob picked up the pace.

"Hey!" she shouted after him, moving from a walk to a trot to a full-on run. "I just have a few questions to ask you." He increased his own speed as he headed back off the entrance steps and down Fifth Avenue, trying in vain to get lost in the crowd. Gaia cut through the masses of pedestrians until she was right on his tail, but he turned off onto the much darker Thirty-seventh Street, probably thinking that the maze of blue scaffolding on the street would hide him better.

Gaia leapt off her feet and connected with his disgustingly sweaty back, slamming him face first into the rugged stone facade of the corner building.

"I asked you to wait up," she hissed, yanking his arm behind his back and stretching it downward at a most inhuman angle. He let out a tragic little yelp. Gaia was certainly no sadist, but she couldn't help taking some small pleasure in any pain she might be causing him. She knew it was nothing compared the torture he'd put her through when he'd stolen her father from her and strapped him onto a metal gurney like he was already dead.

"Where is he?" That was all she wanted to know right now. The rest would come later.

"I don't. . . I'm not sure what . . ."

"Where *is* he?" she shouted straight down his ear canal, cramming her knee into his lower back.

"Who?" he whimpered. "I don't know what you're—"

"Don't. Don't do it. Don't waste my time with that, I'm warning you. You tell me where my father is. You tell me who is doing this right now, and I won't break your arm clean off your shoulder."

"I don't know."

"Don't lie!" She shot a jab into his back and then twisted the arm harder.

"I *swear*. I swear to God. I was just supposed to stand there and let you see. . . . Please don't—"

"What? What are you talking about? What do you mean, stand there? Let me see what?"

"Me. I mean, you were just supposed to see—*ugh* . . ."

A hand suddenly whipped by Gaia's face, smacking Pockmark hard on the back of the head. Gaia flipped around just as an elbow cut across her forehead, knocking her completely off balance and sending her headfirst into one of the blue metal bars of the scaffold. She couldn't even tell if the chimelike sound was inside her head or just the sound of her skull striking metal.

"Just go, you idiot," she heard a man barking at Pockmark. "Get your fat ass back to base. *Run*, you piece of crap."

Gaia leapt to her feet just in time to see Pockmark

huffing toward Madison. But when she turned back to her assailant, the plot thickened so much more, it nearly congealed.

It was yet another face that she'd seen before, though much less bruised and battered than the last time she'd seen it. The same round jaw. The same Hispanic features. The same man she had encountered on the West Side Highway not so many days ago. The man she had first seen beating Sam Moon.

Sam had explained the entire scenario to Gaia once they'd gotten him safely back to her place. This man who was standing before her. . . he was one of the men from Loki's compound. One of the men who had wanted Sam dead. He'd chased Sam all the way from the Berkshires back to New York City. And if Gaia hadn't shown up when she had, he probably would have gotten his wish: a dead Sam, an incarcerated Sam, or both. But what the hell was he doing here now? What had he just said? *Get your fat ass back to base. . . .*

They knew each other. He and Pockmark. They *were* working together.

He threw another punch at Gaia, but she was ready this time. She dodged the punch and yanked his wrist forward, using his momentum to send him the rest of the way into the cold, hard metal scaffold. There was the second chime.

She yanked him up by the lapels of his gray suit and slammed him once more against the metal for a third chime. He croaked in pain as his eyes momentarily fluttered toward the back of his head. And as she stared at him in his painful daze, she didn't even know what to say. Now she wasn't even sure what questions she should be asking.

If the man who'd tried to beat Sam to death knew the man who'd tried to kidnap her father. . . was one person responsible for all of this? Both Gaia and Sam had considered it a very real possibility, but this seemed to be the clincher. This proved for certain some connection between that compound in the Berkshires and the kidnapping of her father. But what was the connection? Was it as simple as Loki? Had it been as simple as Loki this entire time? Someone working for him while he rotted away in that coma, finishing up all his dirty work out of loyalty?

"Who's doing this?" she barked into his dizzy eyes. "Who is doing all this? Is it Loki?"

"I don't know what you're talking about."

"Where's my father? Where the hell is he?"

"I don't know what you're talking about." He repeated the exact same phrase with the exact same inflection. But this time. . . he smiled.

He was playing with her. He was freaking playing with her. And his stupid, robotic loyalty was obviously unbreakable.

Reflex took over. Before she could finish another thought, Gaia had driven her lower palm straight up into her assailent's nose. She could hear the snap as his head whipped back against the bar again. He began to slide slowly from her grip down toward the ground.

"Get up!" she hollered. "Get up and answer me!"

That was when the knife nearly slashed straight across her chest. He was slicker than she'd thought. As he fell toward the ground, he'd pulled a hidden blade from somewhere, and he'd gone down slashing.

Gaia grappled onto the bars above her and swung herself back from his slashing hand. He took two more swipes before she swung back toward him, punting the knife far down the empty sidewalk with a perfectly placed snap of the foot.

And then he just took off. He took off at top speed, slamming his body deep into the crowd on Fifth Avenue. Gaia landed back on the ground and tried to spot him, but with that damn gray suit on, he'd turned into the other thousand men on the street in gray suits. Plus her dimming vision, along with a mild postbattle dizziness, had begun to kick in just enough to leave her disoriented.

No, she shouted at herself. *You're losing him, god-damn it.* She hadn't just lost him. She'd lost herself the last best chance at getting any real information about her dad.

Unless . . .

Maybe she hadn't lost every chance just yet. Maybe, in fact, she'd just discovered the one true lead she actually had. The one place she hadn't thought of to search.

And quite suddenly there were two horrific things she needed to talk to Sam about. She couldn't even decide which one would be more painful to discuss. But it would all be moot if she couldn't get back home without passing out. . . .

YES, SAM HAD FOUND A COMB IN

the bathroom of the maid's quarters and combed his hair. Yes, he had washed his clothes in the washer/dryer while Natasha and Tatiana were away, and he had cleaned his little prison of a room rather thoroughly. But that did *not* mean that he was preparing for his strategy session with Gaia like it was a date. It had been time to clean things up, anyway. Time to introduce at least a little bit of order into his thoroughly chaotic world.

Scampering Dog Syndrome

Okay, yes, he had snuck out and gotten her a gift.

But it wasn't like it was some kind of *gift* gift. Its purpose was entirely utilitarian. Its purpose was only to ensure his and Gaia's safety.

He heard the front door of the apartment open and close. It was almost seven-thirty. It had to be Gaia. And so. . . he began to pace. Which in this room basically meant taking two steps in one direction and two steps in the opposite direction. He didn't want to sit on the chair and he didn't want to sit on the bed.

He felt like a dog whose master had finally come home from a long day at the office. That was what this excited pacing felt like: a dog scampering around with the most vicious case of cabin fever. He could practically feel his tail wagging with anticipation, waiting in his little doghouse for Gaia to walk through the door. Terrific—he had gone from feeling like a five-year-old child to feeling like a dog. He heard the secret knock and tugged the door open, letting Gaia in and then slamming the door shut.

"I am *so* glad to see you," he admitted. He didn't even bother to temper his enthusiasm. "I mean, I've always thought of myself as a pretty solitary person, but this hiding thing is just ridiculous. This is. . . well, I'm just very glad you're here." He smiled at her and tried to free himself of scampering dog syndrome, relaxing his body into a state of near stillness. But something was wrong. Gaia wasn't smiling back. In fact, she was a complete mess. Maybe she'd fallen asleep on the train?

"Sam, we need to talk—"

"Wait, I got you something," he said, reaching

behind him for her gift and handing her the rolled-up paper bag.

Gaia stared dubiously at the bag. "What's this?"

"A gift."

"Sam, this is no time to be—"

"No, it's not a *gift* gift," he explained. "It's nothing like that, just open it."

Gaia still looked rather uncomfortable. Impatient, even. Exhausted, concerned, ornery. . . not what Sam had hoped for tonight. But nonetheless, she reached into the bag, and she pulled out her gift. A brand-new cell phone.

"I got a replacement ATM card at the bank and I got us each a phone," Sam explained. "Don't worry, I was only outside for about a half hour. I just thought for safety purposes, we wouldn't want to risk. . . losing contact again. It's already on and ready to go."

She examined the phone and then looked up at him. "That was. . . Thank you," she said. "It's a really good idea. . . . Thank you."

"You're welcome. Now if we need to get a message to each other, we can just call or text message, and no one needs to know a thing about it—" He stopped himself midsentence and took a closer look in her eyes. A sharp pain flashed through his chest. And it had nothing to do with his healing bullet wounds. Something had happened. Someone had hurt Gaia somehow, or she had just hurt someone, or else. . . she was going to hurt someone. "What happened?" he asked anxiously. "Tell me what's wrong. Is it your dad? Gaia, come on, you're scaring me."

SHE DIDN'T EVEN KNOW WHERE TO

Spinning

begin. She didn't want to scare Sam senseless or break his spirit, which seemed to be improving every day. But he had to know. He had to know just how big this was. He had to know that it was all connected, just as they had both speculated. He had to know that the people who wanted him dead were still out there—maybe right outside the door. They were still watching. And most of all, she needed to make him understand that, all things considered, they only had one lead now.

That compound. Loki's compound in the Berkshires that Sam had somehow managed to escape. If Loki or his people were somehow behind her father's disappearance, then the compound was definitely their best shot for clues. But even if Loki had absolutely nothing to do with the disappearance, Gaia was willing to bet that he might have had some information on the person who did. And that information might still be hidden away somewhere in that compound.

The timing was perfect. With Loki out of commission, his operations had come to a complete standstill there—at least that was how it seemed. And if Sam had managed to find his way out, Gaia was clinging to the hope that he just might be able to help her find her way back in.

But how could she ask him to do such a thing? How could she even break the news about the kind of danger he was obviously still in?

"Sam, listen to me for just a second, okay?"

His eyes widened slightly. He could obviously tell that this was serious. "I'm listening. . . ."

"I saw some things today. . . ," she began slowly. "I had a run-in with a few people, and. . . I'm not even sure what to make of all of it yet, but—"

"People—what people?" he snapped.

"I had a little. . . altercation with that man. The man from the West Side Highway. The one who was trying to—"

"457?" Sam squawked. "You saw 457? Did he. . . What did he do to you? Tell me what he did to you."

Sam looked like his head was about to start spinning with anger. Gaia did her best to keep him calm. She would offer him the facts because he needed to know them, but she was desperate to keep the emotions to a minimum if that were at all possible.

Sam began to get ahold of himself, and Gaia

brought him up to speed. She told him about the connection between Pockmark and 457 and thus the connection between both her father's kidnapping and Sam's. Obviously all evidence pointed to Loki, but Gaia still wasn't absolutely sure. His coma was an unequivocal reality, which meant that even if he was behind all this, there was still some other enemy somewhere out there in the dark making it all happen.

"But I have a plan," she finally forced herself to say. "A crappy plan, but still a plan. And I hate it so much, I don't even want to tell you."

"Try me," he insisted.

"Okay . . ." Gaia's chest tightened as she began to feel the painful weight of what she was about to ask Sam to do. "S-Sam. . . ," she stammered uncomfortably, "if I could do this alone, I swear to God, I'd be gone already. . . and the thought of you in any more danger makes me physically sick. And the thought of you having to revisit that horrible place makes me even sicker, but. . . if we want to solve this thing. . . if we want to find out where the hell my father is and who it is we're trying so hard to hide you from. . . I think that compound is our only lead right now. And you're the only person who has any idea where it is, Sam. You're the only one who can help get me in there and—"

"*Us,*" Sam interrupted. "I'm the only one who can help get *us* in there."

Gaia wasn't sure how to respond. But Sam was way ahead of her.

"We can use my car," he said. "I hardly ever use the thing. I let this guy Todd Cooper drive it and he pays for the garage."

"Sam . . ."

"We've hardly even talked for the last year unless it's about the car. He already graduated. He probably hasn't even noticed I've been gone. But if I call him tonight, then I can get the car for sure, first thing in the morning. That's our deal."

"Sam, you don't have to do this," Gaia offered, backpedaling in spite of everything she'd just said. "If you can try and remember how you got out of there and how you got to the city, I can just retrace—"

"*We* are going first thing in the morning," he declared, leaning his face closer to hers. "If you think I'm going to let you go alone, you're crazy. Besides, I need to get to the bottom of this just as badly as you do, Gaia. I'm not going to live out the rest of my life in this room. If that's our only lead, then that's our only lead. I can get us there."

Gaia nodded her solemn thanks. If he was truly willing to take the risk, then she was currently in no position to argue.

"So perfect," Sam said with a resigned smile. "That leaves us the rest of tonight to go over strategy." He moved back toward the chair and picked up the pad and pencil he'd gotten for their strategy session. "I have a couple of ideas. . . . I was thinking we could even—"

"Sam, wait," Gaia interrupted. "I. . . I can't."

"Gaia, it's already been decided. I'm going with you, that's—"

"No, that's not what I'm talking about now."

Sam looked up from his pad and stared at her, confused. "Well, what are you talking about? You can't what?"

Gaia's stomach began to roll and twist and spasm. Was she *still* going to try to keep that date after everything she'd been through? Was she still going to take this moment—the moment right after Sam had agreed to risk his life—to tell him about Ed?

Remember that look in Ed's eyes, she reminded herself. She was hanging on by a thread with him and she knew it. *You're not leaving until the morning. You can still pull it off. The world's shortest date. For Ed. Jesus, think about everything he's done for you. You're going. No matter what you want right now, you're going.*

She looked back in Sam's eyes and then she dropped her head. She was frozen. Paralyzed from the head down. *You have to tell him now. At some point he's going to have to know.*

It was time. It was time for all her stupid choices to blow right up in her face. That must have been why she was hiding behind her hair.

71

HE COULDN'T UNDERSTAND WHAT HAD

gone wrong. He'd just done the right thing. He'd insisted on taking her back to that compound. So why had she moved beyond quiet into a state of almost complete paralysis? Her hair fell over her eyes as she gazed

Tragically Uncomfortable Smile

at the floor. Finally she tried to look up at him.

"Sam. . . I can't. . . go over strategy with you tonight."

"Why not?"

"Because . . ."

That couldn't possibly be her entire answer. Though knowing Gaia. . . Was she really going to make him say it? Yes, as the seconds ticked by, it seemed she was.

"Okay." He sighed. "Because *why*?"

"You're angry already," she complained.

"No, don't be ridiculous. I'm not angry. You just need to talk to me."

"I'm *trying*."

"You can tell me anything, Gaia. I promise you, you can tell me whatever you're feeling. Whatever is going on. Believe me. There are things I want to tell you, too. Things I need to tell you . . ."

"What?" she asked. "What's wrong?"

"No, you have to talk first, okay? Believe me, you have to talk first. So tell me. Tell me why we can't do this tonight and then I'll talk, okay?"

Gaia took a deep breath, met Sam's eyes with her own, and then dropped her head again. "I can't go over strategy tonight. . . because I have a date." She finally turned her face up and looked Sam dead in the eye. "I have a date with my boyfriend. And I have to keep it. I have to."

The silence in the room was impenetrable. But it wasn't silent in Sam's head. In Sam's head, all he could hear was Gaia's statement, echoing again and again, until it blurred into one loud, muddy noise that rattled his eardrums and left his mouth and his throat bone-dry.

Sam fell back onto his butt and crossed his legs.

"Sam—"

"Shhh." He smiled and placed his finger to his lips, desperately trying to regain his faculties. *Talk, Sam. Talk now.* He was struck by a number of urges. The urge to destroy every piece of furniture within a ten-foot radius, the urge to leave this stupid little room and never come back, the urge to cry like that pathetic newborn. But he discarded all those urges one by one, employing herculean amounts of self-discipline. *You know what you have to do. You know what you're going to do now, so do it. Honesty is not an option. It's not fair to her. So talk, you idiot. Start lying.*

73

"God," Sam squeezed out of his throat. "Is *that* what you were so worried about?" He could feel his heart literally shriveling. "God, you had me so scared after everything we were just talking about. Don't scare me like that again, okay?"

Gaia looked into his eyes and gave him the sweetest, most loving stare she'd given him since his resurrection. He'd finally seen the look in her eyes he'd been dreaming about, and now it was for all the wrong reasons. "I just don't want to hurt you, Sam. Seeing you again is one of the best things that's ever happened to me. You have no idea—"

"Gaia," he said, forcing the corners of his mouth to maintain a smile, "you don't need to be so worried about me getting hurt. I took two bullets in the back and I'm still here. Come *on*. We were already broken up. And, I mean . . ." *Go on. Keep going. You can pound your head through the wall once she's gone.* "I mean, I was dead to everyone. That's not your fault. That's no one's fault but your uncle's. No, I'm just. . . I'm glad you had someone to stick by you through this horror show." *Deep breaths. Deep breaths.* "Wow. . . a boyfriend, huh? I guess I started a trend. Do I know him?"

Gaia's head dipped yet again. Sam was just starting to remember what a horrible sign it was when Gaia's head dipped. He wished he'd remembered that earlier. "Who is it?"

She didn't say a word. She didn't even move a muscle.

But somehow Sam knew. He knew already. Had he always sort of known? Maybe he had. In that totally useless way that people know things they don't know. But whether he'd always known or not didn't really matter much now, did it?

"It's Ed, isn't it?"

Her head shot up in surprise.

"It's okay," he said gently. The gentle part, he wasn't faking. The smiles, maybe. The calm angelic acceptance, definitely. But he wasn't angry. There was no one to blame here, and he knew it.

"We've just gotten... really close...," Gaia began.

"Of course." Sam nodded.

"He's back on his feet again, and he's been—"

"Wow, that's great," Sam interrupted. He wasn't even sure which answers were sincere anymore.

"I know," Gaia said. "And . . ." She trailed off with nothing left to say.

"So... okay... you have a date tonight... with Ed. Your boyfriend."

Gaia barely nodded in the affirmative. "I do," she croaked. "I tried to get out of it. I really tried, but—"

"It's *okay*," he said for what felt like the two-thousandth time. His brain was beginning to throb. "You don't need to explain. I just wanted to figure out... a game plan for us, that's all. For tomorrow. But we can do it after your date—"

"*Yes*," Gaia agreed. "After the date. Definitely. We

75

need to do that, Sam. We need to figure out a game plan for tomorrow. That's really the only thing I should be doing now; I just. . . need to go out on this date."

Sam could feel the conversation coming to a close and he got a bit lazy, actually letting his own head drop forward for a moment.

"But it's going to be the world's shortest date," she assured him. "I swear. I'm going to tell Ed that we need to make it an early night. Okay?"

Please don't do that, Gaia. Please don't try to throw the dog a bone.

"Well, you'd better get going," Sam said, trying to cut off her patronizing offer of an "early night" with Ed. The thought of an early night only made him imagine what the *late* nights must be like. "Keep the phone with you," he added. "Just to be safe . . ."

"Okay . . ." She stood up tentatively from the bed. Sam immediately shot up with her to avoid feeling any more doglike than he already did.

"So I'll. . . see you later tonight, then," she said.

With that, she leaned over and gave Sam an awkward peck on the cheek. She backed out of the room, wearing a `tragically uncomfortable smile,` and then she closed the door behind her.

It took Sam ten minutes to find the will to move. He managed to drag himself over to the chair, where he plopped himself down and then once again lost his will to move.

MISTAKE. THIS IS ALL A MISTAKE.

Freaking Whale Flippers

What am I doing? What the hell am I doing?

Gaia threw yet another one of Tatiana's lipsticks on the bathroom floor and washed her entire face again until it was practically raw. She looked back up at her chalky face in the mirror and seriously considered spitting at it.

She pictured Sam's face again and the pain floating just behind that forced smile of his. Was this what he had come back from the dead for? To hide in the closet while Gaia went out with her new boyfriend? A *date*? A goddamn date? Was that really what she needed to be doing right now? A date while her father was out there somewhere with no one to protect him? A date to rub right in Sam's smiling face? A date that had compelled her to put on a freaking *dress*?

The dress. Jesus H. Christ, the dress. She'd found the black dress that her father had given her in Paris, but somehow it had ended up crumpled into a ball inside a shopping bag inside another crumpled-up ball of clothes inside a shopping bag. She'd tried to unwrinkle the dress by throwing it in the bathroom with the shower running scalding hot, but all that had left her with was a scalding hot, wet, wrinkled dress. Not to mention the need to stretch the top of the dress

77

higher and the bottom lower every fifteen seconds. Not to mention the two pork loins she had for hips that the dress was apparently designed to *enlarge*.

She'd tried to pull her hair back in one of Tatiana's hair things, but navigating a hair thing was like trying to operate a goddamn space shuttle. And shoes? *Please*. She couldn't possibly have fit her `freaking whale flippers` into any of Tatiana's *Sex and the City* shoes, which left her with only the wrinkled-up clunky shoes her father had bought her to go with her wrinkled-up dress.

She shut her eyes and pulled a lipstick back out of the pile she'd created and slapped it on. She shoved her hair under the running water for two seconds, swung her head back up, and rubbed a towel through her hair.

Yes, as she looked at herself in the mirror, she could think of only one word. *Ugly*. The whole evening was all so very ugly. And tomorrow was only going to get uglier. She flipped off the light and slammed the bathroom door shut.

She felt painfully nauseous as she passed Sam's door in the hallway on her way out. She nearly tripped on her own shoes stepping into the elevator. *Why are you doing this to me, Ed? Why?*

She clomped slowly out of her lobby, ignoring the ghoulish stare of her doorman, and then leaned back against the stone wall of her building. She wondered whether or not she looked like a French hooker. She'd have given a thousand dollars to be in jeans and a sweatshirt right now. There was only one explanation for the invention of the dress: public humiliation. That made sense, she supposed. This whole fiasco was just a massive punishment for agreeing to the date.

It was five minutes after eight and still no sign of Ed.

A date. What on earth did Gaia know about a date? What was supposed to be so romantic about putting on clothes and spending a bunch of money on all sorts of elaborate nonsense? Gaia's idea of romance was. . . well, Gaia really had no idea of romance. Love, she knew something about. But what did love have to do with all this dating crap? No, this was ridiculous. This was an unfathomable waste of time that she desperately needed for planning. Whenever Ed showed up, not only would she have to call it off, but she would have to tell him a thing or two about her opinions on dating. She would have to tell him that this kind of crap was for mindless idiots with nothing better to—

"Gaia!" Ed called from the end of the block.

Gaia turned angrily to follow Ed's voice. And then she saw him. She saw him stand up out of an old-fashioned carriage, which was being pulled slowly down Seventy-second Street by a majestic white horse.

He was wearing a suit. A slim black suit, a white shirt, and a gray silk tie. He had a huge bouquet of red roses in one hand, a huge heart-shaped box of chocolates in the other, and between both hands. . . a huge wheel of cheese. And he was grinning from ear to ear.

For reasons beyond her understanding, Gaia was immediately compelled to cover her face in shame. Because a smile had spread across her lips in spite of everything she believed about dating. In spite of everything she'd just been through in the last hour. . . her heart was suddenly melting.

Her boyfriend was a genius. His portrait of cheap clichéd romance had instantly dismantled her defenses. And whatever she might have been feeling exactly one and a half seconds ago, she had already forgotten it.

Gaia quickly adjusted her `embarrassingly gleeful smile` and greeted Ed with a straight face. "Making an entrance, I see," she mumbled.

Never in her life had she seen Ed in a suit. She wondered if he'd ever even *worn* a suit before. But the contrast of his wild, crunched-up black hair and the slim, tailored suit made him look awfully charming. . . . All right, he looked beautiful. `Gaia's boyfriend was beautiful.`

Ed still hadn't said a word as he stood there, staring at her.

"What?" she snapped defensively.

Ed stepped back from Gaia and stared at her, wide-eyed. "You look absolutely—"

"Let's not even go there," Gaia interrupted.

"You're right," Ed said. "I'd never shut up. Well, in

case you haven't noticed, tonight is a night for *romance.*" Ed raised his right eyebrow and rolled his *r.*

Gaia's hand jumped to her mouth to try and cover her chuckle. She was still trying to hide how helplessly enchanted she was by this whole ludicrous production.

"Yes," Ed continued, "as I'm sure you can see, there are red roses, a huge box of chocolates, and a hansom cab driven by a crusty yet benign old salt named Jeeves. We shall dine in the hip, romantic, catacomb-like confines of Chez Es Saada, to be followed by a trip to the Screening Room, where we will see what I consider to be the most romantic movie of all time: *Harold and Maude.* Yes, it shall be the most romantic and cheesiest night of your life, and so I present to you this ceremonial Wheel of Cheese."

Gaia accepted the surprisingly heavy wheel of cheddar cheese and bowed her head slightly in thanks. "No one has ever given me cheese," she noted.

"Oh, there's so much more where that came from," Ed assured her. His eyes suddenly turned just a tad insecure. "You do. . . *like* cheese. . . don't you?"

Gaia looked down at all her gifts and then back up at Ed's inquisitive face. "Apparently I do," she said.

Ed's shoulders slumped forward with relief. "Thank God." He sighed. He turned back to the driver. "Jeeves. She likes cheese."

"Right," the driver replied, shrugging confusedly.

Ed turned back to Gaia. "Well. . . shall we go?" He tossed the roses into the hand with the chocolates and offered his elbow to her.

And they rode off. Clip clopping in the cool air down Seventy-second Street, headed for the brightly lit skyline of the West Side. Gaia had forgotten about absolutely everything but Ed. And she hoped she'd never remember.

The entire restaurant seemed to roll its eyes in unison.

five- foot nose ring

From: ruskiegirl@alloymail.com
To: megan21@alloymail.com
cc: tammiejammie@alloymail.com
Time: 9:22 P.M.
Re: the party

Hello, ladies. Had some ideas for the party.
Let me know what you think:

I saw a beautiful huge parchment book at
Kate's Paperie tonight. I thought it might be
nice to set up a table where everyone could write
encouraging messages to Heather. We could send
the book to Heather at her special school. I can
pick it up tomorrow if you like the idea.

Also, I know this may sound a bit cheesy, but
big bunches of black and white balloons could
look very elegant and help assure people that
this is a festive event and that they shouldn't
feel sorry for anyone.

I'm around tonight if you have any ideas.
(Don't worry, Gaia's not home, so you won't have
to deal with any more awkward confrontations.)

I'm working on a few sketches for possible
decorations. And what do you think about white
roses? I'm a huge fan. I can get a great deal
down on Fulton Street.

Quick Hello

DON'T DO IT AGAIN. YOU'VE ALREADY checked the clock a thousand times. If you check it again, you will have entered the Pantheon of Losers.

It was nine-thirty and Gaia had been gone an hour and a half. That really wasn't a very long time to be on a date, Sam supposed, but from where he was sitting, it felt like it had been about three days.

And hadn't Gaia said they were going to keep it short? As far as Sam could recall, once a date hit two hours, that was no longer "keeping it short." That was pretty much a standard date length. Unless they were going to a movie, too. But going to a movie wouldn't be "keeping it short," either. Or what if instead of a movie, they'd just decided to go back to Ed's place? Was *that* Gaia's idea of "keeping it short"? No. No matter how you sliced it, they'd officially passed the "keeping it short" time limit. Or at least. . . they *would* be past it at the two-hour mark.

But by the time Sam had finished thinking this through, the clock already said 9:34. They were already past the "half hour until two hours" mark. She obviously wasn't going to keep it short. She'd probably made some faint attempt to call it a night and Ed had probably talked her out of it. He'd probably charmed her into some kind of "perfect date" hypnotic trance, and she'd completely lost track of time. She'd probably remember what time it was when she woke up in his bed tomorrow morning. . . .

Okay, now you're overdoing it. Just give her time. She's still got twenty minutes. She'll probably be back before then.

Unless something was wrong.

Maybe she *had* already cut the date short? Maybe she *had* cut it short after an hour and 457 had already gotten his hands on her again? Maybe he had more men with him this time? Maybe she'd finally lost a fight?

Maybe he needed to call her.

Just a quick call. This was exactly what the cell phones were for. Just to check in. For safety purposes. It *wasn't* like he'd be calling to check up on Ed and Gaia or interrupt their date. He was just being. . . responsible.

Sam dropped his book to the floor and ripped the cell phone from his pocket. He had already programmed Gaia's number into his phone and his number into hers. He held his thumb over the send button, and then he hesitated.

But any internal arguments he was having became moot, anyway. His thumb had made up its mind before he had. It had already pressed down on the send button, and he had done nothing to stop it.

Just a quick hello. Just a two-second check-in to be sure she was all right. . .

CHEZ ES SAADA WAS ALIVE AND

Painfully Shrill

kicking with New York's urban elite—couples at the tables, huge parties at the bar, candlelit stone arches, and elegant iron lanterns and even bits of stained glass adorning the walls. The underground atmosphere couldn't have been more perfect. Festive and romantic. Filled with life, yet still private. And Gaia was taking it all in. Enjoying herself, in fact. Immersing herself in the moment. Sipping wine, enjoying her food, even letting Ed feed her grapes every now and again when she was sure no one was watching. It was the quintessential, picture-perfect, ideal New York night on the town.

Until the phone rang.

The ear-piercing electronic shriek of a cell phone seemed to rattle the entire restaurant. But since Gaia had always defined herself as a non-cell-phone person, the entire restaurant was forced to suffer through three painfully shrill rings before Ed finally noticed that they seemed to be coming from Gaia's bag.

"Is that *yours*?" Ed asked.

"I guess it is," Gaia muttered, shoving her hands down into the little handbag she'd borrowed from Tatiana and fumbling with every single unidentifiable button as it continued to scream at her. The entire restaurant seemed to roll its eyes in unison. Gaia was ready to pound the thing against the table like a hammer just to shut it up. "Just let me. . . *Jesus*, how do you turn this *goddamn* thing—"

"Why don't you answer it?" Ed asked, wondering if she knew how.

She glimpsed the flashing green readout. Flashing in bold black letters over and over was one small word:

SAM. . . SAM. . . SAM . . .

He'd programmed his name in with his number. *Oh, crap. Was that really necessary? I've got a photographic memory, for God's sake. I don't need any help remembering numbers.* Gaia cursed the day that some hopeless paranoid bastard had invented caller ID. Now Sam's name was flashing over and over for anyone with decent eyesight to see. She hadn't thought for a second about the phone. She hadn't thought to turn the ringer off before dinner or just to turn the whole phone off. Sam, on the other hand, seemed to have thought of everything.

"Here," Ed said, reaching for the phone. "Let me help—"

"*No*," Gaia snapped, pulling the phone out of Ed's reach He looked positively bewildered, if not suspicious. Gaia felt her entire chest cave in with guilt. "I can do it," she insisted, trying in vain to gloss over the horribly awkward moment with anger. She took one long hard look at the phone and finally realized that there was a small button on the left that read *reject*. She slammed her thumb down on the button to reject the call and finally breathed in the glorious silence.

The diners slowly returned to their meals, all of them shaking their heads in condescending disapproval. But Ed was now frozen in place. He wasn't even breathing. He just stared at Gaia, his mouth slightly agape, and his eyes scrunched into a mild squint. "When did you get a cell phone?" he asked, as if she had just pierced her nose with a five-foot nose ring. "I thought you hated cell phones. . . ?"

"It was a gift," she replied, trying to sound nonchalant.

"From. . . ?"

Gaia had never lied to Ed for any other reason than to protect him. And that was the only reason she was going to lie to him now. At least. . . she was pretty sure that was the only reason. . . . No, of course, that was the only reason. Keeping Sam a secret was protecting everyone—Ed, Sam, even Gaia. Until Gaia could understand exactly who the threat was and exactly how much danger everyone was in, she wasn't going to take any chances. Keeping Sam a secret was a basic rule they had set from the beginning, and if she broke it even once, she knew she would end up regretting it.

That did not mean, however, that lying to Ed didn't make her feel violently ill and even guiltier than she already was, if that was possible. "It was a gift. . . from Natasha," she said, forcing her eyes to stay glued to Ed's even though she was dying to crawl under the table. But Ed knew her too well. He would have picked up on the slightest hitch in her speech, the slightest pause or aversion of the eyes. She had to stare him down on this one. It was her only hope. "Yeah," she went on, "Natasha kind of freaked out after everything that's gone down in the past few weeks. . . and so she gave me this cell phone in order to check in with me. It's kind of a pain in the ass, but you know how it is— sometimes it's kind of hard to track me down. . . ."

"Oh, I know how it is," Ed assured her with increasing sarcasm.

Go ahead, Ed. Just hate me. You might as well.

"Yeah, well. . . that was her calling," Gaia muttered. In spite of all her guilt, she knew she needed to call Sam back. What if 457 had already broken down the door to her house? What if Sam was backed up against a wall, looking for a way out? She needed to call him back right now. "I should probably call Natasha back," she went on. "You know. . . just to . . ." At this point Gaia felt so guilty about the date, she was practically looking to Ed for permission to make a phone call.

"Go ahead," Ed encouraged her. "It might be entertaining to watch you play the role of the dutiful surrogate daughter."

"But. . . I also need to use the bathroom," Gaia added. This had to be her record for lying.

"Well, Gaia . . ." Ed stared blankly into her eyes. "You've gotta do what you've gotta do."

Gaia had no idea what that was supposed to mean.

And she had a feeling that Ed didn't quite know, either. But she knew that his words were cold. And deliberate. And as harmless as it was, Ed's little comment somehow felt like the coldest thing he had ever said to her. Because it was the first time in their entire relationship that Ed had been cold to Gaia without Gaia being cold first. And that was a bad sign. That was a really, really bad sign.

"I'll be *right* back," she promised.

One quick phone call to Sam and then she was going to come back and fix this entire relationship.

HE MUST HAVE SAT THROUGH AT

runaway Psyche

least eight rings before he got transferred to some generic voice-mail message.

Eight rings. *Eight rings.* What was she doing? What the hell were she and Ed doing that she couldn't stop for one second and just pick up the phone?

Sam instantly regretted his own question. He'd only invited in a series of images that he'd been working arduously to avoid.

The cell phone was probably nowhere near Gaia's

person. It was probably lying on the floor of a hallway in Ed's apartment. Inside a purse or maybe in the pocket of Gaia's pants. Which were probably crumpled up next to Ed's pants. Next to their shoes. And their socks. And their underwear. And whatever else they'd left in a long, haphazard trail as they crashed along the walls, kissing passionately on the way to Ed's bedroom. . .

Jesus, Sam, will you give it a rest!

Sam hurled the phone against the cushy chair and plopped down onto the bed. He had to get ahold of his completely inappropriate, totally immature, run-away psyche. The facts were the facts, life goes on, and whatever other clichés he wanted to throw in there. Gaia had every right to be on a date, and to love Ed, and to ignore a ringing cell phone. They weren't leaving until morning, and she could spend this evening however she needed to or wanted to. It was time for Sam to stop clock-watching and shove a stopper in all his nostalgic fantasies.

Sam grabbed the Walkman Gaia had given him and shoved the headphones into his ears, blasting Radiohead deep into his skull at top volume. He tried desperately to drive Gaia out of his head and focus on the images in the songs, but it didn't work. By the middle of the second track every song was about Sam and Gaia. Or, to be more specific, every song was about the fact that there was no Sam and Gaia.

GAIA SLAMMED THE DOOR OF THE

otential Horrors

bathroom stall behind her and dropped down on the closed toilet. Her brain felt like mud as all the Ed-dumping-her scenarios mixed with all the Sam-and-her-father-in-danger scenarios. Being fearless didn't mean she couldn't recognize a slew of potential horrors. But as she'd learned long ago, she could only live her life one horror at a time. She had no choice in the matter. Step one: Call Sam and hear some kind of dreadful news. Step two: Go back and face Ed's cold and hateful stare. Step three: Surely something worse.

She tugged the despicable cell phone back out of her purse. First things first, she finally turned that goddamn ringer off. Once that was done, she punched the send button to call back her last missed call.

She waited through three long rings. No answer. She checked the number Sam had programmed again and tried dialing the full number.

Three rings. And then four. And then five...

"Come *on*..." Muttered curses were falling from her mouth with each additional ring. "What the hell are you *doing*, Sam?" she whispered through nearly closed lips. "You *just* called me...."

On the seventh and eighth rings Gaia's frustration began to skyrocket. This didn't make any sense. He

93

was supposed to be sitting alone in his room. How could he possibly not hear his phone ringing?

Unless the worst-case scenario was true. Someone had gotten in there, 457 or a whole goddamn army for all she knew. Someone had gotten to him, and all he'd had time to do was dial her number. . . .

Oh God, Sam, please pick up the phone. Please.

But the phone just kept ringing. And ringing.

Now the only
sounds were
melodramatic
their short, **feline**
rapid
breaths **scowl**
echoing off
the pale,
white walls.

TATIANA'S EYES DARTED TOWARD THE

bedroom phone. She'd fallen into a half-sleep state in bed, sketching ideas for Heather's party. Her sketch pad had fallen onto the floor, and her pencil was still dangling in her hand. She nearly stabbed herself with it when the phone woke her.

She glimpsed the clock and saw that it was only about nine-thirty, though her lagging body and mind made it feel closer to four in the morning. She dropped the pencil to the floor and reached over to the bedside table to grab the phone.

"Hello. . . ?"

She cleared the nap-induced frog from her throat to speak more clearly. . . but there was no one on the other end of the line. Just a dial tone buzzing rudely in her ear. She hung the phone back up and shook off the remains of her sleepy daze.

But the phone was still ringing.

As she finally came to her senses, she realized that the ring wasn't actually coming from her phone. It was, in fact, a very faint ring floating in from the hallway. She slipped off her bed and stepped out of her room, following the alien ring as she walked slowly down the hall.

She could hear the ring getting stronger and stronger, and as she neared the living room, it finally reached its maximum volume. A shrill electronic ring buzzing in her left ear. It sounded like one of those offensively loud cell phone rings, but where on earth was it coming from?

She turned to her left and realized that the ring was coming from the obsolete maid's quarters. They barely used the room except for storage and some of their bulk supplies—toilet paper, paper towels, and whatnot. At this point the door had pretty much melded into the wall as far as Tatiana was concerned. But now. . . the forgotten room was ringing.

Was Gaia using the room for privacy or something? Tatiana thought she'd earned more of Gaia's trust than that, though she could certainly understand the need for a private space. Tatiana sure as hell wouldn't have minded having her own room. But if it was Gaia's private hiding place, since when had she gotten a cell phone? That was so unlike Gaia.

Tatiana turned down the hall toward her mother's bedroom, wondering if she knew anything about Gaia using the room. But her mother wouldn't even be back for hours. She turned back to the door.

The phone wouldn't stop ringing. Whoever was calling seemed to refuse to give up. And Gaia seemed to refuse to answer. Unless Gaia wasn't currently *in* her private hiding place? Or. . . there were a couple of far more disturbing scenarios—a couple of people Tatiana would most certainly not want to see on the other side of that door.

But unfortunately, there was only one way to find out.

She tapped lightly on the door.

"Gaia?" she whispered.

No reply. And the phone kept ringing.

She brought her hand down to the knob and turned it gently. Locked? Since when did they lock a barely used storage room? It was a flimsy excuse for a lock, anyway. Just the usual indoor variety, easily jimmied open by the simplest of tools. Tatiana stepped over to the coat closet and grabbed a wire hanger, untwisting it quickly and slipping the straight end right into the keyhole. A few careful twists and the lock didn't just click open; it pretty much cracked open. Just one more busted old lock to go with the rest of the useless locks in the apartment.

She let the door fall open naturally, wielding the hanger before her as her sole weapon.

The ringing suddenly ended, filling the room with a loud, overwhelming silence. But Tatiana had already forgotten all about the ringing. The inexplicable sound had given way to a much more inexplicable vision.

There was an absolute stranger hunched over on the bed.

A reddish-brown-haired stranger in a gray T-shirt and boxer shorts was sitting comfortably in Tatiana's apartment, listening to a pair of blaring headphones as if he just. . . *lived* there. As if he were just the older brother Tatiana had never noticed she had.

She was at a complete loss. Her body and mind

stalled. Should she be frightened? Should she run from the strange dusty room and call the police or one of her mother's contacts? It didn't feel that way. The stranger looked so. . . casual, so completely nonthreatening. So unbelievably gorgeous.

But looks could be deceiving.

He still hadn't noticed her standing there. His eyes were so tightly shut. He seemed so deeply ensconced in the music, she was almost afraid to wake him out of his trance. She crouched slightly, readied her hands and feet for trouble, and reached forward slowly with the hanger. She gave the stranger's shoulder one cautious prod. . . .

"*JEE-sus!*" he bellowed, leaping back against the wall like the hanger was a high-powered stun gun. Tatiana let out a sudden scream of her own and slammed her back up against the door, thrusting her hanger forward defensively.

Their eyes locked as they faced each other across the tiny room. Now the only sounds were their short, rapid breaths echoing off the pale, white walls.

His shoulders settled down slightly once he'd gotten a look at her, though his breaths were still coming in short spurts. His eyes drifted down the length of her body before jumping back up to eye level. Tatiana suddenly became very aware of the fact that she was wearing nothing but a stretchy white cotton nightie. She brought her left arm slowly across her chest and thrust the hanger forward again.

"Who are you?" she spat, trying to sound as threatening as anyone with a hanger and a white cotton nightie could. What exactly did she plan to do? Tickle him to death?

He stared at her blankly for a long beat. And then he finally ripped the headphones from his ears, throwing the Walkman down on the floor. "Sorry, what?"

"Who *are* you?" she repeated more harshly. "What the hell are you doing in my apartment?"

"Right," he said, staying glued to the wall. "Right... I'm... I'm a friend of Gaia's."

"Friend? What friend? I've never met you before."

"Well, I've been——" He cut himself off and narrowed his eyes. "Wait, how did you get in here?"

She couldn't believe his gall. "How did *I* get in here? How did *I* get in here? This is *my* apartment!"

"I know, but I locked the——"

"Do you want me to call the police *now*? Or do you want to tell me what *friend* of Gaia's would be... be... *stoving away* in this little secret room?"

He raised his right eyebrow slightly as he stared at her. "I'm... I'm sorry, 'stoving'?"

"*Stoving!*" she snapped, shaking her hanger. "A *stove-away*. Like on a boat. Hiding where you know you don't belong——"

"Oh, *stowing*. A *stow*away..."

"Yes, this——whatever, you still have explained nothing. *Talk*."

"Okay." He raised his hands in truce. "Just calm down, okay?" He took a deep breath and blew it out. "I'm Sam," he said. "Sam Moon. I *am* a friend of Gaia's. And I'm guessing you're Tatiana...?" He smiled cautiously.

God, homeless thief or not, he was still so ridiculously gorgeous. His face looked like some kind of ancient Greek sculpture depicting the ideal male. The more he spoke, the more she found herself giving way before his slim, perfect features and his curly brownish hair and his slightly gravelly voice. This simply wasn't the face of a killer, or even a stowaway. She began to relax in spite of herself. Without her even noticing, her hand dropped down and let go of the hanger.

"I am," she said, confirming Sam's guess about her identity.

He stepped gingerly from the opposite wall and held out his hand. She took one last suspicious glimpse at his kind hazel eyes and then decided to shake.

"Sam," he said as he shook her hand.

"That's what you said," she replied, pulling her hand away quickly.

"Right." He stepped back against the wall.

There was a brief, awkward silence.

"Sam...," she began.

"Yeah?"

"What the hell are you doing in my apartment?"

"*Yes.*" He let out a slight laugh. "Right... well... I, uh... told Gaia that I needed a place to stay—"

"Why don't you have a place to stay?" He might not be a murderer or a rapist, but that didn't mean she was done interrogating him.

Sam paused again. "Right. Well, that's a really long story. You know how it can get. . . with the parents. . . ."

She still couldn't tell if he was a horrible liar or just spoke in strange cadences. "You live with your parents?" she tested. "You look like you go to college. Don't you go to college?"

"I do," he replied, throwing her off again with his smile. "But I'm. . . taking this semester off."

"Hm."

"Yeah, so. . . as I was saying, Gaia gave me this room here, and I think she was just a little worried about. . . you know, freaking out your mother, so. . ."

"Gaia was *worried* about freaking out my mother?" That wasn't the Gaia Tatiana knew.

"I guess so." Sam shrugged, dropping down on the bed. "So, that's what I'm doing here, but. . ." He tilted his head slightly. "How did you find me?"

Tatiana glanced over at the chair in the corner and saw the small blue cell phone lying on the cushion. "I heard your phone ringing."

Sam slapped his hand over his head, scolding himself. "I left the ringer on? How could I be so stupid? I left the ringer on and I had the music blasting and—*wait*—" His head suddenly snapped over to the chair. "The phone was ringing?"

He leapt off the bed and grabbed the phone, slapping his finger down on a few buttons as he stared intensely at the display. He pressed a button and held the phone tightly to his ear, clearly waiting with anticipation for an answer. But he got no answer. A few more long seconds and he threw the phone back at the chair, not even hiding his extreme frustration.

"*Gaia*," he muttered angrily, staring at the phone. He looked back up and saw that Tatiana had been observing his behavior almost scientifically for the past minute. He dropped the anxious frown from his face and quickly composed himself. "I guess she turned off her phone," he said with a forced smile. But there was no point in the smile. Tatiana had already seen everything she needed to see.

Sam was no threat to her. Sam was just a man in love.

And slowly Tatiana began to remember bits and pieces of a conversation she and Gaia had shared late one night in their bedroom. A conversation about a boy named Sam.

She stepped over to the bed and sat down, making herself comfortable as Sam stood awkwardly by the chair.

"You know," she said with a slight smile, "now that I think about it, I remember Gaia telling me about a boyfriend she once had named Sam. Are you Sam, the ex-boyfriend?"

Sam straightened up slightly as he forced another

slight laugh. "Not exactly," he said. "That's. . . that's another long story."

"Oh, you *have* to tell me." Tatiana laughed. "Gaia never tells me *anything*. Especially about boys."

"No." Sam smiled. "There's really nothing to tell."

"Oh, *please*. I have so many questions."

"No, like I said. It's just a long—"

"I *like* long stories. Besides, who knows how long Gaia's going to be out on her date with Ed? It could be *hours*." She leaned forward, almost as if she were sharing a secret with Sam. "Sometimes. . . she doesn't even come home at all."

The smile instantly dropped off Sam's face. For a moment he looked like he'd just been shot in the back. He collapsed into the chair with a thud and locked his cheerless eyes with Tatiana's. "Okay," he uttered in a near monotone. "What do you want to know?"

"THIS ISN'T GOING TO WORK."

Gaia was standing at the table, looking down at Ed. She'd called on her least-favorite skill in the world— the unique talent that she was most ashamed of—her near superhuman ability to turn her heart to stone.

Hateful Glare

She'd been left with no other choice but this—to watch Ed's face turn as stone-cold as her own. To rip down the pathetic remains of the night and eat the consequences later. Because after fifteen rings of a phone flying out into blank space, Sam had disappeared again. He'd vanished into that same phantom zone where her father now resided, and that had finally gotten the better of her. All that potential death had to take precedent over Ed's increasingly unforgiving eyes.

"What's not going to work?" Ed asked coldly.

"This date, Ed. There are just too many things going on right now, and I can't—"

"Right. Good night." Ed turned down to his plate of paella and began to eat it robotically. Gaia's chest began to sting.

"Ed, please don't—"

"Don't what?" he asked matter-of-factly. "Don't eat? I'm at a restaurant."

"Don't talk to me like that, okay? I *tried* to make this work. You have *no idea* how hard I tried."

"Oh God, *thank you*," Ed snapped with a wide, disturbing grin. He stood up out of his chair to face Gaia head-on. It seemed they were doomed to be the spectacle of the evening. "Thank you so much for *trying* to go out on a date with me."

"That's not what I meant." Her teeth were clenched so hard, she was sure she could feel them crumbling away. Candlelight kept flickering under Ed's eyes, revealing a more and more `hateful glare` with each indiscernible flash.

"No? What *did* you mean?" He tilted his head with sarcastic interest.

"Don't do this, Ed." She couldn't even tell if she was begging him or threatening him. What would she even be threatening him with? "Look, there are things going on with my father—"

"Well, thank you so much for *trusting* me with that highly sensitive information. Thank you for everything. I had a lovely evening. Don't forget your cheese on the way out." Ed dropped back into his chair and began to eat again.

Gaia searched herself for some way to put Ed in his place, but the more she thought about it, the less righteous anger she could muster. And the guilt took over. Of all the emotions she'd felt this evening, the guilt was the only one she'd be taking home.

She dropped back down into her chair and grabbed his hand. "I'm so sorry, Ed. I am *so* sorry. I know how important this date is, I know. I would do anything not to ruin it. But. . . it's ruined. It was ruined before we got here. Just please don't. . . You look so. . . It's just one night, Ed. Just one night is ruined, okay?" Silence came from the other side of the table. "*Okay?*" she repeated.

`He wouldn't respond.`

Pulling Teeth

ED DIDN'T KNOW WHAT TO SAY. HE wanted to squeeze out another obnoxious retort, another vengeful little jab just to stake out another inch of personal territory. But he couldn't. Not with her eyes so wide with guilt.

He couldn't have done it, anyway.

He didn't have endless piles of emotional ammunition stockpiled and ready to fire. He'd already shot his wad with a few cold stares and some sarcasm.

Now he was just Ed again. *Ed Fargo, complete sucker in love.* Now he was stuck in her eyes again. And glued to the candlelight that glowed on her cheeks. And tangled up in the tousled waves of her hair. And so it would always be. . . .

"If you have to go, then you have to go," he said. "Don't make me feel like any more of a loser than I already do."

"No, *I'm* the loser," Gaia insisted.

"Mr. and Mrs. Loser." He sighed.

"Oh, you're proposing now?"

"Would you say yes?"

Gaia's entire face froze. Now Ed knew for sure that they were drifting apart. She couldn't even tell when he was kidding anymore. Which, of course, he was. Mostly. No, of course he was kidding. Mostly. . .

"*Kidding*, Gaia," he groaned. "Just kidding."

107

"I *know*," she scoffed. Ed could see her start to breathe again. "I know that."

He gripped her hand tightly and leaned closer. "Gaia. . . if something has happened to your dad, *tell* me what it is."

She looked deeper into his eyes, barely blinking for the next few seconds as she seemed to consider his demand.

"I don't know what it is," she stated.

"What? What does that mean?"

Gaia suddenly pulled her hand away, leaning back awkwardly against her seat. "Look, he's. . . he's been transferred out of the hospital, and we're. . . they're not sure where he is."

Ed's eyes widened with disbelief. "The hospital *lost* him?" He didn't doubt Gaia; it was just the most ludicrous thing he'd ever heard.

"They just. . ." Gaia looked more and more anxious to make a run for it. Ed could see her eyes darting yearningly toward the staircase that led to the exit. He couldn't believe, after everything they'd been through, that getting the truth from her about her struggles was still like pulling teeth. "I just need to find him," she concluded. "That's all."

Ed's stomach twisted itself into a knot. He couldn't fathom how she could have gone all this time without telling him something this massive. "Well, I'll help you find him," he insisted. "Jesus, we've been sitting here having dinner and you don't *know* where your father is? Why didn't you just tell me? We could have been looking for him this entire time. We could have been suing the *crap* out of that hospital. God, I hate hospitals. We should be making calls, we should be calling every goddamn hospital in—"

"Ed, *no!*" Gaia snapped, slapping her hand down on the table.

Ed went silent. He had no idea what to make of her sudden outburst. Every time she opened her mouth, she seemed to make less and less sense. "Gaia. . . what the hell is the matter with y—?"

"Ed, I love you, but you are *out* of all of this, do you understand?" She lowered her voice to an intensely urgent whisper. "I *won't* drag you back into it, do you hear? Not *any* of it." Ed could only sit and watch as tears began to well up in her eyes. She gripped the table tightly as her words became more and more frenzied. "I don't want you to be my trusty sidekick, or my knight in shining armor, or the dead body lying on top of *my* dead body in some tragically romantic Romeo and Juliet *death* scene. I just want you to be my *boyfriend.* My boyfriend who is *alive* and. . . and safe and. . . *here.* Do you understand? I need to do it alone so that when it's done, when it's finally *finished.* . . I can come home to you."

Ed could see a thousand different thoughts tugging away at her mouth for airtime. This had to be more honesty than she had ever spewed out in one sitting, and Ed could tell from the look on her face that it hurt. It was physically painful for Gaia to talk like this.

"Gaia, it's all right," Ed promised her. "I understand, okay? I do. You don't have to be so—"

"I have to go now," she interrupted, swiping the tears too forcefully from her eyes as she stood up out of her chair.

"Gaia, wait," he said gently, standing with her. "Don't go yet. Let me—"

"No, I have to go. I'm sorry. I'm. . . I'm so sorry, Ed. I'm sorry for ruining the date and for lying, and for—"

"Lying? When were you lying?"

She cast her glassy-eyed gaze on him one last time. "I'm sorry for everything," she said. "I'll explain it all to you soon, Ed. So soon, I swear. When it's safe. Just don't give up on me, okay?" She leaned in closer and pressed her lips firmly against his.

She was three feet behind him before he could even kiss her back. She was on the stairs before he could say another word. And she'd disappeared from sight before he could form any understanding of what the hell had just happened.

From: megan21@alloymail.com
To: ruskiegirl@alloymail.com
cc: tammiejammie@alloymail.com
Time: 9:58 P.M.
Re: the party

Love it! Love love love it.

Parchment book sounds beautiful. (I love Kate's. I go there all the time for cards and calendars.) And I'm lovin' the black and white balloons.

Can't wait to see your other decoration ideas. Are you a pro or something? We should totally start a party-planning business. My mom and her partner started when they were sixteen. Can you believe that?

But enough of my yakkin'. Love white roses, too. We are going to make Heather so proud. And party so hard!

Tammie and I printed out awesome invitations on her printer. Card stock, silver on black. (Does that go with the balloons? Oh, hell, yes—we totally think alike.) We'll give you a bunch tomorrow to hand out. I'm pretty sure you'll approve. See you at the caf?

                                        —Meegs

SHE'D ALREADY GIVEN UP ON THE

shoes. Gaia ran barefoot along Seventy-second Street, scraping along the rocky granite, ignoring shards of glass and wads of chewing gum as she increased her speed.

Stinking Laundry

She could still see the ghosts from earlier in the evening as she approached her building. The sweet ghosts of Ed in his suit, and a majestic white horse, and a black iron carriage. She swallowed down another glob of guilt and regret and burst into her lobby. She jabbed the elevator button with rapid-fire precision, sliding through the door before it had even opened fully and pummeling the button for her floor. As the elevator lurched upward, she tried to sort it all out, piece by piece, like a daunting heap of stinking laundry.

Her guilt about Ed went into the "tomorrow" pile. It had to. She had no other choice for now. It was just as she had said—she would explain it all to him as soon as it was safe. But Sam was the immediate matter at hand. Sam and her father. They were the massive pile that towered over her higher than the eye could see and wider than the Great Wall of China. They both needed finding now. No more distractions. No more doubts or delays. Starting right now, and ending with both of them sitting with her at a dinner table or on a park bench. Something normal and banal.

She prayed that the Sam search would end in the

next thirty seconds. He needed to be in her apartment, waiting just behind that closed door of his. He had to be there. And once she found him safe and sound in his room, they would lock every door in the house and make whatever plans they needed to make for tomorrow, and then they would sleep.

One thing at a time, Gaia. You've got to find him first. She burst into her apartment and made her way toward his room as quietly as she could, even though she wanted to jump the two couches in the living room and kick his door down on the fly. She held up at his room and brought her hand to the door to tap out the secret knock. But as her hand grasped the knob, she felt it give way. . . .

Oh God. The lock was broken. Gaia's hands went numb. Someone had broken the lock on the door. Someone had broken in and done God knew what to Sam. She shoved the door open and bounded into the room, ready to rip someone's head off his spine. But once she'd stepped inside, she nearly tripped over her own feet.

Sam was couched deep in the comfy chair in nothing but a thin T-shirt and a pair of boxers. Tatiana was leaned back comfortably in his bed. In nothing but a stretchy white cotton nightie.

Somewhere between shock and confusion, Gaia suddenly found herself in a purely paralytic state. Frozen solid. The only thing she felt capable of moving was her eyes, which continued to shift from one side of the room to the other, taking in this vision that she could only describe in understated terms as *most unpleasant.*

"You're home early," Tatiana said with a smile.

"I'm . . ." Gaia was still at a loss for words as she tried to accept the jolting sight of the two of them sitting happily (and damn near *nakedly*) together in the room.

Sam's eyes brightened with what looked like relief. "You're back," he said, a gentle smile spreading across his face.

"How was your date with Ed?" Tatiana asked. Sam's eyes instantly darkened again.

Thank you, Tatiana, Gaia thought. *Thank you so much for asking. You're making this incomprehensible moment so much easier.* The silence in the room felt as thick as glue.

"Why didn't you stay over?" Tatiana added, tilting her head quizzically. "I hope there were no troubles of paradise. . . ."

"*In paradise,*" Sam corrected her, turning his bitter eyes to Gaia. "I hope there were no troubles *in* paradise. . . ."

Gaia would have paid any sum of money for another chair in this godforsaken room. She needed to sit down.

"Well. . . ?" Tatiana pushed. "Okay, what *grade* would you give the date?"

Was she *trying* to make this the most disturbing, unexpected, and uncomfortable moment of Gaia's

114

life? If so, she was doing a damn good job. Gaia hadn't even managed to form a sentence about this situation, and Tatiana already had her tangled into a painful knot and praying for a seat.

"I'm . . ." Yes, it was official. Gaia was now a mute. If she couldn't form a sentence soon, she was sure this tragically awkward tableau might just be seared into her brain for all eternity. "I'm sorry," she finally uttered. "But what's. . . *what's going on here?*"

For a moment there was no response. But Tatiana finally came up with an answer. "I met Sam," she explained.

"Yes, I *see* that," Gaia replied sharply as fury began to bubble up from her chest and into her throat. "And exactly *how* did you meet him?"

Gaia realized that she was giving Tatiana the most ridiculous 90210 scowl. She had suddenly entered her very own nighttime soap, and she hadn't even realized it.

This was all so uncalled for. She should have just been elated that Sam was all right. She should have given him a hug and started in on their plans for the morning. She should have just accepted that Tatiana had somehow discovered Sam, as was bound to happen at some point in one's own house, for God's sake. And she shouldn't have cared about Tatiana's wardrobe. Why *wouldn't* Tatiana be in her nightie? She always went to bed early, and she'd worn that thing to sleep at least twenty times before. Tatiana certainly

115

hadn't done anything to deserve the melodramatic feline scowl Gaia was shooting at her.

Yet the scowl only deepened as Gaia compulsively scanned Tatiana and Sam's scantily clad bodies again and again, watching their bizarrely friendly smiles flash on and off. That was the thing about jealousy. No amount of rationality could possibly. . .

Wait. . .

Jealousy? Is that why I'm glaring at her like a rich bitch heiress to an oil fortune?

Yes, of course it was. It wasn't the concern or frustration over Tatiana having found Sam; it was the jealousy. Gaia was still rather emotionally naive, but she knew jealousy. She just hadn't expected to be feeling it at this particular moment. Two hours ago Gaia had been breaking the news to Sam about her relationship with Ed, and now she was giving Tatiana the classic stay-away-from-my-*man* look? When had Sam suddenly become Gaia's *"man"* again?

Okay. So maybe things with Sam were a little more complicated than Gaia had thought. Perhaps she was still wrestling with just a couple of denial issues. . . .

"It was kind of funny how we met, actually," Tatiana said, smiling over at Sam.

Gaia began to grind her teeth again.

"More like scary," Sam said.

"Yes, funny and scary," Tatiana agreed.

Can we get on with it? Gaia was happy that her

116

friends were playing together so nicely, she really was, but this whole finishing-each-other's-sentences shtick was a bit much.

"I was half asleep in bed," Tatiana went on, "and then I heard this phone ringing. . . ."

"The cell phone," Sam said, rolling his eyes to Gaia. "I forgot to turn off the damn ring, and when I put on the Walkman—"

"I get it," Gaia interrupted, shaking her head over the pointless double whammy of this evening, thanks to those stupid cell phones. She'd always hated those infernal things.

"But it's okay," Sam said. "Tatiana and I talked."

"We talked," Tatiana repeated, "and now that I understand everything, I hate him, Gaia, I hate him so much."

Gaia knew right away that Tatiana was talking about Loki. Sam really had told her everything. He must have told her about the shooting and even about his time in Loki's compound. For a moment Gaia felt her blood begin to boil again. How could he have let out all their guarded secrets like that? For God's sake, Gaia had just damn near torched her relationship with Ed to honor their secret, and here was Sam blabbing the whole deal to Tatiana? A girl he'd never even *met* before? What the hell kind of honor system was *that*?

But the more Gaia thought about it, the more she

realized how unfair she was being. Tatiana and Sam had both come about as close as anyone could to being a couple of crossed-off names on Loki's list. In fact, very few people had suffered through the war with Loki like the three people sitting in that room. And if Sam and Tatiana wanted to share their war stories, then they had every right. They had every right in the world. Gaia really needed to get her priorities straight.

"Gaia, don't you think we should tell my mother about this?" Tatiana asked. "Don't you think we should tell her what's going on?"

"Not yet." Gaia dropped down on the bed and slid closer to Tatiana. It wasn't exactly a conscious decision, but Gaia let it happen. Because she was shoving her priorities back in line. Tatiana was in this now, whether Gaia liked it or not. And right now there were simply more important things to worry about than immature soap operas and stupid petty jealousies. She knew she had no reason to be suspicious of Sam and Tatiana. It was time to move past the initial shock of walking through that door and get on to the matter at hand. "Soon," Gaia said. "We can tell everyone what's going on soon, but just not yet. Sam and I are going to the compound tomorrow morning, and maybe we'll have a better idea of things once we get back. But we have to wait until we're sure that Sam, and every one of us, is safe." Gaia looked into Tatiana's eyes to make sure she understood how crucial it was to maintain secrecy.

118

"I understand," Tatiana stated, her complete commitment showing in her eyes. It was good to see Tatiana's loyalty and intensity again.

JOYCE, THE RESIDENT ADVISER, HANDED Just Voices

Heather the phone in the hallway and pulled a chair over for her.

"Don't talk too long, okay?" Joyce whispered. "You really shouldn't be on the phone this late, but he sounded so sad. And cute."

"Thanks," Heather whispered. She still couldn't get over how much nicer the authority figures were when you were blind. "I'll try to keep it short." She waited until she heard Joyce's door close, and then she brought the phone to her ear. She had never loved the phone as much as she did now. It was one of the very few activities that was exactly the same whether she could see or not. No eyes required. Just voices in the dark. "Hello? Ed?"

"Hi," he said, sounding like a four-year-old who'd just lost his first goldfish to old age.

"Oh my God, you sound awful." She tried to cup the phone in her hand for optimum hallway privacy. Most of the girls in the dorm were probably already asleep, but they had awfully good ears. "What's the matter, Ed? It's almost midnight."

"I know. I'm sorry. I tried not to call, but. . . well, I actually got out of my cab at the bus station, but there were no more buses to Carverton."

"What? What are you talking about? What happened?"

"I don't think she likes cheese."

Somehow the way Ed said it, it sounded like the saddest fact in the world. Heather suddenly felt like crying, even though talking to Ed on the phone should have been one of the second-greatest delights of her day, the first being his visit just fourteen or so hours ago. "What do you mean? They all like cheese, Ed, I swear. What happened?"

"I don't know," he complained, sounding not all that far from tears himself. "She just. . . left. She just left me there in the restaurant. It was all going so well. . . I thought. But then, I don't know, we started fighting, sort of, and she started acting all weird. . . and then she just left."

"Well, maybe she had an emergency?" Heather knew how lame that sounded, but it was all she could think of to say. Then again, when it came to Gaia, and given everything that had been going on, an emergency wasn't such a far-fetched concept, was it?

"Yeah, right." Ed sighed. "That emergency is called her life. Her life is an emergency."

"Oh, Ed, I'm sorry. I loved your date. I think any girl would think it was the most beautiful date in the world."

"Yeah, well. . . Gaia's not a girl, she's just a. . . teenage. . . armageddonatrix."

"What?"

"I don't know. I don't know what I'm saying. I'm just so freaking depressed."

Heather pushed her chair out of the way and settled onto the rug of the hallway, basking in the normalcy of the moment. Just sitting on the phone trying to cheer up a friend. No new skills to learn or hardships to grin and bear. Helping someone else instead of waiting for someone to show her to the goddamn bathroom.

"Look, Ed, maybe something really did come up, if she was having a good time and then just suddenly had to leave. If you want to be with her, that's the kind of stuff you'll have to deal with."

"I know, but not tonight." Ed groaned. "That was the whole point of the night. We weren't supposed to deal with whatever apocalypse was happening tonight."

"Think about it this way," Heather said, pressing her toes against the opposite wall. "Her life is pretty insane. My life isn't exactly a holiday right now. But *your* life is pretty amazingly normal. You're walking, and you've got your family and school. You're lucky, Ed. You're so lucky that your life is normal. Let Gaia deal with the awful stuff she has to deal with and enjoy your normal life, you know? Ed, I know you remember wanting that, and only that, when you were in the chair. Just to walk around like everybody else.

Just to do stupid teenage nonsense because you can. Because nothing is stopping you."

There was a long pause on the other end of the line. "Is this Heather Gannis? I wanted to speak with Heather Gannis."

Heather laughed quietly. He was joking. That was a good sign. She was getting pretty good at this whole cheering-up thing. "I told you I've changed, Ed. Please don't tell me you don't believe me yet."

"No, I believe. Believe me, I believe."

"Thank you." She nodded graciously as if Ed were sitting across from her.

"And you're right."

"I know I'm right. That part has never changed."

"There's the Heather I know and love."

"Ha ha," she muttered. "But seriously, Ed. Just go to school. Hang out with the freaks. *I know*. Why don't you go to my benefit? That should be good for a laugh. How's that going, anyway?"

Ed breathed out a cross between a sigh and a chuckle. "Well, I wouldn't really call it a benefit. I think it's really more like a party. I'm not really sure what kind of benefit they could throw together if they're doing this thing tomorrow night."

"It's tomorrow night? So soon?"

"Yeah, well, it was the only night Tatiana could get the place."

"Tatiana is putting it together?"

"They all are, but Tatiana's is practically taking the whole sucker over."

"Well, where's the party?"

"Some bar called Pravda."

"*Pravda?* She booked Pravda for the whole night?"

Heather felt herself slipping back into her old persona, but she couldn't help but be impressed and maybe even a little jealous. She'd tried to book a few parties there, and they'd always seemed to diss her. What the hell was so special about Tatiana?

Will you listen to yourself, please? You're regressing.

The more Heather thought about it, the more she realized just how `pathetically shallow` her life had been. The fact that something as trivial as who could book Pravda for the night had been something to steam over was just downright embarrassing.

"Yeah, I guess," Ed said. "You sound just like the girls. They were going nuts about it. They started kissing all kinds of Tatiana ass, and I don't think they've really stopped since."

Heather suddenly found herself flashing back to the day she had basically found herself in charge of the entire group. She hadn't exactly asked for all that power; it had just sort of been handed to her based surely on some combination of her remarkable character and her remarkable wardrobe, not necessarily in that order. And she could sense it immediately, with almost no information: They had set their sights on

123

Tatiana. With Heather gone, they needed a new interim queen. They were, after all, while being extremely stylish and sweet, born followers. That was what made things run so smoothly.

"I bet the coronation ceremony's not that far off," Heather heard herself say. She hadn't even intended to say it out loud.

"What do you mean?" Ed asked.

"Oh, nothing," she said. "But I just have this feeling that they might be looking for a. . . Never mind, let's talk more about you."

"Come on," Ed insisted. "What were you going to say?"

"No, it will sound egotistical, and I'm not like that anymore."

"For old times' sake, then," Ed joked.

Heather figured Ed would take it the right way. He'd known her for a very long time, even at her most shallow and egomaniacal, and they were still friends, after all. "Okay," she agreed. "I was just going to say that it sounds to me like they're looking for a new. . . you know. . . queen. To replace me."

There was a pause on the other end of the line. "Ed?"

"Oh, that doesn't sound egotistical. . . my queen."

"Okay, shut up." She laughed. "I'm just *saying*, Ed, when I, you know. . . *took over*, it only took them, like, two days to roll out the red carpet. I knew I was officially the new leader once there was a closet raid."

"I'm sorry. . . ? A closet raid?"

"Yes, a closet raid, Ed." Now he was making fun of her, thus forcing her to explain, no matter how ridiculous it might sound to a boy. "They all begged to come over to my house and raid my closet. As if I were hosting a Barney's warehouse sale out of my bedroom or something. You have to understand, Ed: When they want your clothes, it basically means they want to *be* you. That's just how it works."

"Huh," Ed grunted.

"What?"

"No, I was just remembering," he said. "I was remembering that day all those girls agreed to dress up like Gaia to try and fake out that surveillance team waiting outside my building. Remember? When you all put on the blond wigs and the army pants and the tank tops? I guess Gaia had her own coronation and she never even knew it."

Heather thought about it for a second. "Yeah," she agreed finally. "I guess so."

Silence on the phone again. "Now I'm depressed again."

Heather let out a long, frustrated sigh. "Look, just go to my ridiculous fake benefit, Ed. Go and hang out and be normal, will you please? Your life is better than mine and Gaia's combined."

"I'm sorry, you're right. You're right, Heather."

"I know I'm right, Ed. I told you, I'm the blind soothsayer you've always dreamed of."

"I know," Ed replied. "But if you don't mind me saying. . . your last prediction about the date. . . it left a little to be desired."

"Well, it was half right, wasn't it? Until she left. I'm new at it, Ed. Give me a little time."

"I'll have to think about it," Ed said. "But if tonight was what half a perfect date feels like, I'd almost rather have no date at all. . . ."

Almost.

as if they
had just
stepped off **the**
the
mother **ultimate**
ship, ready **truck**
to begin
their deadly **stop**
assault on **diner**
earth

THERE WAS REALLY NO LOGIC TO IT.

Everything about this moment should have been painful and nauseating. Traveling toward the ruins of Loki's operation, on a futile search for information about her missing father. Alone in a car with Sam, questioning the underlying meaning of every word exchanged and every pregnant silence. But somehow, in spite of all the gloomy

Semi-invisibl Ghost

circumstances and stilted conversations, Gaia was still breathing better than she had in months.

It was the simple act of leaving the city. Crawling out from under the gray skies and enclosed spaces. Coasting over the world instead of standing under it. She could feel them all drifting away—all the skinheads and faux hippies in Washington Square Park, all the FOHs and their hopeless admirers pledging their allegiance to Abercrombie & Fitch, the Chanel mothers and Ralph Lauren fathers of East Seventy-second Street, the Perry Street town house turned crime scene. . . .

Gaia didn't exactly mind taking a little break from Natasha and Tatiana, either. Surrogate families were simply too complicated, and waiting for them to behave exactly as you wished was like waiting for the sun to set in Scandinavia. Even Ed. . . The truth was, Gaia felt so guilty for the way she'd treated Ed the last few days that physically leaving the city was just about the only way she could feel any less tortured about it.

With a little time to breathe, she would come back from this fact-finding mission with a legitimate lead, a slightly improved attitude, and a much lower stress level. Then she could be something better resembling the Gaia Ed deserved instead of the semi-invisible ghost she'd turned into. With a few substantial facts under her belt, she'd be able to tell Ed about Sam and finally clear the air. That would be all she needed to get her and Ed back on track.

With Sam at the wheel, Gaia was free to drift off into the daze of her choice, and as she watched the crackled green blur of trees pass by her window, she found herself dreaming of being on the road like this with Ed. Of course, she and Ed wouldn't be heading out on some miserable mission. They would just be heading out. Sampling every single Friendly's and Bob's Big Boy, searching for the best deal on doughnuts and the perfect microwave burrito, trying out every indoor pool at every ultracheesy motel they passed, taking deeper breaths as the pollution grew thinner and thinner and watching as the people who gave them directions grew less and less obnoxious and cynical. And then at some point they'd get tired of driving. And they'd find the remotest street they could find and drop down their savings as a down payment on the first house that caught their eye. And presto facto... they would be home.

She lulled herself so deeply into her fantasy future that she actually turned toward the driver's side with an idiotic smile, expecting to see Ed. When she saw Sam's profile, awkward could not even begin to describe the sensation. But when Sam glimpsed her smile and smiled *back*. . .

Welcome to the land of the *über*-awkward.

"My God, was that a smile?" Sam asked, looking momentarily away from the road again. "I don't think I've seen you really smile once. Not since before I. . ."

His voice trailed off slowly as the steady bumps of the highway became the only sound inside the car. Gaia had to say something to fill the silence.

"I was just. . . ," she began. Nope. Nothing. She knew enough to start a sentence, but she didn't have one single idea as to how to finish it. She certainly wouldn't be finishing it with the truth, that was for sure. So she had only answered his silence with more silence. *Nice going, Gaia.*

"You know. . . I, uh. . ." Sam trailed off again.

Don't talk about us, Sam. Please don't talk about us.

Gaia suddenly realized that this mantra had basically been running through her head since the moment they'd fastened their seat belts. She was literally praying he wouldn't broach the subject of their relationship. Or Gaia's relationship with Ed.

Even if he'd asked to discuss this stuff two days ago, she probably could have handled it a little better. But after last night she just wanted to sweep all the questions under the rug. Because until last night she really hadn't been aware that she *had* any questions. Gaia had been beyond elated to see Sam alive. It was the first true miracle she had ever encountered. It meant the world to her. It meant everything. She never wanted to let Sam Moon out of her sight for another second. She wanted to protect him and be close to him and just bask in his resurrection for as long as she possibly could. But their romantic relationship was over. Just like Sam said, it had been over before he'd even disappeared. Gaia was with Ed now. And as painful as it was, she'd finally explained that to Sam. Ed was all she wanted, if he would even have her after last night's debacle. She certainly had no questions about her love for Ed Fargo.

But after going through that altogether icky conversation with Sam—after setting all those romantic boundaries so clearly for him. . . Gaia'd had to go and walk through that door last night and have that *thing*. That *thing* she'd felt when she'd seen Tatiana sprawled out on the bed like a goddamn Victoria's Secret model.

The jealousy. Gaia just hadn't expected the jealousy. It wasn't even that she really thought Tatiana was making some kind of play for Sam; it was just that Tatiana had somehow sparked this bizarre possessive instinct in Gaia—that was all.

"I, uh. . ." Sam was trying again to form his sentence as he squinted out the windshield.

131

Just leave it alone, Sam. Please. It will make things so much easier for both of us. . . .

"I can't quite remember if we came up the Sawmill Parkway. . . or the Taconic. . . ."

Right. Are we feeling sufficiently idiotic, Gaia? She tried to hide the massive exhalation that poured from her lungs. Sam wasn't trying to start some deep emotional conversation. He was trying to find his way back to the compound. Just as he promised he'd do.

"It could have been either," she replied. "You said you remember seeing signs for Great Barrington, right?"

"Right."

"I can get us there," she said, "but once we're onto the little unmapped roads, it's all you."

Sam rolled down his window and rested his elbow on the door. "Gaia. . . about last night. . ."

Oh, no, no. They were supposed to be past this. She'd just suffered through that entire false alarm. *You've got to stop him, Gaia. Just stop him right now. . . .*

"I am *starving*," she groaned, loud and long enough to cut Sam off permanently. "I think we need to stop for something." Of course, the last thing she wanted to do was stop, but it was all she could come up with on such short notice. "Are you hungry?"

"I could eat," Sam said. "I mean, if you're sure you want to stop. Let me know when you see a place."

"Okay."

The car filled with awkward silence again. Until Sam opened his mouth.

"I just wanted to ask you about last—"

"*There,*" Gaia announced far too loudly, thrusting her finger out the window. "That place looks *perfect.*"

She was pointing at what looked like the ultimate truck stop diner. The kind of totally generic and anonymous place where she'd always dreamed of working as a waitress. The kind of place where everyone would be perfectly polite about the weather and the traffic, but no one would ever have to know a damn thing about Gaia except the name on her name tag. Which she would have changed to something like Mavis or Janette.

The place was nothing more than a little block of cement with windows. Its only identifying mark was the word *Diner,* which had been plopped down on top of the cement shoe box in huge, rusted metal letters. Perfect. They probably had the best cheeseburger in the Western Hemisphere.

"*There?*" Sam asked. "You're sure you don't want to wait awhile and find a McDonald's or something?"

"No, *there,*" Gaia insisted. "Come on. What, are you scared of the bikers or something? I'll protect you."

"No," Sam said. "I just. . ." His eyes suddenly darted up to the rearview mirror as if he were checking for something behind them.

"What?" Gaia asked. She turned to look through the back windshield. "What's wrong?"

133

"What?" Sam asked.

"What's back there? You just looked—"

"No—what? Nothing," he said. "No, I'm just checking the traffic...."

Gaia turned back behind them again. "Is there something—?"

"We can eat here," Sam interrupted. "That's fine." He signaled for the turn and pulled into the parking lot across the street from the diner.

Gaia looked over at him for a better understanding of his `blip of weirdness,` but the blip had passed. They got out of the car and traversed the gravel toward the door.

Sam still looked a little preoccupied, but Gaia realized that he was probably exhausted. He was, after all, still recovering from a massive injury, and all this activity couldn't be great for his health. Gaia did her best to keep her guilt in check as they took the two steps up into the diner.

We'll be back home so soon, Sam, I promise. We'll be in and out of that compound and we'll be back before the sun even sets.

Maybe a good meal was exactly what Sam needed. A good meal and the company of some of the finest people on earth, as far as Gaia was concerned. Truck drivers, waitresses, and bikers. She opened the door and stepped inside. And with only one step she realized...

There were certainly plenty of bikers. But as far as Gaia could tell, there were very few of the finest people on earth. Okay. There wasn't one. In fact, judging from the looks that Gaia and Sam got the moment they walked in, she figured it was probably safe to say that the patrons of this particular establishment. . . had probably assaulted, robbed, or otherwise injured many of the finest people on earth.

ED HAD BEEN SPRAWLED OUT ON THE

Post-apocalyptic Puppet

cafeteria table for twenty minutes, watching Megan and Tammie squealing joyously about their benefit for Heather and passing out invitations to "the right people." It was like watching some kind of post-apocalyptic puppet show as they bounced around from table to table, turning on their tilt-and-grin smiles for the privileged few and pretending the other ninety percent didn't exist. That ridiculous benefit. . . now that Ed thought about it, it really was something of a travesty. Had they even talked to Heather once to hear her opinion on all this silliness? Of course not.

The supposed "Friends of Heather" were hardly

thinking about Heather. They were thinking about looking like people who were thinking about Heather. They were thinking about the pictures of their party showing up on the society page of *Manhattan File* magazine. Ed tuned them out completely and returned to his `mental postmortem` on his evening with Gaia.

His chin was pressed down against the Formica table, hands dangling over the other end as he planned the perfectly worded speech that would finally make Gaia "believe in love," as it were. Make her understand that he *wanted* to be there for all her battles and all her struggles and all her crises. The more he imagined this fictional dialogue, however, the bigger the pathetic frown of futility on his face grew.

Never happen, Ed. She'll never get it. Never.

But when Gaia's hands suddenly began to massage his shoulders from behind, he felt an irresistible spark of hope shoot through him in spite of everything. In spite of their abominable evening and all the unfortunate facts of her inevitable nature, all it ever took was one little gesture. One truly intimate gesture like this and Ed was willing to forget it all.

He placed his hands on hers and pulled her down toward him, feeling her cheek press against his from behind. "Let's just forget last night, okay?" he suggested gently.

"What is there to forget?" her sweet voice asked just inches from his ear. In a faint Russian accent.

Ed snapped his head away as his eyes darted to Tatiana's face, so close to his that she had blurred completely out of focus.

"*Whoa.*" He laughed uncomfortably. "I thought you were—"

"Why do you want to forget last night?" Tatiana laughed, dropping down into the chair next to Ed's and leaning closer.

"Okay, close-talking alert." Ed straightened up in his chair and wiped the `zombified yearning` from his face.

"What?"

"Don't sneak up on me like that, okay?"

"Relax." Tatiana giggled, freeing her mane of long blond hair from its ponytail, swinging it all in front of her face and then flipping it back, letting it fall perfectly over her shoulders.

"I'm perfectly relaxed," Ed assured her.

"Tatiana!" The native call of the FOHs suddenly rang out through the entire cafeteria. Ed cringed at the deafening frequency of their joyous squeaks.

"What's *up*, ladies?" Tatiana chirped at top volume. She flashed a massive grin as Megan and Tammie scampered up and dropped down into the two opposite chairs.

Ed turned to Tatiana, arching his eyebrow ever so slightly. He'd heard of fast friends before, but Tatiana seemed to be setting a new record. On the other hand, when the FOHs locked onto their targets, they tended not to miss.

"Oh my God, I *totally* loved your ideas for the party," Megan squealed, ogling Tatiana with wide-eyed admiration.

"Oh, thank you." Tatiana smiled humbly. "I just thought the teeniest bit of decoration would make it a little more special, you know? More tasteful."

"You were totally right," Megan crooned. "They were *perfect*. Perfect. Melanie is out shopping right now at Kate's. Laura is checking on my balloon order. It's all totally coming together. What do you think of the invites?"

"Perfect." Tatiana smiled even more widely, taking one of the invitations. "We really do think alike, uh?"

"Totally," Megan agreed.

"Well, I'll put in the flower order after next period," Tatiana said. "And everything is all set at Pravda. I talked to my friend last night, and it seems the management is going to be out of town, so she's going to help us do a little something special for the alcohol situation, what with it being a benefit and all. . . ."

Ed gave Tatiana another sideways glance. He still seemed to learn new little tidbits about her every day. He'd certainly never seen her with the particular "naughty little smile" she was flashing the girls. Nor was he aware that Tatiana could simply make a call and arrange a private stash of booze. It was actually a relief to see that she had a slightly wild side. Sometimes Ed worried about her perfectionist streak.

"*Genius*," Tammie gurgled, smiling back reverently. "You're a genius. Well, the turnout is going to be *huge*. We've got some NYU, some Columbia, *some* VS, though there's very little point, given the dearth of hot guys here."

"*Nice*," Ed quipped. He couldn't decide which thing to be offended by first. The fact that their concern was how many "hot guys" would attend a benefit for Heather or the fact that he had just been dissed.

"Oh, relax, Ed." Tammie groaned. "You're taken."

"Taken, but still hot." Tatiana laughed, mussing up his hair like a dog. Ed gave her another puzzled glance, and she tugged her hand away quickly.

For the briefest millisecond Ed found himself troubled by Tatiana's recent weirdness. He actually wondered if they needed to have a two-second chat just to go over the fact that their slight unfortunate dip into romance was totally resolved—and more than over. She had completely concurred with the "just friends" plan. Did he need to remind her that he and Gaia were totally, one hundred percent together?

But his worry was quickly replaced by a torturous and spiky rock that landed in his stomach when he caught himself thinking he and Gaia were totally one hundred percent together. That was the overstatement of the century. A cloud of gloom fell over his face before he could even hide it.

"Oh, Ed, don't look so sad." Tammie sighed. "You're hot, okay? You're no Jake, but you're hot."

"What?" Ed uttered, not even sure what Tammie had just said.

Megan's eyes suddenly widened with desperate urgency. "Wait, is Jake *coming*?"

"Of *course* he's coming," Tammie replied. "He's basically the entire VS hot guy contingent. I mean, besides Ed," she added, tossing Ed a patronizing nod. "But I think Jake should count double based on his hotness. . . so that's three. He's hanging out after school/preparty with us, remember?" Tammie suddenly looked at Tatiana with a blinding grin. "Oh, Tatiana, I forgot to even ask you—can we come to your house for that?"

"Of course." Tatiana smiled. "Absolutely—"

"I knew you'd say yes." Tammie laughed.

"*Yes*," Megan agreed with a pronounced nod of excitement. "We are coming to your house and we are raiding your closet."

Ed's eyes nearly bugged out of his head when he heard it. The closet raid. Already. After two days. Maybe Heather *was* becoming psychic?

"Sounds good to me," Tatiana said.

"*Perfect*," Megan chirped. "I am *so* dying to see your entire collection."

"Well, you're all welcome to come over."

"Um. . ." Ed stepped in on Tatiana's conversation and stared at her, trying to give her the appropriate code with his eyes.

"What?" she asked innocently.

He couldn't believe how little she was thinking this through. For Gaia's sake, he didn't want to have to spell it out in front of Tammie and Megan, but judging from Tatiana's blank face, he guessed he would have to. Tatiana seemed to have forgotten that her bedroom and apartment were also *Gaia's* bedroom and apartment. And if Tatiana thought that she could bring a herd of FOHs into Gaia's house without the potential for bloodshed. . .

"Won't, uh. . . Gaia get a little. . . annoyed?" Ed tried to make his point as lightly as possible.

"Oh, Gaia won't be home," Tatiana said, nearly in passing. "I love it. You can all help me pick something out for tonight."

"Where's she going to be?" Ed asked.

Tatiana turned to Ed and went into a bizarre two seconds of `deer-in-headlights syndrome`. She looked like she'd suddenly needed to power down and restart. "Gaia. . . you mean?"

"Yes, *Gaia*," Ed repeated, searching Tatiana's eyes for returning brain function. "Where is Gaia?"

"Oh. . . oh, I have no idea." Tatiana laughed. "But you know she won't be home, Ed. She is never home."

That was certainly true. Gaia was always appearing and disappearing at will, not even telling Ed where the hell she was going. The thought of it made Ed want to drop his chin down on the table again.

Megan turned to Ed. "Ed, you should come over, too."

"To raid Tatiana's closet?" he muttered.

"*No,* Mr. Gloomy-Face. To hang out with Jake. Jake's supposed to hang out with us, but now you guys can do 'boy' things while we do 'girl' things. It's perfect."

However gloomy-faced Ed had looked before, he doubled it. "I'm supposed to sit and do 'boy' things... with *Jake*?"

"He's *cool,* Ed," Tammie insisted. "He's really cool. You'll like him."

"Yeah," Ed uttered in a monotone. "I think I'll pass—"

"Ed, come *on,*" Tatiana moaned, giving his shoulder a jovial shake. "Come over, okay? I will let these girls take my entire wardrobe if I don't have someone there to talk some sense into me."

"She's right," Tammie assured him. "I've already seen her in two skirts that I'm totally borrowing."

"I really don't think—"

"Ed, what are you going to do instead?" Tatiana crossed her arms and stared at him with a well-meaning frown. "Sit in your house alone and look gloomy until the party?"

Ed had no response for that. It was, for the most part, exactly what he had planned to do if he couldn't have that dream conversation with Gaia. Particularly if

142

he couldn't even *find* Gaia for the evening, which he was beginning to think might be the case. But now that Tatiana had announced the depressing plan so publicly, he realized that it was, in fact, *too* depressing. Even more depressing than sitting with Jake and doing boy things, whatever the hell *that* meant.

"Okay." He sighed.

"Perfect," Megan said, standing up out of her chair. "We'll meet you guys in the lobby after school. Let's go, Tam. We need to finish handing out the invites."

Megan and Tammie said their good-byes and drifted back into their puppetlike bouncing, leaving Ed and Tatiana alone at the table.

"They are so *nice*," Tatiana cooed. "I had no idea they were so nice."

"It depends on what you're wearing," Ed mumbled, leaning back in his chair and giving in to the question of where on earth Gaia had gone this time. She was obviously searching somehow for her father. Probably running from hospital to hospital across the city. Of course keeping Ed out of the loop completely.

Tatiana leaned closer to Ed and examined his eyes.

"Ed, I wish you didn't let Gaia's craziness hurt you so much, you know?"

"I know."

"I mean, she is just Gaia. She has *so* many things going on in her life."

143

Ed gave Tatiana his full attention. "What things?"

"Just. . . *things,* you know? She's just. . . out there somewhere, doing. . . whatever she is doing, and. . . You don't need to worry. Everything is going to work out between the two of you."

Ed searched her eyes more closely. "Do you know where she is?"

"*No.* Of course not. When do I ever know where she is? I just wish you didn't have to go so crazy when she is off doing. . . *whatever.* I mean, she's not, you know. . . a *princess.* . . ."

"What are you *talking* about?" Ed sat up much straighter in his chair so that he and Tatiana were face-to-face.

"*Nothing.*" Tatiana giggled, putting her hands on his shoulders and steadying him. "Oh my goodness, *nothing,* Ed. I'm just babbling. I'm speaking through my ass."

"That must be why you're not making any sense."

Tatiana laughed and dropped her head on Ed's shoulder. "Yes, exactly. I have learned English so well that I can now talk out of my ass. Please forgive me, okay? Forgive me."

"I don't know what for."

"I don't know, either." She laughed again. "But forgive me, anyway."

"No problem." Ed sighed. "Forgiving people is what I do best."

"SHOULD WE LEAVE?" SAM UTTERED through the side of his mouth.

'Diner' Diner

The entire diner seemed to have looked up from their meals or their beers. Even the cook and the two waitresses seemed to be staring at Sam and Gaia as if they had just stepped off the mother ship, ready to begin their deadly assault on earth.

Gaia had never seen this many fat leather-clad men sitting in one place. Normally she would have been delighted to finally be surrounded by "real" people instead of the parade of posers back in the city. But the looks on these faces suggested otherwise. The looks on these faces did not elicit delight, but rather suggested the need for a deep understanding of biker gang protocol. Which Gaia would have to pretend she had.

"No way," Gaia said, grabbing Sam's wrist firmly and dragging him toward two open spots at the counter. "I'm hungry."

Slowly but surely, the bikers returned to their meals as the waitress approached Sam and Gaia at the counter. The look on her face hovered somewhere between puzzled fascination and disdain. Gaia peeked down at her name tag. *Doris.* Even better than Mavis or Janette.

I want to be you, Doris.

Doris brought her pencil to her notepad but suddenly dropped it down at her side and just stared for a moment, sizing them up. "Okay, I just got one question," she said. Her voice had obviously been ravaged by three packs a day for at least twenty years. "I got a bet going with the cook. Are you two supermodels or aliens?"

"He's a supermodel," Gaia explained. "I'm an alien."

Doris let out a large, infectious laugh. She pressed her pencil back to her pad with a smile. "Well, what do supermodels and aliens eat?"

"Cheeseburgers," Gaia explained. "We only eat cheeseburgers. And coffee. We drink a lot of coffee."

"Well, I'll start up a fresh pot, then," Doris said. "Coming right up."

Gaia smiled with complete sincerity. Something she rarely did in anyone but Ed Fargo's company. She wondered whether or not she should ask Doris for an application just in case she decided to come back and get a job right here at the "Diner" diner.

So she hadn't been wrong after all. These *were* the kinds of people she'd hoped to find out here in the land of truck stop diners. Straightforward, funny, and unpretentious. She could see Sam start to breathe a little easier, too. Until the door opened again.

All heads turned toward the doorway with that exact same communal glance of death that had greeted Sam and Gaia. This was either the standard greeting for the folks at this particular diner, or, more likely, this was the standard greeting for the nonregulars—something they clearly got very few of.

They must have been particularly troubled to see *two* nonregular arrivals in such a short period of time. And they weren't alone. Gaia found that coincidence a bit curious herself. She and Sam walked in. And then these two other random dudes walked in three minutes later? Could be meaningless. Could be a major problem. Especially since they were clearly criminals, plain and simple. Their faces were obscured by ugly aviator sunglasses. And their black clothes were entirely nondescript.

"You know what?" Sam said. "I'll be right back."

He slid off his spinning stool, but Gaia grabbed his arm and held him close. "Where are you going?" she asked calmly, glancing back furtively at the two men, as they of course had to sit down at the booth directly behind her.

"Bathroom," Sam explained. "I'll be back."

"Okay."

She let go of his arm and watched as he made his way to the rest room. Doris placed the coffees on the counter.

"Here you go. Two coffees. The burgers will be out in a sec."

"Thanks." Gaia had only enough time to bring the coffee to her lips before the worst-case scenario reared its ugly head. Why did her instincts always have to be so good in just this one category? Potential violence. She always seemed to get that right.

"Is someone sitting here?" the man asked, lowering his

aviator sunglasses to introduce Gaia to the hideously black circles under his eyes and the reek of his cigar breath.

"Yup," Gaia replied, turning her eyes straight forward and focusing on the old milk shake machine. She sipped her coffee. This lunch could still come off without incident if he just took his brush-off cue. "Someone's sitting here," she confirmed, "and you're sitting back there."

"Well, maybe it should be the other way around," he suggested, leaning an inch closer to her as he settled into Sam's seat. He seemed to have studied his stupid, loutish accent at thug finishing school.

Gaia rolled her eyes and then glanced down the hall toward the rest rooms. "No, I think it's good the way it is," she said.

"Wait, are you saying that you would rather be with that. . . that skinny *kid* than *me*?" He leaned forward on the counter, trying to make eye contact.

If he wanted eye contact, he could have it. Gaia turned and stared him down over the tops of his serial-killer shades. "Yeah, that's what I'm saying."

"Yeah." The man chuckled dubiously, showing his yellowing excuses for teeth. "Yeah, he looks real tough, that kid."

"Yeah, tough, right," Gaia mumbled. "There's just nothing I love more than a 'tough guy.' Nothing says 'confidence' like a guy babbling about how tough he is."

"Oh, you think I'm babbling? You don't think I'm tough enough?"

Oh, Jesus. Couldn't you keep it in check, Gaia? Challenging an idiot's toughness was the equivalent of flashing a banana in front of a caged monkey.

"You don't think I'm tough, bitch? How's this?" The next thing Gaia knew, the barrel of a gun was jammed against her head. "Is this tough?" he shouted. "Would you call this tough? Does your college boy ever cram a nine millimeter into your head? 'Cause maybe he should."

Gaia barely even noticed the first round of screams and curses that echoed through the entire restaurant. She was too busy trying to plan her next move.

"Shut up!" the man howled. "Everybody shut up and get your asses down on the floor!"

The man's accomplice leapt up out of the booth and pulled his own gun, waving it wildly at all the bikers and truckers. "The *floor*, I said! Get down on the floor!"

Gaia could tell that a few of the bikers still wanted to be heroes. They were grumbling and making slight steps in Gaia's direction. Boy, had she pegged them wrong when she first came in.

"It's all right," she assured them, basically ignoring the gun set against her right temple. "I'm fine. Just do what he says."

Gaia's mind was racing through all of her options, given the spatial relationship of the two men. *Mark their positions. What's the distance from this stool to thug number two? It would take a leap, definitely. He'll*

149

fire from the right, but if I go left, then thug number one has got me from behind. . . . Two guns, Gaia. You've got to shake yours, but you can't leave the other guy any time to fire on one of these people. . . .

And where the hell are you, Sam? You're telling me you can't hear this entire thing in the bathroom?

"Listen to the bitch," the cigar-loving sicko shouted. "Do what I say! Everyone empty your pockets. *You,*" he screamed down to Doris, on the floor behind the counter. "Empty the register!"

Doris wobbled nervously over to the register as he knocked the barrel of the gun against Gaia's head again. He leaned in closer and whispered in her ear, "Now is where it gets good. Tony!" he called to his accomplice.

"Yeah?"

"Kill one of 'em."

"Right."

"*What?*" Gaia whipped her head around to look the deranged son of a bitch in the eye.

"Oh, *now* she's losing her cool." He laughed.

"*Why?*" Gaia shouted.

Tony grabbed one of the truckers, hoisted him up off the floor, and placed the gun right against his stomach. Gaia could see the absolute terror in the poor man's eyes as sweat poured down his face. Tony seemed to enjoy it. "Guess you picked the wrong day to eat lunch here, my friend."

"*Why?*" Gaia shouted again, staring down Cigar Breath. "They're doing everything you say! Everything. Why does he have to kill anyone?"

"You'll see," he said with a disturbing smile.

"Adios, Mr. Dumb Trucker." Tony dug the gun deeper into the man's stomach.

She had to move. She'd have to improvise. All that mattered now was that completely innocent man's life. *Move, Gaia, move! The stool. It's a spinning stool. . . .*

Gaia dropped her hand down and tugged on the seat of Cigar Breath's stool with all her strength. The bastard's gut smacked into the counter and he bounced off onto the floor, but Gaia had already taken to the air.

She grabbed onto Tony's neck, pulling him down to the floor as the gun fired up at the ceiling, smashing one of the fluorescent lights and sending the entire fixture crashing to the floor. Then all hell broke loose.

Tony began to rise up off the ground. Gaia clasped her hands behind his head and smashed his face back down against the floor, hearing the distinct crack of his nose as he cried out. He reached for his gun. Gaia kicked it to the other side of the room. She was about to drop-kick his head back against a table, but before she even got the chance, a mass of bikers had converged on the two of them. It was Tony they were after. Without his gun, he was just one poor thug with a broken nose against ten or fifteen angry bikers. But Gaia was still in the way.

151

She got caught up in the melee and tried to work her way around their flailing fists and their loud angry shouts. She ducked their wild kicks and punches, searching for the daylight in this huge, vengeful brawl— searching for Sam. She somehow got turned around as she worked her way out of the crowd and the deafening noise. She ultimately had to back her way out of the pileup step by step.

But somehow, in spite of all the noise, she was able to hear it. The stupid loutish voice of that cigar-smoking son of a bitch. She heard him utter two simple words right behind her.

"Good-bye, Gaia. . . ."

Jesus, you're dead! she howled at herself. *Move now!*

Thoughts dropped away, and so did sound, and so did light, and somehow. . . so did time. Gaia had never moved so quickly in her life. Faster than she'd even known she was capable of moving. Almost as if she'd found the smallest little rip in time, an invisible gap that left her just enough space to maneuver. She could almost see the gun at her back—hear it hovering behind her as the trigger was being pulled. . . . She shot out both of her arms and whipped her entire body around, slicing at the air until her fists made contact with gun, swatting it ten feet from his hand as it fired off into nowhere. She even had time to see his stunned expression as he watched her complete her backward spin and leave him empty-handed.

And then she laid into him. She pummeled his chest with a blur of jabs, cracked his chin back with an outstretched palm, and then rose up high into the air, spinning three hundred and sixty degrees. As she reached the peak of her leap, her foot snapped out against his jaw, nearly severing his head from his spine as his entire body careened into a row of chairs and tables. She came down on the floor with her fists cocked and ready for a counterattack. But it would never come.

He was out cold on the floor. Covered in ketchup, lettuce, and hamburger grease.

Gaia turned around to get her bearings again. The bikers had begun tying up the bruised and battered Tony, and now they were flying past Gaia with their rope and heading for Cigar Breath.

"Did somebody—?" she began loudly.

"I'm calling the cops now," Doris assured her, clutching her chest and trying to catch her breath.

"Sam!" Gaia called out. "Sam, where are you?" She ran over into the tiny hallway and threw open the bathroom door. But Sam wasn't there. There was another door on the opposite side of the bathroom. A rusty metal door that had been left partially open. Gaia cracked it open farther and saw that it led outside, like the door of a gas station rest room. She turned around and ran back into the restaurant. . . just in time to see Sam out the window. He was walking back from the parking lot.

Gaia leapt to the front door, hoisted it open, and stepped out in front of the diner. "Where the hell *were* you?" she howled.

Sam's eyes nearly popped out of his head in response. "Whoa, there." He thrust out his hands, just to defend himself from her frenzied volume. "Re-*lax*. I just went out the bathroom door to check on the car. There were so many freaks in there. . . and then those two guys that walked in. . . . I just thought I should double-check and make sure the car was locked and secured. Why? What happened?" He looked over Gaia's head and in through the window.

Gaia stared at him a few more seconds, dumb-founded. She couldn't believe that he had somehow missed the entire nightmare. Which was not to say that she wasn't incredibly grateful that he *had* missed it. In fact, with a few seconds to breathe, she realized just how elated she was that he had missed it.

Because "it" was clearly something much more sinister than a couple of thugs trying to rob a crappy diner. *He knew her name.* "Good-bye, Gaia," the bastard had said before he'd tried to shoot her in the back. Not, "Good-bye, bitch," as would have been expected, but, "Good-bye, Gaia."

This entire thing had been an elaborate hit.

Those guys had obviously followed Sam and Gaia all the way from the city and then followed them into the diner with a series of distractions and fake outs to get Gaia right where they wanted her. They knew they didn't stand a chance with her alone. So they wanted chaos. They wanted her caught up in the confusion, focused on saving someone else's life, with her back to the shooter. They had probably come for Sam, too. And it had almost worked.

"Let's just go," Gaia said, looking back through the door. She could hear the sound of police sirens far down the road. Doris and the bikers had the situation under control. She pulled a twenty-dollar bill out of her pocket, strode across the room, and threw the money down on the counter. "Thank you," she called out to Doris.

"Now, wait a minute," Doris called to her. "You need to sit down. You need to—"

"Don't worry about me," Gaia interrupted. "The cops are on their way, okay? I'm. . . I'm sorry. . . ." Here she was, apologizing again.

"Sorry for what?" one of the bikers asked. "You were the one with a gun to your head. Are you okay? Don't you want to—?"

"I'm really sorry." Gaia stepped back outside the door and looked up at Sam. "Let's go. We need to get to that compound *now*. And then we need to get home."

"Gaia, what happened in there?"

"Nothing," Gaia said, tugging Sam back toward the car. "Just a whole lot of nothing."

The only
thing left
in this
horrid
place was
wind.

cool

gray

lines

SO THESE WERE "BOY" THINGS. BEER

Catwalk Struts

and basketball.

Based solely on the fact that Ed and Jake were boys, Megan had insisted that there was no way they wouldn't enjoy drinking a beer and watching a basketball game. So she had basically posed them in front of the TV like her very own boy dolls and handed them their beers before following the rest of the girls into Tatiana's bedroom for the closet raid. Ed didn't know how to tell Megan that he really didn't drink much at all and that the only time he cared about sports was when he was playing them, not watching them. And even then he only cared about sports of the extreme nature. He'd just been too depressed to even go into it.

He sat silently, pushed up against the right edge of the thick white couch. Jake was pushed up against the left. They each had an Amstel Light in their hands (the only beer Tatiana had), and they kept their eyes glued to the TV. There was a "classic" Sixers-Lakers game on, but Ed was more fascinated by the players' giant seventies Afros and freaky short shorts than the actual game.

Incessant annoying giggles kept wafting in from Tatiana's bedroom down the hall as the girls proceeded with their "girl" things. Ed could already picture the FOHs piling out of Tatiana's bedroom with shopping bags full of her wardrobe. He still couldn't believe that group theft was the highest praise these girls had to offer. He hoped Tatiana could keep them from taking advantage, although, judging from the way she had been dealing with them since yesterday, it seemed like she had the situation under control. Complete control, actually.

"You play ball?" Jake asked, keeping his eyes on the TV.

"Not really," Ed replied. He was surprised Jake had even tried to start a conversation.

"Football?"

"Nope."

Silence followed.

"I'm a recovering skate freak," Ed explained.

"*Sweet*," Jake replied, finally turning to Ed. "Did you compete?"

"Um. . . it was more of a city thing."

"Oh, right," Jake said, nodding foolishly. Ed was surprised to find Jake making no attempt to hide the fact that he suddenly felt stupid. From the little Ed had seen, Jake seemed like such a conceited ass. "The 'city thing' is still a complete freaking mystery to me," Jake admitted.

"Why, where are you from?"

"I'm from Oregon," Jake explained. "Not Portland, so don't bother asking me about grunge."

"Not a problem," Ed said. "I'm all about the Backstreet Boys, anyway."

Jake stared at Ed, blank faced.

"Kidding," Ed said, sipping from his tepid beer.

Jake's face relaxed. "I knew that," he joked. "Knew that."

All right, maybe Jake wasn't that bad. Maybe Ed had judged him a little too soon.

Jake surveyed the room slowly and then peeked down the darkened hallway. "So. . . where's Gaia?" he asked, focusing on the TV again and sipping from his beer.

Another silence followed. Ed turned slowly to Jake and examined his generic "stud boy" profile. He was beginning not to like him again. "I don't know. . . why?"

"Huh?" Jake turned with an almost imperceptible twitch of his eye. "Oh. . . no, I just thought—I thought she'd be here. Doesn't she live here, too?"

"It depends on her mood," Ed replied, feeling depressed again as he stared at Jake. "And all the potential casualties."

"Huh?" Jake grunted again, scrunching up his eyes.

"Forget it." Ed sighed, turning back to the TV.

"Okay, are you boys *ready*?" Megan's offensively singsong voice came echoing from the hallway. "These are just the first options, but I think you should be pleased. . . ."

Ed swallowed a gulp of annoyance and sighed heartily. He turned dutifully toward the hallway. *Fashion shows.* This was one of his favorite aspects of Gaia—not having to worry about fashion shows.

Am I "with" Gaia Moore?

Shut up, Ed. Shut up and watch the fashion show.

159

Megan, Tammie, Melanie, and Laura paraded themselves out into the living room in a freakish festival of tastefully revealing tops and short skirts. They gave their best catwalk struts, with their hands on their waists, their cheeks sucked in, and their lips puckered out like a bunch of too skinny well-dressed blowfish. Jake honored their unfortunate display by providing the requisite applause and hooting.

Ed took another sip from his beer and tried to shake off an image of Gaia in her black dress from the night before. That had been beauty in the truest sense of the word. Beauty that was just born out of nowhere—without an ounce of fakery or contrivance. Beauty that wasn't *made*, but just *was*. But these girls. . . no matter how perfect their breeding, no matter how expensive their outfits, no matter how much lettuce they ate, or water they drank, or trips to yoga or Pilates or the gym five times a week they took. . . these girls would still never be truly "beautiful." They would still always look like girls playing dress up in their mothers' clothes. At least, that was how they looked to Ed.

"Thank you," Megan joked, bowing to Jake and Ed as Jake continued to applaud. "Thank you, thank you, thank you. But wait just a moment. . . . Silence, please." She grinned, playing the part of the grateful award winner. "There'll be time for autographs later."

Jake finally stopped applauding, much to Ed's delight.

"Thank you," Megan said again. "We have all done our best to look fabulous. But in truth. . . tonight's not really about us. Yes, it's time to bring out. . . the one. . . the only. . . ladies and gentlemen. . . make way for Ms. Tatiana Petrova!"

Then Tatiana finally stepped out into the living room. And somehow it felt like a bright spotlight had just been turned on.

She was wearing a formfitting strapless black gown that dipped slightly at the center. Her vanilla-colored shoulders and the very top of her chest were totally exposed. She had put some kind of gel in her hair that made it shine like yellow gold and cascade with a movie-star lilt down to her shoulders. The only other things on her body were the two long black velvet gloves that traveled up the length of her arms, ending above her elbows.

Ed felt a sudden gap in his breathing. He quickly attributed it to beer-induced gas. He instructed himself to turn back to the game. But he had never been very good at following instructions.

"*Wow*," Jake uttered, leaving his mouth open as he gawked shamelessly at Tatiana.

"I *told* you," Megan squealed, looking over at Tatiana. "Look at them. They're goddamn *zombies. Ahhhhh . . .*"

Tatiana flashed a smile, and then the girls began to squeal in unison, dragging her farther out into the room and pushing her toward Ed and Jake as she laughed. Megan began to applaud, followed by the rest

161

of the girls and Jake, along with his frat-style hooting. And then. . . in spite of himself, Ed found himself beginning to clap for her. Just to play along. Just out of respect. He still refused to smile, given his state of mind.

"Thank you," Tatiana joked, blowing them all ironic kisses. "Oh, thank you so much. Thank you. . . ."

Megan ran over to the coffee table and pulled a bouquet of flowers from a vase. She giggled as she handed the flowers to Tatiana and began singing her own version of the Miss America theme. "Ohhh, there she is. . . Ms. Superhottieeee. . . ."

"Thank you," Tatiana joked, imitating the `shallow smile` and mechanical waving of a beauty pageant winner as she walked toward Ed and Jake on the couch. "I love you all. I do. I would just like to thank God and capitalism and my plastic surgeon, in that order. . . ."

Ed tried to maintain his self-pitying expression, but he finally gave in to a slight half smile. Tatiana was funny, and she deserved at least some mild props for it.

"I love you all," she went on. She turned back to the girls, crossing her eyes like a hypnotized Barbie doll. "I love *you,* and *you,* and *you.* . . ." She turned to Jake. "I love *you.* . . ." And finally she dropped down onto Ed's lap, dipping herself back as she held on to his neck and posing for an imaginary *Vanity Fair* cover. She came up from her dip and locked her eyes with Ed's. "And I love *you,*" she said, giving him a peck on the cheek.

The entire room chuckled. With the exception of Ed, who was suddenly feeling quite uncomfortable. The half smile fell from his face. He was about to find his way up from the couch when Natasha interrupted the preparty festivities.

"What is all this giggling and singing?" she asked with a laugh. The group turned as Natasha stepped out into the living room, apparently infected by the laughter that was spreading through the apartment. "I thought the party was not until tonight? Hello, Ed." She smiled.

"Hi," he said with the fakest smile he could muster.

"We're just getting ready for tonight," Tatiana explained from Ed's lap. "Is there... any good news yet?"

"No," Natasha said, furrowing her brow in frustration. "Apparently not yet."

The pleasant smile dropped from Tatiana's face. For a moment she looked almost angry. "That is too bad," she uttered calmly.

Ed assumed they were talking about Gaia's father.

"Yes," Natasha agreed. "I know." She turned to address the group. "I'll be at a UN function tonight. They usually last until the wee hours of the morning, so you kids have a good time, okay?"

"We will," Tatiana said.

"Okay." She turned back to Tatiana. "I'll call you when I get the good news, Tatiana. I'm *sure* it will be before the end of the night."

"Good," Tatiana replied.

Natasha pulled her black turtleneck sweater taut over her black leather pants and headed for the door. "Good night," she said. The girls all said good night as she picked up her bag and her long black coat from a chair by the door and headed out for the night.

"Okay, second option!" Megan announced with a grin. "Let's roll!" The girls all broke into laughter again. The FOHs quickly followed her back into Tatiana's bedroom to change into the next outfit. Tatiana stayed seated on Ed's lap, coming down from her laugh. Ed began to shift his legs obviously, hoping she would stand up. But she didn't seem ready to move.

"Oh, no," she started, finishing up her laugh and staring back at Ed. "What happened? Look at your face. I thought I saw at least the *beginnings* of a smile before, no? Now you look like the boy who has lost his puppy again."

"I'm fine," Ed grumbled, trying to subtly remove Tatiana's arm from around his neck.

"This is not what 'fine' looks like, Ed. I know what you look like when you are fine. Come *on*." She giggled, brushing the side of his face with her hand. "I have just made a complete fool of myself for everyone's amusement. Look at me."

Ed wouldn't quite look at her. "What? I'm fine."

"*Ugh*," she grunted, crossing her legs. He felt her strong thighs press more firmly against his lap. "You have it again."

"What?"

"The disease," she said. "The Gaia disease." Ed became all too aware of Jake watching this exchange from the other side of the couch. "Don't be so *gloomy* about her," Tatiana went on. "I'm telling you, everything will be fine. It isn't worth it. I mean, Gaia is so much. . . her own person, you know? You should be, too."

"I don't know what you mean," Ed snapped. He didn't care if Jake was watching. This was the second time Tatiana had started talking in these `annoyingly cryptic terms` about Gaia, and it was truly starting to get on his nerves.

"*Nothing*," Tatiana replied with a reassuring smile. "Nothing, I just mean, here you are pining away, you know? Always sort of 'waiting by the phone,' so to speak. . . and meanwhile Gaia is so. . . you know. . . *independent*."

"And what is *that* supposed to mean?" Ed squawked.

"*Nothing*." Tatiana laughed. "Oh my God, Ed. *Nothing*. You know what? I am being silly. You are just in a bad mood, and I am going to let you be in your bad mood, okay?"

"Okay."

"Okay." She gave him one more friendly peck on the cheek and finally slid off his lap, following the rest of the girls into her bedroom.

Ed tried to shake the tension out of his legs and relax. He took a deep, cleansing breath and tried not to think about Gaia or Tatiana's weirdness or any of it. But he'd barely even finished that breath before Jake opened his mouth.

165

"So. . . stud boy. . ." Jake placed his beer down on the coffee table and turned to face Ed, flashing him a curious smile. "What's the deal there?"

"Where?" Ed asked, dreaming about a ten-pound bottle of extra-strength Tylenol.

"Well. . . are you with Gaia or not?"

"*What?*" Ed couldn't quite mask his anger at the question.

Jake held out his hands defensively. "No, dude, I wasn't trying to pry, okay? I was just. . . you know. . . I was sitting here watching your. . . *vibe* with Tatiana, and I just wasn't sure. Which one is the friend and which one is the girlfriend?"

Now Ed really wanted that ten-pound bottle of Tylenol. So he could use it to crack open Jake's skull. Or maybe he'd just use it to crack open his own.

"Tatiana is just a friend," he stated coldly. "And yes, Jake, I am *with* Gaia. I am definitely *with* her."

IT MADE NO SENSE. HE'D BEEN RUNNING ever since he and Gaia had pulled over at that gas station. That gas station, which only days ago had served as Sam's passageway to the outside. And

Black Viny Body Bag

now he was using it to get back *inside*. He had it all back-ward—like those hostages in Stockholm who'd grown so attached to their captors, they resisted rescue.

What kind of grip could that horrible place have over him? Why would he possibly want to see those ugly stone buildings with their stupidly futuristic glass atriums, where he'd been prodded and tortured and left alone for entire days with nothing but his disturb-ing `morphine-induced` dreams? Why wasn't he moving just a bit more slowly? Biding his time, cau-tiously avoiding the inevitable moment when he would step back into all those nightmarish memories?

Because it was no longer *his* prison. It was no longer the place where he would eventually die, reduced to nothing but the withered muscles of an invalid and a zipped-up `black vinyl body bag`. He would be seeing the place as a free man this time. And that was all he had ever dreamed about while lying on that hospital bed: coming back as a free man and wiping them all out—every single one of those dirtbags. That and seeing Gaia again.

So in some twisted sense, as they stepped through the cold woods, nearing the dreadful place and most likely risking their lives, all of Sam's dreams had come true.

One more step and he knew. They had reached the perimeter. He turned back to Gaia and held her back in silence.

Gaia froze and focused her attention on the mass

of shrubbery and branches just ahead of Sam. He placed his hand on a batch of the low-hanging branches and bent them out of the way.

And there was the first sight of something man-made amidst this towering, dense forest. A wall. A cold and forbidding white stone wall.

"I think this is the back of one of the barracks," he whispered. "I saw them lining up in formations in front of this building when they'd transfer me for tests."

"Do you think they're still here?" she whispered back.

"I don't know. Everything was so chaotic when I made it out. I think some of Loki's men had even turned on each other. They were definitely all piling out, but did some psycho loyalists stay on to defend the place? I have no idea."

Gaia looked into Sam's eyes and nodded. She understood the situation. They were searching through an abandoned ghost town for clues. But Sam couldn't guarantee that they wouldn't run into some ghosts.

They crept through the opening in the branches and walked carefully along the side of the abandoned barracks, then poked their heads around the corner of the building—*ghost town* was definitely an accurate choice of words. Dirty manila folders and documents flew across the empty road in random windblown circles. Piles of unmarked wooden boxes lay cracked open and pillaged all along the side of the road. The splintered wood had scattered everywhere, along with the numerous crowbars and black sledgehammers they'd used to pry the boxes open.

"Weapons," Gaia whispered. "They knew he was gone, so they looted and pillaged all his weapons."

"Great," Sam muttered. "Now we're on the lookout for psycho loyalists with extra weapons."

"I don't think there are any psycho loyalists, Sam. I don't think there's any anything."

The empty hiss of the wind blew across the road, pushing Sam's hair back as if to confirm Gaia's point. The only thing left in this horrid place was wind.

"I think you're right," Sam said. "But we should keep looking. Those papers flying around. . . they must have come from one of the buildings down there. I think there's an office or an archive in that third building."

"Okay, I'm taking the lead," Gaia said, pushing her body in front of Sam's.

"What are you talking about? You don't know where everything is. I've studied this place every chance I had, Gaia. I took as many mental pictures as I could whenever I crossed through the outdoors, planning for an escape I figured would never happen."

"Sam, don't be stubborn," Gaia snapped. "If you think I'm letting you lead the way in the state you're in, you're nuts. Let me be the first round of defense. Just in case."

"In case *what*? There's nobody here. We just agreed that nobody is here!"

"*Shhhhh!*" Gaia slammed her hand over Sam's mouth and widened her eyes as she looked over his shoulder.

"I'm sorry," Sam whispered, shaking his head. "I'm sorry. I know we need to be—"

"*Shhhhh.*" She silenced him again, taking a step back toward the side of the barracks. "No, it's not that. . . ," she whispered.

"Then what?"

"Do you hear it?"

All Sam could hear was that merciless wind whipping through the center of the compound. And perhaps the occasional combination of caws and chirps from the three birds in nearby trees.

"Hear what?"

"A voice, Sam. I hear a voice."

IT WAS COMING FROM TWO BUILDINGS

down. And it sounded an awful lot like one word being yelped out again and again.

Help.

Of course, Sam couldn't

hear it. Very few people other than Gaia would have, but she knew what she was hearing. And she knew she was going to follow it.

"Gaia, wait." Sam grabbed her by the arm. "Whatever you're hearing could be a trap. Let's just get to that office, see if we can dig up some clues, and get the hell out of here."

She was shaking her head before Sam had even finished his sentence. "First of all, in case you haven't figured it out yet, I'm not scared of these so-called psycho loyalists of which you speak. Second, and much more importantly, there's a man's voice calling for help down that road. And I have a thing about saving people, Sam. I know it's a little obsessive-compulsive, but the potential victims seem to like it."

"Well, how would you know if the voice belonged to someone dangerous or not?" Sam pointed out.

"I don't know," she replied defiantly. "I'll just have to find out when I get there."

"Where?" Sam pushed. "Which building is this *supposed* cry for help even coming from?"

"That one," Gaia argued, pointing to a short but sprawling gray building two "blocks" down.

Sam suddenly went silent. He turned a shade paler than he already was as he gazed down the road at the gray monstrosity. "That's the hospital," he uttered. "That's where they had me the entire time. . . ."

Gaia could see the flashbacks playing out in his eyes as his forehead began to crinkle into a series of tense creases. "Okay, look. You should just hang out here and stand guard, and I'll check it out and be back in—"

"*No*," Sam huffed. "I'm fine."

Gaia grabbed Sam's shoulders. "Look," she began cautiously, sensing the fragility of Sam's current emotional state. "If you think about it. . . it doesn't really make sense that you would be the only person being held in that facility. I know Loki, Sam. He thinks big. He probably had twenty potential enemies and pawns and puppets locked away in that place. Do you really think his idiot paid thugs went door-to-door and let them all out before they ran?"

Sam broke from Gaia's stare and looked back at the building, gazing in a long contemplative silence. "Jesus, there's still someone in there. . . ." Out of nowhere he launched into a surprisingly powerful sprint. Gaia took off after him, scattering the dust and ripped-up paper of the empty road as they stomped their way up to the entrance of the prison building.

The place had Loki written all over it—an ornately modern design of cool gray lines layered on top of each other like some hideous modern-day coliseum. Squares of black and white marble hung where the windows should have been.

"There are a few tiny windows on the side of the building," Sam explained. They cut around to the corner of the building and scanned the two rows of eight-inch windows. And now Gaia was sure she heard it. Coming through a tiny golf-ball-size hole in the top-left window. A cry for help.

"He must have broken a hole in the window," Sam said, squinting through the sunlight to get a better look. He turned back down to Gaia with a look of absolute puzzlement. "How the hell did you hear him from back there? I can still barely hear him."

"Good ears," Gaia replied, already trying to figure out how to get up there. "My mother was a musician."

"Right," Sam mumbled.

Gaia sprinted back toward the front of the building.

"Wait a minute," Sam called to her. "What are you doing?" He caught up with her at the front door, which was made entirely out of industrial-strength polarized glass.

"Sam, we need to get up there," she said. She stepped down next to one of the pillaged wooden boxes and picked up a black steel sledgehammer.

"I know we do," Sam said, "but what if the security systems are still—"

Sam was cut off by the deafening smash of breaking glass as Gaia blasted through the doors with the sledgehammer. Giant shards of polarized glass sprayed

173

across the lobby, leaving a gaping hole in the door. She stepped through the jagged remains of the door frame, leaving Sam speechless. His only choice now was to try and keep up with her breakneck pace.

"Stairs?" she barked, stepping into the center of the cold marble lobby. It was obvious that all activity had been interrupted by surprise. Security phones were dangling off their cords. A fly-infested can of half-eaten chicken was lying behind the security desk. But there was at least one small bit of good fortune in this nightmare. The power had been shut down. That meant any high-tech security was a nonissue.

"Behind there," Sam said, pointing to a shadowy corridor.

The door to the stairs was partially open, and Gaia wasted no time, flying up the steps three by three until she reached the top floor. Sam huffed and puffed behind her. She was giving him the biggest workout of his life since his escape from this place. He was working just as hard to get back in as he had worked to get out. The irony didn't go unnoticed.

But Gaia had given him the choice to stay behind while she investigated. And in truth, without him, God knew where she would have been at this point. Probably still traipsing through those woods until the freaking Blair Witch found her.

Gaia was the first to burst onto the floor. Sam

followed close behind. "Hello?" Gaia called out as her echo traveled down each and every hallway.

"What are you doing?" Sam whispered urgently, grabbing her by the shoulders. "There could still be guards around any one of those corners."

"Bull," she said, pricking up her ears for the man's call again. "This place is dead. It's as dead as Loki." She finally picked up the sound of the man's voice and began a series of careful twists and turns down the endless halls.

"Can you hear me?" she called out. "We're here to help you. . . ."

"*Here!*" the desperate voice croaked. "I'm in *here!*"

Gaia turned behind her and realized that the voice was coming from down the hall. "Just hold on," Sam called to him.

Gaia could see the increasing determination in Sam's eyes. This wasn't just a chance to free some stranger from an abandoned prison. Sam had found himself a brother of sorts behind that door. Sam ran down the hall and turned the corner. "Here it is—N 37. The door's open!" he called out triumphantly.

"Door's open?" Gaia asked.

There was no response.

"*Sam?*" She hollered much louder this time.

All she could hear was a `thick and ugly silence.`

GAIA WHIPPED AROUND THE CORNER

to N 37, hammer cocked behind her shoulder, and kicked open the door, coming down squarely on both feet in a crouched position. And then she froze solid in her tracks. She was more thankful than she had ever been to feel no fear.

Virtual Walking Database

Because she was standing before a three-man firing squad.

Three men in black jumpsuits and black combat boots were standing in front of an abandoned prisoner's bed. The man in the center was holding Sam against his chest, with his black-gloved hand pressed firmly against Sam's mouth. His right hand was holding a semiautomatic machine gun about two inches from Gaia's head. He was flanked by two other goons, both of them with their guns stabilized on their shoulders, aiming from only inches away.

The thug on the right looked up from his gun sight and examined Gaia's face. His eyes grew wider the longer he looked. "Is that *her*?" he asked, sounding just as thick as he looked.

The man holding Sam began to nod and smile. "Oh, that's her." He grinned. "That's her."

Gaia had never really stopped to consider just how familiar all of Loki's thugs must be with her face.

They'd all been after her for so long, she wondered if these idiots had even gotten the memo that their boss was brain-dead and that this particular war was over. It had been over for days now. Most of his men had obviously gotten the picture, but these freaks. . . they really put the *psycho* in *psycho loyalist*.

So Sam's fears had been right. There were a few of them roaming the compound like robots that some-one had forgotten to turn off. That's what Gaia got for having no fears—a three-gun wake-up call.

They obviously hadn't abandoned their posts in days. There was not an ounce of sanity in their eyes. They were like those libertarian hillbillies, who thought the best thing they could do for their country was to march around on their crumbling porches, just loading and reloading their shotguns. It almost seemed worth it to Gaia to put these poor bastards out of their misery. But three on one with Sam and the man as their hostages? Not to mention the fact that deranged psycho-loyalist lunatics tended to be trigger-happy. Maybe she could talk some sense into them. . . .

"Okay, look. . . ," she began.

"Let's just kill her and bring Loki the body," one of them said.

"Good idea," another agreed.

Okay, talking sense was out. Action was the only choice, given their very clear and simple plan. She saw their fingers pulling down on their triggers and her plan became equally clear. There was only one way to free Sam and the man and take all the guns out of the picture in one move. She tightened her hands around her hammer, and she swung away.

Gaia's hammer knocked against the barrels of their guns in quick one-two-three succession. She smacked all three weapons into the corner simultaneously as the bullet spray clanged along the metal-reinforced walls. The deafening sound of rapid machine gun fire filled the room, reverberating off every shining key and dark corner.

The thug on the right let out a loud growl as he leapt toward Gaia. He slammed her up against the door as the hammer fell from her hands. He ripped a hunting knife from his belt and pushed forward to plunge it into her stomach, but Gaia grabbed onto his wrist and drove his arm to her side. She shoved her knee straight into his groin and then flipped his entire frame over her head, cracking his spine back as he collided with the door. One down.

She saw the glint of the gun out of the corner of her eye. "Sam, get down!" she ordered. "Down!"

Sam ducked and flattened himself on the ground as the thickest goon fired off the gun he'd retrieved from the corner. The only advantage to dealing with someone who had gone off the deep end: no aim. He was just firing off round after round, hoping he would hit something. Hoping he would hit everything.

Gaia leapt to the far corner of the room, landing in a fast roll that nearly threw her against the wall. But she pushed her hands out against the wall and bounced back under the only table in the room—a fold-out card table. It wasn't exactly bulletproof, but it was sure as hell easy to throw.

She shot up from the ground and hurled the table at the trigger-happy maniac like a rocket. It connected with his gun first, redirecting his gunfire up toward the ceiling and then knocking him to the ground.

Gaia took to the air again, landed by the sledgehammer, and snatched it from the floor. She ran at the goon as he threw off the table and aimed his gun again. She could feel the third psycho running at her from behind. It seemed Loki hadn't done a very good job of combat training.

Never sandwich a target, you idiots. Never sandwich a target.

Gaia waited till the absolute last second. . . and then she dropped. She dropped flat to the floor as the gunfire flew over her head, riddling the man behind her with bullets, forcing back his oversized frame until he tripped and landed in a lifeless heap at the foot of the abandoned prisoner's bed.

The second the gun-toting goon had emptied his mag, Gaia pushed back up to her feet, wielding the sledgehammer with the same craft and discipline as she would a samurai sword.

She charged at the thug's wide psychotic eyes, knowing that mercy was no longer an option. Whoever he might have been at some point in his life, he'd now been reduced to nothing more than a rabid animal, with no intention of stopping until he'd murdered everyone left in that room. And he'd left Gaia with no choice. He dug back down for another gun, but he would never reach it.

Gaia swung the hammer with full force. It struck his chin with a surprisingly blunt thud and drove his entire body back into the corner. He smacked up against the metal wall and then slid slowly down into absolute stillness. He was down but not out. She could still see his diaphragm moving in the slow rhythm of unconscious breathing. But he wouldn't be conscious anytime soon. That was for sure.

Silence filled the room.

Gaia let the hammer hang down at her side as she turned slowly back to Sam on the floor. "Are you okay?" she asked, beginning to feel faint.

Sam looked around at the inert bodies and then back up to Gaia. "I'm—I'm fine," he stammered. He was obviously still a little spooked. He'd seen Gaia fight before, but perhaps not quite like this. "You just. . . how did you. . . ?"

"I just did what I had to," she said, helping Sam back off the ground.

"Yes," he uttered, still mildly in shock. "Yes, you did."

"Come on," she said, motioning to Sam to join her

by the man's bedside. He was wearing only a sagging white T-shirt and institutional-grade black pants. Finally there was a face to go with all those desperate cries. But the face was nothing like she had expected.

First, he was ancient. There was barely a hair left on his head, and any hair that remained around his ears was like the dead white wisps of a dandelion. His face was so pale, it was like translucent ivory. The deep creases through his cheeks looked like mistakes that had been made with a sculptor's chisel. An ugly gray goatee had sprouted around his lips, and his entire frame was hunched over like an old Dutch marionette.

His eyes were the only feature that made him look alive. Bright, ocean-blue eyes that had obviously seen more life and death than Gaia could comprehend. But they weren't so easy to see, because they were clouded with tears.

The old man collapsed into Sam's arms and seemed to hold on for dear life. "You are angels," he cried in a light Russian accent that Gaia hadn't picked up on before. "*Angels.* I thought I'd heard voices in the silence, but I wasn't sure. I thought guards, maybe, but now. . ."

"It's okay," Sam said gently, looking up at Gaia as he held the man tighter. "It's okay."

"Thank God," the man repeated again and again. "Thank God."

Gaia stepped behind the old man and stroked his back gingerly. She was still doing her best to shake off her dizziness and stay alert. "What's your name?" she asked.

The moment she touched him, his eyes suddenly lit up. They opened wide, revealing every millimeter of his sparkling, ocean-blue irises. "My name is Dmitri," he said, seemingly hypnotized by her presence. "Dmitri Gagarin."

"I'm—"

"*Gaia*," he said, finishing her sentence as he stared at her with that frozen, enthralled expression. "I know who you are, of course." He smiled almost submissively. "I worked for the Organization for almost forty-five years. You and your mother. . . you know. . . you are somewhat like royalty to us. . . ."

Gaia pulled away the moment she heard the word *Organization*. The Organization was synonymous with Loki. The Organization had killed her mother. She did not want to even touch a man who worked for that horrid agency, no matter how old or frail or desperate he might be. She even considered leaving the old man in his filthy cell.

"Oh, no, please," Dmitri begged, searching deeper into Gaia's eyes. "Do not misunderstand. I *hated* Loki. I hated what he did to the Organization. I *hated* what he did to your mother. And what he tried to do to you. That is why he had me locked up in here. Because he knew I was his enemy. He knew how well I knew him."

Now Gaia wasn't sure what to think. But she knew this much: Any enemy of Loki's was a friend of hers. The next question fell from her lips before she could even stop it. "You knew my mother?"

A grand, wistful smile spread across his withered face. "I knew *of* her," he said. "Of course. We all did."

"And my father, too?"

"Yes, of course. I knew of your father. I still know many things, you know. Many people. I am not as *obsolete* as Loki would have liked to believe."

Gaia darted her eyes up at Sam. She didn't have to say a word for him to understand what she was thinking. Maybe they didn't need to search an entire building full of ransacked files. Maybe they had just found themselves a `virtual walking database` of information. Maybe they had just found exactly what they had come for. And they had just saved his life.

"Your mother," Dmitri went on, sweetness taking over the anger in his voice. "She was. . . *special*, uh? We all thought so. Like a queen. And you, I think. . . you are like a princess." He smiled. Gaia did not quite know how to respond to this either. "I am. . . honored, Gaia," he said. "I am so very honored to finally meet you."

"We should get him out of here," Sam said. "I'd really like to get out of here," he added. He turned to Dmitri, who was now managing to stand on his own. "I was locked up here, too."

"*You?*" Dmitri sighed. Gaia could see the pain in his

eyes as he looked at Sam's face. "So *young*. . . Why?"

"They shot me. . . ."

Sam didn't even seem to know why he had shared this fact, but for an imperceptible moment he almost looked on the verge of tears. It suddenly occurred to Gaia that he had never actually said this out loud before. He had never been able to share it with anyone other than Gaia, but it must have taken on so much more significance when spoken to a complete stranger.

"Loki shot you," Dmitri repeated, years of regret pouring through his fraying voice. "Then that is *two* things you and I have in common, my friend." He stared solemnly at Sam.

"You too?" Sam asked quietly.

"I will not show you the scars," Dmitri said. "It is much too ugly a sight."

Sam turned back to Gaia with an urgent stare. "We have to get him out of here right now."

"Can you walk?" she asked. "Can you make it down the stairs?"

"To get out of this place?" He smiled desperately. "Oh, yes. To get out of this place, I would throw myself down the stairs. I will go wherever you are going. *Anywhere* that will get me closer to New York City."

"Oh, I think we can get you pretty close," Gaia said. She ducked under his arm to support him with her shoulders. Sam ducked under the other arm. "Just hold on," she said. "It's going to be a long walk. But once we get to the car, I think we can all be home before dark."

"*Home.*" Dmitri savored the word. "That would be something. . . ."

Slowly but surely they began to walk Dmitri down the hall, keeping their eyes peeled for any more riffraff.

"Thank you," he uttered, giving in to his tears again. "Thank you both." He looked up at the two of them and then settled his glassy eyes on Gaia's face. "You truly are a princess," he said. "A princess. . ."

The rich
scent of
expensive
lipstick
was
floating
from her
lips.

killer of a day

Epic Proportions

HAD ED BEEN ANY LESS DEPRESSED, HE would have noticed that Heather's benefit had turned into a party of epic proportions. Tatiana and the FOHs had handled the thing like seasoned professional publicists, cranking up the hype for the last forty-eight hours, building up the buzz, and then delivering. They'd decorated the place with black and white balloons, white roses, and funky candles. Tatiana had sketched an amazing abstract portrait of Heather. It looked and felt like a very real party. Pravda seemed to be literally rocking from side to side with thumping music, a giant crowd of beautiful people, and enough alcohol to get the entire state of Rhode Island soused.

Yes, there was a picture of Heather and a turnout that would have made the Hilton sisters envious, but what this party had to do with Heather's blindness. . . Ed had no clue. And the fact that there was a sign-in book at the doorway, with a placard hung over it inviting guests to write "encouraging messages," only added to Ed's confusion. Was it some kind of twisted joke, or were Tatiana and the party-planning club so caught up in themselves that they'd actually forgotten that Heather couldn't read?

But Ed's skepticism didn't keep him from giving in

to a few beers. All right, maybe more than a few. He was now officially the world's most pathetic cliché. A country music cliché sitting at the most urbane gathering he had ever had the unfortunate privilege of attending. The lonely man hunched over the bar, drinking his sorrows away as he pined for the lady who had run off to God knew where.

It was just as Ed had figured. There was no sign of Gaia. No sign at the party, no sign at her house, no message, no e-mail, no nothing. She was off somewhere searching for her father. Alone, of course. Always alone.

What a shocker. Gaia disappearing on some lonely mission. When has that ever happened before?

This was an all-time low for Ed. He was being sarcastic with himself.

"*Okay,* Mr. Fargo!" Tatiana's voice screamed straight into Ed's ear from right behind his shoulder. He jumped slightly and tried to pretend he hadn't heard her. Even at this close distance, that was a legitimate possibility, given the deafening thuds of house music and the penguinlike chattering of the crowd.

"Hey!" she barked. "Mr. Fargo! I'm *talking* to you."

Ed had never in his life heard Tatiana barking like this. She sounded like a professional wrestler trying to taunt her competition. But once he turned around, he understood why he had never heard her talk like this before. He had never seen her drunk before.

Tatiana looked at him and grinned from ear to ear. She still looked just as ridiculously stunning as she had at the impromptu fashion show. Same black dress. Same vanilla shoulders. Same movie-star hair. Ed tried not to notice. One thing he did observe, however, was that she seemed to be swaying ever so slightly from side to side as she smiled.

"Well, it is official," she declared, speaking successfully over the din of the party. "Gaia has reduced you to rubble."

Ed frowned and grabbed his beer from the bar, taking a long swig.

"And do you know how this makes me feel?" Tatiana asked. Her voice was so animated, she almost seemed to be singing her words up and down. "Do you? I'll tell you how it makes me feel, Ed. I am mad as hell, and I'm not going to take it anymore!" She giggled slightly as she looked into his eyes.

Ed couldn't help but break a smile. "*Network.*" He chuckled. "Did you just quote *Network*? That's one of my all-time favorite movies."

"Mine too." She nodded.

Ed tilted his head slightly, staring at her with pro- gressively increasing puzzlement.

She tilted her head to mirror his. "You don't really know me very well, do you, Ed?"

"I guess not," Ed admitted with a deferential smile.

"Well, I am pleased to make your acquaintance," she bellowed, sticking out her hand. "Tatiana Petrova."

"Ed." He laughed. "Ed Fargo. Nice to meet you."

"Nice to meet *you*." She nodded. "Though I must tell you. . . even though you are a *complete* stranger who I have never met before, I hope you do not mind my mentioning that you look awfully sad."

"Women," Ed grumbled. "You know how it is. Can't live with 'em. . ."

"Blah, blah, blah."

"*Exactly*," Ed agreed. "I think the only crucial point is that you can't live with 'em." The more Ed actually thought about this point, the sadder he became.

"Oh, *no*," Tatiana moaned desperately. "I am losing you again. Well, fear not, Mr. Fargo, I have brought you medicine."

Ed had been so busy wallowing, he hadn't even noticed what Tatiana had been holding the entire time. Not until she raised her hands. In her right hand was an unopened bottle of Stolichnaya vodka. In her left hand were two shot glasses.

"Secret stash." She smiled.

"Oh, Jesus," Ed groaned, running his hands through his crunched-up hair. Four beers was already way more than his average alcohol intake. "I think I'll pass. I'm not really a vodka man."

Tatiana took a step closer. "Let me tell you about

vodka," she said, shaking the bottle with pedantic authority. Drunk, Ed realized, would not begin to describe her at this point. "In my country vodka is the primary cure for *all things*. You *need* to get your mind off Gaia right now, Ed. For your own sanity. And *nothing* gets your mind off things like a few stiff shots of Stoli. Believe me, it works. In my country we need to get our minds off *many* things. And a shot of Stoli makes Prozac seem like children's aspirin."

One thing about a drunken Tatiana. She didn't mince words.

It was a little strange to see her so out of character, but on the other hand, with four beers to his credit, Ed wasn't exactly in character, either. And at this particular moment he didn't really mind that so much. The truth was, `out-of-character Tatiana` seemed to be the only person who could make Ed smile for any decent period of time right now. She was the only person capable of taking his mind off Gaia for even a few seconds. And if he added that to her staunch advertisement of vodka. . . that could equal some rather substantial time without this pathetically clichéd case of self-pity. All in all, it was a rather tempting combination.

"Okay, you win." Ed threw his hands up and stepped off his chair at the bar. "Let's be drinking buddies. Where to?"

"Come, drinking buddy," she said. "I have secured us a secluded spot."

THEY HAD ALREADY SURVIVED A SERIES

of agonizing trials in what should
have been a simple journey back to
the city. The walk through the
woods to the highway felt like a
marathon hike, mostly due to the
snail's pace required for Dmitri's
aging, ravaged body to keep up.

Nervous Twitch

Once they'd finally found their way back to the car
after three hours, they had neglected to consider the
fact that they would be hitting bumper-to-bumper
commuter traffic on the highway. That was another
two or three hours of unbearable slow going—two or
three hours of Gaia basically slipping in and out of
consciousness in the front seat, checking on Dmitri
every time she awoke.

But there was no point in checking on Dmitri. He
had fallen into a deep, near cadaverous sleep the
moment he'd laid his head on the backseat. He probably hadn't slept a wink for days, trapped in that abandoned cell, praying for his rescue. Now Gaia had a
feeling that his frail old body would need about a
week of nonstop sleep just to try and recuperate, if
recuperation was even an option for him at this point.

Gaia was eternally grateful to Sam for somehow
being able to still stay awake and drive. He had, after all,
not only been through the same life-threatening ordeal
as she, and the same marathon walk through the

woods, and the same traffic from hell, but he was also still recuperating from serious injury. And judging from his strained, half-open eyelids, he was just as painfully exhausted as everyone else in that rickety car.

But that, as it turned out, would be the final dagger. The rickety car. Gaia had been so exhausted that she'd nearly forgotten about the noise. The clunking that she had noticed right after they'd left the diner that afternoon. The clunking that had turned into a rattling once Sam finally cleared the traffic and sped up.

"Sam. . ." She spoke quietly, not wanting to wake Dmitri. Which was rather ridiculous, given the fact that a thirty-piece orchestra couldn't have woken the old man out of his bearlike hibernation. "Tell me you hear that noise this time."

"Isn't that just the highway?" Sam croaked, doing his best to hide the fact that he was driving a car while half asleep.

"*No*, it's not the highway; it's the engine. The engine has been making that noise since we left the diner."

"Well, I'm sure we'll make it back," Sam mumbled. "We're only about an hour away. . . ."

As if on cue, the loudest clunk yet sounded from under the hood. And then the car began to slow down.

"If you're not worried, then why are you slowing down?" Gaia's frustration was getting the better of her after this day of endless trials and tribulations.

"I'm not slowing down," Sam said, sitting up

193

straighter in his seat and pounding his foot harder on the gas pedal. "The *car* is."

"What?" Gaia scanned every readout and display on the dashboard. Every needle was dropping bit by bit—most importantly, their speed. "Well, what the hell is wrong?"

"I have no idea," Sam whispered, his own frustration mounting. "The car is just. . . dying." He tried to pump the gas again, but the pedal was becoming nearly nonresponsive. "We need to get off the highway, Gaia. We need to get off now before we go belly-up in the middle of the road. . . ."

No, no. They needed to be *on* the highway. This day from hell had to come to an *end.* They needed to be home. Dmitri needed to be home. Gaia needed to get home so she could straighten things out with Ed, and Tatiana, and even Natasha.

Sam flashed his eyes up at the rearview mirror with that same nervous twitch she'd seen earlier—that half-second glimpse behind them, just like he'd made before turning off to the diner. Was it just the turnoffs that still made him a nervous driver?

"What's going on, Sam?" Gaia whispered urgently. "What's going on with you? Why are you so nervous?"

"What? What's going on with *me*? Nothing! I'm just trying to pull a dying car off a highway and force it down the road to that motel. What's going on with *you*, Gaia?"

194

She had rarely seen Sam get so openly angry, but she realized that she'd chosen the wrong time to quiz him on his awkward driving habits. He was right. Whatever had happened to their car, it was now running on fumes, and if he couldn't gun it a hundred more yards to the blinking neon light of the motel at the end of the road, they'd be pushing that pile of junk themselves. This nightmare day had turned into a nightmare evening. And it still wasn't over.

The car did manage to putt its way up to the tiny office of the S-Stay Motel, and then it simply died. Two plumes of black smoke streamed out from either side of the hood. The engine let out a series of horrid coughs and burps and groans, and then all the sound gave way to a complete and deadly silence.

Sam and Gaia sat motionless in the front seat for quite some time, just staring at the smoke—just trying to accept the inhumanly cruel nature of fate. Dmitri's steady snoring didn't make this any easier. Nothing said "cruel twist of fate" like the sound of a snoring ninety-year-old man in a `crappy motel parking lot.`

"What time is it?" Gaia muttered in a monotone, staring out the smoky windshield at the S-Stay Motel's garbage dumpsters.

"It's almost eleven," Sam replied just as numbly, not moving an inch.

Unbelievable. Simply unbelievable. Just problem solve,

Gaia. All you can do is keep problem solving. . . if you ever want to get home.

She didn't want to admit it out loud, but she had no choice. Because no one in the car had a triple-A card, and there sure as hell wasn't a twenty-four-hour mechanic in the neighborhood. "We're never going to get it fixed tonight," she announced bitterly. "I don't know *what* the hell happened to the car, but I know we are never going to get it fixed until morning. . . . We have to stay here. We have to get rooms at the freaking S-Stay Motel, and then we get the car fixed first thing in the morning and we drive the rest of the way home. That's it. That's the whole thing. That's all we can do."

"I know," Sam replied, staring straight ahead at the overloaded dumpsters. He let out a long, painful sigh and slid down farther in his seat, shaking his head. "I know."

Gaia would have to accept Dmitri's snoring as his vote of agreement. "Come on."

Gaia and Sam just about fell out of the car with exhaustion, closing the doors behind them quietly and dragging themselves into the three-foot "office" of the motel. A middle-aged Pakistani man had fallen asleep at the front desk with a newspaper still open on his lap. Gaia cringed when she realized he'd been reading the Macy's underwear ads.

She slammed her hand down on the bell on the counter, watching as the man nearly fell out of his seat from the rude awakening.

"Yes, hello. . ." He dropped the paper to the floor and forced a smile.

Gaia pulled a credit card out of her wallet and Sam pulled out his bankcard. "How much for three rooms for the night?" she asked, laying her card on the desk.

"Thirty dollars for three-hour stay," the man said. "Fifty for the whole night." He stared at Sam and Gaia, and then a lascivious grin spread across his face as he turned to Sam. "Hey, man. . . you sure she's eighteen?"

"*What?*" Sam squawked.

Gaia's jaw nearly dropped from a combination of shock and disgust. The flashing neon sign of the motel had been nothing other than a safe finish line for their dying car, but now that she had a chance to look around, she was beginning to understand the nature of this particular motel. It gave new meaning to the term *seedy*. The handwritten price list on the desk even had pricing for a one-hour stay. The price was, of course, higher if you wanted twenty-four-hour porn on TV. One-hour stays, three-hour stays, and plenty of porn—she hadn't really stopped to consider what the *S* in *S-Stay* stood for. She had thought perhaps that it stood for "short," as in a "short stay," but now she realized that the *S* most likely stood for something far more disgustingly blatant.

She looked back down at the man's repulsive little knowing grin as he stared at Sam and Gaia. In his perverted eyes, they were a guy and an underage girl who had just pulled up in the middle of the night, asking for an all-night "S-Stay." She was too tired to even know which emotion hit first: her embarrassment at what this lowlife was insinuating, her totally irrational sense of disloyalty to Ed just for what it *looked* like, or her very serious desire to reach over the counter and pound most of the teeth out of the pervert's face.

"*Three* rooms," she repeated, feeling her fists begin to clench. "Three *separate* rooms."

The man looked mildly confused, and then a dour expression took over his face. "Whatever," he grunted. "Three rooms for the whole night, one-fifty. No credit cards."

Gaia's hand froze as she was handing him her card. "What? What do you mean, no—?"

"*Cash only,*" the man insisted, pointing at the block letters in faded blue ballpoint ink at the bottom of the handwritten price list.

Of course. Of course, cash only. This just kept getting worse. And with a dead car outside, it wasn't as if they had any other options for the night.

"How much do you have?" she asked Sam, digging into her pockets.

"How much do I have? I have nothing," he said, staring angrily at the man for making this night still more complicated. "I have twenty bucks."

"I have eighty left," she said. "That's enough for two rooms. One for Dmitri and one for. . . us." The moment she'd said it, both her and Sam's eyes seemed to drop down to the floor.

"That's. . . that's fine," Sam uttered uncomfortably. He tossed his twenty on the counter and shoved his hands in his pockets, stepping away from the desk.

The pervert smiled again as if he knew exactly what Sam and Gaia were "up to." What he didn't know was that he would be dead in ten seconds if he didn't wipe that grin off his face.

All those damn questions were bubbling up again. The questions Gaia had absolutely refused to entertain for the entire car ride up. Nagging questions about her and Sam's murky, unspoken, leftover feelings. Sharing a motel room was not exactly the best way to avoid those nagging questions.

This is not a big deal, she chided herself. *Don't be ridiculous. After the day you've both had, this is nothing. You'll just go straight to sleep. No conversations, no questions. Besides, cheap motel rooms have two beds. All cheap motel rooms have two beds.*

"That's *fine*," Gaia agreed, staring angrily at the clerk as she threw the cash down on the counter. He handed her the keys to the two rooms, and Gaia and Sam slammed the door behind them.

They were operating almost completely in silence now. Maybe out of awkwardness. Maybe out of exhaustion. Probably out of both. They were able to wake Dmitri just enough to carry him out of the car and into his bed, though he seemed to stay basically asleep the entire time. Dmitri's room, Gaia noticed, had only one bed.

That's just one of the rooms, she told herself as she and Sam silently dragged their tired bodies down a few doors to their room. *Your room will have two beds.*

But the moment she unlocked their door, she saw the bed. The one and only bed in the tiny brown room. The bed with the `coin-operated vibrating function`.

Sam immediately turned to Gaia. "I can stay in Dmitri's room," he offered nervously. "That's no problem...."

She hated that he'd even offered it. He was confirming the weirdness, and the last thing she wanted to do was confirm the weirdness. If they didn't acknowledge the weirdness, then the weirdness wasn't there. That was Gaia's theory.

"No, it's fine," Gaia said as nonchalantly as possible. She made a beeline for the bed and collapsed on it. She shoved herself as far to the left side as she could without falling off. "We just need sleep," she said. "Let's just get some sleep, and we'll take care of the car first thing in the morning." She shot back up in the bed and ripped her shoes and her jacket off before diving back under the covers.

"Okay. . ." Sam stepped over to "his" side of the bed. "You're right. I'm going to drop if I don't get some sleep. We'll just. . . get some sleep."

He sat down on the side of the bed and hunched over on his knees, probably just trying to collect himself.

A calm silence took over the room.

Gaia turned away from Sam and squeezed her eyes shut. There was no weirdness if she did not acknowledge the weirdness. No weirdness if she did not acknowledge the weirdness. . .

I'm coming home, Ed. I swear to God I'm coming home. Just wait for me, okay? Wait for me.

THE MUSIC AND WORDS HAD ALL

Spinning and Spinning

started to blend together. The thumping bass drum and the incessant chirping. The howls of laughter and the drunken shouting. The plush couches and the harsh white lights. It was all melting into one huge ugly and sensational mass. Even Tatiana's face had begun to blur, as had her black dress, and her vanilla shoulders, and her rather stunning blond hair. They were all just parts of the same overwhelming whole. Or, to put it more specifically, they were all parts of Ed being totally plastered.

Tatiana had been right about the vodka. It had made him forget about Gaia—although now that he remembered that he'd forgotten, he sort of remembered again. Though not really. The thirty or forty thousand vodka shots (more like four) had made him forget just about everything, including his middle name and address. Actually, his last name had become a little blurry, too.

Fargo? Is my last name really Fargo? What the hell is that about?

All he was absolutely sure of right now was that his name was Ed and that he was drunk. And that a beautiful girl named Tatiana was sitting next to him in a dark, secluded corner of Pravda with her beautiful face far, far too close to his.

"Ed, are you drunk?" she asked, breathing warmly onto his cheek as he stared out at the blurry shadows and light.

He held his hand out in front of his face and spoke slowly. "Well. . . how many fingers am I holding up?"

"All of them." She laughed.

"Okay, I'm drunk, then. I thought it was my foot."

"Shut up." She giggled, slapping him hard on the shoulder.

"Owww."

"Oh, no, did I hurt you?" She held a guilty hand to her mouth.

"No, I'm just kidding," he said. "I actually can't feel anything."

"Aha! It works!"

"Oh, it works," Ed agreed.

"Then here is to the great Russian medicine! Did I tell you or did I tell you?"

"You told me," he said, holding out his glass and letting her pour him another shot. "To vodka," he said. "And to a fine drinking buddy." They clinked glasses and downed their shots. Ed couldn't even feel the burn going down his throat now.

"So then, drinking buddy. . . you are clearly drunk," she said.

"Clearly."

"Good. Because I wanted to tell you something. But only if you are drunk."

"Well, then, you're in luck," he said, realizing how close he actually was to slurring his words. He couldn't believe that. He'd really thought the word-slurring thing was only for bad drunk acting, but apparently one could in fact be drunk enough to slur one's words. Live and learn. . . .

"See, if you are *really drunk*," she said, "then you probably won't remember what I am about to say. And if *I* am really drunk. . . which I am. . . then I probably won't remember, either."

"Of course," Ed said, tilting his head ninety degrees to experience the sideways view of the world. "It's always good to say things that no one will remember."

"Well, in this case it is. . . ."

"Go ahead," Ed offered. "I've already forgotten what you said." He lifted his head back upright, and the entire room seemed to spin the rest of the way around. And then it wouldn't stop. Spinning and spinning. . .

"Perfect." She placed the vodka bottle down on the floor and took Ed's face by the chin, turning it to face her own. With her face this close, Ed suddenly felt a rush of strange heat drop down through his chest.

"Whoa, there," he slurred, seeing that his face was now about three inches from hers. "Close-talking alert. We need to have a talk in which we talk about your close talking. . . ."

"When we're sober," she said.

"Right. But just let me say that this is too close for talking even if—"

"Ed," she interrupted, gluing her eyes to his. "Here is what I wanted to say that you should forget. You know that. . . I have come to care for Gaia almost like a sister, you know?"

"I know."

"And believe me, Ed, I really do care for her."

"I know. . . ."

"And I know that you and I have been through all of our. . . *whatever*. . . and now we are just good friends."

"Right. . . ?"

She slid her glossy hair behind her ears. It was an opportunity for Ed to pull back, but he found himself glued at this point to her eyes. Her eyes kept the room from spinning.

"But all I wanted to say. . ." She sighed and leaned closer. ". . . while drunk and knowing that we will forget I said it. . . is that. . . well. . . if there were no Gaia, then I would probably tell you. . . that I am a bit in love with you."

The music suddenly seemed to double in volume. Ed couldn't feel much, but he could feel all the blood rush to his head. Or maybe it wasn't blood. Maybe it was vodka. That or the loud music cutting into his brain. Or it might have been that he was so drunk, he could actually *feel* the confusion swirling around in his brain. The confusion mixed with his depression and his pitiful lack of any assurance with Gaia. But for a deeply unfortunate combination of reasons, he didn't turn away from Tatiana or stand up. Actually, he probably couldn't have stood up if he'd wanted to. "I, uh. . . I think I should just—"

"Don't *worry*, Ed," she assured him with a smile. "I am not making a pass here, okay? We are only two drinking buddies talking. I *know* that we have already been through this. I know that I am officially supposed to stop liking you like that; I know that. But there is nothing official about feelings, Ed, you know? I can help what I *do*, but I can't help what I feel. . . ."

"Well, I. . . I understand," Ed said, having absolutely no idea what else to say.

Tatiana's face suddenly seemed to have moved closer.

The perfect tip of her nose was nearly touching Ed's as the words fell from her lips—so close now that he could hear every word no matter how softly she spoke. The light scent of flowers and sweet lemons was floating up from her neck, and `the rich scent of expensive lipstick was floating from her lips.`

"For instance, right now," she said softly, "I feel like kissing you."

He could hardly move now. Every ounce of his drunken focus was on her warm breath and her naked shoulders. "But you wouldn't," he said.

"No," she whispered, leaning her lips and her body toward his. "No, I would never. . . ."

Her lips were so close, Ed could nearly taste them. . . .

What are you doing, Ed? What the hell are you doing?

"Whoa!" Ed lurched backward like he'd just been hit with a thousand volts of electroshock. He jumped up out of his seat, tripping over his own feet and stumbling his way back to a standing position. "No more vodka," he announced, waving his hands wildly in front of him. "That's it for the vodka."

Tatiana shot up, too. "Sorry, sorry, sorry," she moaned. She buried her face ashamedly in her hands. "Oh my God, Ed, I am *so* sorry!"

"It's okay," he insisted, taking a few steps farther away from her. "It's okay. No harm, no foul. . . *no vodka. . .*"

"No more vodka," she agreed. "I promise no more vodka for me."

"Or me."

"Oh God, I'm *terrible*. I know I'm not supposed to do that anymore, I *know*."

Ed was having major problems maintaining his balance. A horrid dizziness had begun to take over. Or maybe he could just *feel* the guilt spinning around in his head. He'd stopped them both before anything had happened, but somehow, at the moment, that didn't seem to make him feel any better.

"Oh God, Ed, please don't tell Gaia about this; I feel just *so. . .* Oh *God*—"

"Don't even think about it," he said, leaning his hand against the wall for balance. "Just forget it, okay? It never happened. Just two **very** drunk drinking buddies. That's it. Never happened."

"It never happened," she agreed.

"Nothing *did* happen!" he reminded her. And himself.

"That's right. Nothing *did* happen."

"Nothing."

"Nothing."

Come home, Gaia. Wherever the hell you are, just come home. Please.

"What's going on, you two?"

The next thing Ed knew, Jake was standing right behind his shoulder with the world's most annoying sly grin. "You two having a cozy 'just friends' moment over here?"

Had Ed been even a little more sober, he would have socked Jake `straight in the mouth`. But considering Jake's rather formidable karate skills and Ed's being a walking bottle of vodka, he opted to just sock Jake with his eyes. "Nothing is 'going on' here, Jake." Had he actually *liked* Jake for a second earlier in the day? What a freaking joke. Gaia had it right. Jake was clearly the loser of the century. And what was up with his new-found obsession with Ed's screwed-up love life.

Tammie stepped up behind Jake, wrapping her arms around his stomach and peeking over his shoulder. "What's *up*, girl?" she squealed at Tatiana. "Are we not the party geniuses of the decade?"

"Geniuses. . . ," Tatiana echoed, still bathed in guilt as she stared helplessly at Ed.

It's okay, Ed wanted to tell her. *I was drunk, too. Let's just not think about it anymore. Let's not think about it ever again.*

"Well, I think they're finally shutting us down here," Jake said. "Any ideas where we can move the party? How about your place, Tatiana? Wasn't your mom going to be out all night?"

"Sure," Tatiana said, still only half paying attention. "My place is fine."

"Excellent!" Tammie squeaked. "I'll rally the troops! You coming, Ed?"

"Sure," Ed snapped defensively. "Why wouldn't I come?"

Jake and Megan both widened their eyes, shifting their gaze from Ed to Tatiana and back to Ed. "What*ever*," Tammie said, sharing an infuriating little knowing smile with Jake.

It took every ounce of Ed's remaining self-discipline not to scream at them both. He wanted to scream that there was no need for their stupid, knowing smiles. Because there was nothing to know. Because *nothing* had happened. Nothing.

AT FIRST SHE THOUGHT IT WAS A

No Dream

dream. Gaia just hadn't expected it. After all they'd been through, after she'd explained about Ed, it just seemed like they'd put it all behind them. Or at least as if they'd silently agreed to *pretend* they'd put it all behind them.

But now, as she lay beside him in this creepy motel room. . .

Now the palm of his warm hand had just crept up on her back. And after resting there for a moment, it had slid upward and begun to caress her shoulder. This was no dream.

She couldn't have been asleep for that long, because all he did was touch her ever so lightly. And Sam might not have even fallen asleep for a moment. For all Gaia knew, he'd been battling in his head the entire time she'd been asleep, trying to make the right choice, trying not to let himself touch her the way he must have wanted to so badly. The way, if she was completely honest with herself, she had come awfully close to wanting to touch him, too . . .

But she couldn't go back. She couldn't let herself fall back into all that nostalgic confusion. No matter how strange and electric his touch made her feel, she knew in her heart that she wasn't going to give in to it. It was wrong, and she knew it. And she'd thought that Sam knew it, too. Maybe not.

Her entire body tensed up as his hand slid up along her neck and then into the tangles of her hair. She couldn't bring herself to say anything. She just didn't want to reject him like that. She'd hoped she wouldn't have to—that he'd pull his hand away any second and just leave it at that. She'd hoped that he could understand that whether or not those feelings were still there for her, she had to ignore them now. Because of Ed. Because of the time that had passed. Because everything had changed.

But she couldn't wish it away. He wasn't going to stop. His other hand pressed up against her back. But this time he didn't slide it toward her shoulders. This time his hand began to slide downward. Farther and farther down her back until. . .

"Sam, don't," she finally heard herself say. She had

to say it. Before he'd crossed that line she'd worked so very hard to be sure they didn't cross. His hands had left her with no choice but to speak up.

But her words didn't seem to matter to him now. Because he didn't stop. His hand moved even farther down....

"I said *stop*." Her eyes shot open, and she flipped around to say it to Sam's face.

Only it wasn't Sam's face. And they weren't Sam's hands.

You scum. You repulsive lowlife scum of the earth.

All she needed was a glimpse of his black ski mask and she knew. Her mind had processed the entire disgusting scenario in a split second. She knew that Sam was nowhere to be found. She knew that this whole disgusting time, it had just been another one of *them* touching her, damn near molesting her, trying to do God knew what else to her while she *slept*.

She flipped out of the bed, bouncing up off the floor and facing the hulking son of a bitch down in the dark. So now they weren't just pond scum murderers—the kind you scraped from the bottom of your shoe. Now they were wanna-be rapists, too.

Goddamn them. They weren't done. Whoever they were, they weren't giving up. They were still on her tail—still sending in these pathetic hired thugs to take her out, no matter where she was. There couldn't be a moment's peace. Not a moment.

The only light in the room came from the glare of

the parking lot lampposts, beaming through the slight opening in the windows. She could just make out the hideous smile on his lips, framed by the circular mouth hole of his mask. He jumped off the bed and pulled a knife from his jacket, staring her down with dead eyes that were just as black as the mask.

The thought of his disgusting hands actually touching her body made her skin feel like burning sandpaper. But with one more moment to think before he made his move, the fact that those had *not* been Sam's hands touching her raised one very simple and horrifying question: Where the hell *was* Sam?

No more time for questions. He lunged, and she jumped left, letting him charge into the ugly brown wall. But when she'd moved left, she hadn't been ready for the other one. Yes, there were two of them. There were always at least two of them now. It was nice to know that whoever was out there trying to have her killed wasn't completely underestimating her. But still, considering the mood she was now in, considering the fact that this would now be the *third* attempt on her life in one day, not to mention the fact that these assholes had done something with Sam. . . she wasn't going to waste her time making this fight interesting.

These two losers in their pathetic black masks had taken the wrong assignment tonight. They simply had no idea what they had signed on for.

The second thug tried to wrap a wire around her throat

from behind, but he was about as slow as they came. She jabbed her elbow deep into his solar plexus, located his wrist in almost complete darkness, and flipped him across the tiny room. The paper-thin walls of the entire room shook as his body made a deep dent in the plaster.

She turned to the one with the knife. "What did you do with Sam?" she demanded. But his only reply was another bull-like charge with his knife pointed at her chest.

Forget it, she shouted at herself as the point of his knife flew toward her. *Forget the questions. Just get them out. Get them the hell out of here.*

Gaia quickly mastered all of her boiling frustration and channeled it into a series of deadly precise moves.

She zoomed in on the gleam of the knife in the dark and shot her leg out with a swift forward kick. The knife snapped out of the thug's hands, and then she swung around for a roundhouse kick that bashed his face hard against the wall.

"Get out!" she barked, snapping another kick to his face and another to his back. She knew it was wrong to lead with her anger, but there was simply nothing left of her self-discipline tonight. Now it was only about what would be quickest and most effective. "I'm through with this crap today. You go and tell them that. This is your one chance to leave."

He grabbed onto her leg and toppled her to the floor, but she countered by jabbing his back with her elbow in three spine-cracking blows.

She shot up off her shoulders, landing squarely on her feet, and trounced him with two more kicks to the back. "I'm *telling* you," she growled. "You *want* to get out of here. Believe me. You want to get out of here *now*."

The other one had risen back to his feet and decided it was his turn to attack. He lunged for her, but she simply sidestepped him, using all his momentum to send him crashing into his friend on the floor. They still apparently were not getting the picture. She would to have to be a bit more forceful with her point.

She spotted the knife across the room, took one bouncing step over the bed, and swiped it up off the floor. They stumbled up together and made another foolish attempt to rush her. This time simultaneously.

Good. She could make her point much quicker that way.

She wasn't going to kill them. She was simply going to give them their last warning. She bent her knees slightly as they lumbered toward her, and then, with perfectly calibrated pressure, she swiped the knife across the chest of the one on the left, shoving him quickly out of the way. Then she ducked down and swiped the knife across the leg of the other, checking him into the wall in almost the exact same spot where she had tossed him to begin with.

They both let out rather pathetic cries as they writhed around on the floor, holding tightly to their harmless flesh wounds. They could always dish it out so much better than they could take it.

"That was only the warning," she spat, flashing the knife before each of their pained faces. "The next one will cut so much deeper. And the next one deeper than that. . . and the next one—"

There was no need to utter another word. Without either of them even exchanging glances, they simultaneously opted for the retreat. Gaia followed them out onto the walkway as they piled out the door, nearly knocking it off its hinges. She stood there in front of the open doorway with the knife extended, watching as they scampered out into the parking lot and then disappeared into the darkness of the road.

Gaia stood there for another ten seconds just breathing heavily with the knife at her side. And then, finally, her thoughts turned away from violence and back to the much more important matter. *Sam.* What the hell had they done with Sam?

All the ugliest possibilities began to flash before her eyes, but she wouldn't have to indulge those awful images for very long. Because Sam suddenly appeared at the end of the walkway, stepping out of the motel's office. He saw her standing in front of the door, and he smiled at her. That was it. A smile. He smiled the most innocent, nonchalant smile she had ever seen, and then he began to walk toward her.

Gaia couldn't believe it. It had happened again. She could see it in his face. He seemed to have no idea what had just happened. Somehow he had missed the entire battle *again*. Somehow, just as it had happened at the diner that afternoon, Sam had stepped out just before the violence had begun and then stepped back in just after it had ended. What on earth were the odds of that happening *twice* in one day...?

And that was really the first time it hit her. At least it was the first time it had hit her consciously.

An ugly, ugly thought. One of the ugliest thoughts she had ever had.

What *were* the odds of Sam being conspicuously absent for Gaia's attempted murder twice in one day? They were abysmal, that's what they were. They were damn near impossible.

Unless, of course, Sam knew. Unless he knew exactly when the attempted murders would take place.

STOP IT, GAIA. SAM IS NOT THE enemy. Don't even think of it. It's ridiculous. You've got to stop that entire line of thinking right now.

But once the line of thinking had started, she had to take it to its logical conclusion. No one with any amount of intelligence could ignore it. And the longer she looked at Sam's oddly

Oddly
Innocen
Smile

innocent smile, the harder it was to discount.

In one lightning-quick moment the chain of unfortunate facts flashed through her head. And the longer she let the horribly paranoid theory develop, the more evidence she seemed to find to back it up.

Twice he'd disappeared right before her attacks. *Twice.* And what had preceded the attacks both times? That look. Sam's nervous glimpse into the rearview mirror. Like he was checking for someone. Checking to make sure someone was following them and knew where to pull over. Someone, for instance, like a couple of contract killers.

And the *car*. Where had Sam mysteriously disappeared to during the attack at the diner? Gaia had seen him walking back from the parking lot. He'd said he'd gone to check on the car. But it was right after Sam's visit to the car that it began to make that strange noise, like someone had tampered with the engine. . . .

And how convenient that the broken-down car would force them down the road to this seedy motel in the middle of the night. . . where there were probably no cops for miles. A perfect place to catch Gaia off guard, wasn't it? Asleep and confused in a strange motel room, in bed with Sam. Wouldn't that be when she was least prepared for another attack?

And how had those two thugs gotten into the motel room so easily, anyway? Without a noise? Without breaking a single window or a lock? Almost as if the door had been left open for them. Almost as if they'd been invited in. . .

The longer she stared at Sam's smiling face as he walked toward her, the more it all began to make a most disturbing kind of sense. Every single little puzzle piece seemed to fit together.

He could have been slowly and professionally brainwashed during all his unbearable isolation in Loki's compound. Loki's people could have offered him a deal. They'd set him free if he would just agree to do them the simple favor of leading Gaia directly into their trap—leading the lamb to the slaughter.

Even the psycho loyalists at the compound could have been a setup. . . .

Think about it: Sam disappears behind a corner, and you follow him straight into a three-man firing squad?

It was like another trap. Like they'd already known she was coming before she even got there. Like every other attempt on Gaia's life today. Sam had never made a move on them, and they'd never made a move on him.

And now here he was, walking out of that motel office. Why the hell would he have gotten out of bed right after he'd supposedly gone to sleep? And when exactly had he suddenly become best buds with that pervert in the office? What could they possibly have to discuss at this hour?

By the time Sam stepped up to her, she had completed his vilification in her head.

"Where were you *this* time?" she snapped, staring at Sam with unabashed accusation. "And don't *lie* to me, Sam. Whatever you do, do *not* lie to me."

Sam nearly fell backward with a look of utter shock. First he seemed shocked by the sheer aggression and volume of Gaia's demands. But as his eyes dropped down to her hand, his shock tripled. He'd caught a glimpse of the large, bloody knife still gripped tightly in her fingers.

"What. . . what the hell is that? What the hell is going on?" He took a giant step into their room and flipped on the overhead light, darting his head from side to side before turning back to Gaia. "What happened?" he demanded again. "Where did you get that knife? Was there a fight? Jesus, did somebody try to hurt you?"

And suddenly Gaia was confused again. She was at a loss for words.

He stepped back up to her and grabbed her by the shoulders, probing her eyes with a desperate brand of concern. "Talk to me," he insisted. "What *happened,* Gaia?"

She'd painted an entire picture of him in her head for a moment—a picture of pure, sadistic evil. A crystal clear picture of betrayal and coldhearted calculation. But nothing about the actual Sam matched that picture at all. As she stared at all the intense, heartfelt compassion in his eyes, and all that deep-rooted concern, and all that bright, hazel-colored innocence, she realized that she had simply fallen prey to a trauma-induced spasm of temporary insanity. That was all that had happened. She'd lost her mind. She was looking for someone to blame, and she'd patched together a bunch of useless coincidences and blamed the first person she'd laid eyes on. But in reality, he was the last person in the world who would ever want to hurt her or even see her get hurt.

"Gaia? Why won't you talk to me?" he pleaded. "Are you injured? Should I call a—"

"No," she said, finally snapping out of her insanity trance. "No, it's. . . there was a fight. . . but I'm fine. I'm fine, Sam."

She wrapped her arms around his shoulders and hugged him tightly. It was her version of an apology— an apology for the batch of awful thoughts she had just stupidly indulged in. She pulled away from him and tossed the knife deep into the woods behind the motel.

"Gaia, I don't understand," he said. "Whose knife was that? Whose blood? Why won't you tell me what happened? If something happened to you while I left you alone, I swear to God, I'll. . ."

"Calm down," she told him. "Someone is after me, but it's not your problem."

His eyes nearly popped out of his head. "*Of course* it's my problem! They're after both of us, Gaia. That's what this is all about. I should have been in the room with you. I shouldn't have left you alone for a second; that was so *stupid*. . . ."

She could see him going down the same self-punishing road she'd been down herself a hundred times before, and with each new word out of his mouth, she regretted her ridiculous accusations more and more.

"Sam, stop it," she insisted. "Everything's fine now. I'm fine. We're fine. Everyone is fine. But where *were* you? I still don't understand what you were doing out of bed."

"I was in the office," Sam explained, coming awfully close to slapping himself upside the head. "I just. . . I felt so crappy that we couldn't get you home. . . that your dad is still. . . out there somewhere. . . . I wanted to try to do something about the car before you woke up. . . ."

"You didn't need to do that—"

"I know, but. . . well, now it nearly got you *killed*—"

"No," Gaia insisted. "No, it didn't. Nothing even close. Did you have any luck?"

"What?" He was clearly punishing himself again in his head.

"With the *car*," she said, trying to keep his head in the right place. "Did you have any luck with the car?"

He looked down at her for a moment, and then a half smile finally appeared on his lips. "Yes," he said. "Yes, I did. The guy in the office. . . the pervert. . ."

"Yeah?"

"It turns out he's not such a bad guy." He smiled. "And he knows something about cars."

"What are you saying?"

"He checked the engine for us," he explained. "Someone had drained all the coolant out of the car, Gaia. And they'd dropped a quarter in the tank just to really screw things up."

"I *knew* it," she said. "I knew someone had messed with the engine."

"But all we had to do was get the quarter out of there. And then he filled it up with some coolant from the trunk of his truck and now we're good to go."

Gaia stared at Sam for a confirmation. "Say that again," she uttered.

"We're good to go." He nodded firmly. "Without the traffic, I can get us back home in an hour."

Gaia dropped her head for a moment. She gave thanks to the Fates for this one bit of good fortune they'd been kind enough to grant her on an otherwise killer day. Literally.

"Wake Dmitri," she said. "We're going home. Right now."

A dark
rain
cloud in **strange**
her **psychedelic**
brain had
blocked **hell**
out the sun.

HOW THE HELL DID ALCOHOLICS DO

it? Were they completely insane? Ed couldn't fathom feeling this ridiculously messed up and disoriented on a nightly basis. That would be like consigning oneself to some kind of strange psychedelic hell every single night and then waking up the next morning and doing it all over again.

God-Awful Dizzines

Was it the next morning yet? Ed couldn't even find a clock amid the crowd that jammed Tatiana's apartment. He couldn't find anything. It was just an ugly whirlwind of disgustingly beautiful faces and bare midriffs and muscular arms. Bad pop music was blaring from the stereo, and then there were the screams. The constant screams. What was it with drunken girls and screaming? Why did drunken girls think that all emotions needed to be expressed with the high-pitched screech of a brutal murder?

"Shhh," he found himself mumbling, basically to himself. "Quiet down, now."

He stumbled over to the kitchen area, cutting through a crowd of what seemed like thousands, and ripped open the fridge. Somehow, in spite of his god-awful dizziness, and his increasing nausea, and the buzzing in his ears from all the whooping and screaming, and the general sense that the world was soon to explode into a billion pieces. . . Ed had decided to have another beer. Because why the hell not? Because did it really matter, anyway? He'd probably never drink another drink for the rest of his natural-born life, but tonight. . . tonight required a numbness the likes of which he had not encountered since losing feeling in his legs.

Now there was even more to forget than there had been only hours ago. Not only did he need to forget about Gaia—forget that their relationship was melting like a nuclear accident and forget that she was out "there" somewhere for some indeterminate period of time, something between ten hours and ten years. But now he also needed to forget about Tatiana. He needed to forget about that stupid almost kiss. He needed to drown it out until its totally trivial, inconsequential nature revealed itself permanently. Until his brain had successfully placed it in the "total and complete nothing" category where it absolutely belonged.

But one thing was making that very difficult. How could he drown out that stupid drunken moment with Tatiana if Tatiana wouldn't stop following him around?

"I just wanted to apologize again," she called into his ear from behind. She had developed this unfortunate habit of sneaking up on him. He nearly banged his head on the inside of the fridge as he searched for a decent beer.

He grabbed a Sam Adams and slammed the door closed, pressing his back up against the fridge to keep his distance. "Don't," he said in a clipped tone, flashing his best approximation of a smile, given that he could barely feel his lips. "Don't apologize anymore. Because it's nothing."

"Okay, but. . . are we cool?" She slurred her words slightly as she tilted her head back and swigged from her own beer. Ed couldn't even fathom the fact that she was actually ahead of him in drinks. If he'd had as much booze as Tatiana had imbibed tonight, he would already have been passed out somewhere beneath the screaming midriff girls and the hooting biceps guys.

"Sure, we're cool," he replied, wishing he could just disappear into the crowd and not have her find him for a few hours. "We're totally cool. I just—"

"Hold on," Tatiana said, holding her finger up in his face and looking at her pager.

"Do you always carry around your pager at parties?" Ed laughed.

"I'm waiting for news from my mother," she said, reading her new message.

"About Gaia's dad?" he asked.

She looked back up at Ed, registering mild surprise. "Right," she said.

"So she's not really at a UN function, is she?"

Tatiana rolled her eyes as if that was the most naive thing she'd ever heard anyone say. Ed took her point in stride.

"Well. . . ? Any news?"

Tatiana dropped her head back down to her pager

and blew out a long, frustrated sigh. "No," she complained. "Nothing yet."

The beer suddenly fell from Tatiana's hand and spilled all over the kitchen floor.

"Oh, *no*," she moaned, slapping her hands to her face. The crowd quickly made way for the spilled beer. Nothing got those girls moving like the threat of beer-stained shoes.

"It's okay," Ed said, grabbing a few paper napkins from the counter and dropping down to the floor. "No big deal."

"I know where there are more paper towels," she said. "Wait here, okay? I'll be right back."

"We don't really need. . ." Ed tried to stop her, but there was no point. Tatiana was already off on her hypercommitted quest for paper towels.

GAIA COULD BARELY BELIEVE IT,

aveman-like Moos

but her eyes hadn't deceived her. The slim green signs overhead were real, lit up by the amber hue of a New York City streetlight.

Seventy-second Street and Madison Avenue.

They turned the corner and slowed down, pulling closer and closer. . . .

The limestone façade was real. And so was the uniformed doorman behind the latticed windows of the front door.

Home. Gaia was finally home. After all the attempted murders and bizarre suspicions and romantic confusion. After thinking it might never really happen, here she was, pulling up slowly to her front door. Sam had done it. With a little help from the perverted desk clerk of the S-Stay Motel, he had finally gotten them home.

The car came to a halt in front of her door, and then Sam put on the brake and flipped off the ignition. Gaia and he both let out almost inaudible sighs and slid down slightly in their seats, leaving no sound in the car but the steady wheeze of Dmitri's snoring in the backseat.

In fact, Dmitri's snoring had really been the only sound in the car for the rest of the ride home. Sam had perhaps been too freaked out by the sight of that `bloody knife` to utter another word to Gaia. And she had been too freaked out by her own sudden suspicions to make any further conversation. Or perhaps it was just the deeply uncomfortable aftermath of their moment in bed that had left them speechless. Most likely it was a toxic combination of all the strange revelations of this day.

But one thing was for sure: Making it back home

hadn't done a thing to relieve the awkward tension in the car.

"We did it," Gaia said, realizing how idiotic she sounded.

"We did," Sam agreed, giving way to another long silence.

And then, quite suddenly, out of the clear black sky, Dmitri awoke from his marathon sleep. Perhaps it was the sudden stillness of the car, or just some internal antenna that told him they were home.

"Where. . . where are we?" His voice was blocked almost completely by the phlegm in his throat, which he proceeded to clear with a loud and intense effort. "Is this. . . ?" He peered out the side and back windows, and then his face began to light up with the innocent awe of a five-year-old child. "This is the city," he marveled. "This is my city. . . ." The smile on his face looked almost permanent.

"I told you we'd get you pretty close," Gaia said, smiling back at him.

"I cannot believe it," he said, staring gleefully into her eyes. "You are an angel. Both of you. The angels have brought me home. Delivered, uh? I have been delivered from bondage. . . . I cannot believe it. . . . My home, my apartment. . . it is not even so very far from here."

Gaia noticed the look in his eyes begin to darken slightly. She couldn't quite read the shift. Was it sadness? Or maybe worry? But a moment more and Gaia was sure she understood. "Dmitri," she said, searching his eyes. "Is there anyone else at home? Is there someone who can help take care of you?"

"Oh," he muttered, averting his eyes. "Oh. . . I will be fine. You don't need to worry, Gaia. I am perfectly capable of taking care of myself." He let out another long, phlegm-ridden cough, wheezing slowly to regain his breath.

Gaia turned her eyes to Sam. He seemed to know exactly what she was thinking. He even seemed to understand that there were a hundred different reasons she was thinking it.

"Maybe. . . I should stay with you tonight," Sam suggested, still glancing from her to Dmitri. "Just to make sure you're okay. You've been through an awful lot these past few days."

"Oh, *no*." Dmitri smiled, waving Sam off. "I would never ask such a thing. Never. You don't need to be tending to some poor old stranger, Sam. . . ."

Sam's eyes drifted back to Gaia. It was as if they had an entire conversation in just that one long glance. A conversation about the many reasons it would be so much better for Sam to leave Gaia's apartment tonight. Especially if there was a truly safe place for him to stay. A place where no one would ever think to look for him. In a complete stranger's Upper East Side apartment.

For one thing, now that Tatiana had discovered Sam, hiding him in the apartment would become so much more complicated. It was only a matter of time before

Natasha discovered him, too. And besides, Sam was clearly going stir-crazy in that tiny maid's room, surrounded by nothing but dust and supplies.

But even that wasn't the main reason he needed to go.

Things had simply gotten too weird. There was no way Gaia and Sam could spend another night in the same apartment after that moment of confusion she'd had in the motel bed. Sure, she had only *imagined* that Sam was touching her, but the response she'd felt had been shockingly real. And after her suspicious freakout, she wasn't even sure she was totally comfortable with him in the apartment, even though she *knew* that was completely irrational. There were just too many reasons for him to go. Dmitri needed the company. And at this point Gaia had to admit that she would be a little happier to be *without* Sam's presence.

"No, I insist," Sam said finally, turning to Dmitri. "I mean, if you don't mind the company, then I really think you shouldn't be—"

"Mind the company?" Dmitri wheezed his way through another laugh. "Oh my goodness, *no*. The company would be. . . But I don't want to impose on you like this, Sam. No, you are being too kind. You have been kind enough already—"

"Then it's done," Sam interrupted, flashing a smile that looked only slightly fake. "We can help each other recuperate," he said. "I'll just get my things from upstairs and we'll go, okay?"

Dmitri conceded with a smile. "Okay," he said. "I am grateful to you, Sam. So grateful."

Sam turned to Gaia with another pregnant glance. "Okay?"

"Okay," she said, breathing an internal sigh of relief.

She still had a million questions for Dmitri. She still needed to quiz him on everything he knew about her father, any clues he might be able to provide. But not tonight. Tonight was done. Tomorrow. She would start with him fresh tomorrow.

"Stay here, Dmitri," she said. "Sam will be right back with his stuff." She turned back to Sam. "Let's go." They took the elevator in complete silence, both keeping their eyes glued to the flashing numbers above the door. But the moment Gaia stepped off the elevator, she could hear it. Who on earth would *not* hear it? The offensive muted bass of a loud stereo. The horrible din of a teenage crowd. The yammering chirps of the girls and the cavemanlike moos of the boys.

A party. There was a goddamn party going on in Gaia's apartment.

"Oh my God," she groaned, grabbing Sam's arm at the front door. "Heather's benefit. It has to be. The freaking *after-party*," she whispered. "They're having the after-party at *my* house. *Tatiana. . .*" She nearly banged her head against the door with frustration.

"What do we do?" Sam whispered. "I can come back for my stuff—"

"No, it's okay," she said, turning to the door at the end of the hall. "This is nothing. This is not a big deal. We can go straight to your room through the back door. We won't even pass through the front of the house. It's a service entrance. Come on."

Gaia led Sam through the halls of her building and then unlocked the back door, leading him quietly through the service hallway and into his tiny room.

The sounds of the drunken crowd grew louder and louder. God, she hated parties. Particularly parties that starred the FOHs. Tatiana would have to be sufficiently reamed tomorrow for bringing the entire New York teenage community into Gaia's only remaining safe haven. But for now, her only goal was to gather Sam's things and get him out of there as quickly as possible.

"Let's just take what you need for now," she whispered. "I can bring you the rest later." She scanned the room for necessary items, but Sam suddenly seemed completely uninterested in gathering his things. He stood in the center of the room, staring at Gaia as she moved back and forth.

"Gaia. . ."

"Where's your toothbrush and stuff like that?"

"Gaia," he repeated again at a slightly louder volume.

Gaia shot her finger up to her lips to keep him quiet. "What?" she whispered impatiently. "What's wrong?"

"Come here," he said.

She paused and stared at his solemn expression.

"Please," he said. "Just for a second. I just want to say something, and then I'll go, okay?"

She could see the necessity building in his eyes and she was compelled to respect it. She stopped her frantic movements and stepped up close to him so they were standing face-to-face.

"What's wrong?" she asked, trying her best to let go of her discomfort at such close range.

"I just wanted to say that I know that you're with Ed now, and I'm sorry if anything I've done has made you feel uncomfortable," he said. "I know we're not going to go back in time. And I have to find it in my heart to accept that. And I will. I will accept that. What we had is—"

The sound of the raucous crowd suddenly burst into the room in a giant gush of air, cutting Sam off and assaulting Gaia's eardrums. They whipped their heads toward the open doorway.

And there was Tatiana. Standing half in the door with a massive sheepish grin on her face.

That stupid lock. Gaia had completely forgotten about the broken lock on the door.

"*Uh-ohhh,*" Tatiana sang, ducking her head down into her shoulders like a guilty turtle. "I think I've just int'rupted a romantic moment. So sorry. So, so, so, *sor-reeeee.*" She giggled slightly and changed her footing to maintain her balance. She was slurring every other word.

Tatiana was so obviously plastered. Gaia could honestly smell her breath from across the room. She was almost drunk beyond recognition, if there was such a thing.

Gaia felt her entire body seize up with anger. "Will you *close* that door?" she whispered through clenched teeth.

"What?" Tatiana belted out at top volume.

"The *door*," Gaia hissed.

"Re-*lax*, my sister." Tatiana laughed. "I am just here for some supplies. I need extra paper towels. It seems I have spilled my beer." She leaned in farther with a winking glance, nearly falling over. "But I think maybe my sister has gone a bit boy-crazy tonight, uh? Look at you two—"

"You don't know what you're *talking* about!" Gaia stepped past Tatiana and slammed the door shut. Her instinct was to push Tatiana out herself, but that would have been way too violent. Instead she simply barked into Tatiana's drunken face, nearly ripping her vocal cords to maintain a whisper. "You're drunk, Tatiana. You're disgustingly drunk. Now will you do me a favor and get the hell out of this room! Get out!"

Tatiana's eyes suddenly glazed over with rage as she stared at Gaia.

"Don't you talk to me that way," she spat. "Don't you accuse me. *You* are the one in here with your secret boyfriend. You are the one making Ed some kind of fool, making him mope around with his head dragging across the floor waiting for you to come home when here you are *already* home, whispering sweet nothings in your secret hideaway. I think *that* is what is disgusting, Gaia. Not how much I have had to drink, but the way you treat your boyfriend. He deserves so much better than this. *So* much better. And in case you were wondering who I meant by 'your boyfriend,' I meant *Ed. Not* this one," she hissed, pointing her finger out at Sam. "*Ed.*"

With that, she stormed out of the room and slammed the door behind her.

Gaia stared at the door, breathing heavily, burning from Tatiana's offensive and totally misguided accusations. But she would have to let it go for now. She would have to. At this point the only imperative was to get Sam through that back door and out of this house for good. With that broken lock on the door and a house full of drunken freaks, it was all getting just a little too close for comfort.

She stepped back over to Sam. "I'm sorry," she told him, shaking her head. "I am *so* sorry about that. I've never seen her like that in my life. I guess I've never seen her drunk."

"It's okay," Sam assured her.

"You've got to go, Sam. You've got to go now."

"I know," he said. "I know I do. Look, forget about my stuff, all right? We can deal with the stuff tomorrow. I just. . . Okay, I know I can't pick up where we left off, not after that, but . . ."

Given a moment, Gaia was beginning to feel slightly ill about everything Tatiana had said about Ed. Even if Tatiana had no idea what was going on here, Gaia could still feel a well of guilt beginning to spread through her chest like a fungus. Sam picked up on it immediately.

"Don't worry about Ed, Gaia." His kind eyes were actually a little soothing. "You'll fix everything, I'm sure of it. Look, just. . . just give me hug, all right? A *friendly* hug," he assured her. "And then I'll go. And we'll move forward. And you'll fix things with Ed, and we'll find your father, and everything will work out. It will, Gaia. I *know* it will."

Gaia looked deep into Sam's eyes, and for a moment just the slightest bit of his optimism actually rubbed off on her. She wrapped her arms around his shoulders and squeezed him tightly. It was the first hug they had ever shared purely as friends, without an ounce of remaining confusion.

And that was when Gaia realized. . .

She desperately needed a new friend right about now. And maybe she had just found one in Sam Moon.

Living nightmare

ED COULD SEE TATIANA STORMING through the living room like a Nintendo warrior. She was practically bumping kids out of the way as she headed back toward the kitchen. What the hell had happened to her in the last four minutes? Had she just crossed over into "angry drunk" mode?

"Did you just have a fight with the paper towels?" he joked. "What the hell happened to you?"

"Forget it, Ed!" she snapped, stepping up to him at the fridge. "It's not even worth it. Just forget it!"

"Whoa!" Ed grasped Tatiana's shoulders. "I cleaned up the beer already. Don't worry about it, okay?"

"It's not the beer! I don't care about the beer!"

"*Okay*, okay. Relax, will you please? I think you might be just a little too drunk at this point—"

"I am *not* that drunk, okay! My *God*, you sound just like *her*!"

"Like who?"

"Gaia!" she shouted, flailing her arms drunkenly in the air. "'Disgusting'? How *dare* she call me disgusting? Maybe a little *obnoxious*, but I'm sorry, I just don't think it's right, Ed. It's not right!"

She swung her arm down with anger and nearly fell over. Ed caught her and then pulled his hands away as quickly as possible once she'd regained her balance.

"I have no idea what you're talking about," Ed complained. "You're not making any sense."

"You're goddamn right you have no idea what I'm talking about. You're goddamn right! I'm so *sick* of the way she treats you, Ed. So sick of it! I've been watching it happen since I *came* to this stupid apartment. And now she tells me I don't know what I'm talking about *again*.

Oh, I'm *sorry*. Am I just too 'disgustingly drunk' to know what I'm talking about? No! I know what I'm talking about, Ed! Believe me, I know what I'm talking about!"

"Wait, wait, what do you mean, *now* she tells you? Is Gaia *here* now?"

"Yes, she's here!" she slurred viciously. "She's here giving me more of her stupid attitude! I thought she and I were getting better, Ed. I thought we were really starting to become—"

"Where?" Ed felt his chest nearly close up with excitement and confusion. "How long has she been here?"

"How the hell should I know? Why don't you ask her yourself?"

"Where is she?"

"In her *stupid* little maid's room down the hall." Tatiana waved her hand behind her and continued with her out-of-control drunken tirade. She seemed to be talking to herself at this point. In fact, she seemed to have been talking to herself the entire time. "I don't know why I put up with her attitude, I really don't. I don't deserve that. I don't deserve. . ."

But Ed had stopped listening completely. His head darted up, and he gazed across the crowded living room at the dark hallway.

Maid's room? Did she just rant something about a maid's room? What maid's room?

Ed pushed his way through the crowd and into the hallway as the music pounded in his ears and the screams

239

went on and on. He was still not even sure if there was actual meaning to any of Tatiana's stumbling rant.

He stepped into the hallway and had walked a few steps when he realized that there was a painted-over doorway that he had never really noticed in the hall before. And there was a light shining through under the door.

"Gaia. . . ?" He pushed open the door, assuming he had simply found a closet.

But he hadn't found a closet. What he had found was a very bad dream. A kind of living nightmare that left him completely paralyzed and unable to breathe.

He had found Gaia. She was, in fact, there. And he had also found a boy. A boy who looked just exactly. . . like Sam Moon. It was hard to tell, though. Because his face was slightly obscured. . . what with Gaia's head being nestled so lovingly on his shoulder.

Gaia and this boy—who looked so very much like a boy who was supposed to be dead—both turned toward Ed at the exact same time, ripping their hands away from each other's bodies. And they stared at him, speechless. Just as he was speechless. With dumbfounded shock on their faces. Just as there was dumbfounded shock on his face.

For a moment it was almost as if they were playing some kind of children's mirroring game. But that moment passed away quickly. And Ed woke up to the fact that whatever he was witnessing—however surreal and impossible their romantic embrace might have seemed. . . it was not in fact surreal. And it was not in fact impossible. And it was most definitely not a game. It was real. It was disgustingly, heart-crushingly real.

Ed turned away from the ghost of Sam Moon and burrowed his unabashedly sad eyes into Gaia's paralytic stare. There were a thousand things that he could have said. And a thousand more things that he wanted to say. Anything to help revive his flat-lining heart—to administer some kind of CPR to his slaughtered ego and his overloaded brain. But before anyone in the dusty little room was able to muster a word, Tatiana came bounding in, using Ed as a bumper to break her stride.

"Oh God," she whimpered, catching her breath. "I'm sorry. I'm so drunk. I just realized what I. . . I'm so drunk, I didn't even. . ." Tatiana leaned back against the door. It actually looked like she might just be about to pass out. "You're right, Gaia. I think I am disgustingly drunk. It just came out when I was. . . Our secret. I'm sorry."

Ed stared at Tatiana for a moment more and then turned his head slowly back to Gaia. The look on Gaia's face was indescribable now. Anger, pain, and helpless regret all mixed together and heated up to a boil. And she *still* couldn't utter a word. But Ed could certainly understand why she would be so upset. Tatiana had, after all, accidentally revealed "their secret."

Ed decided that words wouldn't do him any good, either. He decided that words were, in fact, an utter waste of his time. All he needed were his legs.

241

Which, thank God, he had now. His legs were the one thing in this world he had left. And he used them. He used them to run as fast and as hard as he had ever run.

GAIA TURNED TO TATIANA ONCE MORE.

She gazed at her tragically, pathetically, drunken, pitiful face. She indulged briefly in visions of beating Tatiana to a bloody pulp and dragging her by her hair back to Russia. But that passed rather quickly.

Sadistic Blow

Because it was really herself that she wanted to beat to a bloody pulp. She was the one she wanted to punish. For building this horrible mess of misunderstandings piece by piece. For telling just enough stupid secrets and lies to end up in this situation. Whoever Gaia had been trying to protect, the lies were still her fault. Tatiana was just the messenger.

So she put all her rage toward Tatiana aside, and she forgot about the pointless remainder of her goodbyes to Sam, and she ran. She ran after Ed because it was all she could think to do. Because it was all she wanted to do.

Down the stairs, out the front door, and down onto the street. She spotted Ed headed toward Park

Avenue—spotted his back, actually, down half a block from her and still running.

"Ed! Ed, wait! Wait!"

Ed slowed down and turned around, his entire body obscured in the dark shadows of the towering buildings. He stood his ground, not taking a single step toward her, only staring from afar.

Gaia took a few steps toward him.

"Don't," he called to her. "Stay there, Gaia. Just stay there."

Gaia honored his request and stayed put. She had already let him down in so many ways, she felt compelled to do anything he asked of her.

"Alone," he called to her. She could hear his voice quavering slightly. If she had been able to see his eyes, she had a feeling she might have seen tears. "You said you had to do this *alone*, Gaia. . . ."

"Ed, I swear to God, this is not what it looks—"

"Shut up. Please. . . just shut up." She watched as his head dropped down in silhouette. "I'm wondering how many things you've told me were lies."

"Ed, no—"

"That's what I'm wondering," he said, pretending she hadn't even tried to speak. "That's what happens when you find out about one lie, Gaia. You doubt everything else the person has ever said. But you probably know that already. You've been lied to so many times. But not by me, Gaia. Never by me."

243

Gaia felt her chest give way to a sudden rush of tears. They shouldn't have been a surprise, but somehow they were.

"Ed," she uttered aimlessly. She didn't even have any words prepared to follow his name. She just wanted to say his name. To connect to him somehow again.

"I'm wondering. . . I'm wondering where you really were tonight. I'm wondering if there's anything really wrong with your father."

"Of course there—"

"I'm wondering if Sam has anything to do with why you've been so distant with me half the time. . . that whole time after our first night together. . . and every time after that. I'm wondering if that was Sam on the cell phone last night while we were on our *big date*. . . ." Ed laughed bitterly. "I'm wondering if that even *was* Sam upstairs. I'm wondering if you were *lying* when you told me he had *died*. Is that possible? Could you possibly lie about something like that?"

"Ed, *no*, don't be—"

"Ridiculous?" he scoffed. "This is all ridiculous, Gaia. All of it. You and Sam? Ridiculous. Me and you? *Ridiculous*. You and anybody? Utterly ridiculous. You know what, Gaia? You're right. You've been right this whole time. You *are* supposed to be alone. I wish to God I had just listened to you. You were *born* to be alone. Or maybe you were born to be with the apparently undead Sam Moon, I don't really know. But I know you're not supposed to be with me, Gaia. I do know that much."

"No. . ." Useless one-syllable words were all she could manage now. "Ed, listen—"

"Hold on!" Ed interrupted coldly. "Dead man walking. . . ."

Gaia had no idea what Ed was talking about until she heard the footsteps behind her. She turned around and realized that Sam was now leaving her building. He glanced at Gaia for a moment and then turned away. Who knew why? Maybe because now he hated her, too. Maybe because he was trying to respect her dying relationship with Ed. She didn't even care right now. She simply watched as he got into the car with Dmitri and drove off toward the park.

As she turned back toward Ed, she realized that a huge group of gossip-hungry rejects had gathered in front of her front door. Just to revel in someone else's pain, as they all loved so much to do. Many of them were complete strangers. And of course there was Megan and Tammie and all the FOHs. Of course Jake wouldn't want to miss this, either. And of course Tatiana was nowhere in sight. She wouldn't dare show her idiotic face right now.

Gaia turned back to Ed, just like she was turning to face a bullet. A public execution of sorts. She couldn't even manage another word. There was no point now.

"You see this distance here," Ed called to her, slowly

regressing into a full monotone. "From now on, I think we should maintain this approximate distance from each other at all times. I don't think we need any kind of court order or anything; we'll just stick with the honor system on this one. Because I trust you, Gaia. I *trust* you."

With that last sadistic blow, Ed turned around and began to walk—moving at a cold and steady pace, farther and farther into the shadows.

Gaia couldn't feel herself crying now. She could only note the tears pouring down her face. She turned around to go home, only to come up against the captivated faces of her drunken audience.

She stared at all of them for a moment, examining each of their clueless, disgusting faces. And then she let it rip.

"GO HOME!" she howled, frightening the daylights out of every one of them. "Get the hell out of my house!"

The entire crowd dispersed in seconds, running every which way to escape Gaia's wrath. Even her doorman ducked for cover back inside the building.

But one person remained. Gaia couldn't believe it. She could not believe that he could be such cruel and obnoxious asshole that he would actually stay behind just to witness a few more delicious seconds of Gaia's suffering.

"Jake. . . I swear to God. . ." Now she could hear her own voice quavering. She was running on emotional fumes. Complete breakdown no more than a few minutes away. "If you do not clear out of here in ten seconds. . . if you say one harsh word to me. . . or give me one proud chuckle or one half of that disgusting hideous grin. . . I will crack your skull so wide open—"

"Look, you seemed so upset. I just wanted to be sure you were okay," Jake said, standing in her doorway with his hands sitting deep in his pockets. Now she could only stare at him. His unexpected kindness was making her dizzy and a little bit nauseous. She wasn't altogether sure that she wasn't about to faint.

"Are you?" he asked, checking her eyes. "Are you okay?"

Gaia was trying to come up with an answer to this question when her cell phone suddenly buzzed inside her pocket.

Cell phone? Now? Why the hell would Sam be calling me now? He just left two minutes ago. . . .

Unless. . . maybe Dmitri had already given Sam some pertinent piece of information on their way back to his house? Maybe Sam was trying to do her the incredible service of reminding her that no matter what kind of stinking hole her life was becoming, her father's life was still much more important. The search for her father was the one and only thing that mattered—the reason that this apocalypse of a day could still be worth something.

Gaia pulled the phone out of her pocket and looked down at the flashing green display. Sam hadn't called her. He'd sent her a text message:

247

Don't be sad. Just received some new information.
Meet me at the Ukrainian church on Eleventh Street.
Tomorrow. 8:00 A.M.

Gaia stuffed the phone back in her pocket.

Thank you, Sam. Thank you for keeping me alive tonight. I will see you in the morning.

"Was that Ed?" Jake asked.

"Jake. . . go home, okay? Just go home."

Jake gave Gaia one last look. He shook his head slightly with a sardonic smile, and then he turned away and started down the street toward the park.

"And thanks," she heard herself say. She hadn't exactly planned to say it.

He turned his head back over his shoulder with his hands still in his pockets, and he smiled. He looked like some goddamn blue jeans ad you'd see on a subway poster or at a bus stop. But at least his smile wasn't quite so repulsive this time.

He turned his head back and walked off into the glare of the corner streetlight.

Gaia ducked her head and dragged herself upstairs to bed. She tried not to think of Ed. She pretended that Tatiana wasn't even there, and she collapsed onto her mattress fully clothed. She allowed herself only one thought as she drifted off to sleep.

The Ukrainian church on Eleventh Street. Tomorrow. 8:00 A.M.

I had you figured for so many things, Gaia. A psycho. A freak. Thoughtless. Selfish. Misguided. Coldhearted. And it was still all so meaningless to me. I still loved you more than I've ever loved any- one or anything in my life.

But I never had you figured for a traitor, Gaia. Never.

I know you've lied to me before. But I'd always thought that the only lies you could tell were noble lies. At least noble in your own screwed-up head. All those stupid lies to protect me. Pretending you didn't love me. Pretending you didn't care. Thinking that would keep me safe. Thinking that made a damn bit of difference in either of our fates. . .

But now I know. Now I know you can tell real lies. The kind that destroy people. The kind that make people hate themselves for being such trusting, idiotic fools.

Or maybe that's wrong, too? Maybe all those "noble lies" were actually the truth? Maybe you

never did love me? Never cared?
Never gave a crap?

I'm drowning in maybes again,
Gaia. Drowning, suffocating,
choking, dying. . .

Maybe this, maybe that, maybe
the other thing. Maybe Sam never
died. Maybe your father is fine
and you've just been off on a
romantic holiday with Sam while
I've been sitting here like a
freaking idiot, pining for the
queen of maybes.

Maybe I'm so exhausted, Gaia.
Maybe I am so utterly tired of
being there for you when you have
never been there for me. Maybe
I'm beginning to realize that
I've spent all of my will and all
of my heart on you. . . and I
have absolutely nothing to show
for it.

I don't know, Gaia. I think
maybe. . . just maybe. . . I'm
ready to hate you.

From: shred@alloymail.com
To: heatherg@alloymail.com
Time: 1:34 A.M.
Re: the blind leading the blind

I'm assuming they've got those voice-activated e-mail reading programs at your school. Otherwise you won't be able to read this, which would make me just as dopey as those devoted friends of yours who put a sign-in book at the entrance to the party without realizing that if you could actually read it, they'd be one idea short of a party theme.

Anyway, a bit of loving advice:

You might want to think about quitting the soothsaying business. Because, with all due respect and love, you suck at it.

Sorry, I don't know what I'm doing. I'm just taking my crap out on you. You're a good friend. Bad soothsayer. Good friend. You were right about one thing, though. It is definitely time to start my normal life. My normal life without anyone who is crazy and a liar to screw it up. I'm going to find me a normal girl and get started with that normal life first thing in the morning. Right after I pass out.

This has been the worst night of my life. No part of it was good.

Did I mention I was drunk off my ass? Yup.

But not so drunk that I can't do THIS. . .

* DELETED *

SHE HAD ONLY SLEPT FOR ABOUT

two hours. The other four had been spent waiting. Waiting for 8 A.M. Waiting for another hint, a clue. Anything to lead her an inch closer to her father. Anything to give her life the remotest bit of purpose. She was doing everything in her power to block the rest out. She could do that for about an hour at a time. She could certainly do it at this very moment.

Cold Hollow Air

Gaia stepped out of the bright, glaring sunshine of Eleventh Street into the cold, hollow air of the church, listening as her footsteps echoed from the large wooden doors all the way down the aisle and through the pews.

The doors had been open, but the church was empty. She scanned her eyes across the dark pews and the shadows of the altar, searching for a sign of Sam, but there was nothing.

Minutes went by and still nothing. Not a soul had walked in or out of the church.

Gaia sat her aching body down in one of the front pews, trying to master her impatience—trying to give Sam as much time as he needed to show up.

And then finally she heard footsteps behind her.

"Sam?" she whispered, turning around. But there was no sign of him. Nothing. Just the sunlight obscuring the doorway at the end of the aisle. Like they had been the footsteps of phantoms. Like there were ghosts roaming the Ukrainian church. Only Gaia didn't believe in ghosts. And she didn't like the uneasy feeling that had begun to build in the pit of her stomach.

This is wrong. Something about this situation is wrong. . . .

She shot up out of her pew and began to walk slowly down the aisle, back toward the wooden doors. But her instincts told her to speed up. She checked behind her more than a few times as she increased her speed, her rapid footsteps echoing louder as she came down harder with each step.

She was about a foot from the bright sun when someone slammed the doors in her face, trapping her in a sudden pocket of total darkness. She grabbed onto the handles of the door and shook with all her strength. But they were locked. Slammed in her face and locked.

Move, Gaia. It doesn't matter in what direction, just move!

The first gunshot whizzed right past her face, popping a hole in the wooden door as the sun shot through like a laser beam. And then another beam and another, as the deafening crack of gunshots exploded through the enclosed space, echoing like thunderclaps from the airy turrets of the ceiling.

Gaia leapt to her right in a series of consecutive

rolls, tumbling away from a string of gunshots that chased her into a corner of the church. And finally she heard footsteps. Running toward her faster and faster as the gunshots grew in volume and frequency. They had no intention of letting her make it out of this one. This one was clearly to be the successful assassination—the simplest of plans that would leave her with nowhere to run and no one to fight off.

She rose to her feet and sprinted back for the opposite side of the church as the bullet holes erupted closer and closer to her head. She wasn't sure this time. She wasn't sure how the hell she was going to make it out of this one.

Gaia suddenly realized that the shots were coming from *two* different places now. The shots from down on the floor and now another stream of shots raining down from somewhere up above. . .

Strength, Gaia. That's all you have left here. Your strength and your speed. Find a way out. Look for the light. . . .

She dropped down on her back behind the last row of pews and scanned the wall.

There. . . in the back corner. Light under the door. . .

She didn't hesitate. She shot up to her feet, took a running start down the aisle, and slid from the front of the church all the way to the back, ending with a forward roll to her feet and a leap to that back door. A barrage of shots followed her every step of the way as she kicked the door open and rolled through the doorway.

She found the light source above a decrepit wooden door. A filthy little window, just big enough for her to fit through. But there was no way she could jump high enough to reach it, and those footsteps were coming closer again.

Gaia grabbed a wooden chair from the corner and positioned it just below the window. She stepped back a few steps and then ran for it at full speed, pushing up off the chair and grabbing onto the window frame with both hands, hanging by her fingers.

A shot flew in below her feet, but Gaia hoisted herself up with the sheer strength of her wrists and upper arms, shoving herself through the open window and landing on the rugged pavement outside, finally back in the glaring sunshine.

She took off at a full run, leaping all obstacles until she was on the crowded morning sidewalk, dodging the suits and briefcases as she ran quite literally for her life.

"Watch it!" she shouted, weaving her way farther and farther from the church. "Coming through!"

Alive, she assured herself. *Still alive.*

She slowed to a fast walk at Eighth Street, panting for breath as sweat poured down her temples. It was as close to certain death as she had come in a long while, and escaping certain death had left her with an actual blip of appreciation for her life. But a moment more and a dark rain cloud in her brain had blocked out the sun. Given a few seconds to think of anything but pure survival, Gaia's brain crashed up against the inevitable truth. The unbearable truth that she had pushed away so successfully in the last twenty-four hours. But now. . .

Sam was the only person on the planet who knew her cell phone number. He was the only person on the planet who could have written her that text message telling her to come to that death trap of a church. And when the shots had been fired. . . he'd been nowhere to be found.

Again.

Three strikes, Sam. That's three strikes.

Gaia slowed down on Sixth Street and collapsed on the stoop of a brownstone. She dropped her head in her hands and stayed in that exact position for what felt like hours.

Why, Sam? How could you possibly? What did they offer you? What did they make you believe?

But that wasn't really her question. Not for long.

The real question wasn't what they had told Sam to make him betray her. The real question was much simpler and of a far more pressing nature. The real question:

Who are they? Who the hell are they?

I am so tired of hidden enemies.
My whole life has been about hidden enemies, and I am done with
it. I am so done with it.

I wish you would just *show*
yourself. Whoever you are, just
come out from behind the goddamn
curtain and let's put our cards
on the table already.

Do you work for Loki? That
just wouldn't make any sense. He
knows he's not my father now.
That stupid battle for me is
over. He's a goddamn vegetable.

Do you work for someone else?
Who? And how did you get to Sam?
How did you brainwash him? And
what the hell have you done with
my father?

I just want to understand why
you're hiding. I want to understand why you're doing this to
me. There has to be a *reason*.
There's always a reason. People
don't just assassinate for sport.
There has to be an agenda. I can
sense it now. Something floating
high over my head that I'm not

even beginning to understand.
Clue me in, you son of a bitch.
Or is it sons of bitches?

Who *cares?* I don't even care.

All I really care about now is
Ed. Ed and my father.

God, Ed, I wish you were here
right now. I wish I could explain
it all to you right now. Because
you have it all wrong. You just
have the whole thing wrong. I
need to make you understand that.
I need to sit you down and make
you understand.

All we need is a car, Ed. And
a diner for me to work in. And
there's this house out there,
waiting for us in some random
suburban neighborhood that no one
has ever even noticed. And we're
going to put a down payment on
it, and we're going to throw a
couch and a bed in it, and we're
going to live there, Ed. That's
where we're going to live.

When I find my father. When
this is all over. When I find the
enemy.

here is a sneak peek of Fearless™ #27:

SHOCK

Some mornings I wake up and everything seems okay. It's something my brain does. I suppose everyone's brain does it. You're in dreamland, and the wish-fulfillment fairies take over and douse you in their bogus happy-dust. Peek into your hidden desires and make you believe that you've satisfied them. Paint pictures that your eyes, flicking back and forth behind your closed lids, devour with an embarrassingly ravenous greed. And by the time you open your eyes, you're full of ill-gotten endorphins, convinced that all is well with the world.

Sometimes I can float there for thirty seconds, a minute, two minutes. I can will myself to believe I'm just a regular teenager whose biggest problem is figuring out how to sneak out after curfew. I can look at the sky outside my window and think, "Good morning, sunshine! Are we ready for another fabulous day?"

But reality always gets me in the end.

Before I can even wipe the

boogers out of my eyes, I start to
remember.

That's when the fairies take
off. The minute they see my eyelids
flicker, they start laughing like a
bunch of punky eight-year-olds and
take off out the window. And all
the good feelings they gave me get
slowly squished by the lead-and-tar
mixture of the very real mess that
is my life. I sink under the weight
of reality. And pretty soon the
bright colors of my dream fade to a
dismal black-and-white of facts.

Fact one: Ed, my boyfriend up until
last night, but more importantly, the
person who's been my closest friend
through all of this—well, he hates
me. Wants to keep distance between us,
where there used to be nothing but the
best of friendships.

Fact two: Sam, my first love—as
in the person you never fully get
over—turns up just long enough to
ruin things with Ed, and then turns
out to be a two-faced killer. Just
like George Niven and everyone else
I tried to trust.

And worst of all, fact three: My

dad is missing. A particularly gut-
wrenching fact that should make all
boyfriend troubles irrelevant. He's
out there somewhere, and nobody
seems to know the first thing about
how to find him. I might be his
only hope. Which only makes me that
much more of a target for whoever
is trying to kill me.

Oh yes. Trying to kill me.
Shots fired, life in jeopardy.
Someone actually wants to take
this dismal life from me, and I'm
damned if I'm going to let them.
My father needs me too much.

For one brief moment, I had
everything I wanted: a family—two
parents and a sister. A
boyfriend. And I let myself
believe it was mine, that those
stupid dreams had really come
true. And it all fell apart.

Note to self: Never fall for
that one again.

Period.

End of story.

Beginning of day.

"Rise and shine!"

This was so WEIRD. Like a new reality show: *When* **human** *Best Friends Go Bad.* **obstacle** They didn't speak to each other like this.

GAIA MOORE EXITED THE BUILDING

she lived in, on East Seventy-second Street, in a foul mood. She didn't even know where she was heading; she just knew she had to get out of that apartment and go somewhere, anywhere. It was stupid to stay in one place for long if her would-be killers—with or without the help of Sam—were looking for her. She wanted to search for her dad, but with nothing to go on, her energy just floated around in a hyperhaze. It made her feel wired and weird.

Electronic Dork Tool

To make matters worse, some moron was letting his cell phone ring. Probably an idiot yuppie fresh from his morning workout getting a frantic call from the office asking what was going on with the Hooper account. Or a frazzled mom with two bratty kids who left her phone in the diaper bag and couldn't find it. Or some "boutique" dermatologist avoiding her needy patients jonesing for their Botox fix.

What Gaia couldn't understand was, why did people carry cell phones if they didn't want to answer them? And if they knew they were going to blow off a call, why not turn off the ringer and save everyone from having to hear that incessant, bleating whine? The worst part was, whoever the phone belonged to seemed to be following Gaia down the street. She glared at the people passing her, trying to shame whoever it was into turning off that annoying ring, but it kept going and going. Jesus, it sounded like it was coming right from her own backpack. Who the hell. . . ?

Crap. It was Gaia's cell phone. She kept forgetting she was one of the wirelessly enhanced masses!

She dropped her backpack to the ground and quickly unzipped it, yanking the zipper up so that the grimy pack flopped against the ground. She spotted the cheerful silver phone in the dank recesses and reached in to get it, at which point it finally stopped.

Aaaah. Sweet silence.

She checked the incoming-calls screen and saw that the phone number came from Dmitri's apartment. She hit the TALK button twice, and stood in the middle of the sidewalk, legs planted on either side of her open backpack, listening intently. She'd never get used to this tiny electronic dork tool. It clicked a few times, then beeped. She tried again, but the damn thing wouldn't connect. She waited to see if the little envelope would pop up—maybe he was leaving a message—but after about a minute and a half she realized that nothing was happening. Maybe Sam had signed her up for one of those low-rent plans.

Sam. As she closed up the phone, Gaia was disturbed to realize that her heart was thudding. Despite all evidence that he was a two-faced, double-crossing, wanna-be killer, there was still a part of her that just didn't get it. That wished it was him calling. How dumb was that? The guy had given her instructions to meet him at a Ukranian church the night before, and as soon as she'd gotten there, *bam*, gunshots were headed straight for her gut. He had to be involved. He'd obviously been the willing bait to bring her there. But some small, idiotic part of her still felt a connection to the guy she had long ago fallen for.

The human heart was undeniably the stupidest organ in the body.

Forget it, she thought. *There's nowhere to go, and nothing to do. I may as well go to school.*

Packing her nonworking phone into her backpack, she disappeared down the yawning maw of the concrete subway tunnels. She'd try calling Dmitri again when she got to school.

. . . A GIRL BORN
WITHOUT THE FEAR GENE

FEARLESS™

A SERIES BY
FRANCINE PASCAL

PUBLISHED BY SIMON & SCHUSTER

3029-01